"*New Lots* is prime-time cri[...] fast, roving past drug-ravaged [...] ers hunting their next target, jamming a zoom lens on a world at whose feet many have suffered. Clarkson writes with fierce reality, pages filled with characters tabloid-fresh, corner dialogue vibrating with the fear which populates the hard zones of the city.

"*New Lots* is a roller coaster thrill ride, from the opening riff down to a pulse-shredder of a climax. As with many of the characters he has created, Clarkson has bagged himself a hit. *New Lots* is the proof."
—Lorenzo Carcaterra, *The New York Times*
bestselling author of *Sleepers* and *Apaches*

"Gritty, streetwise reading. . . . I will be looking forward to his next book."
—Hugh Holton

"Thrillingly complex. . . . Steel-edged dialogue and intensively researched. . . . Hard-driving realism."
—*Kirkus Reviews*

"Snappy. . . . *New Lots* will satisfy readers looking for a fast . . . cop thriller with sympathetic leads."
—*Publishers Weekly*

"Clarkson has created an assortment of vibrant, realistic players—not exactly likeable but certainly watchable. . . . Recommended for fans of gritty crime dramas."
—*Booklist*

"Tough, complex."
—*Staten Island Advance*

"Well written. . . . Believable . . . terrific dialogue. . . . This is a really terrific, 'can't put down till the end' read."
—*The Ellenville Press*

"*New Lots* by John Clarkson is a top-notch, adrenaline-charged, action-packed thriller. . . . [A] gritty, explosive tale. . . . Carefully orchestrated."
—*Lansing State Journal*

JOHN CLARKSON

NEW LOTS

TOR®

A TOM DOHERTY ASSOCIATES BOOK
NEW YORK

NEW LOTS

A Tor Book
Published by Tom Doherty Associates, LLC
175 Fifth Avenue
New York, NY 10010

www.tor.com

Tor® is a registered trademark of Tom Doherty Associates, LLC.

ISBN: 0-812-56476-6
Library of Congress Catalog Card Number: 98-19395

First edition: September 1998
First mass market edition: October 2000

Printed in the United States of America

0 9 8 7 6 5 4 3 2 1

To Ellen,
who reminded me at a crucial moment
that she married a writer

Thanks to Detective Michael Greene, without whose help this book could not have been written. Also to Kathy and all the other cops who shared their time and information with me. Thanks to Abdul Karim. Thanks to Norm Siegel for his invaluable technical advice. And thanks to Andy, for everything.

NEW LOTS APARTMENT COMPLEX

Christmas lights in April.

A little out of season, thought Loyd Shaw.

The miniature, multicolored lights framed the front window of an old neighborhood bar. Behind the window, a sign displayed the words, EARL'S PLACE, in glowing red neon script. Behind the neon, black velvet drapes completely blocked any view into the bar.

Shaw tried to push open the heavy front door. Locked. Yep, he thought, this must be the place.

Shaw rapped on the door. It opened just wide enough to reveal the scowl on the dark, broad face of a white-haired black man.

"Loyd Shaw, friend of Jake's."

The frown disappeared, and the door opened.

Shaw stepped into a bar like none he had ever seen. His head bumped into a Christmas ornament hanging from the ceiling. He noted a spray of cardboard St. Patrick's Day shamrocks plastered on a wall, a HAPPY NEW YEAR sign drooping over the back bar, birthday streamers, Valentine's hearts, tinsel, and more multi-colored lights, tacked on, hung up, or draped over walls and fixtures.

But it was still a bar. Shaw breathed in the smell of beer, whiskey, and smoke and listened to the good old Motown music that filled the air.

While Shaw looked around trying to spot Jake Bennett, he thought about all the holidays and occasions represented by the jumble of decorations. Everything but weddings, he thought. This is a place where wedding vows are broken.

He spotted Big Jake Bennett, sitting at the far curve of a long wooden bar. Shaw politely made his way through the crowd, noticing that as the only white person in the bar he made a few heads turn his way.

Jake spotted him before he reached the end of the bar and boomed out, "Shaw! Get your ass over here, boy!"

Shaw walked into a bear hug. Not surprising since Jake Bennett very much resembled a medium-sized, bald black bear.

"I didn't think you'd come, man."

"Well, it was either that or try to get a piece of ass from my wife. That's when I knew I had to do something drastic."

"You talkin' 'bout Jane?"

"Well shit, man, technically we're still married. . . ."

"Jane."

"Yeah. I know. That bad, right? So I came to my senses. Said to myself, enough of this shit. But hell, I couldn't sleep. Can't sleep a lot of nights lately. So I said, what the hell, go on out to Brooklyn and drink down some birthday booze with Big Jake."

"And here you are, goddamn it."

"Here I am. Where am I, exactly, Jake?"

"Flatbush."

"Fuckin' Flatbush. Whose place is this? This is no regular bar, Jake."

"No, this is Earl's place. He only opens it up when he feels like it. Mostly for private parties. Goddamn, I'm glad you came out, Shaw."

"Private parties. Like your birthday."

"Right."

"Thanks, Jake, I'm glad to be here. How old are you, man? You been around for so damn long it seems like everything else came after you."

"Old enough. Older'n even you, Shaw. How'd you get out here?"

"Drove."

"Shit, now you be careful drivin' back, man. Don't get so drunk you can't drive."

Shaw knew that as big and tough as Jake Bennett was, Jake really would worry about him driving back.

"I don't have the energy to get really drunk."

"Yeah, we'll see about that. What the fuck you lookin' around at?"

"All these women you've got here, Jake. Christ, man, how'd you get such attractive women out here in the middle of the night for your birthday?"

Jake looked sideways at Shaw. "Who you talkin' to?"

Shaw shouted, "Big Jake Bennett. Three hundred pounds of fun for everyone!"

"Goddamn right. What're you drinkin'?" Jake shouted at the bartender, "Eddie, get my friend a drink."

The bartender leaned close to Shaw to hear his order above the party noise.

"Jack rocks, soda back."

The bartender nodded, grabbed glasses and ice, and started pouring. Shaw looked at his friend, Jake, sitting on his bar stool as if it were attached to his broad rear end, set in, smiling, sipping double shots of Johnny Walker Black out of a heavy-bottomed old-fashioned glass. Shaw noticed that even though he had plenty to do, the bartender never allowed Jake's glass to become completely empty.

Shaw's drink and chaser landed in front of him. He took the first cold swig of icy whiskey, leaned back against the bar, and watched a steady stream of friends and relatives come by to wish Jake a happy birthday.

Jake would smile and nod and shake a hand or

accept a kiss, and his guest would move on.

Shaw remained standing at the bar, next to Jake, mostly because he didn't know anybody else in the bar. The partygoers were polite to him, but mostly because he stood with Jake.

Shaw didn't interpose on the well-wishers, but he couldn't help notice one of Jake's friends seemed to take special notice of him. He had no problem returning her curious gaze, and it certainly didn't seem to make her the least bit uncomfortable.

She was nearly tall enough to look the six-foot-two Shaw eye to eye, and was mature enough to do it without a hint of shyness. She wore a black, spaghetti-strap dress that ended high on the bottom, about midthigh, and low on the top revealing plenty of flawless, *café au lait* skin.

Shaw particularly enjoyed the view when she bent over to kiss Jake's cheek.

She reached out to shake Shaw's hand.

"I'm Denise."

"Loyd. Loyd Shaw."

"Pleased to meet you."

Denise smiled, revealing a right front tooth rimmed in gold. Her smile made Shaw wish she would kiss his cheek, too. The warmth of Denise's smile lingered over him as she turned and melted back into the party. For a moment he felt less like an outsider.

Jake looked at Shaw watching Denise saunter off, and said, "It's all that sperm backed up into your brain."

"Maybe I need a black woman, Jakey."

"Why?"

"I have the feeling they are more understanding of a man's needs. A man such as me."

"Man, you crazy."

Shaw leaned over the bar and took a long sip from

his tumbler of iced bourbon. "I suppose."

The cold whiskey warmed his belly and he swung an arm across Jake's broad shoulders. "You are one big happy fucking birthday boy, aren't you?"

Jake laughed a big, booming, birthday laugh that made Shaw laugh, too.

Shaw looked around the bar enjoying the sight of Jake's other guests. All the women were dressed for just the right amount of show, as were the men. There were no jeans in the place except the black pair Shaw wore. And although most of the people were Jake's family and close friends, they weren't typical family and friends. Jake Bennett didn't attract typical people. These were people who partied in after-hours clubs until dawn. The kind of people who knew about a bar like Earl's Place. And who would be admitted once they tapped on the locked front door.

Suddenly, Shaw wished he weren't such a stranger.

"Keep lookin' you might find something, Shaw. You welcome to anything I don't want."

"Oh, Jakey, how marvelous it would be . . . a young, toned, smooth-skinned voluptuous black girl, snuggled up next to me, naked, in postcoital bliss, in some quiet little Flatbush bungalow."

"What kind of bliss?"

"After-fucking-me bliss."

"After-laughin'-at-your—"

"Hey, no racial stereotyping, please."

"And they ain't no innocent women in this bar, Shaw. At least none that I know of."

"Forget innocent. Young is good enough. Young and wicked. Twenties. Late twenties, I don't care. Maybe thirties. Like Denise."

"Oh boy, here we go."

"What do you think?"

"Hey. It could happen. I saw the way she smiled at

you, all nice and friendly. Ask her husband over there, maybe he'll say okay."

Jake's big laugh boomed again. Shaw smiled, but didn't laugh back.

"Story of my life, Jake. I find no humor in tormenting a man already in torment."

"You wanna get laid, Shaw, just stand where you are and keep drinking with old Jake. I'll get you laid. Maybe not some tight-assed, smooth whatever, but I'll get the job done."

"Yeah with some poor, sloppy, old, fat-assed, nasty, worn-out woman that you stopped fucking about ten years ago."

"So?"

This time they both laughed. But Shaw's laughter faded quickly. He reached over and picked up his drink from the bar and drained it. The ice had watered it down to the point where it had no bite, but he finished it off anyway.

"Fuck it," Shaw said. He reached over and squeezed Jake's meaty shoulder and told him, "So long, big guy. You have a happy birthday."

"What's the matter, man? We just gettin' started."

"I don't know. Don't have the energy to stand around drinking and bullshitting with you all night waiting for a miracle. Don't mind me. Your fat ass is gonna be sittin' in that spot for a long time, and I want you to enjoy every minute of it."

Jake answered, " 'Til the dawn's early light, brother."

"Yes, sir, you must meet the first day of your new birth year all drunked up, smellin' of perfume and pussy and smoke and booze."

"Sounds good to me."

"We don't do that often enough anymore, do we?"

"Wouldn't still be here if we did."

"Well there you go. Blow out the candle brother, you're gonna get your wish. See ya."

"You okay?"

"Yeah, of course I'm okay."

"You know where you are?"

"Yeah, and I know the way home. Have fun."

"How's that other thing, Shaw?"

Damn, thought Shaw. Old Jake had to slip in the question, quick like that, just as I'm about to leave.

Shaw answered, "I'd say it's pretty much over. It shits, what else is new?"

"Hang in."

"Oh yeah. Not to worry, brother. Take care, Jake. I love you. Happy birthday, man."

"Thanks for comin' out to see me." Jake began to rise from his stool. "Come on, I'll walk you to your car."

Shaw pushed him back down. Shaw knew the offer was mostly a gesture on Jake's part and wouldn't think of taking him away from his party.

"Sit. Relax. Enjoy yourself."

Jake eased back down and gripped his scotch. They shook hands so that no more could be said about the sadness that suddenly surrounded them. Shaw held on to Jake's solid hand for a couple more beats than he normally would, then released his grip and headed for the front door. He eased his way through the party-goers. Nobody stopped him or urged him to stay.

He unlocked the front door himself and stepped out onto the darkened street.

He stood for a moment, letting the cool April early morning air clear his head a bit, listening to the faint bass beat of the music emanating from the bar. A muffled laugh penetrated the closed door. Denise? Laughing at something her husband said? Shaw heard the lock snapping behind him.

Now what? he asked himself. Drag my ass out here in the middle of night. For what?

He checked his watch. Almost three in the morning. To hell with it, he thought, I'm going home.

He pictured crawling into bed with Jane. He didn't relish waking her and facing that steely silence that continued to separate them.

Should have built that second bedroom in the back of the loft, he told himself. Nah, no way. That would've just brought open warfare. She'd have had to get the divorce rolling just to save face. No, he told himself, just go home and get it over with. Just keep your distance, pal. Now is not the time to negotiate a divorce.

He had parked four or five blocks from the bar. After two blocks, he started looking for his seven-year-old, dark green Mercury Marquis, trying to remember exactly where he'd parked. He passed two black men standing under the streetlight. Seeing them brought to mind that he was a white man walking in a poor black neighborhood at three in the morning. The two men checked out Shaw. Shaw looked at them for no more than five seconds and judged them to be working men. Maybe four-to-midnight guys getting home after eating a late dinner or an early breakfast. Not a problem.

He started thinking about Jane again, and the loneliness her presence caused, and the unfulfilled needs. He frowned. And then the frown deepened into a scowl as he heard the unmistakable low-pitched thud that seemed totally and specifically created to annoy.

Shaw turned and saw the car coming his way. Even at a distance of a city block, he could hear the music. . . . Gangsta rap. Loud. With that booming, thudding bass and the angry, insistent lyrics.

Shaw shook his head. What the hell is that incomprehensible shit? Yelling like that, over and over and over again.

As the car approached, the music blasted out so loudly, the bass boomed so deeply that Shaw could feel the sound waves thudding against his chest. He thought, this is fucking ridiculous.

The car passed by and three dark faces glared at him, daring Shaw to say something.

He wanted to yell back, Turn that fucking shit off. He didn't, but he did say the words in his head. And when they glared at him, Shaw didn't look the other way. He didn't look down. He lifted his chin and defiantly stared right back at the dark threatening faces. And in his head he said, "Fuck you, assholes." In the middle of the night, alone, on the streets of Flatbush.

Less than a mile from where Shaw walked glaring at the rolling boom box, six bearded black men wearing knit skullcaps stood in a dark stairwell inside Building A of a five-building housing complex called New Lots Apartments located on Rockaway Avenue in Brownsville, Brooklyn.

Each of the six men occupied a step. At the highest step stood an ex-convict named Walter Harris, who had changed his name to Rachman Abdul X during his last stay at Ossining Prison in upstate New York. His conversion to Islam had required the change in his name and his life.

The five men standing behind Rachman Abdul X were also Muslims. Rachman knew their Muslim names, but referred to them as simply "gunmen." When Rachman pictured each of the men, he thought about how they fired their weapons more than he thought about their names and faces. Efram fired steadily, but always squinted at the discharge. Achman, a small man, employed a strong, two-handed grip to compensate for his slight size. Abdul, Mahmoud, Suli... Rachman held an image for each gunman based on how he used a gun.

On that particular April night, Rachman had matched each gunman with a particular weapon. The three standing directly behind him gripped Tec-9 machine pistols. The next two held Glock 17 9-mm semiautomatics. Rachman, the only one strong enough to fire one single-handed, gripped a powerful 50 Magnum

Desert Eagle. All the weapons were loaded with full clips. And each man held a second clip.

Rachman turned to check his gunmen one last time, but the narrow, unlit stairwell was too dark to see anything but indistinguishable, shadowy forms. He finally decided they were ready when he heard the last gunman chamber a round.

Once the weapons were cocked, Rachman slowly led the way up the stairs. He headed for the fourth floor, but by the time Rachman and the gunmen reached the second floor, the blood thudding in Rachman's ears made it difficult for him to hear the shuffling footsteps of those behind him. It wasn't just the walk up the stairs that made the blood pound. The last prison doctor had called it hypertension.

"What's hypertension?" Rachman had asked.

"High blood pressure," the doctor had told him.

More poisonous words from the white devil trying to weaken him. Rachman had ignored the doctor, just as he had ignored all the other prison doctors who had examined him throughout his nearly lifelong sojourn through the New York prison system—at Sing-Sing, Dannemora, Attica, Rikers, all the way back to the Spofford Juvenile Detention Center, which he had entered at the age of sixteen.

Rachman remembered that word now: hypertension. High blood pressure. He didn't need a doctor to tell him living in a New York prison would cause pressure and tension. What he felt standing in the darkness with his five gunmen coming up behind him, automatic weapons pressed against their legs, hands on the stair railing, slowly climbing the dark stairs, ready to do what they were about to do . . . that went way past tension.

Rachman thought about one of those doctors standing there with him now, knowing what was about to happen. He pictured how their guts would ache and their teeth would grind from the tension. Rachman pictured one of his gunmen tripping on one of the damn stairs they couldn't see, jerking a trigger and told his imaginary prison doctor . . . you'll see some damn tension if that happens. A whole lot of blood in New Lots, too.

Rachman pushed all such thoughts out of his mind and concentrated on climbing up onto each invisible step, slowly, carefully up, up, every so often catching a bit of light seeping out from doors that opened onto the hallways of each floor.

A few more steps up and Rachman stopped outside the door to the fourth-floor hallway.

The sudden stop caused the gunman directly behind Rachman to bump into him. For a moment, the gunman thought he had bumped into the door itself. Rachman's two hundred-thirty-pound frame hadn't moved an inch.

Rachman hissed, "Careful."

The column stopped without further mishap and stood in the order Rachman had determined: first, Rachman with the .50 Magnum. Then the three Tec-9s. And finally the two Glocks.

Out in the hallway, about twenty feet from the stairwell, a man named Ellis slouched next to one of the few functioning elevators in the entire five-building complex. Ellis belonged to the crack gang that had taken over New Lots Apartments four months previously. The gang called themselves the Blue-Tops after the color of the caps on their crack vials. They were the ones who had smashed all the lights inside the hallways and stairwells of New Lots Apartments. Less light meant more terror for those who walked the halls of New Lots. The more terrified people were, the easier it was for the Blue-Tops to control New Lots. The darkness also made it easier to keep the cops out of their business inside the dark halls of New Lots.

Ellis was chosen for his job because of his bulk. Even if someone shot him, he was so big he would block the doorway to the crack apartment.

Rachman stood in the dark, waiting patiently. He knew Ellis stood outside two empty apartments being used by the Blue-Tops. One apartment for selling crack, the other for smoking it.

He also knew how the Blue-Tops ran their operation. Police pressure and rivalries had driven much of the drug business indoors. It was simply safer and easier to sell inside rather than out on the street. Steerers surrounded the five-building complex directing customers into the main courtyard, known as The Pit, where gang members would direct them into one of the five downstairs lobbies. From there, the buyer would take the elevator up to a designated floor, money in hand. No one reached inside a pocket inside New Lots. The customer handed the money to Ellis, who slipped it into a slot in one of the apartment doors. The proper amount of crack would come out.

Rachman knew everything there was to know about how the Blue-Tops ran their operation. He knew exactly where to send six more of his gunmen outside so that they could cover each of the Blue-Tops working the complex, in The Pit, and in the lobby.

Soon now, Rachman told himself. Soon. He breathed slowly, willing the blood to stop pounding in his ears. For the hundredth time, he pictured the layout of the two apartments. The selling apartment, two rooms, unfurnished except for a couple of chairs and a table. In the room behind the front door, two armed Blue-Tops guards protecting the entrance. The room next to that held the counters, baggers, and probably one runner to bring in more supply as needed.

Then there was the smoking apartment, next door to the selling apartment: dark, littered with filth, stifling. The only piece of furniture in it being a battered old couch that had been pulled in off the street, something dogs and derelicts had slept on. The windows in the apartment had never been opened. Rachman curled his nose at the memory of the stench that he knew permeated the place, a gagging combination of burning crack, rank body odor, and the human waste deposited in a bathroom that no one ever bothered to clean. He didn't bother estimating how many people might be in there. They did not concern him.

One of the occupants, a glassy-eyed, wasted woman who had been smoking for almost two days, worked the crack den. At one time in her life, before she lost twenty pounds and her teeth loosened and her skin began to look like dirty clay and her hair like filthy brown steel wool, she had been an attractive girl with a lovely shape. Even on that night she somehow managed to conjure up a smile that helped, but wasn't the main attraction. The main attraction was her unbuttoned blouse and lack of a bra.

She had run out of money one hour into her binge and continued to finance her habit by offering oral sex for five dollars. She'd shuffle on her knees between the legs of whatever crackhead would allow it, kneeling there, stroking his thigh, smiling at him, exposing her breasts so they could be easily fondled while she gently cupped his genitals, softly whispering the required graphic sexual pleas as she asked for five dollars, describing what she would do and how good it would feel and how much she wanted him in her mouth. She'd let them grab her breasts and pinch her nipples for free, no matter how much it hurt. Anything to engender an obligation. She asked for five, and some of the men would simply push her away after abusing her for as long as she, or they, could stand it. But others gave her money. Maybe five, maybe only one dollar. And as soon as she had sucked enough to get ten dollars, she turned those dollars into rock and sucked her crack pipe with frightening need.

Rachman didn't know about the woman working the den, but he knew the misery crack had caused her. And when he heard the elevator open out in the hallway, he knew it was almost time to end that misery. For her and for everyone else in New Lots. At least for tonight.

John X stepped out of the elevator and smiled at Ellis. Ellis did not smile back. Nobody smiled when they saw John X. Like the others, John X was bearded, but he wore his beard to hide his pockmarked skin and diminish a pronounced underbite that exposed a badly misshapen row of teeth. Not only that, John X was bigger than Ellis, which made him very big. Ellis did not like anyone John X's size and demeanor and might normally have pulled his gun the second he saw John X, but John X had been in and out of New Lots buying crack enough times to be familiar to Ellis. Ellis simply put out his hand for the money.

Unfortunately for Ellis, this time was different.

When John X stepped out of the elevator, he grabbed Ellis's throat with his extra large left hand and shoved a long-barrel .38 revolver far enough into Ellis's gaping mouth to make him gag.

With the long barrel pressing into the back of Ellis's throat, John X swung the guard around and backed him up against the wall next to the elevator. Ellis instinctively grabbed John X's wrist, but when John X pulled back the hammer of the .38, Ellis froze. John X brought his big, ugly, pockmarked, under-bit face closer to Ellis and just kept nodding at him as if to say, that's right, that's right, don't move. Don't move and I won't squeeze this trigger and blow off the back of your head.

Rachman had heard what he had been waiting for—the sounds of the elevator and Ellis choking on the gun barrel.

Rachman shoved open the hall door and walked quickly into the dim corridor, moving fast along the outside wall of the two adjoining apartments. The others followed him as he raised the Desert Eagle and fired three booming shots. The high-caliber explosions deafened everybody in the corridor.

Ellis flinched at the booming blasts, likely wondering what the hell Rachman was shooting at since only he and John X were in the hallway.

But Rachman wasn't shooting people. He was shooting walls. Three shots opened up three holes: one in the cinder-block wall and one in the front door of the selling apartment, and a third in the wall of the smoking room.

The exploding walls and door had the desired effect on the people inside. They dropped as if they had been shot. If they could have burrowed under the surface of the hard floors, they would have. One of the Blue-Tops sitting at a glass table doling out crack rocks and counting money, dove under the table so quickly that he caught the corner with his forehead, splitting open a gash that ran from just above his eyebrow to his scalp.

The only person who didn't immediately drop down was the strung-out woman in the smoke room. She froze in her kneeling position, hands covering her ears, and began screaming nonstop.

Her screams were not audible for very long.

3

Loyd Shaw might have preferred the crack addict's screams to the booming rap that blasted him as the car rolled by. His angry scowl had not pleased the car's occupants. Shaw saw the passenger in the backseat lean forward and say something to the driver. The car sped up to the corner, only fifteen feet in front of Shaw, turned right, and stopped short, blocking his way.

Shaw muttered a curse. "Shit." And then said, "Shit, fuck," as he felt the first sickening blast of fear hit him, walloping his chest as if someone had thrown a bucket of ice water on him, penetrating right down to the depth of his intestines, creating that sickening loose bowel feeling. His heart began pounding. He ruthlessly suppressed the fear, shutting off any image of vulnerability. He made it a point to step toward the car. He stopped. He looked behind him. He was too far away from the bar to run back, and they were too close to let him. He looked around. Nobody on the street. Not even a passing car.

"Shit."

Shaw found himself short of breath. The adrenaline had kicked in. He knew he would be very strong for a short time, and then a shaky weakness would set in. One way or another, whatever was about to happen, it couldn't last long.

He muttered, "Fuck it," and walked forward.

He looked into the car, a Chevy Nova tricked out with chrome and add-on trim and wheel covers and ridiculously large speakers in the back window well.

He could make out a driver and two passengers. All black. All young.

Now that the car had stopped right in front of him, the music sounded even louder. Shouting at him, beating him with that pounding bass, like a weapon they were using on him. Shaw felt as if someone were smacking him in the head with the Brooklyn phone book.

Now it started. The two passengers opened their doors and stepped out. The driver stayed behind the wheel, but leaned forward to watch with a malicious grin.

That's right, Shaw said to himself. Smile, you cocksucker. This is very funny—whitey about to be maimed.

With the car doors open, the music boomed out even louder. The two young blacks moved toward Shaw, blocking his passage. They seemed to Shaw like a George and Lennie act: one big, one small. The big one responsible for the heavy work, the small one giving directions.

Shaw did not miss noticing how the Nova had visibly lifted when the big one stepped out. He wore his homeboy uniform: a hooded black sweatshirt, baggy denim pants, untied Timberland boots. His face reminded Shaw of a very stupid heavyweight fighter, nose flat and eyes blank. The sides of his head shaved. A short pile of dreads sprouted like a nest of fat black worms coming out of the top of his skull.

He tilted his head back to look at Shaw and said, "What's your fuckin' problem, bitch?"

Shaw knew which of the two he would go for, but first checked the smaller one to make sure he didn't have a gun pointed at him. In two seconds, Shaw saw everything he needed to, and more. The smaller one stood behind his partner, lean and nasty, nothing extra on him, with a face that reminded Shaw of a Doberman. Every angle of his bony skull stood out underneath his skin. Shaw checked the smaller one's hands, saw that they were empty, but the heavyweight . . . he had his right hand stuck in the front pouch pocket of his sweatshirt. He was the one with the gun. Shaw could already see the big, stupid kid dressed in those ridiculous baggy clothes, surrounded by that awful booming din, pulling out the gun and squeezing the trigger, shooting him, alone, on this strange street in Flatbush. Squeezing the trigger, no questions, no statements, without thought or concern, mindlessly inflicting terrible pain and damage on him. Or killing him. And with that horrible music so loud, no one would hear the shots.

Just the idea of it made Shaw so furious that the anger inside him blossomed like something alive. Like a dark hand reaching up his spine into his head, pushing aside everything: good sense, fear, caution, all of it. He went for the heavyweight powered by a fierce red wave of anger.

The heavyweight didn't see the anger take over. He was much too accustomed to terrifying people to worry about their anger.

He said, "I axed you a question, motherfucker."

But Shaw was already moving for him, very fast. It confused him. A white guy, alone, middle of the night, coming at him. No way. It confused the heavyweight and made him hesitate.

The smaller one behind him yelled, "Yo, Dread, cap this crazy motherfucker."

But by the time Dread started pulling out the gun, Shaw was already too close.

The gun came out of the sweatshirt pouch. Shaw already had his left hand coming straight up from his hip, open, twisting as much thrust and power into it as he could, he slammed the crook of his right hand into the heavyweight's throat.

The contact jarred Shaw's wrist and arm all the way to his shoulder. It felt as if he'd hit a small tree. The big kid barely moved back, but the blow hurt him enough to paralyze him where he stood. As he instinctively reached for his throat, without any hesitation between blows, Shaw made his next and last move.

Shaw circled a closed-fisted, overhand blow right at the heavyweight's collarbone. He put everything he had into the strike. All his strength, up from the balls of his feet, twisting his hips, sending the power into his shoulder and arm, concentrating everything into one fast brutal overhand smash. Shaw knew he couldn't let this turn into a fight. He had one chance, just one blow, full strength, the side of his tight fist coming down on the heavyweight's collarbone.

He heard the crack and felt the heavyweight's thick bone break under his fist. It was at once both sweetly satisfying and sickening.

Shaw heard a short, choking scream and watched the big kid deflate. The pain hit so intensely, so suddenly, the scream didn't last long. The heavyweight dropped to his knees. Moving either arm now would grind the broken ends of his left collarbone, so he didn't move.

But Shaw moved fast, ripping the gun out of his attacker's limp hand just as the smaller one swung at him. Shaw thought it was a punch, but the hand coming at his face held a hooked, carpet cutter's knife. He just managed to duck under it before the blade could tear the left side of his face open.

Shaw came up out of his crouch fast, the gun in his right hand. With no time to aim, he backhanded the gun barrel across the smaller one's nose hard enough to break it. The smaller one's head snapped around, blood flew out of his nostrils, and he went down hard on his left hip.

Now the driver came out of the car, pointing a revolver. Shaw pulled back the slide on the gun he'd taken from the heavyweight, a 9-mm semiautomatic.

The driver fired wildly, too pumped up and rushed to aim. The bullet went wide. Shaw returned fire, but he did not shoot at the driver. He shot at the back speaker in the Chevy Nova. That idiotic noise had been booming at him the entire time he had been fighting for his life. His shot blew out the back window. The driver ducked and ran, and the two others somehow made it to their feet and disappeared. But not the music. It still pounded out at Shaw, driving him even further over the edge. He pumped another shot at the speakers, yelling at the car in between shots. Shouting, "Turn off—that goddamn—fucking—music!"

He emptied the gun into the speakers and the dashboard, and the music finally died.

Shaw stood staring at the car, breathing hard. It took a few seconds, maybe longer, for him to come back to present time and space. He was just about to toss the gun, a beat-up old Browning, into the wrecked Nova and stumble off, find his car and drive out of the neighborhood when the first police car screeched to a halt behind him. The second blue-and-white appeared two seconds after the first, stopping in front of him.

Shaw stood motionless, frozen in the glare of four headlights, and forgot about tossing the gun. He dropped it right where he stood.

For some reason, as he dropped the gun he noted that it was an expensive weapon, probably stolen. Strange thoughts to be having standing there with his hands raised while at least four cops, four nervous cops, all had their guns drawn pointing at him. He wondered who'd called the cops. Maybe those two black guys under the street lamp. He supposed it was good of them to do that. Too bad the cops hadn't arrived sooner. Now, Shaw knew, that even though he'd survived the other three, if he made any sudden move, one of these four would shoot him.

4

After firing the deafening blasts from the Desert Eagle, Rachman Abdul X could not hear the hysterical screams of the crack whore, nor could he hear the pounding footsteps of the three rushing gunmen behind him. Each of them shoved the muzzle of his Tec-9 into the holes Rachman had created and fired short ripping bursts into the two Blue-Tops apartments. Bullets banged and ripped and ricocheted in the confined interiors. Fire from the muzzles burned the walls. Acrid smoke filled the rooms. The exploding nine-millimeter ammunition roared. Everyone alive in the rooms expected to die.

But they didn't. Rachman had made sure to blast open holes about six feet high. And the gunmen made sure to aim level or slightly upward. So the nightmare erupted over the heads of the dealers and buyers.

The Blue-Tops, the crazed crack addicts, all of them squirmed and writhed on the floor, expecting to die any second under the withering gunfire. Cringing, clinging to the floor, the assault seemed to go on forever.

Finally, the Tec-9s ran out of bullets. But it still wasn't over.

The two trailing gunmen with the Glocks stepped up to the two holes in the selling apartment and began methodically pulling their triggers. There were fewer bullets, but each of the nine-millimeter shots blew a withering blast into the rooms, forcing the Blue-Tops inside to cover their ears in order to prevent their eardrums from bursting.

Finally, out of a desperate survival instinct, the two

Blue-Tops guards inside started shooting back. They lay on their backs, cowing under the gunfire, and blindly shot at the exploding hole in the door in front of them.

The Blue-Tops bullets slammed into the metal-clad door. Rachman saw his gunman duck and step back. Rachman rushed to the door, pushed the gunman aside, shoved the barrel of the Desert Eagle into the hole, and fired. The big gun bucked and banged into the top of the door hole. Rachman growled and kept on firing, aiming downward because those inside had dared to shoot back. He tried to envision the position of the shooters on the other side of the door, willing his bullets to hit them, tear into them, and kill them.

Rachman grunted and yelled with each pull of the trigger. Inside both guards scrambled out of the line of fire as the big .50 Magnum bullets slammed into the floor around them and the wall behind them, tearing out chunks of wood and Sheetrock. One of Rachman's bullets caught the side of a guard's leg and tore away a wad of flesh the size of a fist. Both Blue-Tops stopped shooting.

And then, just as suddenly as the hellish assault had started, it ended. Suddenly, nothing could be heard but the screaming crack whore in the smoking apartment and the hollow click of Rachman's empty Desert Eagle. The gunmen with the Glocks had already stepped away from the wall, turned, and walked back to the stairwell. The gunmen with the Tec-9s had reloaded and stood pointing their weapons at the apartment door in case anyone dared to come out shooting.

Rachman stepped back from his firing hole, slid a fresh clip into the Desert Eagle, and motioned for John X to leave. John eased his long-barreled revolver out of Ellis's mouth, while Rachman pressed the hot muzzle of the Desert Eagle into Ellis's chest and brought his face up close to the Blue-Tops guard. While Ellis stared at him, he told the guard, "Lie down on your face. Ask Allah to forgive you. Don't look up for a long time, or I will come back and kill you."

Inside the smoking room someone finally punched the still screaming crack whore. Her jaw broke with a quick brutal snap, ending her hysterical shrieks.

After a few moments, the others slowly rose from the floor, touching themselves, squinting in the smoke-filled rooms, deafened from the gunfire, unable to comprehend what had just happened except that somehow, they were still alive.

As Rachman and his men rumbled down the inside stairwell, his gunmen assigned outside, as if emerging from the very night air, appeared next to each one of the Blue-Tops working around the complex. Every member of the gang felt a gun pressed firmly into the side of his head. If they had weapons, practiced hands found them and stripped them away. Then each Blue-Top heard a message hissed into his ear: "Tonight, we shoot above your heads. Next time, we shoot *in* your heads. Get out. New Lots belongs to MS-Two."

By the time Rachman and the others reached the bottom of the stairwell, the outside gunmen had converged near the rear door of Building A. Rachman and the others burst out the door, the muzzles of their guns still smoking, their clothes still stinking of gunpowder. All of the MS-2 gunmen gathered around a small man holding open a canvas bag. Each of them carefully placed their weapons and the confiscated Blue-Tops weapons in the bag. Rachman watched the final disciplined act, made sure all the weapons were carefully placed in the trunk of a beat-up '86 Ford LTD that looked like any of the other gypsy cabs that plied the Brownsville neighborhood. Only then did the gunmen quietly scatter and walk away from the scene. All except for Rachman. He stood and watched until the last gunman had disappeared.

5

Loyd Shaw stood on Tilden Avenue, hands lifted in the air. The beams of three police squad cars illuminating him. Six cops yelled, "Get down, get down. Down. Down."

Shaw slowly dropped to his knees, keeping his hands raised. When they continued screaming, "Get down!" he carefully placed his hands on the pavement and lowered himself to the street, arms and legs spread wide.

The gritty asphalt felt cold against his cheek. Better than a hot bullet slamming into my head, thought Shaw. He knew that cops called out in the middle of the night to a black neighborhood where shots had been fired were going to make damn sure they didn't get shot. And there he had been, standing in front of that shot-up car with a gun in his hand. Shaw thought about what would have happened to him if he'd have been a black man. I'd be dead already, he thought.

He lay on the damp, cold, dirty street motionless. He wasn't about to give anybody a reason to launch a kick or pull a trigger now.

At least a couple of the cops held their guns pointed at Shaw while two others knelt next to him and cuffed his hands behind his back. They roughly lifted him to his feet, pulled him over to a squad car, and shoved him into the backseat.

They left him in the squad car and started carefully checking over the scene.

Shaw leaned over and rested against the side door of the squad car. He couldn't sit back comfortably with his hands cuffed behind him. He carefully rolled his shoulders, testing to see if ligaments had been torn or joints dislocated when they lifted him off the street.

"Assholes," he said to himself.

Outside, the cops prowled around the wrecked Chevy Nova and confirmed the area was free of witnesses or damaged bodies.

After about ten minutes, one of the older cops came over and squatted down next to the back window of the squad. He held up the empty Browning by the trigger guard so Shaw could see it.

"This your gun?"

Shaw suppressed an urge to say, What the fuck do you think? and simply answered, "No, it's not my gun."

"Whose is it?"

"Two guys came out of that car, approached me, and one pulled out that gun. I took it away from him."

The cop raised an eyebrow. "You took it away from him?"

"Yeah."

"Uh-huh. How'd you manage to do that?"

"Very quickly."

"Oh really."

Shaw clamped his mouth shut instead of saying, yeah, really, so the cop asked him another question.

"That's their car?"

"Yeah. There were three guys in it. The two, plus the driver."

"And they came after you."

"Right. When I got the gun, the driver came out and pegged a shot at me."

"Why?"

" 'Cuz I had his pal's gun, I guess."

"No, why were these guys after you?"

Shaw thought about the answer for a moment. Because I dissed them? Because I was white, alone, in the wrong neighborhood? Because they weren't nice guys?

"I didn't like their music."

"You didn't like their music."

"I'm using the term music very loosely. I don't consider rap exactly music. Maybe musical, but not music."

"What are you, a fucking critic?"

Shaw didn't answer.

"I see. So you shot up their car?"

"Not the whole car. Just the speakers and the dashboard."

" 'Cuz of the music?"

"It was self-defense."

"Uh-huh. The guys with the guns you didn't give a shit about. It was the music that was killing you?"

Shaw smiled at that one.

The cop said, "Yeah, well, maybe, but shooting up cars ain't allowed. I'm going to have to take you in."

When they brought Shaw into the 77th Precinct, the Desk Sergeant didn't do much more than glance at Shaw. He saw a well-built white guy, brown hair long enough to go over the collar of his blue shirt, a dark brown leather jacket, black jeans. He noticed that Shaw was bigger than the cops on each side of him, but he didn't bother to look beyond that. The Desk Sergeant looked down at his logbook and made an entry.

Shaw, on the other hand, recognized the Desk Sergeant from a long time ago, but didn't feel like reminding the old cop. The arresting cop waited for the Desk Sergeant to make his few notes and hand him a report form. Then he walked Shaw over to the property clerk's cage, handed over Shaw's wallet, keys, pocket change. Next, he walked Shaw to an empty desk, sat down, and pulled out an arrest form from the bottom desk drawer.

Shaw sat and took it all in. The cop pulled an old IBM Selectric typewriter into position, shoved the arrest form in the roller, kicked shut the drawer.

Midnight to eight shift, thought Shaw. All pissed off now that he can't get out of here on time. Not this shift, pal. Not for a long time, Shaw thought.

Shaw said to the cop, "Well, at least you'll be getting some overtime."

"What?"

"Nothing," said Shaw.

The cop ratcheted a form into position and began poking at the keys.

Shaw looked around the precinct, noting that it was the same as most he'd been inside. Cement-block walls. Green paint. Cheap fluorescent lighting. Gray metal desks and a motley assortment of desk chairs. They never got the chairs coordinated, he thought. Shaw noticed that this precinct seemed particularly messy. Piles of papers lay everywhere—in folders, on desks, in piles next to desks, on bulletin boards. Lots of paper, lots of forms, one of which his arresting cop labored over. Shaw watched him peck away with two fingers and wondered if the NYPD would ever fully computerize their precincts. So many useless words pecked into mountains of forms that sat in mute phalanxes of old file cabinets.

Shaw turned sideways in his chair and leaned his shoulder against the back. His hands were still cuffed. He couldn't comfortably sit back. Shaw decided he'd about had enough of the damn handcuffs. He was about to tell the arresting cop to uncuff him when the property clerk appeared and told the cop, "We got a problem here, Joe."

Joe kept hunting for typewriter keys as he said, "What?"

The property clerk said, "You arrested a cop."

"Huh?"

"His ID is in his wallet. This is Detective First Grade Loyd Shaw."

The cop stopped poking at the typewriter keys. He looked up and stared at Shaw for about three seconds, then asked, "You're a detective?"

"Yeah."

"First?"

"Yeah."

"Where's your fucking shield and gun?"

"I don't have them."

"Who does?"

"My CO."

"You're on the rubber-gun squad?"

Shaw nodded.

"And you're out on Tilden Avenue shooting up cars?"

"Not cars. One car. Singular. One piece of shit Chevy Nova."

The cop grimaced, "Whoa. Fuck me, man." He stood up and said, "This one's outta my hands." He told the property clerk, "Watch him."

The clerk looked at Shaw. For a moment, he didn't say anything. Then he asked, "Whyn't you tell 'em you're a cop?"

"I don't know. There was a moment when it seemed appropriate to mention it, then it somehow slipped away."

The clerk looked at Shaw again and said, "Are you really Loyd Shaw?"

"Yeah."

The property clerk blinked twice, mumbled something about deep shit, and sat down.

Within five minutes, the cuffs were off and Shaw was locked away in a small office on the second floor of the precinct.

Shaw sat in the cramped office trying to figure out who worked in it. Probably the detective booking in assignment calls for the precinct's detective squad. There was the old green ledger used for such purposes sitting on the desk. On the far wall, someone had taped a map of Brooklyn showing the various boundaries of each Brooklyn precinct. Phones would be ringing all over Brooklyn about now, thought Shaw. In other boroughs, too.

Shaw began to make a mental list of the law enforcement personnel that would be called in the next hour or so. He knew the precinct commander wouldn't be on duty now, so they'd call in the zone commander to handle the situation. The zone commander would call Shaw's CO, Captain Richard Parnell, commander of the Special Investigation Division that had jurisdiction over Shaw's unit . . . the Major Cases Squad.

Shaw pictured Parnell being awakened by a four A.M. phone call. Parnell reminded Shaw of a bulldog, both in appearance and demeanor: squat, dour, tough Irish cop who had been around and knew the ropes, and didn't suffer fools easily. Nope, Shaw told himself, old Richard won't be happy about this.

Parnell would call the Detective's Endowment Association and talk to the head delegate who would probably call the local delegate who would call the lawyer assigned to Shaw's restricted duty case, Morton Siegel. The zone commander would call the Internal Affairs Bureau and the Brooklyn District Attorney's Office. Both entities would send personnel.

Shaw figured there would be anywhere from six to ten people assembled to figure out what to do with him. The possibilities ranged from letting him go home to locking him up and indicting him for attempted murder.

"Shit," he muttered to himself. That was going to be

one room full of disgruntled fucks. Dealing with this shit at five in the morning.

Shaw leaned back in his chair, propped his feet on the desk, and laid his head back, shifting until he achieved a somewhat comfortable position. It would be some time before the Assistant District Attorney and Internal Affairs investigator interviewed him. Nothing he could do until then, except try to catch some sleep.

Three hours later, Captain James Raiford sat at the precinct commander's desk writing notes on a legal pad. The commander's office wasn't much bigger than the second-floor office Shaw occupied.

If Raiford had been wearing a judge's robe instead of his police captain's executive white uniform, he would have perfectly fit the image of a stern, no-nonsense criminal court judge. Everything about him communicated rectitude: his hawklike features, his ramrod-straight posture, his thinning hair combed straight back. Even the meticulous way he scrutinized his notes reminded the men who sat before him of a judge.

Shaw's estimate of six to ten proved accurate. Eight men were crowded into the small office, sitting or standing, looking at the zone commander, James Raiford. But Raiford's interest focused on three men only: Shaw's CO, the bulldog Richard Parnell; Shaw's lawyer, a disheveled bald, gnomelike man named Morton Siegel; and the assistant district attorney, an intense young black man named Philip Johnson whose white shirt and blue suit seemed remarkably crisp and wrinkle-free, as if kept that way by sheer force of Johnson's will.

Raiford finally looked up from his notes.

"All right, you know the drill, gentleman. It's my job to decide what happens to Detective Shaw tonight.

After tonight, Internal Affairs and the DA's office will do whatever they decide, but the next move is my call. I want your input, but I'm not looking for arguments or extended debates. You've all read the report. I think Captain Parnell has made Detective Shaw's personnel file available. Internal Affairs and Mr. Johnson have completed their interviews. Mr. Siegel, you've finished?"

"Yes, sir."

"All right. The union delegates have already given their opinion that Detective Shaw should be awarded a commendation and sent home. Mr. Johnson, you represent the District Attorney here, what's your recommendation?"

"I'm looking at an indictment for attempted murder."

A voice from the back of the room commented, "You gotta be kidding."

Johnson's head snapped in the direction of the voice and said, "You think I'm kidding, just watch me. First of all, this line about a twenty-year veteran who never had a problem is bullshit. The man's already on restricted duty for what, assaulting a superior officer?"

Siegel gently interrupted, "Excuse me, Mr. Johnson, I happen to be handling that case. It's not assault. In fact, it's not at all clear who struck the first blow in the altercation."

Johnson shuffled his papers and referred to a report on the incident. "Well it's damn clear who ended up with a broken jaw and chipped teeth." Johnson held up a hand to preclude Siegel's response. "Hold on. I haven't even started. This other report says this isn't the first shooting incident he's been involved in. I'll want the details on this, but it says here he saw Psych Services after that incident for two weeks. Now three years later, he's back in Psych Services, been going twice a week for three months. What the hell is that all about?"

Siegel tried to get a word in, but Johnson continued over him.

"Now the guy shows up on Tilden Avenue at three in the morning, drunk, shooting a gun, while he's on restricted duty. The man shouldn't even be touching a gun, and he's shooting up a car, which for all I know, was filled with civilians. Hell, at the very least I've got weapon's possession and property damage. If there were people in that car, I've got attempted murder. You folks have a cop out of control, Captain Raiford. He should be held for arraignment. Let a judge set bail and give the Department of Corrections custody of this man and let my office go in front of the Grand Jury and figure out just what we want to indict him for."

Raiford turned to the lawyer. "Mr. Siegel?"

Siegel grimaced as if in pain. As if he couldn't imagine how the ADA could say such things about Loyd Shaw. Siegel spoke at half the volume of Johnson, but with just as much intensity.

"This *man*? Turn this *man* over to the Department of Corrections? This *man* is not some common criminal. Loyd Shaw is a nineteen-year, not twenty-year yet, Mr. Johnson, a nineteen-year veteran of the NYPD. A first grade detective. Gentlemen, some perspective, please."

Siegel looked around the room as if to assess for himself whether everyone was keeping the proper perspective before he could continue.

"Where is the criminal case against this officer? Mr. Johnson refers to a shooting incident three years ago. *Three* years ago? In the line of duty. What does that have to do with anything? Psych Services counseling is *mandatory* after shooting incidents. A full and proper investigation was conducted. There were no charges.

No improprieties. Officer Shaw was awarded a commendation for God's sake! And this is now being turned against him? That's outrageous. Not to mention irrelevant. As is his recent use of Psych Services. The department encourages its officers to use those services. You don't know why Detective Shaw is seeking counseling. Perhaps Detective Shaw is dealing with a marriage problem, a death in the family, the loss of a fellow officer, there could be any number of reasons. It's this kind of prejudicial attitude displayed by the assistant district attorney that discourages cops who need help from getting it. Detective Shaw should be commended not condemned.

"And this characterization that Detective Shaw was drunk? Based on what? There's no evidence of intoxication. The arresting officer made no mention of it. I just interviewed Detective Shaw, and I can assure you the man is stone-cold sober. Detective Shaw attended a birthday gathering for a fellow police officer. He was present for a total of a half hour. And suddenly he's running the streets of Brooklyn in a wild drunken spree? Hardly. He was walking back to his car, and he was assaulted.

"If there's a crime here, Detective Shaw is not the one who committed it. There's no evidence of a crime. The gun was not Detective Shaw's. There was no sign of injury on the street. No blood in the car. No witnesses. There is no case. By all means, Mr. Johnson, I encourage you to go back to your office and figure out what charges to bring. A closer, more dispassionate appraisal will reveal there are none. Captain Raiford, send this man home. He shouldn't have even been arrested."

Johnson responded, "Mr. Siegel, you are being disingenuous at best. You know the relevance of his Psych Services record. Whether it's fair or not, you know as well as I do that once a cop does that, he's basically kissing off his career. A cop who doesn't give a damn about his career anymore is a dangerous cop.

"Now, there might not have been any victims on the scene, but the man fired off eight rounds. *Eight.* If he intended to drive off these so called assailants, one or two warning shots in the air would suffice, don't you think? The man unloaded a nine millimeter at a car. You consider that rational behavior? He claims he was assaulted by three black men, but there's not a mark on him. No sign of a struggle. How do I know that gun wasn't his? How do I know he didn't just decide these kids were making too much noise and felt a little street justice was in order. I think you've got a cop out of control here. He should be locked up."

Raiford raised a hand. He knew that exaggerations aside, Johnson had finally stated the critical issue.

"All right, gentlemen, thank you."

Raiford's demeanor precluded any further comments by Siegel and Johnson.

"Mr. Siegel, I tend to agree with you that without witnesses or victims, there isn't much of a chance that any criminal proceedings will go forward. Of course, if Internal Affairs comes up with the owner of that car and a victim, Mr. Johnson might be able to make a case.

"However, Mr. Johnson does have a point. Detective Shaw, by any standards, went way over the line tonight. Most of us in this room are familiar with the shooting incident Detective Shaw engaged in a few years back."

Johnson interrupted. "Enlighten me."

Raiford held up a hand. "I don't have time for that. I've got to decide if this cop is stable enough to be let out of here. He is seeing Psych Services. He seems to be acting a bit crazy out there, even given the circumstances. Captain Parnell, you're the one in this room who knows him best. I don't want to turn a good cop over to the Department of Corrections, but I can't let him back out there if he's lost it. Is this Detective Shaw a danger?"

Parnell rubbed his jowly face as if he were trying to rouse a response from somewhere deep inside. Raiford watched him carefully, calculating how much of Parnell's answer would be contrived to distance himself from Shaw, and how much would be the simple truth as he knew it.

Parnell started with an equivocation.

"I don't deal with Shaw on a day-to-day basis. But I've known him for a lot of years. I put him on Major Cases."

Parnell shifted in his chair. He knew whatever he said would be the deciding factor for Raiford.

Parnell continued, "Fact is, Shaw's a damned good detective. Not exactly a team player, but he gets the job done. Maybe a little too smart for his own good. Does things his way. Always has. But like I said, he gets the job done. I don't know if he's about to go off his nut. How the hell do you know that? Who knows how all this shit we deal with affects a guy. Maybe you should have dragged his shrink in here and asked her. But I do know one thing."

"Yes?" asked Raiford.

"I know the guy wants to finish his twenty and get the hell out. He's made no bones about that to anyone. Told me that himself. He's got a place up in Massachusetts. Weekend place. I don't think he deserves to sit in some goddamn cell until he gets arraigned. I'd tell him to get the hell out of town. Go up to his place out of state and stay there until his departmental trial. Suspend him. Tell him if he shows up inside the city before his trial, he goes into the can. If he's gonna go off his nut and shoot something or somebody, let him do it up in the woods."

Parnell crossed his arms and sat back in his chair.

Raiford looked around the room one time to see if anyone had anything else to say.

Johnson saw the decision coming and simply announced, "Do what you want. I'm pursuing an investigation."

Raiford responded, "Fine. Detective Shaw is suspended pending a departmental trial and investigation of tonight's events. I suggest IAB get his departmental trial on the books as soon as possible.

"Captain Parnell, I'll give Shaw the news, but I want you to accompany him out of here and take him home and tell him if he doesn't leave town, I'll have him locked up. And I want you to keep a tight rein on him until he does. Don't let him near your squad. They work out of One Police?"

"Yes."

"He shouldn't even go in there to clean his desk. Tell him to get out of town and stay out until his trial. That's it, gentlemen. Thank you. Go home and get whatever sleep you can."

6

As Parnell and Raiford slowly walked up to the second floor of the 75th Precinct house to deliver the news to Loyd Shaw, a phone rang in Saddle Brook, New Jersey, bringing news to Archie Reynolds.

Archie lay sleeping in a queen-size bed, dressed only in purple silk boxer shorts, his slim, muscular, mocha-colored body contrasted against the white sheets. Before the first ring finished, Archie snatched the receiver from the cradle.

"What?"

"Ar-Man, we, we, we got hit."

Archie knew the stuttering voice belonged to one of his three managers, Reggie Whack.

"Slow down, motherfucker. Where?"

"New, New Lots?"

"New Lots?"

"Yuh, yuh, yeah, man."

"Who? Cops?"

"Nuh, nuh, no. Wasn' no cops."

"Who? What they get?"

"Nu', nu', nuthin'. The crew got the rocks and money out."

"What the fuck you talkin' about?"

"A hit, homes."

"Anybody dead?"

Reggie answered, "No. Mayon guh, guh, got, hit in the leg. He messed up, but he ain't dead."

"So what you so fucked up about, man?"

" 'Dis wasn't no regular thing, Arch. This was different. They didn't *try* to shoot nobody, except for Mayoñ 'cuz I guess he wa, wa, was shootin' back. They unloaded all kinds a shit into the place, coulda kilt everybody, taken everything, but they didn't. This was a warning kind of thing."

"A warning? What the fuck you mean, a warning?"

"They had guys inside, outside. Got the drop on everybody. They said New Lots belong to them now and we got to get the fuck out or the next time they shoo, shoo, shoot us in the head."

"Wait a minute, wait a minute. Who's 'they'?"

"Don't know, man. Some initial shit."

"Some what?"

"Initials. Like em, em, MSG or M-Two, I don't know. Some shit like that."

"And they tellin' *us* to get the fuck out?"

"Yeah."

"What they hit us with?"

"Ellis said it was Tec-nines and Glocks. A shi, a shi, a shitload of firepower, man."

"That's drug-gang guns."

"Yeah, but it wasn't no drug gang, Archie. They didn't kill no one. And they had everybody covered, man. The guys in The Pit. The steerers. The lookouts on the roof. They could have kilt all of 'em, but they didn't. Just said 'get out.' "

Archie said, "Yeah, okay, I got it."

"Got what? Who the fuck are these guys?"

"You suppose to know that, motherfucker. Somebody puts a gun up and tells me and mines to get out, you suppose to know."

"Yeah, man. I know. I knu, knu, know."

"No you don't fuckin' know. That's the trouble. You call everybody walking. You get everybody over to the shop. You make sure Little Marvin is there. He's lieutenant of the operation, ain't he?"

"Yeah."

"You suppose to be the manager, right?"

"Yeah. Get your people, your wagons, your shit over there now. I be leaving here after I shower and dress an' shit."

Archie dropped the receiver back into the cradle and lay back in bed. A frown marred his otherwise handsome, dark face. Archie stroked the slight goatee that decorated his upper lip and chin.

"What the fuck is goin' on now?" he asked himself.

He thought about it for a few seconds then jackknifed himself out of the bed in one quick move and headed slowly for his bathroom. Archie did not rush through the hour he spent showering, shaving, slipping on his matching gold chains on wrist and neck, and dressing. Archie moved casually, stepping into light wool pleated pants, buttoning his stylish silk and rayon shirt. But his mind ticked off several scenarios trying to explain what had happened at New Lots that night.

By the time he slid behind the wheel of his Saab 900 SE convertible, he had stopped trying to figure all the angles and concentrated on two facts: his Blue-Tops had not seen the attack coming. Whoever had attacked them told him to get out of New Lots. The first fact made him angry. The second drove him into a slow, simmering, barely suppressed rage.

The rage simmered and burned as Archie drove along Route 80 toward New York.

When Archie had first checked a road map to figure out the way from Saddle Brook to Brownsville, he thought Route 80 looked like a long, fat blue vein. A fat, blue vein that ran right next to his condo in Saddle Brook, headed straight to the George Washington Bridge, crossed the bridge, and merged with another highway vein that pulsed through the Bronx, curved over to the Whitestone Bridge, continued into Queens along the Van Wyck, looping slowly around in a lazy

J along the Interboro Parkway right into the heart of Brooklyn, right into the misery of Brownsville.

Archie rode the vein to Brownsville, checking the Saabs speedometer to make sure he stayed between fifty-five and sixty mph. It didn't matter that there was very little traffic on the road. Archie Reynolds knew better than to give some eager state trooper a reason to pull him over.

Archie knew Jersey troopers or Port Authority police didn't need genuine probable cause to stop him. To them, a young black man in a new car was cause enough.

Archie reminded himself, fuckin' crackers be smacking and crackin' my nappy head and slappin' me in cuffs before I know it.

Nope, just be cool, Archie told himself. Don't want nothing to stop me from getting into Brownsville tonight, baby. Not tonight, baby. Not tonight.

7

Zone Commander James Raiford walked into the small, second-floor precinct office. He didn't sit down while he told Loyd Shaw he'd been exiled. Raiford recited the verdict while Parnell stood behind him. Shaw glanced at Richard Parnell while the zone commander spoke in an official monotone. Parnell's fleshy face displayed no emotion.

Shaw found himself surprised that he looked for something more from his commanding officer. A look of regret. A scowl of anger. Anything. Something to convey that Parnell cared.

Raiford's speech to Shaw ended. He turned to Parnell and said, "Please see that Detective Shaw leaves the precinct immediately."

The zone commander left without another word. Shaw hadn't bothered to rise from his chair. Parnell simply said, "Let's go."

As they walked down to the ground floor of the precinct, Parnell said, "I don't have to bother telling you they mean business, do I?"

"No."

"Don't even think about hanging around, Shaw. When can you leave?"

Parnell's seemingly simple question deeply offended Shaw.

He said to himself, that's the best you can come up with, Dick? When the fuck are you leaving? Shaw opened his mouth to answer and felt the anger and bitterness well up in him. But he shut off the words.

He wouldn't give Parnell the satisfaction. Instead he merely said, "Now."

"What?" said Parnell.

"Now. Give me a ride back to my car in Flatbush. I'm leaving now."

Parnell heard a tone in Shaw's voice that told him, don't push it. He shot a quick sidelong glance at Shaw, and decided to keep his mouth shut.

Parnell's deference mollified Shaw just enough so that he endured being led out of the police precinct like a criminal. He caught the looks of the uniformed cops as he walked into the main entrance area of the precinct. For a moment, he considered turning to Parnell and telling him, no thanks. I don't need a fucking ride. I'll find my car myself and leave when I damn well feel like it. But just then they reached the ground floor and Shaw spotted big Jake Bennett standing in the precinct lobby. Jake's smiling birthday face had turned glum and worried.

When Shaw saw that look on Jake's face, he forgot about Parnell. Shaw thought, goddamn it, they went and pulled him out of Earl's. Shit. Shit.

Jake stood there, brow furrowed, head down, looking as if he had done something terrible. Shaw turned to Parnell and said, "Wait a minute."

Parnell didn't try to follow him.

"Don't even say it, Jake."

"Damn, Shaw. I'm sorry."

"I told you don't say it. This had nothing to do with you."

"I should have walked you to your car."

"Oh, bullshit. It just happened, that's all."

"Yeah, but you can't be—"

"Forget it. I told you in the bar it's over."

Jake shook his head once or twice, forcing himself

not to comment on it or belabor the fact that Shaw's career was over.

"Jake, listen, damn it, don't stand there feeling sorry for me. You want to do something, I'll tell you what to do."

"What? Name it."

"You heard about what happened?"

"Yeah."

"Three knuckleheads. In a Chevy Nova. Get the plate from the arresting officer. Find those fucks."

Shaw described the three assailants, making sure to mention one of them would be walking around with a broken collarbone.

"Jake, find them before the ADA's investigators or IAB guys. Make sure those pricks don't show up at my departmental trial with some bullshit story."

Jake listened closely to what Shaw told him.

"No problem, man. It's done."

Shaw knew if his attackers were still in Brooklyn, Jake Bennett would find them. Jake had been on the Brooklyn Warrants Squad for a long time. He knew how to find people. They shook hands, and Shaw headed out of the precinct. Parnell followed two steps behind him.

After speaking with Jake, Parnell's presence didn't bother Shaw nearly as much as it had. It suddenly didn't matter so much what the brass wanted to do. Shaw never paid much attention to the brass anyhow. The guys you work with in the trenches, thought Shaw, those are the ones who determine whether or not you make it. Always have been. Always will be. Fuck Parnell and Raiford and all the rest.

At that moment, all Shaw wanted to do was get into his car and get the hell out of there

Parnell drove Shaw back to Flatbush. They quickly located Shaw's car.

Neither of the men spoke during the ride. When Shaw stepped out of Parnell's car, he didn't offer his hand to his CO. Clearly, they had ended up on opposite sides.

Parnell felt compelled to reiterate the order to get out of town, but this time Shaw didn't even bother to say, okay. He just nodded. Their positions had become clear. Parnell was in. Shaw was out.

Shaw climbed into his seven-year-old Mercury Grand Marquis, shut all the windows tight, turned on his CD player, and headed north. He stopped once for gas and coffee on the Merritt Parkway and to call Jane. He timed his call about fifteen minutes before her regular wake-up time. The way she answered gave him the impression that she had been dead asleep. Could have probably snuck in and grabbed a couple of hours with no problem, he thought. Too bad.

He simply told her that something had come up on the job and he would be gone for a few days. He told it in a voice that said, don't ask me any questions about it.

As he walked back to his car, Shaw pictured Jane hanging up the phone. He tried to imagine the look on her face. Would she be concerned? Would she even think about it? Did he give a shit?

He told himself, not really, as he climbed back into the Mercury.

Shaw sped along as dawn came up over the highway, running at about seventy-five mph. He decided he didn't care about speeding tickets either.

By the time Archie Reynolds drove the Saab convertible 900 SE off the Interboro Parkway and hit the bleak streets of East New York and Brownsville, the night had turned into a gray, dull dawn.

He had driven from Saddle Brook, New Jersey, an area comprised mostly of trees and houses, through the Bronx, dominated by apartment buildings, and through Queens, a mix of both. Now he entered Brownsville, most of which was nothing but long stretches of waste and rubble interrupted by structures that had collapsed under the weight of abuse and neglect and the final ravages of fire. The houses and apartments and commercial buildings still in use were so run down and decrepit that they seemed to be discarded versions of what the rest of the city used.

There was too much waste in Brownsville, particularly wasted lives. Angry knots of young men collected in between the rubble and ruin, standing in front of bodegas or newsstands or subway stations; or roving in bands looking for something amidst the nothing.

As soon as Archie hit the streets of Brownsville, he tuned his radio to 106 and pressed his turn signal switch down three times. A hidden door built into the driver's side door popped open. He glanced down to make sure a loaded Taurus .40-caliber PT 101 sat within reach. The gun fit in the car door, but could hold twelve bullets that Archie would shoot into the face of any knucklehead who might decide to sidle up to the Saab at a streetlight and take the shiny, middle-class car for himself. Not everyone knew the car carried Archie Ar.

Archie turned the Saab into an alley that ran alongside the elevated Canarsie line tracks. A high-intensity streetlight that should have lit up the area had been broken years ago, so the only light that filtered down into the alley was a gray, predawn glow that made everything look even more dirty and dismal than usual.

One of Archie's gang, a slim Jamaican kid sporting dreadlocks, stood slouched against the door of a body shop located in the alley. When he saw the black Saab rumble into the alley, he tapped twice on the corrugated steel door, and it began to slowly winch open so Archie could drive the Saab inside.

There were several cars in various states of repair or reconstruction scattered around the ground floor of the body shop, including two cars used by the gang to transport guns and drugs. Cars that had been chopped up and reassembled with hidden compartments in the floor, side panels, under the backseat, and inside the trunk. Opening the hidden compartments required a similar series of complicated moves as with Archie's Saab. Turning the radio to the secret frequency, pushing down door locks, flipping the turn signal.

In addition to the cars, sixteen gang members lounged around the shop, the expected assortment of angry, young black men who had taken up the brief career of crack dealing. There were enough gold teeth and jewelry, dreadlocks, tattoos, dark glasses, baggy Phat clothes, and quarts of malt liquor for any respectable crack gang. But the Blue-Tops differed from other crack gangs in their degree of viciousness and violence. All but two of the young black men standing around the body shop had killed another human being. Each of the sixteen faces bore a sullen, dangerously aggressive look as if they constantly had to prove to themselves and each other that they were bad men.

None of the killers appeared happy to be in the body shop. Particularly Little Marvin, who hung back from the main group.

Reggie Whack stood in the middle of the body shop dressed in his usual attire: black knit cap bearing a New York Knicks logo, sweatshirt, baggy khaki pants, and black boots. Reggie hardly ever smiled or talked, thereby concealing his missing right front tooth and his ferocious stutter. Reggie had earned his street name, Whack, by killing seven men, two of whom died laughing at his speech impediment.

Nobody in Brownsville laughed at Reggie Whack now.

Archie stepped out of the Saab and Reggie Whack handed Archie a .22-caliber Beretta Model 21A, a short-barreled, deadly, little gun that weighed just over half a pound. Every member of the gang felt the gun to be much too small for a respectable thug. But experience had taught Archie what small bullets could do when fired into a human body.

Archie hardly looked at any of the men except Little Marvin, who was little only in comparison to his older brother, Big Marvin. Archie stepped out of the Saab and motioned for Little Marvin to come over to him, even before he closed the driver's side door.

Archie had stepped out quickly, not bothering to pull the keys out of the ignition, so with the door open, the car emitted an annoying, incessant, electronic bing-bing sound to remind Archie to take his keys.

Little Marvin did not hurry to reach Archie and the irritating bing-bing-bing sounded insistently, annoying Archie so much that he shot Little Marvin from a distance of five feet. He had wanted to press the small gun into Little Marvin's head, but shot him without waiting for that pleasure so he could slam the car door and stop the damn binging.

Archie shot Little Marvin and muttered, "Bing that, motherfucker."

Not surprisingly, for a good time afterward the word *bing* became synonymous among the Blue-Tops with the word kill. As in, "he binged the motherfucker."

Because Archie shot Little Marvin from a distance, the small .22-caliber bullet didn't hit Little Marvin in the center of the head. It hit him just above the right eye, snapping Little Marvin's head backward and spinning him around. Little Marvin lost his balance almost instantly because the small bullet tumbled and bounced and ripped around inside his skull, turning his brain into a useless, bloody, ten-pound piece of meat.

Little Marvin's legs twitched in a short, spastic, little dance, then crumpled underneath him. All his nerve impulses shut down, except for a few basic ones that kicked and twitched for a while. In two seconds, Little Marvin's brain died. The rest of his body tumbled into death shortly thereafter.

Archie turned to his men, now acknowledging their presence and said, "See, that motherfucker was already dead even before I got here. I just put him out of his misery, see, 'cuz any motherfucker in charge of an operation like we got here, don't see it coming when someone is planning to hit you, anyone don't see when somebody scoping you out so damn close that everybody all at once is under the gun? They be dead and don't know it. You all dead. You all be motherfucking, walking dead men. Somebody comes up and puts a gun to your heads, and you don't see it coming? They do that to you last night; they can do it tonight. They can do it tomorrow night. Any motherfucking night.

"So you motherfuckers better find out who the fuck

these guys are, then git yo' asses out there and put a bullet in their heads before they put one in yours."

End of speech. Having told them why, Archie did not need to tell his gang of murderers how.

Less than five blocks from where Little Marvin's body dropped to the concrete floor of the body shop, Whitey Williams sat at the window of his New Lots studio apartment in Building D. Whitey, one of the original tenants in the complex, puffed on his morning White Owl cigar and watched. Safety dictated that, like most senior citizens in Brownsville, Whitey spent most of his time in his apartment. Whitey had made an art of being inconspicuous. Although he was in good shape for an eighty-two-year-old, Whitey moved his wiry, five-foot-eight frame slowly and methodically. When he was outside his apartment, Whitey did nothing to attract attention. It was safer in Brownsville for a man Whitey's age if you did not attract attention. Few people took notice of Whitey. There wasn't anything to notice, except perhaps his close-cropped, white hair.

The morning after Rachman's raid on the Blue-Tops crack apartment provided Whitey with a great deal more to watch than the usual. Change had come to New Lots, hauled in by two five-ton trucks loaded with pre-fabricated sections of iron fencing. Serious fencing— square iron rods an inch wide and ten feet high, joined together by thick horizontal bands of iron.

A heavy equipment backhoe roared and shoveled and scraped out trenches in between each of the five buildings in the complex. A cement truck sat on New Lots Avenue, its huge drum turning, ready to pour concrete into the trenches. Even from his fourth-floor perch, Whitey could tell this was a serious installation. By the looks of it, once the work crews scrambling around the perimeter of the complex sunk that iron fence into the trenches, nothing would get through except a tank.

Whitey had already heard about the shooting in Building A the night before. Now the next part of the plan became obvious to him. Not only had the management decided to do something to get the Blue-Tops out, they had decided they would keep them out.

Whitey sat and watched New Lots change. Who the hell is doing this? wondered Whitey. He decided the squat agitated white man wearing a rumpled brown suit and a knit yarmulke standing near a burly black man wearing combat boots, camouflage pants, an army field jacket, and a Kinte cap must be behind this.

A white man with a bodyguard, thought Whitey.

Shit, thought Whitey, bad as New Lots be, it's gonna get a lot worse around here.

Leon Bloom and Rachman Abdul X stood near the main entrance to the complex where the iron fencing would be turned into the new main gate for New Lots Apartments.

Despite the chilly midmorning April air, Bloom perspired profusely. Not just because Bloom carried an extra fifty pounds on his short, squat frame, not just because the fifty-year-old man was in terrible physical shape, Bloom dripped with sweat because he knew how dangerous it was to be standing in front of New Lots the morning after Rachman's warning attack.

The fear made him anxious to get the fencing job done quickly. Bloom kept telling the workmen around him to keep moving, to work faster.

In between bothering the workmen, Bloom rushed around shooing away the dozens of kids who were a perpetual presence at New Lots. Bloom wasn't surprised that although most of the kids were school age, so many were not in school. Most of the kids barely listened to the portly white man, but Rachman's baleful stares kept them at a distance.

Bloom pushed and yelled. Rachman stood where he was, kept his mouth shut, and watched.

Mostly, Rachman watched the street. Even when Bloom bothered him with nervous questions, he kept an eye on the street. There were no gunmen on the premises, only two of Rachman's regular, unarmed security guards. No police had responded to the early morning shooting because no one in New Lots had bothered to report it.

Rachman, too, wanted the fence up as soon as possible, but he knew bothering the workman wouldn't help.

Rachman kept his distance from Bloom. Bloom's questions annoyed him. As did the faint odor Bloom exuded. Rachman's strict vegetarian diet made him particularly sensitive to Bloom's body odor. Bloom ate meat—fatty, heavily seasoned meat—smoked at least two packs of filtered Camels every day, and drank, mostly gin—cheap, back-bar gin sloshed with cheap vermouth to make the three double martinis Bloom consumed every day with lunch.

Bloom did not fit the stereotype of the Orthodox Hasid. Not in habits or appearance. Bloom had red hair and freckles, and a scraggly red beard much too sparse for his moon-shaped face.

Bloom, of course, didn't care at all about Rachman's desire to keep his distance.

For the second time that morning, Bloom asked, "So, you did what you said?"

"Yes."

"Everything went all right?"

"Yes."

"Your people got out okay?"

"Yes, Mr. Bloom."

"Anybody hurt?"

"Maybe. They shot back at us."

"They what?"

"Shot back."

"How? From where?"

"From inside the apartment."

"And you shot at them? You said it would only be a warning. Nobody hurt."

"We will always defend ourselves."

"*Oy*, this I don't need."

"I explained our methods to you, Mr. Bloom."

"All right, all right. I don't want to hear about it. Let's hope, God willing, it doesn't happen again."

"It will. Be sure of that, Bloom. Before this is over it will."

"At least that place is cleaned out, right? They left?"

"Yeah."

"Out of the complex?"

"No, Mr. Bloom. Not out of the complex. Just out of their poisonous crack den. Just out of one place in one building. You know it's going to take more than warning them."

"Okay, okay. Just keep moving them out of any apartments they use in there until there's no more left."

"Do you know how many empty apartments they use?"

"How many? *Vay iz mer*, how the hell do I know? Who can tell in that dark. They're in, they're out, like rats in a hole, in a maze. One day you see some bum in one place, the next day he's gone, the next day you got some dreck doing drugs, some street whore doing her business in there, who knows? I got more people wandering those hallways than walking on Atlantic Avenue. You got to get 'em out."

"We'll start getting squatters and wanderers out tomorrow. The Blue-Tops won't be as easy. You have to board up the empties as soon as we clear them out."

"Tomorrow. We start first thing. I bring workmen in tomorrow. But once you get 'em out you got to keep 'em from going back in, Mr. Rachman, or they just tear off the plywood and throw it out a window where it lands on some poor schmuck's head."

"I know that, Mr. Bloom."

"I have two crews coming in tomorrow to start boarding up empty apartments."

"Doors and windows, right?"

"That's what you said, Mr. Rachman, that's what I'm doing. You have men to go with the crews?"

"A team of three with each crew."

"Armed, right?" asked Bloom.

"One armed and two regulars. But they're not shooters, Mr. Bloom, not gunmen."

"You said you'd have a given percentage of men with arms."

"Licensed men with the regulars, Mr. Bloom. But remember, they're legal. The legals don't want to lose their licenses. They won't shoot."

"Yes, yes, Mr. Rachman. The ones who have the guns legally, won't shoot them. The ones who aren't suppose to have guns, they shoot."

"We've been through all this."

"I have to pay extra for people with guns who won't shoot them."

"They don't want to lose their license."

"Yes, yes."

"They're worth the price, Mr. Bloom. They'll discourage arguments and intimidate most of the people who want to cause trouble. We don't need the gunmen for that."

"I know, I know. I don't want to know. The rest is

your business. Start with the squatters and keep the crack heads out."

Rachman simply nodded this time, because he didn't want to discuss it further, and because he saw a five-year-old Lincoln Town Car turn onto New Lots Avenue up the street to his left. The car appeared to be filled with passengers. Rachman moved two steps away from Bloom to get a better look at the car. For a brief moment, he felt sure it was a drive-by, but hesitated because the car moved toward them so slowly.

Rachman's experience told him the driver should be too excited or too nervous or too ready to kill to keep coming at them so slowly. But he didn't know that the car never sped up because the driver had been smoking marijuana and drinking malt liquor ever since the early dawn gathering of the Blue-Tops at the body shop. The alcohol and pot made him too stoned to care or worry about the fact that he drove at ten miles per hour.

It wasn't until Rachman saw the first shotgun barrel poke out of the rear window that he shoved Bloom to his right and yelled for the others to get down.

Most of the workman heard him yell, but few understood him.

Bloom hit the ground just before the first loud bang and blast of shot cracked into the iron fence and bricks of Building A. The first lone blast stunned everyone into a deadly instant of paralysis. And then the entire area around the front entrance erupted in gunfire. Shotgun blasts intermingled with the popping of 9-mm handguns and a ripping crackle of a machine pistol. Dozens of bullets slammed into everything: the welder's truck, the concrete sidewalk, the fencing. Glass broke, chips of brick and sidewalk zinged through the air. Rachman just managed to dive behind the welder's truck. So many bullets slammed into the truck that the generator bolted to the truck bed exploded in an eruption of spark and smoke.

Rachman pulled out one of the Glocks he had kept from the early morning raid, braced the gun on the fender of the truck and shot back at the Town Car.

The gunfire from the drive-by never even paused. Rachman unloaded five shots at the flashing windows of the Town Car to no effect. He realized that with all the gunfire and spent cartridges that must be flying around inside the car, the Blue-Tops probably didn't even realize someone had returned their fire.

Rachman heard someone behind him grunt and gag.

The welder's truck suddenly dropped as bullets blew out both front tires. Rachman kept his gun braced on the fender, growled, and emptied the Glock at the Blue-Tops car.

And finally, finally the shooting stopped, only because the Blue-Tops ran out of ammunition.

The Town Car simply rolled down New Lots Avenue at the same slow speed it had rolled up to the complex. The driver made a lazy left turn at the next block as if he were driving his elderly mother to church.

They had executed the drive-by as if they owned the street. If Rachman's bravery had accomplished anything, it might have only been to prevent them from stopping the car, getting out, and emptying their weapons from a standing position.

For a few moments after the explosive chaos, a stunned silence reigned. And then, it seemed everyone alive began yelling and shouting for help. Wounded men cried out, both commands and cries mixing together in an unintelligible clamor that only communicated pain and fear and panic.

Two of the workmen had been hit. One of them, flung onto his back, his chest blossoming blood, his head thrown sideways, appeared to be dead. The other casualty began cursing and yelling incoherently. Shotgun pellets had sprayed his face, neck, and the top of his shoulder. Shredded skin hung off his jaw and neck. It looked as if half his face had been blown away. The man screamed continuously about his eyes.

Rachman's first concern was his guards. He had expected them to be hit because their dark blue MS-2 jackets emblazoned with the word SECURITY in big, block, gold letters across the back made them obvious targets.

Both guards lay on the ground behind a pile of iron fencing, still covering their heads with their hands. No sound came from them. At first, Rachman feared they were both dead, but he saw no blood. And then, slowly, they started moving, cautiously lifting their heads. Rachman muttered a brief prayer of thanks to Allah, acknowledging his will. But in the next instant, Rachman's prayer turned to a curse when booming shotgun blasts and the chilling crack of automatic-weapons fire exploded on the other side of the complex

Rachman turned and looked past The Pit toward the back of the complex. A second Blue-Tops car had stopped in front of the work site. Shooters in the front and back seats blasted fire and shot at the workmen. A third shooter on the far side of the car had leaned far enough out of the window so he could sit in the window well, rest an automatic rifle on the roof of the car and calmly fire off streams of bullets toward the complex.

Rachman saw one of the workmen absurdly standing up on the back of his truck trying to see what was happening. Rachman turned back and saw Bloom on his knees frantically attempting to wrench a cellular phone out of his suit jacket pocket that was too small to accommodate both the phone and his fat hand.

Rachman had expected Bloom to be too terrified to

do anything except soil himself. His respect for Bloom increased as he watched him struggle to his feet, cursing, concentrating on getting his phone out so he could call for help.

Rachman slammed a fresh clip into the Glock. As he ran toward the gunfire, he yelled at Bloom, "Call for ambulances first, then the cops."

The assault in the back of the complex raged even more furiously than the attack at the front. There were more workmen back there, but fortunately the two trucks and backhoe provided more cover. Most of the men made it behind the vehicles. Then, just as suddenly as the second attack had started, it ended and the second Blue-Tops car roared away. One workman had been hit with a bullet, in his shoulder, nearly severing the arm from the shoulder joint. Miraculously, no one else had been hit.

The Blue-Tops shooters, of course, had not aimed carefully. They had simply pointed their weapons in the general direction of the complex and pulled the triggers until their shotguns, handguns, and rifles stopped firing. The bullets could have hit anyone or anything: cars, walls, women, children, dogs, anything, innocent or guilty.

Since Rachman's gunmen had left the complex hours ago, there were no guilty people in New Lots that morning. That fact didn't even begin to bother Archie Reynolds.

He had sat in his black Saab about a half block from the entrance to the New Lots Apartments back parking area, sipping coffee and watching his men drive by and shoot. He had watched the workmen drop to the ground so quickly that it seemed like all of them were hit. Their desperate attempts to avoid the gunfire had amused him.

Beyond instant retaliation, Archie had had another reason for ordering the drive-bys. Archie wanted the shooting to cause enough chaos and commotion so that he could slip out of his car and duck unseen into a narrow gangway that opened into The Pit. From there he had walked ten yards and entered the lobby of Building D.

By the time Rachman Abdul X reached the scene of the second drive-by, Archie Reynolds was strolling past the broken lobby elevators of Building D headed for the stairwell door. As he opened the door, the full stench of New Lots Apartments hit him: urine, excrement (both human and animal), cat spray, and rancid cooking smells. And garbage. Garbage at the rotting stage, food for rats and cockroaches. New Lots Apartments swarmed with both. Archie heard them scurry as he walked up the dark stairwells.

Archie breathed through his mouth and sprinted up the stairs, light-footed, sure of himself, taking the stairs two at a time.

"Now we see what the fuck is going on here," Archie told himself.

He pounded on Whitey Williams's door. From inside, he heard Whitey's old-man voice ask, "Who is it?"

Archie said, "Open up, goddamn it. It's me."

It took Whitey a bit of time to shuffle over to his door and unlatch all the chains and locks.

He pulled his door open and slowly walked back to his chair by the window, not bothering to greet Archie. He picked up his dead White Owl cigar and gazed back out the window as if to demonstrate his devotion to his lookout post.

Archie stood near the doorway and watched Whitey watching, sitting near the window in his old green cardigan sweater with the elbows worn out and his faded canvas work shirt buttoned to the collar.

"You get your checks this month, old man?"

When Whitey spoke, he spoke quietly, revealing a country Southern accent. "You mean my government checks?"

Government came out sounding like guvmint.

"Yeah."

"I got 'em."

"How much that amount to?"

"One thirty-six social security, plus one eighty-six from disability."

"Shit, Whitey, you a rich man. That why you don't need my money?"

"Who said I don't need it? How's a man supposed to live on three hundred dollars a month?"

"Three hundred twenty-six dollars, motherfucker. Yeah, that's why I be so surprised that you quit your job."

"Not me. No, sir, I never quit."

"Then how come all this shit come down last night and I don't know about it? How come they be putting up this goddamn fence around my place, and I don't hear about it?"

For the first time Whitey looked away from the window and faced Archie.

"No way to see this comin', Mr. Archie. Nobody knew 'bout it until it was here."

"Who is it?"

"Far's I heard it's a new security company the complex hired."

"They brought in a security company?"

"I heard it be Muslims."

"Muslims? What fucking Muslims? No Muslims come along and shoot shit up like they did here last night. Who the fuck are these guys?"

Whitey turned back to his window as if gazing out might bring in the answer. He saw the first flash of emergency vehicle lights coming up Rockaway Avenue. Police and ambulance sirens sounded, forcing Whitey to speak louder.

"I don't know. Maybe some kind a hard-core bunch. Take a look out here and maybe you see who it is. A burly fella run through there jes' after you come in. Look like he runnin' toward the trouble in the back while everybody else runnin' away. Had on military-type clothes, field jacket and all, combat boots and one of them skull caps the Muslim brothers wear. Had a gun in his hand, too."

"This is bullshit, man."

Archie walked over to Whitey's window and bent low so he could see out. The angle gave him a clear view of the back parking area. He could see that at least one man had been shot. Other workmen surrounded him. Even from the fourth-floor window, Archie could see the dark pool of blood seeping wider near the fallen men.

He picked out Rachman based on Whitey's description. He watched him checking to see how many men had been shot, directing the others back away from the street, holding his Glock pointed up, ready to shoot if the Blue-Tops shooters decided to come back and do it all over again.

While Archie watched Rachman, Whitey checked the apartment windows facing The Pit. There were more faces peering out than he had seen in a long time.

Archie followed Whitey's eyes and yelled at the people across The Pit, "Get the fuck away from the window. I come over there and kick your fuckin' eyes out yo' heads."

Nobody heard Archie, but if they had, they would have instantly disappeared from their windows.

Archie stepped back and asked, "What else you see?"

"Not much. That fence they puttin' up is gonna make a difference."

"How long you live here, Whitey?"

"Since they opened the place."

"How much rent you pay?"

"One-eighty a month."

"You still pay it?"

"Yes, sir."

"Shit, you must be one of the only ones. How many regular people you figure still left?"

"Maybe half of what used to be. Not counting the squatters and riffraff and such that come in and out."

Archie turned away from Whitey, chewing on his lower lip, thinking. Whitey didn't interrupt him. Finally, Archie spoke.

"Motherfuckers who got this place now can't wait to make their money off the ghetto. Fill up these empties."

Whitey nodded, "I'd say so. May be time you picked an easier place to work out of."

Archie turned back to Whitey. "That's what you think, huh?"

Whitey shrugged. "I don't know. Seems like it might just be easier for you to avoid all this mess. You hit 'em back for last night. Showed 'em they can't push you around. Might make sense to take the easy way for a while."

"Just pack up and leave."

Whitey shrugged again. "Alls I'm saying is, it ain't easy runnin' your business with all this trouble around."

"You never mind about my business. I'll find a way to run my business, trouble or not. And where I'm going to go, old man? How many niggers I got to kill to get another setup like this?"

Whitey knew better than to respond.

"You want to kill 'em for me?"

Whitey didn't move. Archie stepped over to the window and looked out again. He seemed to calm down a bit.

"That's what's wrong with you nappy-headed, old motherfuckers. Always ready to put your goddamn head down and shuffle off."

Archie turned back to Whitey, "You keep your goddamn advice to yourself, old man, and just find out who the fuck is in this security company. How many, where, when, whatever."

"Yes, sir."

Archie shouted, "Don't fucking sir me. Just fucking do it."

Whitey realized he should never have told Archie to leave New Lots.

Archie ranted at Whitey, "You know how I started in this neighborhood? Huh, old man? Do you know?"

Whitey knew quite well how Archie had started in his neighborhood, but he just sat at his table, head down, silent.

"That bodega across the street on the New Lots side. That little piece of shit corner. I had to buy that fucking spot in my own fucking neighborhood from the Terell brothers three years ago. You know how much it cost me?"

"No."

"Everything I had, motherfucker. All my time scrambling and hustling and selling on every fucking corner in Brownsville to get my stake. Looking over my shoulder, ready to shoot any motherfucker who come after me. And even after I paid for the corner Reggie Whack and me had to kill three motherfuckers before they let us have the goddamn corner. Took our money, piss all over us, try to kill us, and tell us it wasn't them. Motherfuckers."

Archie bent close to Whitey. His voice dropped from a shout to a whisper. His face twisted into an ugly, evil grimace.

"You know how long it took me to kill that last Terell?"

"No."

"Took me almost two years before I got the last one. Two years, old man."

"I understand."

"You understand? I hope you fuckin' understand, Whitey, 'cuz if you want to fuck with me I'll kill you right now and save us a lot of time and trouble."

"I ain't fuckin' with you, Mr. Archie."

"Goddamn right you ain't."

Archie turned back to the window, looking, watching the police and ambulances arrive, doing his job, hoping Archie would see that he was doing his job. Hoping if he didn't move or speak out of turn, the storm would pass without hurting him.

Archie paced the small apartment, seeming to calm down a bit.

"May be time to leave here, may be not, but I goddamn guarantee you one thing, Whitey, I'm gonna kill that burly Muslim motherfucker you talkin' about before I do go. Yes, sir, *salaam aleichem*, my ass, motherfucker. Gonna be hell to pay around here for some other people, too, before I go anywhere. If I go. You hear me, old man?"

"I hear you."

"You fuckin' right you hear me."

Whitey sat in his place, making sure he didn't move. He felt a single droplet of sweat slide down the right side of his rib cage. It made him feel like shivering, but he held himself still.

Whitey knew the blood in the street outside had ignited something in Archie. The silence from Archie unnerved him even more than the rants and threats.

But then just as suddenly as it had blossomed up, the murderous aura around Archie eased away.

Archie began to walk around the room, looking carefully at everything in Whitey's small apartment. The place was clean and simply furnished. It seemed to amuse Archie that an apartment as clean and neat as Whitey's could exist within the filth and chaos of New Lots. But Whitey knew there was more than one apartment like his in New Lots, some occupied by old people like him, others by women and children. Some even occupied by families struggling to stay together. Islands of civility in the midst of degradation and danger. Apartments hidden away, locked up, and used carefully by the people who lived there. People who still worked or quietly collected their welfare checks and tried to keep their children alive in the Brownsville–New Lots world of sudden death and danger and grief. People who could have easily been hit by one of Archie's drive-by bullets.

"You said you still pay rent, right, old man?"

Whitey nodded.

"So you'll be a keeper, right?"

"I suppose so."

"And you gonna stay right here, ain't you?"

"I ain't goin' nowhere."

"And you clear about who you working for?"

"I'm clear."

"Okay, good. So how you gonna find out what I need to know?"

"Just about everyone talk to me aroun' here. I'll find out whatever there is to know about these security fellas. You know these Muslim boys believe in what they doing. They all be talkin' to people themselves, I suspect. They think it's a divine mission or somethin' to clean up their neighborhoods."

"I give a shit what they think. Let's see how divine they think it is getting they ass shot up."

"Okay."

"Damn right, okay. You just get the information I need."

"I'll find out. Lots a people with eyes and ears around here."

Archie dropped one hundred dollars in tens and twenties on Whitey's kitchen table. The money collected from the ravaged hands of the New Lots people. Crack money.

"Don't forget who you working for, Whitey."

Whitey nodded.

Archie turned toward the door, but Whitey interrupted his exit. "I'll tell you something you ought to know right now."

"What's that?"

The old man had a trump card, and he decided now was the time to play it.

Loyd Shaw made it to his renovated barn, situated on a twenty-five-acre farm in Massachusetts, just about the time the first Blue-Tops drive-by hit New Lots. The trip had taken under three hours, but Shaw was in another world. Instead of bloodshed and bedlam, Shaw only heard the sounds of birds and the occasional bark of old Mrs. McGovern's black Lab.

The caffeine he had consumed during the drive from Brooklyn didn't have a chance against his fatigue. Shaw lay down to close his eyes. He felt grungy and out of sorts from his night in the precinct house, but he didn't bother to shower or change clothes. He just wanted to rest awhile with his eyes closed and try to dispel some of the tension that the night's events and hard drive had filled him with. Within minutes, he fell dead asleep until midafternoon.

Mrs. McGovern owned the twenty-five-acre property surrounding Shaw's renovated barn. She had seen Shaw arrive, but wouldn't think of intruding on him. Mrs. McGovern's reserve stemmed from her staid New England personality, a poor Irish background, and eighty years of hard times.

Shaw had met Mrs. McGovern on a chilly September Sunday evening a year and a half before. For two months prior to that, he had been taking weekend excursions, trying to find a country place he could afford. Finding a retreat out of New York had been the second step in constructing a life after the NYPD. The first step had happened two years before that when Shaw began to pursue one of his dreams: learning to paint.

During the last few years, in between being a police detective, Shaw had attempted to construct a life as an artist. He spent almost all of his free time either trying to create art or look at art. He took drawing courses at the Art Students League, spent hours laboring over live figure studies in a basement studio in Soho, haunted art galleries and museums from one end of Manhattan to the other. During the last year, Shaw had finally begun putting paint to canvas.

The weekend Shaw met Mrs. McGovern, he had already spent all of Saturday and most of Sunday looking at places that either didn't fit his needs or cost too much. Before he headed back to the city, he decided to check in with a real estate agent. He stood at a highway pay phone, the sun low in the sky, the engine of his Mercury running, fully expecting the call to be a short one, just to tell her he would be leaving and returning the following weekend.

But the agent told him not to leave before he saw one more place.

"She must have just gotten home and heard my message. You should see this place, Mr. Shaw. I think it could be exactly what you want."

Shaw checked his watch and figured, what the hell.

After three or four wrong turns trying to follow the real estate agent's directions, Shaw finally found the farm, a small one situated on the edge of a scrub pine forest. As soon as he saw the little half-renovated barn, even before walking inside it, Shaw knew he wanted it. The barn sat off in a corner of the property surrounded on three sides by forest and by a big open field between it and Mrs. McGovern's old farmhouse.

When he drove up, he saw his real estate agent standing near the owner's front porch waiting for him.

Shaw reached out to shake her hand.

"Hello, Joan."

Joan Cummings was a petite woman who looked even smaller next to Shaw.

"Hi, Loyd. So here's the situation. Mrs. McGovern is getting on. Her husband died about four months ago. She loves this place, but she needs cash for probate expenses and taxes. The price is right. Not a steal, but fair. It's in your range. The place needs some work, but you said that's okay. Main thing, it's a beautiful setting."

"So what's the downside?"

"She's a little stubborn. Mostly she's choosy about who she sells this to."

Shaw shrugged. "I'll be nice."

"Well, just be yourself. There's no telling what she likes."

"Okay."

Shaw never decided exactly why Mrs. McGovern sold it to him. Joan introduced them, then left them alone on the front porch while she sat in her car. The old lady didn't invite him inside, giving Shaw the impression that she didn't like him at all.

She stood at her front door, dressed in what looked like men's clothes: a plaid flannel shirt, corduroy pants so worn the cord was gone at the knees, and suede Birkenstock sandals over wool socks.

"What do you do for a living, Mr. Shaw?" she had asked.

"I'm a cop."

"I'm sorry, I'm hard of hearing."

Shaw raised his voice, trying not to shout at her.

"I'm a cop. Detective. New York."

"Oh," she said. "In New York?"

"Yes."

"In the city?"

"Yes."

"Are you married?"

"Yes."

Shaw didn't explain the state of his marriage to her. He didn't expect Jane to ever come up to the country with him, but he couldn't see why that would matter to Mrs. McGovern. Shaw let her assume whatever she wanted to concerning his marriage.

"My husband died four months ago," she said.

For a second, Shaw felt like congratulating her, but instead gave the usual, "I'm sorry."

"Any children?" she asked.

"No."

"Ah."

Shaw had a feeling that "ah" was meant to communicate a sympathy that they were supposed to share about being childless, but he didn't feel he needed sympathy on that score. He wasn't about to tell her that Jane had long ago made it clear she didn't want any children, and that he had conceded to it without nearly the fight he should have waged. Nor did he want to air the realization that if he and Jane had become parents, he would have never saved the money for the down payment that Mrs. McGovern needed for her estate taxes.

"So it's a weekend place you're looking for?"

"Yes. For now. But I plan on moving up here permanently when I retire."

"Retire?"

"Not retire from work. Just from the force."

"The what?"

"The force. The police force."

Shaw felt like retiring from the conversation, so he didn't mind it when Mrs. McGovern suddenly stopped talking. She stood there looking at him. Most people would have been uncomfortable with Mrs. McGovern's chilly New England reserve and her blatant staring. Most would have needed to fill in the silence. But Shaw knew the silence came from her attempt to make a decision. Shaw knew as long as she didn't turn and walk back in the house, there was a chance.

Finally, Mrs. McGovern spoke, but not the words Shaw expected.

"Do you carry a gun?" she asked.

Instead of asking, what the hell do you care? Shaw simply said, "Yes."

"Is that legal for you in Massachusetts?"

"I don't think it would create any problems for me here."

And then, she waved her freckled hand as if to say it was a stupid question. She looked out at the barn, then back at Shaw.

"All right, you might as well take a look at the place. It's solid. My husband started a renovation back there. Never finished it, but it's got the wiring and new roof and all. I expect you'll know more about that than me. He never wanted me back there. If you want it, talk to Joan. She knows the price. I suppose I'll bargain a little since it's expected, but not much. And I won't take a mortgage. Get your money from the bank. Joan will help with all that."

It took another week of haggling and two month's worth of mortgage applications and red tape with the bank, but eventually Shaw secured his mortgage and his safe haven.

Once he had his country place, Shaw looked forward to his retirement more than ever. He poured the rest of his savings and most of his free time into finishing the renovation of the barn. Now it looked like his last year on the force was going to be the worst one yet.

When he woke from his long nap, he stripped off his clothes which still smelled of gunpowder and cigarette smoke, showered, shaved, and scrubbed his teeth for a good long time. As he cleaned his body, he tried to clear his mind of any thoughts relating to his life on the Job.

He dressed in his comfortable, paint-stained country clothes, loaded his CD player with music, took a few minutes simply to sit and gaze at the sun as it slowly settled down behind the pine trees and mountains in the distance. Then he poured about four ounces of Jack Daniels over ice, took the first sip to banish the taste of toothpaste from his mouth, and began working on the painting he had left propped up on an easel, positioned under his skylight to catch the constantly changing daylight that poured into the second floor of his renovated barn.

For the next two days, Shaw's activities remained much the same. He only added eating an occasional meal and taking an occasional walk to the drinking, painting, and listening to music. Sometimes he slept in his bed. Sometimes he simply sat in his chair, looking out at the changing light of day, and napped.

It would have been nearly perfect had Shaw been doing it voluntarily.

12

Archie Reynolds turned to Whitey Williams and said, "What's that? What you saying I ought to know 'bout, old man?"

Whitey motioned Archie to come back to the window. "You see that lady out there by all the mess?"

Archie peered out. Cops and EMS personnel swarmed around the drive-by victims. Amidst all the uniforms, crackling radios, and flashing lights, Archie picked out a young black woman dressed in a dark blue business suit and white blouse. Her height nearly matched that of the men surrounding her, and she possessed a definite air of command. Despite the emergency situation, several of the policemen on the scene had stopped to respond to her. Archie could tell, even from the fourth-floor window, that she had their attention.

"Who's that mouthy bitch? And why those cops takin' shit from her?"

" 'Cuz that mouthy bitch is the Police Commissioner's daughter."

Archie turned to Whitey. "Fuck you say."

"It's true."

Archie looked back down. "What the hell she doin' around New Lots?"

Whitey pointed into the distance, "You see that set of trailer buildings they put up over there?"

"What? Those prefab things they dump down on empty lots?"

"Yeah, they use 'em for temporary classrooms and such."

"What about 'em?"

"That's some kind of shelter for homeless women and kids. She's runnin' it."

"She is?"

"Uh-huh."

"For women? What women? Ain't nothing around here except a bunch of worthless crackhead bitches and whores and shit."

Archie stood back from the window, shaking his head, talking more to himself than to Whitey. "I see it now."

"See what?"

"Why they cleaning this place up now."

" 'Cause she's out here?"

"What do you think?"

"I don't know. Maybe so."

"What the fuck she think she's gonna do in New Lots, man?"

"I s'pose she figures she's doing some good out here. Make a reputation for herself."

"Let her do good in her own motherfucking neighborhood, 'stead of bringing her Uncle Tom ass out here and mess with my shit."

Whitey turned back to his window. Five seconds later he heard his front door slam as Archie left without another word.

Three minutes later, Archie crossed the street behind the complex and stood in front of the prefabricated structures Whitey had pointed out. They were five simple, one-story structures that had been hauled into an empty, rubble-strewn lot, set up and placed together end to end, creating one long, narrow, temporary building. In front of them, a large sign somewhat grandiosely announced: CARING COMMUNITY SHELTER AND

SOCIAL SERVICE CENTER. EXECUTIVE DIRECTOR JUS-
TINE BURTON.

Archie gazed at the sign for a few moments. Then
he looked behind him at the police and emergency vehicles clustered around the shooting site. He peered
past the emergency vehicles and personnel and stared
at the New Lots Apartments complex, then back at Justine Burton's community center. He spit on the ground
once and turned away, walking toward the far side of
the complex.

Archie had figured out who his enemies were. And
by the time he walked around to the front of the complex, he had come up with a plan to hurt them all.

When Archie reached the New Lots Avenue side of
the complex, he crossed the street and entered the bodega he had told Whitey about. By then he knew that
the police commissioner's daughter, Justine Burton,
had finished her head-to-head with the police and had
returned to her Caring Community Center. He knew
that two more workmen had been shot in front of the
complex. And he had looked closely enough at the
burly guy in the military garb and Muslim skullcap so
that he could identify him later.

Inside the bodega, Archie picked up the phone behind the counter. As he began dialing the first number,
he mumbled to no one in particular, "Shit, fucking
drive-bys be a picnic compared to what I got for you
next."

At the same time, across the street, Rachman Abdul X
had finished making his own set of phone calls.

Leon Bloom saw him, broke away from the group
clustered around the dead workman, and walked over
to Rachman as quickly as his short, fat legs would allow without running.

He hissed, "What the hell is this?"

Rachman looked at Bloom, narrowed his eyes, and said, "What do you think? It's payback for last night."

"Last night was suppose to intimidate them."

"Hey, you think they'd be doing this if we didn't shake them? But it's not going to be easy to really teach them what they have to learn."

"Easy! You want to talk about easy. How easy do you think it's going to be to get somebody to work on this job now? Who's going to risk getting killed to put up this damn fence now. I can't have this."

"Don't yell at me, Mr. Bloom. You want us to leave, tell me now. This is just the beginning."

"Leave? You start this mess and you want—"

Without warning, Rachman grabbed Bloom by the lapels of his jacket and turned him away from the others nearly lifting him off his feet. He put his face down close to Bloom's and spoke softly but intensely.

"I told you not to yell, Mr. Bloom. We don't want people to hear our business, do we?"

Bloom swallowed once and took a deep breath.

"No. We don't. Sorry. I apologize. But we can't have this."

Rachman slowly released his grip on Bloom, but kept his face close to Bloom's and his body between Bloom and the others.

"Every man, woman, and child in New Lots lives under danger here. A bullet can hit any of them, almost anytime. Now every one of them is under the protection of MS-Two. We didn't put these people in this situation. But we will help them get out of it. This is war, Mr. Bloom. Do you understand? Don't play innocent or surprised. You know damn well more people might die here before this is over. We either turn back now or see it to the end. Tell me now if you want to quit. Don't pull out on me later."

"Can you do this, Rachman? Can you handle these animals? These killers?"

"Do you think anybody else can?"

"I don't know."

"We'll handle them. They will learn, Mr. Bloom. They will learn that if they spill one drop of our blood, we will spill a gallon of theirs. They will learn."

"Then do what you have to do. Just do it."

Bloom turned away from Rachman and walked out of New Lots.

Rachman turned in the other direction looking for his guards. He walked past the dead workman. Someone had covered the dead man with a green jacket. A bloom of red had already seeped through the cloth. Rachman realized he never really understood why people covered dead bodies like that. Out of respect? Or simply because the living didn't want to see the faces of the dead? Rachman thought it much better to look at the faces of the dead, whether they were friends or enemies or even strangers.

Across the street, Archie finished his phone calls. He sidled up to Oscar who stood at the doorway of the bodega watching the cops and EMS personnel. Archie stood with Oscar, calmly gazing at the scene across the street.

"Lazy fucks. Look like nothing but dead meat over there. Nobody worried about rushin' that to a hospital."

Archie turned back into the bodega.

"Okay, Oscar, my man, I'm going to catch some z's back in the storeroom. When Reggie come in, tell him to wake me roun' lunchtime. Make us some sandwiches. No bologna and cheese shit. I want turkey on whole wheat. You got it?"

"Yes."

Oscar headed back to the counter, wondering how

Archie could sleep after what had happened.

Archie turned and, called out, "And we ain't moving nothing but groceries today, Oscar."

Oscar had already shoved the crack stash into the floor safe behind the counter. Oscar knew the cops would be coming in to ask questions or, if not that, to get coffee. The image of cops in the bodega made Oscar's stomach turn sour. He walked behind the counter looking for his bottle of Pepto-Bismol.

Rachman had no more interest in talking to the police than Oscar. He reached the spot where his regular guards stood and motioned for them to follow him. He led them away from the police toward The Pit. Once they were off by themselves, he took a moment to see how the drive-by had affected them.

One of the guards, a short, stocky boy, just eighteen years old, stood hunched over, looking at the ground, his hands thrust deep into the side pockets of his MS-2 jacket. The shooting had so unnerved him that he could not stop his teeth from chattering.

The other guard, an older, thin, balding man, seemed to Rachman to be a harder case. He didn't display any outward signs of fear, but Rachman sensed that given a chance, the man would walk away from New Lots and never return.

Neither one of the guards were Muslims. They were just black men looking for a job. Some of the "legitimate" people Rachman used for the day-to-day security work.

Rachman stood close to them so they couldn't avoid the power of his physical presence. It wasn't Rachman's thick muscular body that intimidated, as much as his demeanor. Rachman always appeared to be seconds away from reacting with a blow or a shot. He didn't look at someone, he glowered. When he spoke, he made sure to lock eyes with whomever he spoke to.

As long as Rachman stood in front of them, neither guard had any thoughts of walking away.

Rachman spoke to both men, but concentrated on the younger guard.

"You're all right, now. It's over."

He waited for a response, but neither guard agreed with him.

"Allah protected you. You weren't hit. You made it. Didn't you? Didn't you?"

Rachman waited, staring at them until they both nodded.

"You stood up to the evil around you. Allah protected you. You're blessed. He will continue to protect you. You've done a good act. Goodness will come to you. Don't turn your back on it."

The younger guard's teeth stopped chattering as he spoke, but his voice shook from the fear and shock.

"I can't do this, Mr. Rachman. No disrespect, but I just took this job 'cuz my momma got on me to get some work. I know she didn't think I'd be getting shot at."

Rachman cut him off. "That's over now. By the end of the week, you'll be inside a bullet-proof guardhouse. Right over there. Behind an iron gate. Nobody will get near you unless you push a button to let them in. There'll be a phone in there, too. Phone for anything you need. You won't have to go out. You'll be safer here than at home."

The other guard spoke, "Then I'll be back when you got that built."

Rachman stepped in front of the older guard.

"No," said Rachman. "You stick it out. You don't let evil drive you off. You've got to earn the right to be here and be protected and earn clean, honest money, and do good work."

The younger guard looked over at the older man, waiting to see if he would argue with Rachman. The older guard acted as if the young man weren't even there. He shook his head and turned away from Rachman, but did not say anything.

Rachman let the man move away, knowing he had probably lost him anyhow. But he didn't want the younger one to succumb to his fear.

"Stop worrying," he told the young guard. "You're under the protection of righteous men. Men who will give their lives for you and for others. Our men. Our gunmen. Who else will do that for you?"

The older guard turned back to them and said, "I don't see no gunmen around here."

"Then stand there and wait and see. They're coming. Stay here and do your job. Don't let them drive you off. Don't let them take this job from you. I promise you, you'll be safe."

Rachman told them, "Go stand by the entrance there. Talk to the police. Tell them what you saw. Then stay until your shift is over. My people are already on their way."

The two guards walked off, following Rachman's instructions. Rachman did not delude himself. He assumed they would both disappear the first chance they got. But for now, they kept their MS-2 jackets on and stayed.

13

Three hours later, Archie Reynolds, fresh from his nap in the back room of the bodega, finished his turkey sandwich and chased it with the last swallows of a sixteen-ounce can of Ballantine Ale.

He sat with Reggie Whack in the bodega's backroom. Archie had assumed a new identity. Over his good clothes he wore a jumpsuit-style set of overalls, the kind car mechanics or janitors wore. On his head, he wore a black knit ski cap.

Reggie had on the same clothes he had been wearing at the body shop: a blue knit cap with a New York Knicks logo sweatshirt, and baggy pants.

Archie asked Reggie, "Our guys ready?"

"Yuh, yuh, yeah, Arch."

"Everything set up like I said?"

"Ju, ju, just like you said."

"Any problems inside?"

"Nope. Those muth, muth, motherfuckers be runnin' around outside, we do, uh, do what we want inside. Couple a cops maybe in there try, trying to find out if anybody seen anything. But no more'n that. No, no nobody comin' in there after us."

"Not yet, anyhow." said Archie. "Okay. Just you make sure you be ready where you supposed to be."

Reggie nodded, "Fu, fu, fuckin' count on it, homes."

Reggie pulled out a 9-mm Smith and Wesson automatic, chambered a round, and gently clicked the hammer back into position. "Any motherfucker get clo, clo, close, I cap their ass."

*　　*　　*

By the time Archie and Reggie had finished eating, New Lots had almost returned to normal. All the emergency medical service people had left and almost all the police. Most of the tenants remained indoors except for a few of the older kids drawn to the possibility of further violence. They stood in clusters near the doorways of the five buildings in case they had to duck inside. Most of them watched Rachman and his two shaken regular guards. It was clear to everybody that if the Blue-Tops came looking for another target, it would be Rachman and his guards.

Outwardly, Rachman Abdul X didn't show it, but each minute he had waited for reinforcements to arrive seemed like ten. When the two cars filled with MS-2 gunmen finally screeched to a halt in front of the complex, Rachman displayed no sign of relief other than taking his hand off the butt of his Glock, stuck in the waistband of his pants.

Five gunmen and two "legals," guards with legal gun-carry permits, quickly piled out of the two MS-2 cars. John X and three of the gunmen from the morning raid had returned along with a fifth gunman, Walli X, a man who displayed a nearly constant smile, brought on by tension rather than any jovial nature.

All the gunmen were Muslim. All sported dark beards except for Walli X. All five wore skullcaps and military-style garb, camouflage pants or field jackets and combat boots. The two legals were not Muslims and like Rachman's regular guards, they wore conventional street clothes, and unlike the regular guards, did not wear the MS-2 jackets.

Rachman pointed to John X and one of the legals named Solomon. "You two, go over to the east corner and stand guard. Anybody you see headed for the entrance, you call in."

Rachman paired Walli X with another legal and told

them, "Go into the courtyard. Keep watch more toward the back. I'll watch over the front."

To the other three gunmen he said, "You three circle the complex. There's no telling what direction they might come from, if they come back. Keep moving. That way at least one or two of you will be close to a possible trouble spot. Call in if you see anything. Anyone shows up looking for trouble, anywhere in or around this complex, shoot first."

Rachman nodded once for emphasis then said, "Go."

Rachman remained standing in front of the entrance to New Lots with the two regular guards as the others broke off to their assigned areas. All the gunmen carried two-way radios.

Rachman held up his radio and said, "Call in to me every five minutes. I'll be walking around every so often to check on you. If these infidels return, I want to see them before the get near this entrance. Stay alert."

As Rachman dispersed his gunmen outside, inside the complex, a team of two detectives from the 73rd precinct went about the thankless task of trying to find witnesses to the drive-by shooting.

Detective David Meeb, a big, blunt Irishman who favored cheap sport coats and slacks led the way through the dark, foul smelling hallways. Meeb did his job, complained just enough to be one of the guys, but not enough to anger any of his bosses. He carried about thirty extra pounds on his six foot frame, not including his snub-nosed .38 revolver.

His partner, a whip-thin black detective named Jimmy Silver, always dressed meticulously in one of his six suits carefully acquired at the Sy Syms discount outlet.

The two detectives knocked on every door they

passed, but only about one in four opened to them. Jimmy Silver tried to be polite; David Meeb simply tried not to insult anyone. It didn't matter. People either claimed not to have seen anything or asked more questions than they answered.

After about the twentieth door, Meeb asked Silver, "Hey, Jimmy, you think if this had been some crackheads or dealers got shot, we'd be doing this?"

"Nope. At least not still doin' it."

"Then why don't we get the fuck out of here?"

"I don't know."

"Come on, fuck it. We ain't going to learn anything in this shithole."

"All right. Finish this floor and we're out of here."

Archie Reynolds, dressed in his mechanic's overalls, stood just inside the bodega, watching the entrance to the complex, watching Rachman's gunmen on patrol. He waited patiently, picking turkey meat from between his teeth with a toothpick, until Rachman set out on his route to check his men.

Nobody noticed Archie cross New Lots Avenue and head for the front entrance. Not even the two regular unarmed guards posted near the unfinished gate, standing, wearing their MS-2 jackets bearing the word SECURITY in large gold letters, just trying to make it through the rest of the afternoon. They didn't notice Archie until he approached them and even then they took Archie for an ordinary working man, maybe coming home from his job in the neighborhood for lunch or a quick midday visit with a girlfriend.

As Archie approached the entrance the older guard stepped in front of him and asked, "Sir, can I help you?"

"Help me do what?" asked Archie.

"Are you a resident, or are you visiting someone?"

Archie smiled, checked the MS-2 logos on their jackets, and gave them a quizzical look.

"A resident? You mean do I live here?"

"Yes, sir. Do you live here?"

"What's this? You some kind of guards or something?"

The older guard answered, "We work for the security company that's guarding the building. What apartment are you in?"

Archie noticed the young guard coming over to stand on his right. Archie looked to his right at the younger guard, then back left to the older guard. He cocked his head and smiled at them both.

"You guys really guards?"

"Yes, sir," said the younger guard.

"Whoa," said Archie. "Since when did anybody give a shit about guarding this place? You gonna keep all those nasty crackheads and drug dealers out of here?"

A block away, Rachman finished checking with John X and turned back onto New Lots Avenue. He looked toward the entrance a block away and noticed the two guards talking to Archie near the entrance to the complex. Rachman watched them, but the three men seemed to be having a normal conversation, like the many that would take place as his regular guards explained the new security procedures at New Lots Apartments.

Archie said, "So what'd you say the name of this security company is? Muslim what?"

"Muslim Security Two," said the younger guard.

"Two? What's that? Why two?" Archie smiled, "What the fuck happened to one? When did they tell you to come in here?"

The older guard put on a hard face and again asked, "Sir, which apartment are you in?"

Archie turned to the older guard and pointed at him, "Yo man, what you getting an attitude for? Don't be interruptin' me. I asked a question."

"Sir, do you live here? If not I'm going to have to ask you to leave."

Archie snapped his head around and looked at the older guard.

"What the fuck did you say to me?"

"You'll have to—"

"No, no, motherfucker, I don't *have* to do anything."

The younger guard instinctively took a step back from Archie and the aura of rage that had sparked around him without warning.

"Anybody gonna get the fuck out of here it's gonna be you, motherfuckers."

Archie barely raised his voice, but moved his head with every word for emphasis as he spit out each word.

"You think some shuffling house nigger like you gonna tell *me* to leave? Come on, motherfucker, I want to see you reach up your hand and put me out of here. Pull this phony *sir* shit, on me. You gonna sir *me*, motherfucker? You know who the fuck I am?"

Rachman couldn't hear Archie, hadn't ever seen Archie Reynolds before, but he didn't have to be any closer than a block away to clearly see that the conversation had turned ugly. Rachman immediately headed for the entrance, moving quickly, trying to make his movement and approach attract the attention of the man giving his guards a hard time. And then it happened without nearly enough warning.

Archie pulled his .22-caliber Beretta from the back pocket of the overalls and shot the older guard in the middle of his forehead. This time, unlike with Little Marvin, Archie shot when he wanted to, with the gun inches away from the man's head, just the way he wanted to, just when his anger flared to the right pitch. This time, the bullet blew right through the back of his victim's head, spraying a fine mist of red blood against the unfinished, new, black, iron fence.

For a moment, Rachman thought Archie had punched his guard's face, hoped Archie had, but the snapping crack of the exploding cartridge, the sudden puff of smoke, and Archie's extended arm told him differently. Rachman reached for the Glock and broke into a run.

The younger guard, the eighteen-year-old who Rachman had promised would be safe, flinched and ducked from Archie's gun, turning away, instinctively covering his head. From a block away, Rachman yelled, "No."

Archie glanced at Rachman, turned back to the young guard and said, "Little punk bitch."

He pulled the trigger three times. Three quick cracks without even a second thought, and three bullets exploded into the boy's back, tearing, burning through skin, muscle, and bone. The last bullet tore into the boy's spine, severing it just below his neck, instantly condemning the young man to a life of total paralysis from the shoulders down. Eighteen years old and, in a second, the young man whose mother had sent him to work that morning faced a lifetime of pain and paralysis.

Archie didn't waste any time viewing his carnage. He glanced to his right at the onrushing Rachman. He held his position, waiting insolently, as if he were daring Rachman to catch him. Then, seemingly without effort, Archie bolted, gliding away from the fresh scene of blood and mayhem he had created.

Archie still held the Beretta in his right hand. With

his left hand, he pulled down on the knit cap he wore, revealing that he had another layer with holes for the eyes and mouth. The knit cap covered his entire face.

Rachman roared after Archie, his combat boots pounding on the pavement, his bulky body straining to close the long distance between him and the arrogant, murderous enemy who dared to shoot his guards.

Inside the complex, Detectives Meeb and Silver had heard the first shot. They knew that sound, a faint but sharp pop. They looked at each other. Meeb cursed. Silver frowned. They headed as quickly as they could in the dim light toward a stairwell, listening for more shots, but not wanting to hear them. Then the three fast shots echoed in the courtyard, and the two detectives ran for the stairs, pulling out their guns, their hearts suddenly pounding.

Archie had disappeared from his view, but Rachman estimated he had to still be in The Pit. He yelled into his radio, "Close the courtyard. Everybody head for the courtyard."

Rachman charged ahead. Everything in him concentrated on catching and killing Archie. When he reached the front entrance, he didn't pause to check the injured guards. Rachman knew he had to trap the killer in the courtyard. If the killer made it into one of the buildings, it would be nearly impossible to find him in the dark maze of apartments. If he made it to the street out back, they could easily lose him.

In the rear of the complex, Rachman's shout squawked over Walli X's radio. The licensed guard, the legal, immediately handed his weapon to Walli X and ran for cover. Walli X moved quickly into The Pit, saw Archie running with a mask on his face and a gun in his hand, and opened fire with both his gun and the licensed guard's gun. At the same time, John X on the eastern corner out front and the three gunmen patrolling the perimeter ran for The Pit in response to Rachman's command.

The sound of Walli X firing two guns told Meeb and Silver they were now rushing toward an ongoing gunfight. Silver fumbled for his radio to call in backup. Meeb continued pounding down the last set of stairs. Silver yelled into his police radio a report of shots fired at New Lots Apartments and called for backup.

Archie continued running, angling away from Walli X, who tried to run and shoot at a moving target, even though he knew his chance of hitting the target was slim.

Archie ran quickly, moving with the light, quick strides of a man who carried no excess weight. He never even looked at Walli X, or the gunman who appeared in the back parking area, or at Rachman charging after him from behind.

Rachman entered The Pit, taking in everything at once. Walli X shooting from the far side of The Pit, his gunmen closing in from the back, John X and the last legal coming up fast behind him.

He watched Archie run past the entrance to Building A, headed for Building E at the north end of The Pit. The gunmen coming out of the parking lot should cut him off. If so, the shooter wouldn't be able to turn back without running into Rachman's gun. They had the shooter trapped.

And then the trap snapped shut, not on Archie, but on the Muslims.

From the top floors of the buildings on the east and west sides of The Pit, the barrels of two AK-47 automatic rifles emerged from open windows. Just then,

Detective Meeb shoved open the lobby door of Building B, ducked behind it and held his shield out yelling, "Police! Put down your guns."

As if in a mocking answer to Meeb's command, both shooters opened fire from up above and the crackling sound of automatic rifles filled The Pit.

Burning half-inch projectiles of pointed steel screamed into the courtyard at six hundred meters per second. Walli X turned toward the sound of Meeb's voice just as a stream of bullets ripped through the Muslim's chest, neck, and head sending fist-size chunks of flesh, blood, and bone flying away from his body. He died before his remains slammed into the ground.

Meeb jerked back behind the door, yelling to his partner, "Fuck, Jimmy, they got AKs. Get back. Tell 'em they got fucking heavy weapons out here."

A spray of bullets ripped into the heavy door that Meeb leaned against. He felt the door buck and shatter as bullets blasted through above him, plowing into the lobby floor. Meeb twisted away from the door, but not in time to avoid a bullet that just caught the top of his left shoulder, tearing out a finger size groove of flesh.

Jimmy Silver dove away from the door, banging his head into the wall, and dropping his police radio.

The first of the three Muslim gunmen who had been patrolling around the complex ran into the rear of The Pit. He moved fast, hunched over, creating a more difficult target to hit. The Blue-Tops shooter in the west window of the courtyard took lazy aim in his direction and squeezed off a burst, missing him. A second gunman appeared close behind the first. The shooter aimed more carefully this time, tracking the running man. The second stream of bullets hit his legs, shattering both below the knees.

The first gunman dove for cover behind the remnants

of a wooden bench set on a concrete stand. He landed on his back and fired blindly in the direction of the fourth-floor window in the west building. In response, the Blue-Tops shooter emptied the rest of his clip at the bench and concrete stand. The faded, green, wooden slats exploded. Chips of concrete flew up from the base. The gunman stayed down on his back behind the concrete. The shooter in the east building aimed a spray of bullets at him, but the angle was too acute. He gave up and raked a stream of fire at Rachman who continued charging after Archie.

One gunman, Walli X, lay dead. The second remained motionless behind cover. The third had turned into an inert heap, legs shattered and bleeding. In a split second they had changed from shooters to targets.

Rachman, however, had never taken his eyes off Archie, had never hesitated one step in his mad dash after the killer. He saw Archie run into a narrow gangway opening at the ground floor of the far north building, Building C. Despite the wild bursts of assault-rifle fire, Rachman had managed to stay close enough to the east building that the shooter on that side hadn't spotted him. The second Blue-Tops shooter on the west side ran out of bullets just as he had figured out the range between him and Rachman. He immediately grabbed another full magazine, but in his excitement for the kill he fumbled as he tried to shove it into his automatic rifle.

Rachman did not know or care how close to death he ran. He would kill Archie or be killed trying. Either way, it would be Allah's will.

The last of Rachman's gunmen who had been patrolling the perimeter came running around to the north side of the complex just as Archie emerged from the gangway onto Rockaway Avenue.

The Muslim was not sure if Archie was the one they were after. Archie skidded to a stop and looked back at him, giving the gunman a chance to see him. Then he raised his Beretta and pegged three shots at him. The gunman threw himself on the ground and fired back at Archie as Archie ran across Rockaway Avenue.

Rachman just made it into the gangway tunnel as the west shooter finished loading the AK-47 and opened up at him. The shooter had the rifle on full automatic and the bullets seemed to hit everywhere around the gangway entrance, chipping brick, breaking windows, tearing up dirt from the ground, but Rachman was gone. He charged into the gangway just in time to see Archie fire his third shot at the last gunman.

As Archie broke into a run, Rachman raised the Glock and fired. The booming explosion inside the gangway deafened him. He had to aim low to clear the ceiling of the gangway near the exit, and his bullet zinged off the street and angled past Archie's hip.

Archie turned and fired his last shot on the run, aiming for Rachman as the big man emerged from the gangway. The shot screamed past Rachman's left ear. Rachman didn't even flinch.

The last gunman jumped to his feet and ran for Archie, too. He and Rachman were less then twenty yards behind Archie.

Archie never ducked or dodged or changed directions. He headed straight for the front door of Justine Burton's Caring Community Center.

He burst through the double doors, turned right and ran down a corridor. One of the women who worked in the center stepped out of her office and Archie rammed a forearm into her chest, knocking her down with such force that she cracked the tip of her tailbone when she hit the floor.

Archie ran over her body, stomping on her stomach and shoulder. The woman screamed. He never even looked at her. He knew the Muslims were close now. Almost too close

Archie skidded into the center's main waiting area as Rachman and his gunman thundered through the entrance back down the corridor behind him. Two women and five children sat against the far wall of the waiting room. They all cringed at the sight of a running man, gun in hand, face covered by a black ski mask.

An intake worker sat at a desk to Archie's left, in front of the only window in the area. Justine Burton came storming into the waiting area from her office located through an archway across from where Archie stood.

"Get out of here!" she yelled.

Archie aimed the Beretta at her, yelling back with such fury that Justine felt his spit spray her face.

"Fuck you! *You* get the fuck out of here."

Archie aimed the Beretta at Justine's face. She put her hands in front of her face, turned away from the gun, and screamed. Archie pulled the trigger. Nothing. Justine continued to scream, and Archie continued to pull the trigger of the empty gun, each time cursing the commissioner's daughter.

Finally, infuriated that he couldn't kill her, Archie smashed Justine with the back of his hand. His time was up. The Muslims were seconds away from him. He turned from Justine, picked up a folding gray metal chair set against the wall behind him and heaved it over the head of the woman sitting at the intake desk.

The heavy chair smashed through the double-pane window behind her. She dropped to the floor.

Rachman and his armed gunman, pounding down the

narrow corridor, had almost reached the waiting area. Rachman, running hard, raised the Glock and yelled, "Don't move!"

Archie turned, grabbed Justine's arm and spun her toward the corridor opening just as Rachman burst into the waiting area. Rachman slammed into Justine with such force that her feet left the ground.

Archie jumped up onto the desk and dove out the broken window.

Justine landed with a sickening thud, and slid across the floor, right into a shard of glass which tore a two inch groove of flesh out of her chin.

The collision with Justine knocked Rachman off balance, but he stumbled forward and banged into the wall next to the broken window. By the time he twisted back around and looked out the window, Archie had already landed on the sidewalk, rolled over once, and jumped to his feet. He ran toward the passenger side of his Saab. The convertible top was down. Reggie sat in the driver's seat, gunning the engine, his Smith & Wesson in his free hand. Archie jumped in.

Reggie floored the accelerator and the car roared down the street, tires squealing, rear end fishtailing, Reggie blindly shooting behind him to cover the escape.

Rachman recovered his balance and fired two shots at the fleeing Saab. It was too late. He would not shoot at a target he could not hit. He forced himself to stop shooting, pointed the Glock up, and roared in frustration and rage.

Sunday, two days after the ambush in New Lots, Loyd Shaw rolled out of his bed shortly past noon, relieved his full bladder, skipped the shower and shave, and decided it might be time to cut back on the Jack Daniel's. The hangovers were becoming bothersome.

He stepped out to a cloudless blue sky and determined to sweat out the remains of the alcohol in his system and pump an extra blast of oxygen through his fuzzy brain. A three mile jog-hike should do it.

He headed toward the main farmhouse angling toward a dirt trail across the road that led through a scrub pine forest to a small lake about a mile and a half away.

As soon as he came within a hundred yards of the farmhouse, Mrs. McGovern's black Lab came bounding toward him.

Shaw waved at the dog and called out, "Ellie!"

Shaw had grown fond of the Lab, as she had him. Her owner wasn't able to take her on long walks, so whenever the Lab spotted Shaw, the dog bounded out, ready for an outing.

Ellie would run ahead of Shaw, searching and sniffing, but she never let Shaw out of her sight for long. Every few minutes, Ellie would run back to check on him. Shaw found the dog's attention quite endearing.

By the time they returned from their walk, both felt better. Shaw had worked up a decent sweat.

Ellie bounded up onto Mrs. McGovern's porch and inhaled her bowl of water, then stood on the porch panting, looking, waiting for Mrs. McGovern to bring her food.

Mrs. McGovern came out of her kitchen holding the dog's food in a chipped brown bowl and waved Shaw up onto the porch.

Mrs. McGovern rarely engaged Shaw in conversation. She surprised him even more when she motioned toward her kitchen and asked, "You have breakfast yet?"

Shaw checked his watch. Breakfast time had long past. It never occurred to him that Mrs. McGovern would have known he hadn't eaten, much less invite him in for breakfast.

"No, thanks."

"Well, suit yourself. You came up early this weekend."

"Yep."

"Everything all right?"

Shaw didn't mind when the friendly Labrador checked on him, but he was not at all sure he appreciated Mrs. McGovern's attention. It hadn't occurred to him that the older woman kept such an eye on him.

"Why do you ask?"

She waved a hand as if to apologize for being nosy. "I'm not trying to pry, Mr. Shaw. . . ."

"That's all right."

"Well, you know, I get up two or three times a night. Woman my age. Couldn't help noticing your lights on."

"Just caught up in my work, Mrs. McGovern."

"Oh. Well. That's good."

Shaw felt an exit might be too abrupt at that point, but didn't feel like offering any further explanation.

"Well, Ellie and I had a nice walk. I'm going to clean up."

"Oh, hell, I'm too old to be coy, Mr. Shaw. Fact is, you look awful. Haven't ever seen you look this way or stay up to all hours and sleep until noon. It's none of my business, of course, none at all, but I just thought I'd inquire. Say what's on my mind. In case you . . ."

She left the offer to listen unspoken.

Shaw rubbed the stubble on his cheek wondering just how much his appearance had deteriorated. He realized he hadn't done much to ameliorate a long night in the Brooklyn precinct three days ago. Did he look the way he did because he had been more shaken by his exile than he realized? Had he fallen into a depression aggravated by too much bourbon?

"I'm fine, Mrs. McGovern. Fine."

He knew even as he said the words they sounded like an attempt to convince both himself and Mrs. McGovern.

"But it's nice of you to ask. It's just as well that you did, because you'll be seeing more of me for the time being. There's . . . well, it's a little complicated. But, I'm fine. Thanks for asking."

"Listen Mr. Shaw, you can tell me whatever you want, or not tell me. But don't tell me you're fine because you're not fine. You're a long way from *fine*. If you don't know that, then that's about the best I can do for you. If you do, well, then, you'll do what you can or you won't. That's up to you."

Mrs. McGovern closed the issue with a half wave of her hand. Ellie had watched her short speech and now knew that her mistress was done. She barked sharply once to remind Mrs. McGovern she was still holding her bowl of food.

"Oh, look at me," said Mrs. McGovern. "Forgot about you didn't I, girl?"

Mrs. McGovern bent down quickly and lay the bowl on the wooden floor of the porch. The Lab set about wolfing down her food.

Mrs. McGovern looked at Shaw, but said no more. Shaw knew she didn't have to.

"Thanks, Mrs. McGovern. See you later."

She nodded and allowed Shaw his quick exit, but he had the feeling Mrs. McGovern would be keeping tabs on him whether he liked it or not.

Shaw began to wonder what she might be speculating. He told himself, she's probably decided it had to do with my marriage. He had never brought Jane to the see the place, and he never intended to. They had both accepted the flimsy excuse that the renovation wasn't complete. It provided a polite means to avoid admitting neither of them wanted to spend a weekend together in the country.

Thinking about it, Shaw winced at the discomfort he envisioned if Jane had forced the issue.

"Fuck that," he said out loud. "Fuck all of it." But despite his attempt to dismiss his situation, as he walked back to his studio, Shaw found himself making a mental list of things he would do come Monday: check with Jake Bennett to see if he had run down the punks who had attacked him in Flatbush, call the lawyer Siegel, contact a few guys he knew who would sniff around and give him the word on the assistant district attorney, Johnson.

Maybe he wanted to prove Mrs. McGovern wrong, maybe the thought of Jane viewing the demise of his career with one more galling ounce of pity drove him, but by the time he returned to the studio, Shaw had almost convinced himself that he might be able to hang on to the tatters of his career for the one final wretched year he needed to make his twenty.

By Sunday, Rachman's rage over the Friday afternoon ambush had settled into a constant, festering
wrath. Almost every thought he allowed himself cen-
tered on vengeance.

On Saturday, Rachman and the MS-2 members had
attended to the dead and wounded. Now, Sunday morning, one of the quietest times in Brownsville, the three
top-ranking members of MS-2—John X, Yousseff X,
and Rachman Abdul X—sat around an old Formica-
topped kitchen table in an unoccupied apartment on the
top floor of Building A, planning vengeance. Three
hardened felons with minds bent from years in maxi-
mum security prisons, without futures in normal society, sat planning the next move in their holy war, a war
they felt completely justified in waging. A war that
now had obligated them to avenge the deaths of Walli
X, the regular MS-2 guard shot through the head, and
the brutal wounding of two others.

Rachman and John X were warriors. Yousseff X
functioned as intelligence officer. Yousseff X was a
small man. He wore an old black suit at least two sizes
too big for him, a white shirt buttoned to the neck, and
the requisite Kufi skullcap. There was a sparseness
about the man, as if prison and hate and fanatical dis-
cipline had excised everything extra. Yousseff carried
no extra baggage, no fat, no sympathy, no softness of
any kind. Even his skullcap had been knit out of simple, unbleached cotton string.

The only things Yousseff X held in extra measure
were fanaticism, intelligence, and hate.

Rachman opened the meeting.

"Tell us what your people found out."

Yousseff lit a cigarette with the burning stub of another, as if taking that time to organize his thoughts. Rachman and the others tolerated his chain-smoking, a violation for most Muslims. But Yousseff X was not most Muslims. Their disapproval did not make the slightest difference to Yousseff.

"We know most of what we need to about their operation. Actually, they're a little bit more organized than most scum like them who deal."

Yousseff reached into his breast pocket and extracted a photocopy of a map showing the section of Brownsville surrounding New Lots Apartments. He had enlarged it to the point where the lines and letters had turned grainy, but it was easier for everybody to see the street names and landmarks.

He laid the photocopy on the table and the MS-2 inner circle leaned toward it. Yousseff pointed out areas on the map he had circled with a red pen.

"This is their headquarters. It's a body shop in the alley that runs alongside the elevated tracks at the New Lots stop. They keep weapons and at least one of their stash cars in there. It's also the main supply point for their poison. It goes from here into various apartments. Then from those apartments into whatever hole they are selling out of. So they always have people in there. Four or five, sometimes more.

"In addition, there are usually two lookouts guarding the outside, here and here. They will be armed."

Yousseff pushed the map toward the others and sat back.

"Friday and Saturday are their biggest selling days. Today, most of them and their customers will recover from the weekend. Monday, they start to gear up. It's the day they bring in their biggest supply." Yousseff leaned forward and pointed to a red X on the map. "They'll have the most people in there, the most supply, tomorrow."

Yousseff outlined what tomorrow would bring. For a few moments, no one spoke. Even Rachman seemed to be taken aback by the brutality of it. Yousseff knew there'd be questions. He sat back, hunched in his chair, ready to give the answers.

Loyd Shaw had spent the rest of Sunday afternoon painting. When the daylight dimmed, he switched on artificial light and kept daubing at the canvas, laying on different tones of acrylic red. Over the last months he had become intrigued with the color. No matter what he painted, even the shapes suggested by the deep dark greens and grays of the pine forest around him, it all came out red.

The painting kept his mind off what the department had in store for him, but by the time the Massachusetts moon rose high enough to gleam above his second-floor skylight, Shaw's anger and dread seeped into his consciousness like an annoying stain reappearing after yet another coat of paint.

Sundown was the catalyst for the anger. Shaw couldn't shake off his realization that it was Sunday evening. On every previous Sunday he had spent in his country studio, Shaw found himself resenting the fact that he had to pack up and be back in the city for work on Monday. Sometimes his schedule varied, but Shaw generally worked Monday through Friday. Saturdays and Sundays, Shaw painted under the skylight, surrounded by big double-paned Anderson windows. Mondays, he returned.

He had grown accustomed to recognizing the different light of each hour of each day, changed by the time and season and weather. And now he knew, just by the shade of darkness and the gleam of the moon that time had marched to that Sunday moment when he normally would have packed up and driven back to the city.

Each Sunday, when he left his painting and returned to the Job, his level of discontent crept up one more notch.

But now, on the Sunday after the department had told him *not* to come back, Shaw felt no relief of animosity and resentment. In fact, Shaw felt even more resentful. Shaw realized that, now, he wasn't even good enough for one of their stinking Mondays.

Shaw dropped his paintbrush into the coffee can filled with paint thinner, walked to his kitchen area, and filled a glass with four fingers of Jack Daniel's.

Once again he told himself, "Fuck it."

Yousseff X had described an extremely brutal, yet incredibly efficient plan. Its success depended on timing and the viability of information Yousseff had gathered. Rachman Abdul X trusted that Yousseff's information would be correct. After all, who better to gather information on the dealings of a black ghetto drug gang than black ex-convicts, many of whom had dealt in exactly the same crimes in the same types of neighborhoods? As to the timing, he trusted only himself and the will of Allah.

At six o'clock Monday morning, all was quiet in the back alley where the Blue-Tops body shop was located. As usual, two of the gang guarded the outside. One of them, a gangly young man, with bad skin and a worse attitude, named Nelson slouched against the brick wall next to the large steel garage door. The other guard, a squat weight-lifter type named Beal, sat on the step that led up to the small entrance door next to the big rolling garage door. Beal cradled a loaded Uzi in his lap. Both of the men were alert, watching, mindful of the fact that a shipment would be arriving soon.

A mongrel dog entered the west end of the alley, loping toward them with a sideways gate. About ten feet before the dog reached the guards, he lifted his head in the air, sniffed, then abruptly turned, disappearing between two ramshackle buildings.

Behind them, up on the elevated platform, the Canarsie line subway train pulled into the New Lots station. The old tracks rumbled under the steel wheels and squealing brakes.

Between the dog and the train, the guards didn't see the hunched-over bum enter the alley at the west end. He wore a long raincoat bearing stains and dirt that looked as if it had taken years to accumulate them. The bottom of the coat had reached the shredded stage. Under the raincoat, the derelict wore a filthy hooded sweatshirt despite the warmth of the April morning. Behind him, the bum dragged a banged-up shopping cart jammed with assorted junk: a milk crate, broken pieces of iron pipe, a black plastic bag filled with cans, more dirty plastic bags wrapped in tape, an old quilt.

Nelson noticed him first. He sneered at the human wreck, another loser in Brownsville, looking for worthless shit in a back alley.

Beal cradled the Uzi and told Nelson, "Go tell that old motherfucker to get the hell out of here. I don't want him close enough I can smell the piss on him."

"What makes you think I want to get close enough to smell him?"

"Go on. Get him out of here."

Muttering to himself, Nelson headed off. The bum stood at the wall of an abandoned building, feeling the edges of a piece of tin that had been nailed over a busted out window. He seemed to be trying to figure out how to pull it off so he could add it to the collection in his cart.

Nelson yelled, "Yo. Old man."

The bum kept looking at the sheet of tin.

Nelson pulled out his gun and walked closer.

"Yo. I'm talking to you."

Nelson had closed the distance to five yards, and kept coming.

"Hey!"

Finally, the bum turned.

"Get the fuck out a here, man."

"What?"

Nelson raised the gun, pointing it at the bum, coming close enough so that he could point the piece right in front of the filthy face buried inside the hood of the sweatshirt. He extended the gun, but kept his head bent back away from the bum, not wanting to smell him.

"I said—"

He never really saw the club come out from under Rachman Abdul X's filthy raincoat. He just caught a flash of it before the wood shattered the left side of his skull and cracked his eye socket. One instant of intense pain, and then everything turned black.

Beal had been watching it all, impatient, a scowl on his face, the Uzi cradled in his lap. And then, inexplicably, suddenly, the bum had Nelson in his arms.

"What the fuck?"

Beal stood, gripped the Uzi, moving toward them quickly as Rachman bent Nelson over the shopping cart.

What the fuck had that bum done? thought Beal. It was the last conscious thought he had. The last he would ever have.

John X stepped out from between two buildings, just as Beal passed him, and swung a baseball bat at the back of the guard's head. The hollow crunch of the bat connecting against the skull was loud enough for Rachman to hear it at the other end of the alley.

From between the decrepit buildings, gunmen materialized, gathering around the two fallen guards. No one spoke a word. Rachman shucked off the filthy clothes. The gunmen stripped the Blue-Tops down to their underwear. Two of the Muslims pulled on the clothing, while the others loaded the inert bodies into Rachman's shopping cart.

Within minutes, two of Rachman's gunmen had replaced Beal and Nelson, dressed in their clothes, holding their weapons, standing guard at the entrance to the body shop.

Rachman, John X, and the others disappeared. Thirty minutes later, the car pulled up bearing the Blue-Tops Sunday shipment.

The gunman who had taken Nelson's place banged on the steel door. An electric winch kicked in and slowly the door lifted. The car entered. The large rolling steel door immediately began to close. Before the door fully closed, Rachman and John X were standing at both ends of the door with short sledgehammers and coal chisels. Two blows from each and the chisels were irrevocably jammed into the door's track, stopping it a foot above the ground.

Four gunmen appeared, each carrying five gallon plastic jugs filled with gasoline. They slung forty gallons of gas under the jammed door in seconds. Another gunman jammed an iron bar across the second door.

Voices inside began shouting. Someone inside began pounding on the steel door trying to free it.

Calmly, Rachman took the Uzi from the gunman who had replaced Beal. He bent over and unleashed a spray of bullets under the jammed door. Red-hot lead skimmed and skipped on the concrete floor, ricocheting off the hard brick, engine blocks, and cars. The first bullet to ignite a jug of gasoline created a fiery explosion that seemed rather muffled. But within seconds, a series of concussions exploded and instantly built into one long horrible rolling blast.

The screaming started before the last explosion of

gasoline. The screaming continued and rose with the greasy, black smoke that suddenly poured out of every porous opening in the body shop. Billows and plumes of the deadly black smoke rose from under the jammed door. One of the gang members managed to squeeze his head under the door, scraping with bloody hands on the concrete, pulling himself outside, tearing the skin off the back of his head to escape the flames that were burning the flesh off his back and legs.

A single gunshot exploded his skull, ending his misery.

Rachman had already motioned for his gunmen to leave the scene. He stood outside the burning massacre, listening to the last screams, letting the heat that emanated toward him sear his face, hoping that the one they called Archie Ar was inside burning.

All that would be left to do now was to walk to the empty lot where his men had taken Beal and Nelson and supervise the final task, beating the two men to death, then putting their barely recognizable bodies on display. Rachman wanted the residents of New Lots to witness what happens to those who harm any member of MS-2.

Rachman watched the destruction and nodded. Youseff's plan had worked. All praise to Allah.

When the phone rang at nine the next morning, Shaw was not ready to answer it.

He wouldn't have, except that the phone would not stop ringing. The ringing went on and on, as if the caller on the other end knew Shaw was lying there, stubbornly refusing to answer. Finally, Shaw leaned out of his bed and snatched the receiver, yelling, "What!" into the mouthpiece.

Shaw heard Richard Parnell's voice, undeterred by Shaw's bellow.

"Shaw."

"Yeah."

"Parnell."

"Yeah?"

"Report to the Chief of D's office, today, noon. I suggest you wear a suit."

"What time is it?"

"Nine."

"Are you crazy? I'm up in Massachusetts."

"The Chief of D, Shaw. When can you get here?"

Shaw tried to focus, to concentrate. What the hell is going on? he asked himself.

"What the hell does he want with me?"

"Shaw, you got 'til one o'clock. You have to speed, show 'em your badge. Be here."

The line went dead.

The Chief of D's office. Just like that. No explanation. Just a flat-out order.

Shaw yelled into the dead mouthpiece, "Fuck you, Parnell, you stiff-ass shanty Irish bastard!" Then slammed the phone down.

Shaw sat on the edge of his bed, deciding if he dared defy the Chief of Detectives. He knew that if any detective in the NYPD refused the chief of the division it would be tantamount to defying God. Parnell, sure. The District Attorney's office, why not? But the Chief of D?

Shaw looked at his watch. If he waited five more minutes, he'd never make it.

At exactly two minutes to one, Shaw walked into the foyer of the Chief of Detective's office at One Police Plaza. He wore his best suit, adjusting his best tie over his last clean dress shirt. He ran his fingers through his hair, still damp from the hurried shower he'd taken at his loft.

He announced himself to the administrative assistant guarding the entrance to the office of the person Shaw considered the most powerful man in the NYPD— Chief of Detectives, Albert J. DeLuca.

Most people assumed the Police Commissioner held the most powerful position. Shaw knew that on an everyday basis, when it really counted, the Chief of D held more power. The Chief of the Detective Division controlled the investigative arm of one of the world's largest and most powerful police forces. No crime in New York City could be solved or prosecuted until investigated. Police commissioners set policy, commanded thousands of men. But only the detective division could investigate and gather evidence. Without investigation, there could be no prosecution, no punishment, no justice. Controlling that process made DeLuca a powerful man. The ability to focus a full-scale police investigation on both the innocent and the guilty meant Albert J. DeLuca could save or condemn both the innocent and the guilty.

When he told him to take a seat, the administrative officer studiously avoided eye contact with Shaw. It reminded Shaw of how jury members avoid looking at a defendant they are about to send to prison.

After a ten-minute wait, Shaw heard a very slight tone sound at the desk of the assistant. He looked up and told Shaw, "Okay."

Shaw walked down a short corridor. He caught the rich aroma of cigar smoke. At the end of the corridor a door opened onto a corner office designed to impress. Shaw walked in, his footsteps muted by thick, blue carpeting. The Chief of Detectives, Albert J. DeLuca, sat behind a massive wooden desk, hunched over a pile of papers like some turn-of-the-century scrivener. The office walls were crowded with police insignia, memorabilia, pictures of the chief at various ceremonies with police and public officials. Shaw felt as if he had entered an inner sanctum of officialdom.

DeLuca did not bother to acknowledge that another person had entered the room. He continued reading various pages spilling out of a red folder. Shaw watched, noticing that DeLuca seemed to be reading two or three pages at once. Shaw wondered if the red color of the folder meant anything significant. Top Secret? Beware? Or maybe red was DeLuca's favorite color, too.

Without raising his head, DeLuca reached over and picked up a Churchill-size Cuban El Rey del Mundo from a thick, marble cigar ashtray. He puffed thoughtfully while he perused his papers. Two kings of the world, thought Shaw—DeLuca and the El Rey.

The cigar had the rich, deep, earthy aroma of a Cuban. Shaw suddenly had a fierce desire for one.

When DeLuca finally looked up at him, Shaw was reminded of DeLuca's nickname, The Shark. DeLuca's pale skin blended in with steel gray hair, slicked back tight on his big skull. His head, neck, and shoulders all seemed to taper into a thick body. DeLuca had a piercing gaze, yet his eyes were strangely lifeless as if he could not afford to display the slightest emotion. At public affairs DeLuca tended to flash a smile intended to charm, but which succeeded in merely displaying a brutal set of brilliantly white teeth. Shaw didn't expect any smiles from The Shark today.

DeLuca pushed the papers aside and looked up at Shaw, staring at Shaw as if he had just finished reading about him.

"What are you, Shaw, some kind of psycho?"

"No, but if I were actually psychotic I don't think I would know it, would I?"

DeLuca looked at Shaw to make sure he wasn't being flip, decided he wasn't, then told Shaw, "Sit down."

Shaw sat.

"What prompted you to shoot up a car full of African-Americans at three o'clock in the morning while on restricted duty?"

Shaw looked at DeLuca for a moment to see if he were asking a serious question or just baiting him. Bait from The Shark? Shaw wondered. DeLuca's deadpan stare revealed nothing. For a moment, Shaw considered answering, I don't know, but he wasn't ready to play games with the Chief of Detectives.

Shaw told the Chief his version of what had happened without exaggeration or affectation.

"So you shot up the car to stop the music."

"Right. And drive those guys off."

"Sounds foolish. Why not just shoot the pricks who jumped you? According to your record, you don't mind shooting people."

Shaw decided not to rise to that comment, keeping his face deadpan, too.

"I figured it would cause me less trouble if I shot the car."

"Uh-huh. And what was this 'look' you gave them?"

"I looked at them like they were assholes."

"Assholes? Or criminals?"

"Both."

"Right. So you were pissed off?"

"Very."

"At them and their music."

"Yes."

"Black guys."

"Yes."

"Black music."

"I suppose. I guess some white people listen to it, too."

"And you're seeing Psych Services. What's the problem, Shaw? You got a thing about black people."

"Maybe it's some sort of white-rage syndrome."

DeLuca's chin lifted just a few degrees. His eyes narrowed slightly. Without saying a word, Shaw knew without any doubt that another smart answer like that would not be tolerated.

DeLuca's tone hardened slightly, but the smart answer seemed to bring him to his point.

"Detective Shaw, are you a racist? You hate blacks?"

"No."

DeLuca stared at him, not responding. After several moments of silence, Shaw asked, "Are we finished?"

"You're finished enough, Shaw. Your whole career is finished."

"Then why am I here?"

"Because I say so. And I'm the one asking the questions, Detective. Don't think because your career is over you have nothing to lose. And I'll tell you when you've given me enough answers. Or do you want to say fuck you to me and get up and walk out of here?"

The hard words were said without DeLuca raising his voice, but with a clearly higher level of intensity.

"I want to find out why I'm here more than I want to say fuck you. At least so far."

"We'll get to that. Couple of more questions. Anything more you want to say about the black issue?"

"Not really. Ask some black people who know me if they think I'm a racist."

"So some of your best friends are black?"

"Some good friends."

"All right. Were you drunk when this happened?"

"No. I'd had a grand total of one drink. I didn't feel much like drinking that night."

"You have any trouble with alcohol? You an alcoholic?"

"No. I like to drink, but not when it's going to get in my way."

"You went all the way out to Flatbush for one drink."

"I went out there to wish someone happy birthday. The drinking was incidental."

"You must have really hated those guys who jumped you."

DeLuca's sudden change in topic gave Shaw pause. What was DeLuca trying to do? Catch him at something?

Shaw did not respond for a few moments, but decided he didn't care to attempt figuring out exactly what DeLuca was up to. He did find it interesting to gauge the amount of hate in him and where it was directed.

DeLuca didn't wait for Shaw to finish his introspection.

"All right, never mind. I don't think you're a racist. Nothing in your record indicates it. I don't think you have a thing for blacks. I'll tell you why you went after three black guys in the middle of the night, two of which according to your testimony had guns."

"Okay, why?" Shaw was interested to know himself.

"You did it because you were scared shitless, or close to it. You did it because you were scared of those murderous bastards and you didn't want to die. And you got angry not at them, but at yourself because you were so terrified. So you had to risk your life with that crazy move you took."

Shaw realized that DeLuca was right, but didn't feel like admitting it.

"I had no choice."

"Nonsense. You could have run. Run like hell. You know how damn hard it is to shoot a running target. Those guys might not have even run after you."

"No, just gotten back in the car and run me down."

"I don't think so. I think running was an option."

"Maybe you're right, Chief. Maybe you got it right."

"Are you patronizing me, Detective Shaw?"

"I don't think so."

"Don't avoid the truth here. It's important. Don't concede if you think I'm wrong. Of course, you were afraid of them, that's the easy part. The harder part is admitting that your fear made you angry. That's what was going on out there."

Shaw said, "Sounds right," and meant it.

DeLuca nodded, picked up his fat cigar, blinked at Shaw a few times and rewarded himself with a couple of puffs. "Okay. Next question. Any ideas on how you're going to save your pension?"

"Excuse me?"

"You heard me."

"You mean—"

"You know what I mean."

After a few moments, Shaw said, "I guess that depends on what my lawyer and the union guys tell me."

"Your lawyer and the union guys?"

"Yes."

"Fuck your lawyer and the union."

Shaw hadn't expected that. Hadn't expected any of this.

"Detective Shaw, have you done the numbers?"

"The numbers."

"The numbers. Your pension. Your time in. Do you know what it means if they throw you out before you make your twenty? Do you know how much you lose?"

"No. I haven't gone over the numbers."

"Why not?"

Shaw started to answer, but DeLuca kept talking.

"I'll tell you why not. Because you don't think you'll lose it. You think they'll just suspend you. Shove you way off behind a desk in the Property Office or somewhere horrible for . . ." DeLuca looked at the papers in front of him. ". . . what is it? Eighteen months if you throw in your accrued vacation time. That's what you have left. You figure they'll hide you for eighteen months, maybe make your life miserable, take away vacation days, then let you out to pasture. But if they don't, if they strip you and throw you out, it means you're too old to start a career, assuming a cop like you has another career possibility, which you don't, but if you did, now you have to do it without your base, without your twenty-five percent. With nothing. You're out and you have nothing but your savings and your infinitesimal chance to get a job. Shaw, do you have any savings?"

"Isn't that listed somewhere in your pile of papers."

"No. Just your credit history, spending history, that sort of thing. I didn't bother to get your financial status. I think I already know it. I think even with a pension and a few odd jobs, you're going to live a very simple life. Without it, you're going to be a poor old man."

Shaw thought to himself, what about Jane? He must know I'm married to a lawyer. A successful, tough, woman lawyer. How the hell does he know that she and I are quits? How does he know that if I retired and got my pension, plus her earnings and whatever jobs I got we wouldn't be comfortable? How does he know Jane is gone from me?

Shaw did his best to keep his thoughts hidden and simply said, "I guess I'd better look at the numbers." But he felt himself losing his usual control and perspective. Somehow DeLuca had overwhelmed him with his quiet, monotone delivery, his blinking gaze devoid of emotion, his horrible barbs discharged between puffs on his fat, expensive, illegal Cuban cigar.

"Yes," said DeLuca, "But that's not what the real problem is."

Shaw yelled to himself, inside, That's not the *real*

problem? I'm going to stripped and left with nothing? That's not the fucking problem, you cold, heartless, rotten, fucking fish? What the hell is the problem, you prick?

"The real problem is, once we throw you out, nobody else will hire you. Not even to watch a damn candy store at night."

"Why is that?"

"Because when we throw you out, we'll make sure to label you as a rogue cop, a psycho racist rogue cop who got tossed off the force. It'll ruin you forever."

Shaw felt a constricting feeling in his throat and chest, a kind of sickening, paralyzing heartburn that had nothing to do with anything in his stomach and everything to do with the knowledge that even though DeLuca had delivered the threat without a hint of emotion, his ability to make good on it was undeniable.

DeLuca puffed and squinted, looking as if he had effortlessly engineered the meeting to a point where he could equally effortlessly deliver his coup de grâce.

"I'll compliment you on your ability to keep your mouth shut. Not bawling needlessly. Acting stupid. Arguing about any of this. I only hope you're not sitting there thinking this is an empty threat."

"Absolutely not, sir."

"Good. Good. So the only thing left for me to say to you, to drive this painful reality home is this—you might walk out of here and call the lawyers and the union and hear the line, 'they can't do that to a twenty-year, first-grade, veteran detective.' Or, 'they wouldn't try that shit.' Now, normally, *normally* they would be somewhat correct."

DeLuca looked at Shaw making sure he followed.

"But in your case, no. It doesn't apply."

"Why is that?"

"Without even getting tricky, we could twist your

record around. It's not all that difficult. You had that crazy shoot-out a few years back that made you notorious. You're off center enough to need a shrink. Now you're shooting up cars in the middle of the night."

DeLuca shrugged as if it would be the easiest thing in the world. "We could probably even sell that to the union guys. Watch them walk away from you. But here's the bitch, Shaw. I don't have to sell anybody. Normally, like I said, you can't screw veterans like that. But you, you're no problem."

Shaw swallowed hard, trying to fight off the anger and nausea that overwhelmed him. He didn't want to hear this, but DeLuca kept right on rolling.

"You? You never fit in here, Shaw. I know you. I don't know you as well as some, but I know you. I know the men you worked with and the people you worked for. You never fit in. You were always above it. You stink of an above-it-all attitude. An attitude that says, I don't want to be here because I'm better than the rest of you. I can do this to you and not demoralize anybody, not start any grumbling or worry in the division. I could ruin you because nobody gives a shit about you."

"Nobody gives a shit about anybody on this Job, and you know it. All you're saying is it would be easier with me."

"Okay. If that's the way you want to look at it."

"But since I'm sitting here listening to this, you aren't going to do that to me, are you?"

DeLuca didn't bother to reassure Shaw.

"Not only that, you're telling me you can make it all go away. The departmental stuff, that asshole ADA Johnson, all of it."

"How successful do you think any ADA is going to be without the cooperation of the detective's division? You think I'm worried about him?"

"No."

"So?"

"So what do you want from me?" Shaw asked.

DeLuca leaned back, picked up the El Rey and blinked and puffed. He pushed his chair back from his desk and half turned away, puffing, thinking. He crossed his legs and absentmindedly flexed his ankle, turning his foot counterclockwise.

He said, almost as much to himself as to Shaw, "It's much easier working with smart people. I've always said that."

As DeLuca turned his ankle, Shaw caught glimpses of the bottom of DeLuca's shoe. Hardly a scuff marred the surface of the leather soles. It was as if DeLuca had spent all his time walking on carpet. It struck Shaw as a very sheltered life for a cop. But it hadn't dulled DeLuca's ability to put Shaw exactly where he wanted him.

"So we agree that A, I know you better than you know yourself, and B, I control your fate." DeLuca swiveled around on his chair and faced Shaw again. "That's clear?"

"Clear."

"And do we agree that you are willing to help me out so that I will not do these terrible things that will ensure a life of poverty and subsequent misery for you?"

"Yes. Providing we agree that 'helping you out' doesn't get me sent to jail. I'll be poor on the outside before I'll be anything on the inside."

DeLuca puffed on the El Rey and dipped his head slightly to the right.

"That's certainly not my intent. I don't want to see you locked up. I intend to do the right thing here, not the wrong thing, but how you do it is up to you. You may have to cut a few corners. I'll cover for you as much as possible, but obviously I can't guarantee everything. You go too far, you'll have to live with the consequences. We still on the same page?"

"Yes."

"You want to say fuck you and walk now?"

"No."

"Okay, you'll have to sit there and listen to me for a few minutes."

Albert J. DeLuca spoke without interruption, without emotion, reciting the story as if he were dictating facts to a stenographer, even though the worst of it, the slaughter at the Blue-Tops headquarters, had happened just that morning. He puffed his Cuban cigar and dispassionately related the details of a community in the process of destroying itself.

Shaw sat and listened without interrupting, trying to envision the New Lots housing complex, the Blue-Tops crack gang, the Muslims. His years on the force had exposed him to enough situations so that he could see in his mind what DeLuca's words conveyed, but had a hard time understanding why the Chief of Detectives took such special interest in the situation. As DeLuca talked, Shaw tried to figure it out. Was it political contributions coming from the real estate company that took over the project? Was it simply too many bodies falling in Brownsville too fast? Had the press gotten wind of it?

When DeLuca casually mentioned that the woman injured at the community center was Justine Burton, Shaw asked his first question.

"Did you say Burton?"

"Yes."

"The same Burton? You're talking about the commissioner's daughter?"

DeLuca nodded.

Shaw sat back in his chair and scowled.

"Shit. That's why I'm sitting here? That's why you're threatening to ruin my life, because the fucking commissioner's daughter got her chin cut?"

DeLuca watched Shaw's reaction without commenting on it.

"That's part of it. The commissioner is naturally upset."

"Then why doesn't he tell his daughter to get out of there? What the hell is she doing out in Brownsville, anyhow?"

"Maybe she's trying to help some people? What's the matter, Detective, don't you think she should be able to help people who need it?"

"Not if she's going to get killed doing it. Sounds like she's in a war zone out there."

"That's nothing new. The area has had a war zone mortality rate for years."

Shaw asked, "What did the Muslims do about the drive-bys and the other shooting?"

"Oh, that's right, you've been hiding out up in Massachusetts. You didn't see the papers today."

"No. I came straight here."

"Didn't listen to the news when you drove down?"

"No, I prefer driving to music."

DeLuca reached over and dropped the morning editions of *The New York Times* and *Daily News* in front of Shaw. Both headlines screamed: SEVEN DIE IN BROOKLYN ARSON FIRE.

Shaw scanned the front pages.

"What did they do?"

"I haven't gotten full reports yet. Apparently they went in, shot up the place, locked the doors, and burned them. That's not all of it. Just before you walked in here I received a report of two bodies found propped up on benches in a little triangle park across from the complex. The bodies appeared to have been beaten to death. There's more to it, of course."

DeLuca dropped a red folder on top of the newspapers.

"That folder contains copies of the reports I've received. You'll get a few more details from them. That's all I know so far. Obviously, it's not all of it. This situation has to be stopped."

"So the commissioner's daughter can play Mother Teresa in Brownsville."

For the first time in the meeting, DeLuca raised his voice. "For a lot of reasons, Detective. She's just one of them. Some of us still think that people don't have the right to kill each other whenever they want to. Some of us still think the police department should do something about this. Maybe other people think blacks should just have at it out there and kill each other off. Save us a lot of trouble. I don't think so. What do you think, Detective?"

"I think you're right. I think people shouldn't be allowed to kill other people."

"Good." DeLuca pointed his cigar at Shaw. "So now we move from thinking to doing. You're going to shut this war down. Now. Whatever it takes. Or you're going to live to regret it. Regret it in more ways than you know. Is that understood?"

"Yes."

"From this moment, you're under my command, on special assignment. The only person who knows that is Parnell. That's it. You can live or die on this thing and nobody is going to give a shit. But you have a chance to get yourself back in and deserve the life you've earned." DeLuca dropped another folder on the pile. "You're going to need help, get it from the men on that list. Decide who you want before you leave. Then talk to Lieutenant Conklin two doors to the left, down the hall. He has your gun, badge, and ID. Work what you need through him. Don't waste his time. Do you have any questions?"

Shaw had hours of questions, but he simply said, "No."

"Then I suggest you get on with it. I want this fixed, yesterday. I'll expect to hear from you."

DeLuca turned to his desk and put his head down. The meeting had ended.

Shaw walked out of the chief's office, his folders and newspapers in hand, and wandered to Conklin's office.

A police lieutenant in his officer's white shirt and insignia looked up at Shaw as he entered. Shaw looked at the older cop thinking, if Fred Gwynne had a brother, this guy would be it.

Without a word, Conklin pushed Shaw's ID, gun, and badge at him, along with a form to sign. Shaw scribbled his signature without reading the form.

Shaw said, "I need an office. A place to sit and read. Make some phone calls."

Conklin pointed out his door and said, "Across the hall. Keep the door closed."

Shaw found the office, dropped DeLuca's reports on the desk, but he couldn't bring himself to sit down and begin. Suddenly, breathing felt difficult. He loosened his tie and unbuttoned his collar. He needed air.

The ride down in the closed-in elevator, the walk through the lobby, past the security turnstiles, seemed to take twenty minutes instead of five. Finally, he strode out into the cool air and sunshine. Shaw took several deep breaths.

He bought a cup of coffee at one of the food stands set up in the plaza and sat on an uncomfortable plastic chair sipping bitter black coffee from a Styrofoam cup.

"Shit." He asked himself, What the fuck have I gotten myself into?

He watched his fellow New Yorkers stroll by, thinking they didn't have a clue. Not a goddamn fucking clue what's going on. Asking himself, Are these the people all this is for?

And then Shaw thought about killing or being killed, about violent young black men shooting and burning one another.

Shaw sat and sipped the coffee, deciding whether or not he would walk back into One Police and do what he said he would. DeLuca had tried to make him feel as if he had no choice and done a good job of it. But Shaw knew full well he could walk away. Just put the coffee down, stand up, and walk away. Leave those reports in that empty office and simply walk out of the plaza, find a cab, go back to his place, and get in his car. Just head up the West Side Highway. Call the lawyer or Parnell, or not call anybody. Just go. Take his chances. Certainly, DeLuca would do what he said. But he could still survive. It wouldn't cost much to live in his studio in Massachusetts. Maybe he would sell a few paintings. Hell, maybe he'd sell a lot of paintings. He'd survive.

Shaw knew he could have said "fuck you" and if at the very worst it didn't work out . . . he could still drink a half bottle of good bourbon, stick his Glock in his mouth, get it positioned just right, pointing up so that it would blow his brains out the top of his head, then squeeze. One last, dramatic, messy red painting. At the very least, Shaw knew he could determine who would kill him. He could have said "fuck you" and walked out.

But he didn't.

Why? Because Shaw knew DeLuca had told him the truth. Somebody had to shut down the war. Somebody had to stop the mindless murderers. Civil society required civilized killers to keep the uncivilized killers at bay. And Albert J. DeLuca, the closest a detective gets to God on earth, had just told him he had been picked to pull the trigger.

Shaw stood up, drained the cold dregs of his coffee, and walked back into One Police.

Loyd Shaw picked four others. Four and no more. Four who seemed able to provide what he needed.

He walked across the hall and stepped into Conklin's office, handed him the list.

"Do you think you can get all of them together for a meeting tonight."

"What time?"

"Say eight o'clock."

"Where?" ·

"Restaurant in Tribeca."

"Yes."

Shaw gave Conklin the address and left. Shaw didn't repeat anything to make sure Conklin understood.

At ten after eight, Shaw sat alone, waiting in the place he had chosen, a bar-restaurant selected because it offered a quiet back room, and because it had aged into a comfortably rundown state long before the neighborhood gained its trendy name, Tribeca.

He checked his watch, wondering if the lateness was a show of independence, deciding they were probably having trouble finding their ways in the confusing downtown streets.

As Shaw waited, he drank a Bass Ale, spicing it with sips from a double shot of Jameson Irish whiskey.

The first of the group arrived at eight-fifteen: Detective Anthony Impelliteri, a nine-year veteran who worked homicide out of the 75th precinct in East New York, neighboring Brownsville.

Impelliteri looked much as Shaw imagined he would

from reading his file: early thirties, six foot, slim, well built. He wore black jeans, black T-shirt, and a dark green vest. Impelliteri's thick black hair was cropped short enough to look like a skullcap. He needed a shave, but Shaw decided the dark stubble looked good on him. Shaw noticed that Impelliteri carried his Glock shoved into his pants behind his right hip and didn't seem to care that his vest didn't cover it very well.

To Shaw, Impelliteri looked like a cop the average citizen would think was a criminal, and the average criminal would make as a cop immediately.

Impelliteri gave Shaw a half-wave instead of a handshake and said, "If you're Shaw, this must be the place."

"I am and it is. Have a seat. What are you drinking?"

Impelliteri looked out at the bar, as if to assess the possibility of getting a decent drink in the place.

"I'll take a glass of red."

Shaw yelled the order out to the barmaid. It reminded him to take another swig of his ale and sip of Irish. Once that was done, Impelliteri ignored Shaw and busied himself with looking at the menu.

Shaw wasn't interested in any small talk either.

A few minutes later, two more detectives walked in behind the waitress bringing Impelliteri's wine. Shaw knew one of them very well. The other he had never met. One was black, one white. One big and meaty, the other not much more than a frame for his clothes.

The black detective, the bigger and the older of the two, was Orestes Mason. The younger man was James Sperling. Shaw couldn't help but notice that the gaunt Sperling displayed absolutely no expression on his face. His expression was so free of affect that Shaw couldn't tell if Sperling had achieved a deep, Zenlike calm or if he had arrived at a deep state of depression. Considering the circumstances, Shaw decided

Sperling's appearance might be due to depression.

Mason's big, broad face spoke volumes even with his mouth shut. At the moment, Mason's face said he was not happy.

Sperling nodded at Shaw and took a seat. Mason stood pointing a large finger and asked, "What the hell have you gotten me into, Shaw?"

"Have a seat, Mase. I'll tell you when the last of our group gets here."

Mason sat next to Shaw at the round table. Sperling sat between him and Impelliteri, but seemed to be sitting all by himself. Impelliteri and Sperling nodded to each other, but didn't bother to introduce themselves.

Shaw said, "We've got one more coming. What're you guys drinking?"

Mason asked, "Who's paying?"

"The Job."

"I'll have what you're having."

Sperling said, "Club soda."

Before the drinks came the last member of the crew arrived, Walter Wang. At twenty-six, he was the youngest in the group. Impelliteri and Sperling were in their thirties. Shaw represented the forties. Mason hovered somewhere on the other side of fifty.

Shaw had heard of Walter Wang even before his name appeared on DeLuca's loser list. Wang had run a particularly audacious scam using NYPD personnel records.

Walter fit the image of the archetypal Asian math-computer whiz right down to the cheap suit, white shirt, and wire-rimmed glasses. But Shaw knew that Wang was a scammer, a con artist, someone who would not be constrained by rules and regulations. Which was one reason why he had chosen him.

Wang quickly took a seat at the round table to Shaw's left. He bobbed his head up and down and said,

"Sorry, sir. I had a few last minutes things to clean up."

Shaw didn't take to the con. He waved off Wang's excuse.

"What are you drinking, Wang?"

"Uh, Rolling Rock, sir."

Shaw snapped, "Hey drop the fucking coolie act, all right? Don't call me sir, and don't come in here trying to bullshit me about taking care of last minute job obligations. You want to be late, just fucking be late."

Shaw looked at all of them and said, "Which brings me to my first point. As you might have already figured out, this is not a normal situation here, so for the next hour or so I'd appreciate it if we leave the bullshit at the door, guys. Anybody got a problem with that?"

Wang lifted his head from its half-bowed position and dropped most of his Chinese accent.

"I guess that depends on why we're here."

"Then I might as well get right to it. Check the menu fellas and order some food and whatever else you want to drink. I don't want any interruptions once I start."

Shaw watched each man give the waitress his food order. Impelliteri couldn't resist flirting. Sperling, looking more like a prep-school teacher than a cop in his button-down white shirt and khaki pants, didn't seem interested in either the food or the waitress. Mason, dressed in the old-style detective uniform of sport jacket, tie, and slacks, displayed his usual politeness and attention to detail. He looked at the menu with his reading glasses propped on the end of his broad nose, asked the waitress a couple of questions about the food, and ordered a sizable amount for his sizable appetite.

Wang didn't ask any questions, but made two specific requests about how his hamburger should be prepared.

Shaw gave his order last and asked the waitress to

keep everybody's glass full so they wouldn't have to bother asking. Once the waitress left the dingy back room, Shaw addressed the others.

"All right," Shaw said, "here's the deal. I'll take my pants down and show my ass first. I'm about a half step from getting kicked off of the force, losing my pension, and having Albert J. DeLuca do whatever he can to make my retirement years painful."

"What does that mean?" asked Impelliteri.

"It means not only is he promising to kick me off, he's vowing he'll make sure I never get another job."

Mason asked, "What did it this time?"

"My basic attitude, plus a run-in I had while on restricted duty."

Mason asked quietly, "You shoot somebody?"

"No. If you want the gory details, Mase, I'll give them to you when I have time. Let's just say the chief has me where he wants me."

Impelliteri chimed in, "All due respect, Shaw, but why should we give a shit?"

"Because according to DeLuca, all of you are in similar situations. He threw me a lifeline. Told me he'd give me a chance to pull myself up out of the shit. He's throwing you guys the same line."

"Same line of bullshit," said Impelliteri.

Mason countered, "Chief of D don't bullshit. Believe me. What's the deal, Shaw?"

Shaw looked around the table. The food hadn't arrived yet, so he still had everybody's attention. He had the feeling they would have been paying attention even if a four-star meal had been set in front of them.

"The deal is, if we do his dirty work, we get a clean slate. All sin's forgiven. If we don't, he shits on us from a very high place. Needless to say, what he wants done before he extends us absolution is not going to be easy to deliver. Still interested?"

Impelliteri responded, "I guess that depends how deep in shit each of us is."

Shaw answered, "That's for each of us to decide. We don't have to play true confessions."

Impelliteri asked, "Anybody here bugger small boys or beat their women?"

Nobody responded.

"Good enough. You're right, Shaw. Anything else isn't going to make me decide not to work with you guys. I know what I done to fuck up. Question is, how much of it does the Chief of D know?"

Wang asked Shaw, "Do you know?"

"I can tell you what the file he handed me says. Which may or may not be all of it."

"What's he got on me?" asked Wang.

Shaw could see they needed to know what DeLuca had on them before they made their decisions.

"All right, let's just get it all out. You should know what DeLuca knows, and we should know that about each other. Then you guys can decide if you're in or out. Since you came last, we'll start with you, Walter."

"Fine."

"Walter is one of the department's resident computer geniuses. He works in Operations. Personnel Division, right?"

"Right."

"You pulled a scam that shows me you know your way around the bureaucracy. What buttons to push where. What form you need for what. How to access personnel records, among other things. According to DeLuca's file, Officer Wang used his talents and NYPD records to run some sort of insurance sales program. Apparently he sold a shitload of disability and life insurance to his fellow police officers."

Wang interrupted, "Which by the way is something

each of you should look into. I've figured out a very easy way to finance the—"

"Hey!"

Wang stopped. Shaw glared at him for a second.

Mason asked, "So what's so bad about that? You could survive that."

Shaw added, "Not if you fiddled the payments and skimmed from the premiums."

"They'll never prove that."

Shaw responded, "I suppose that depends on how well you covered your tracks, Walter. According to DeLuca's file you're looking at the possibility of criminal, civil, and departmental prosecution. I got a feeling this might be an offer you can't refuse. Otherwise, DeLuca will make sure you get hit with all three. But, as you say, maybe even DeLuca can't prove it. At the very least, you won't be a cop for much longer."

"Big deal," said Wang.

"Maybe. That's not my call. But apparently you must be considering this offer since you're still here."

Wang said, "If you want me to keep thinking about it, tell me what I'm going to have to do?"

"If you sign on, I want you to be our operations manager. If we need equipment, you get it. If we need computer searches, you do them. Requisitions, liaison with other elements of the department, out-of-state databases, whatever we need, you're the man. You work the system. Your contact is one of DeLuca's people, a uniformed lieutenant. Name is Conklin. You organize it, find it, arrange it, get it. If you get jammed up, work it through this guy Conklin. That's it."

"Doesn't sound too tough."

"I don't think it will be. For you. Plus one other thing."

"What's that?"

"I want you to keep activity reports for us. You write

our fives based on what I give you. I want a tight paper trail covering all our asses. We'll give you enough information to pull something together, but you make up the rest. I don't trust DeLuca. This gets shitty, and it will, nobody is going to cover for us. I hope to hell nobody knows about us, but if it comes down to it, I want a record that says what we want it to say."

"How's your English?" Impelliteri asked.

Wang answered, "Fuck English. I speak Police as good as anybody."

"Fine," said Impelliteri, "but listen Kung Fu, just because you write it don't mean I ain't gonna read 'em. Don't fuck me up if I'm in on this."

Wang shrugged. "Whatever."

Shaw nodded toward Impelliteri.

"Detective Impelliteri is from the seven-five out in East New York. He works homicide so I'm sure he's very busy since East New York usually vies for the precinct with the most murders in the city. Homicides are part of the problem that we'll be dealing with, so I figured Tony—is it Tony or Anthony?"

"Either one."

"I figure Anthony will be helpful to us. The record says he's a very effective cop. However, apparently you've fallen into the worst shit there is."

"What's that?" Mason asked.

"A sexual harassment charge filed by a female officer."

"Ouch," said Wang.

"There's more," Shaw said. "Turns out the female officer is the wife of a deputy inspector."

"Oh Lord," said Mason.

Impelliteri spoke up. "You assholes don't know anything. You have no idea the shit that's going on. That bitch didn't get sexually harassed. She and her dumbass husband know it. I fucked her every which way including up the ass three times a week and her damn husband found out about it. He's the one who forced her into that sexual harassment thing so he could save face and get revenge on me. He keeps up this shit, he's going to find his head in his fucking lap."

"Then DeLuca will have you for murdering a deputy inspector. That ought to do it," said Mason.

"My lawyer will beat this bogus harassment shit. I'll testify to every mark on her body including places where the sun definitely don't shine."

Shaw commented, "I'm sure that will endear you to the deputy inspector. Do you need DeLuca to explain to you what's going to happen when you pull out that information about screwing a superior officer's wife? He'll have Commissioner Burton fire your ass in about ten seconds. Either way, your career is over. You shut up and take the harassment charge, it's over. You tell the truth, it's over. If the Deputy Inspector doesn't shoot you first."

Impelliteri sneered. "Yeah, and DeLuca can wave a magic wand and make it all go away."

"Without a doubt," said Mason. "Without a shadow of a doubt."

Impelliteri turned to Mason and said, "Yeah, so what's your deal, Uncle Remus? Why is your ass in a sling? You must have fucked up pretty bad. Black cops really have to fuck up to get nailed."

Mason's face turned hard. "Mind your manners, son. You don't know me well enough to talk to me like that."

"All right, all right. No offense. Guy your age and seniority, the force being run by a black commissioner, how bad could it be for you?"

"You got a problem with there being a black commissioner?"

"Not really," answered Impelliteri. "You still haven't

answered my question. What's your deal? What'd you do?"

"Mason doesn't have a deal," Shaw said. "He's not in danger of getting thrown out like the rest of us. In fact, his name wasn't even on DeLuca's list. I put it there. Mason and I worked as partners a while back. He got caught in the middle of an operation that I fucked up. He ended up being associated with a disaster he didn't create. He became damaged goods. He's still riding a desk. I know it's driving him nuts."

Shaw turned to Mason, "I figured I owed you a shot to clear things up, Mase. It's your call if you want to take it."

"What happened?" asked Impelliteri.

Shaw told him, "Never mind." He turned to Mason. "Like I said, I figured I owed you this shot, Mase. It's your choice, but we could use you. Finding guys is part of what we have to do, and you're about the best at that of anybody I know."

Mason nodded as if he understood, but he didn't come out and tell Shaw he would accept the opportunity.

Impelliteri interrupted. "All right, so Detective Mason here is squeaky clean, huh? Fine. We're the scumbags. But just for the record, that deputy inspector's wife was a lousy piece of ass. Unless she was drunk. Then she could be lots a fun for the ten or fifteen minutes before she passed out."

Sperling finally spoke up. "Thank you for sharing that with us Detective Impelliteri."

"No problem. Speaking of sharing, it's your turn."

"What do you want to know?"

Shaw interrupted. "Sperling is a detective specialist formerly with the Emergency Services Unit. Started out in the old Neighborhood Stabilization Units, then Narcotics, then a stint with a Federal Task Force. Trained at Quantico. I assume that's when you got into weapons. Now assigned to the shooting range in the Bronx."

"Sounds like Siberia," Impelliteri said.

Sperling said, "It is. I'm not interested in who did what to get in trouble with DeLuca. I want to find out what we supposedly have to do to get out of it."

Sperling's simple statement focused the issue away from him and back on Shaw. Shaw nodded and began talking. The food came. He kept at it throughout the meal telling them about New Lots Apartments, the Blue-Tops, the Muslims, and the police commissioner's daughter. And how the Muslims had responded to Archie Reynold's ambush in The Pit.

The others didn't seem to mind Shaw talking with his mouth full.

19

When he got to the part about Rachman's revenge, Loyd Shaw hesitated. He finished the last finger of Irish in his glass and downed the dregs of the Bass Ale. The waiting made his audience restless.

Orestes Mason finally asked, "So what did they do?"

Shaw said, "I don't know all the details. Apparently it made the headlines today. I just got back in town."

Anthony Impelliteri spoke up. "That body shop thing in Brownsville. That was those Muslims?"

"Yeah."

"Christ," said Impelliteri. "That was a fucking mess. What'd they do, drive 'em into that place and just burn them up?"

"Read the reports. I don't want to go into it."

"How many died?" asked Mason.

"Nine altogether. Seven in the body shop, plus two they beat to death outside."

Impelliteri added, "These boys don't play around."

Mason wiped his broad face. "Lord Almighty. Same old crap. Black boys slaughtering each other."

"Fucking animals," said Impelliteri.

After the ambush in The Pit, Archie Reynolds had laid low in motel off Cross Bay Boulevard near Kennedy Airport. He'd spent most of the weekend partying with his managers and lieutenants and planning his next moves, reorganizing his operation at New Lots.

By Monday, Archie had been ready to check out of the motel and hole up in a new place. When the call from Reggie Whack came, Archie had expected Reggie to tell him he would be coming by to pick him up. Instead, Reggie had told him, "It's ba, ba, bad Arch. They, they, they, got si, si, six or seven of us. Burned down the body shop."

"What?"

Reggie had stuttered out the details he knew, but Archie didn't hear them. Something inside his head had snapped. Red and black dots had swarmed in front of his eyes. A pressure had built at the base of his skull and blossomed in his head, passing through him with such vehemence that he had not been able to speak for about five seconds. When his control returned, he had said, "Get the Jeep. Pick me up."

After a few moments of silence, James Sperling finally spoke up, his voice flat and matter of fact.

"So what are we supposed to do about this insanity?"

"Stop it," said Shaw. "And make sure nothing happens to the commissioner's daughter."

"And exactly how we gonna do that?" asked Mason.

"Maybe we better first figure out who's wants in on this thing."

"Christ," said Impelliteri. "I think I'd rather face the deputy inspector and that bitch wife of his than deal with these maniacs."

Without warning, Sperling announced, "I'm in."

Impelliteri looked at him, "That was quick. What, you got some sort of death wish?"

"No."

Shaw turned to Mason. "What about it, Mase? You want in?"

Mason hesitated then answered, "I'm in, unless I hear some crazy scheme you got cooked up."

"And you Walter? You with us?"

"Yes. Why not?"

"Fucking A right, Fu Manchu, what have you got to

lose? Doesn't sound like you're going to be anywhere you can get shot at."

Walter didn't bother to respond to Impelliteri.

Shaw said, "All right, Anthony, that leaves you. In or out?"

Impelliteri shrugged, "Fuck it. Why spoil the party? I'm in."

Shaw pushed on.

"All right, that's settled. Now, getting back to Mason's question about how we should do this. Obviously, I don't have all the answers. It depends on what we find out when we get there. I want to know more about this real estate company, what the hell the police commissioner's daughter is doing and so on, but as of now my plan is simple.

"First, we shut down this Muslim security company, which shouldn't be too hard if we speak to the right people in the right way. Then we concentrate on taking out this crack gang. They aren't that big. According to DeLuca's files about thirty or forty guys. Not that I'm going to go after thirty or forty guys."

"Yeah," said Impelliteri, "particularly since there's thirty more ready to take their place in about two seconds."

"Right. I figure we take out the leaders, the rest will disappear or at least go fight with somebody else and sell their drugs some other place. We start with Archie Reynolds. There's a second in charge, two managers, a couple of enforcer types. We take them out, the rest should fold. While we do all that, we make sure the commissioner's daughter stays out of harm's way."

"She must already have a shitload of police protection."

"We'll see."

Mason offered, "Intelligence Division takes care of security for the commissioner's family. They work in teams of three. Probably got three on her 'round the clock with this mess. Plus uniforms from the precinct."

"Right," said Shaw. "I'm not looking to provide any more personal protection for her. I'm keeping our little task force as small as possible. The less people know what we're doing, the better.

"Okay, obviously there's a lot to this. I'm too tired right now to go into all of it. The next step is we meet tomorrow at the seven-three out in Brownsville and I'll give everybody specific assignments. It's on East New York Avenue."

Mason asked, "That's the new seven-three precinct house, right?"

"Yeah. We have an office there we can work out of."

Shaw reached beneath his chair and picked up four manila folders. He slid one of the folders to each of his team.

"These are copies of everything DeLuca handed over to me. Pretty much what I told you. Your personnel files are in there in case you're curious, plus more details on that Blue-Tops gang. Let's meet at noon tomorrow. That should give you all time to read this file and get at least one night's good sleep before we start."

Shaw turned to Wang.

"Walter, in that report you'll find four names, including Archie Reynolds. According to the information DeLuca got from Gangs, those are the four top guys in this Blue-Tops outfit."

"The four top Blue-Tops?"

"Exactly."

"Sounds like a fucking singing group."

"I didn't name them, Impelliteri. Anyhow, Walter—"

"Yes."

"Before you come out to Brownsville tomorrow, I

want you to stop off at Central Records and check for any outstanding warrants on those four. If you find any, get copies of them."

Mason asked, "You gonna use the Warrants guys to execute 'em?"

"We aren't using anybody but us, if I can help it. Like I said, the fewer people know about what we're doing the better."

"I hear ya."

"What if there aren't any warrants?" asked Impelliteri.

"Then it's going to be somewhat more difficult to come up with a justifiable reason to arrest them, isn't it, Anthony?"

"So who says we have to arrest 'em? Why not just shoot 'em and say the fucking Muslims did it?"

"Why don't we see if there are warrants outstanding before we commit murder?"

Impelliteri shrugged. "Have it your way."

"Also, Walter—"

Wang seemed to have drifted off into his own thoughts, as if Shaw weren't speaking right at him.

"Walter."

"Yes?"

"Inside your packet is a list of supplies. I want two cars, two unmarkeds in good shape. I want shotguns, vests, cellular phones, portable radios, scanners . . . and a few other things I've listed."

"Yeah, how about a tank with a flamethrower?"

Shaw stopped responding to Impelliteri.

"Organize it, find out where we can get everything. If you get jammed up, use Conklin. Otherwise keep this to ourselves, if you can."

Wang looked at Shaw's list.

"This isn't easy."

"If it were easy, I wouldn't need you."

"I'll see what I can do. I know some guys at Emergency Services who probably have everything you need."

"Don't see what you can do. Do it. Okay?"

"Okay."

"Good. Next, what guns are you all using?"

"Glock," said Impelliteri.

"Seventeen?"

"Yeah. I carry a nineteen for a backup."

"Sig," said Mason. "I don't carry a backup."

"Thirty-eight. Revolver," said Walter. "No backup."

"Okay, before you go, have a quick conversation with Detective Sperling to make sure your shit is up to par. And I want everybody to carry a backup. Everybody, including you, Walter. Mason, you and Walter fill out forms for backups. Make it simple. Just get another of the same gun you use now. Sperling, can you get weapons for them quickly."

"If I have the right paper."

Mason said, "Hell, man, those forty-nines take weeks, months."

"Not for us, Mase," said Shaw. "Walter, work that one through Conklin and see how good he and DeLuca are at getting rid of red tape. Start on that and the equipment tonight. Sperling, get the guns tomorrow before you come out to the seven-three. We'll fill in the paper later."

The dinner had reached the coffee stage. Impelliteri drank regular with Sambuca. Shaw had a Grand Marnier with decaffeinated coffee, and Mason, Remy. Sperling stuck with just coffee.

Mason fired up a cigar, an unbanded, double-corona size hard smoke. Impelliteri dropped a pack of Marlboro reds on the table and lit up. Shaw bummed one from him, wishing he had a decent cigar, knowing that whatever Mason smoked wasn't.

The attempt at after-dinner conversation faded quickly. No one had any interest in being cordial.

Impelliteri tossed down his Sambuca, said "see ya," and left.

After a quick discussion about firearms with Mason and Wang, Sperling unfolded his bony frame and said good night.

Shaw told Wang to get some sleep, and he took off.

The waitress looked in and brought Shaw and Mason one more round and the bill. Shaw knew the night wasn't over yet.

Mason finished his first snifter of Remy and waited for the second. He seemed just as sober as when he had entered the restaurant. Shaw was feeling the liquor but liking it. He rolled a little of the Grand Marnier around his snifter, and took a sip, waiting for Mason to start in on him.

It didn't take long.

20

"Y̲ou see how crazy this thing is, don't you?" Orestes Mason asked.

Loyd Shaw attempted to shrug off the question.

"It is what it is."

"What the hell does that mean?"

"I don't know."

"Shaw, what's so important we got to go out there and risk our necks for it? End up killin' people for it?"

"Nobody said anything about killing anybody."

"You think these crack boys won't put a bullet in you? The gangs left out there are the worst of the worst. These kids don't care about anything. Most of 'em don't expect to ever see thirty. Even if they know you're a cop, they'll shoot you as soon as look at you. You think there's any way we can get out of this without killing somebody?"

"Maybe. Look, Mase, I don't know where all the pressure is coming from. But the goddamn Chief of Detectives doesn't pull a move like putting together this kind of operation unless there's a shitload of heat coming down. How much pressure you think the commissioner is putting on this with his daughter being involved?"

"That's it? The commissioner's daughter?"

"A good part of it. There's the money, too. You know how much money is at stake here?"

"How much?"

"Millions. I called a friend of mine works in the Housing Department."

"This a public project?"

"No. It's private. Hell, I think it'll all be run by private companies before long. But most of the rents in there are subsidized. It's a potential money machine. The place got built with HUD money. The original group couldn't run it. Rents went down. The place went in the shithole. HUD foreclosed. They ate most of the loss. My friend figures the bank just about gave the place away. There's no debt. This company that took it over, Arbor Realty, if they clean it up and fill it with people getting subsidies, the rents are secure. There's half the usual overhead without a big mortgage underlying it, Mase, they stand to make millions. That much money at stake, who knows what kind of pressure is going down.

"DeLuca also gave me a pretty decent version of the 'thin-blue-line' speech, maybe he really believes that, too. Whatever the reasons, he wants it done."

Mason sipped his cognac and nodded. "So what you think of this crew of yours?"

"You should have seen the others on that list. I know this whole thing is fucked up. Impelliteri sounds like a damn wild man. But he could be just what we need. Sperling knows his stuff, but I don't know how he acts out in the field. Wang—"

Mason interrupted. "That boy looks like he's in another world."

"Yeah, but that's the kind of guy we need, someone to sort through all the computer databases, plus coordinate all the shit we're gonna need. You know the department runs on paper. Always has."

"I suppose."

"You tell Muriel about this?"

"No, the good wife don't want hear about this mess. She'll start buggin' me to quit and go find that house in South Carolina she wants."

"So why don't you?"

Instead of answering, Mason asked, "Is what you told them really the plan?"

"At the moment."

"If we find these crack guys, how long you think we can keep them off the street even if there are old warrants out on them?"

"Hey, they're young black men. Locking up young black men in this city isn't a big problem. Most of 'em I'm sure have records. Most of 'em are probably already predicate felons on probation. We get them with drugs, or parole violations, or violating any terms, they go away for a long time."

"So you saying we set them up?"

"I'm not saying anything, Mase. Maybe we should just kidnap them and lock 'em in your fucking garage. I don't know. I'm going step-by-step on this. I got my ass in a ringer and DeLuca's turning the fucking crank; I'm working with a bunch of dangerous fuckups; and I gotta go up against some vicious motherfuckers in Brownsville who'll shoot me in the face without even breathing heavy. Not to mention what these Muslim guys are capable of doing. They killed nine guys in one morning. Beat two of them to death up close and personal. You think I want to walk into this shit storm? What the hell you want from me? You want out, get out. I thought I'd give you a shot, that's all."

Mason took a long pull off his cigar. He looked at Shaw and said. "I can't get out."

"Why?"

"DeLuca is too damn smart. He called this thing all the way."

"What do you mean?"

"He had it figured you'd call me in. He contacted me before you did. Said when you call, go do it. Didn't ask me, *told* me. Said I'm supposed to watch you.

Make sure you don't go off like last time. Said I'm the only one you'd listen to."

Shaw took the news in for a few moments then simply said, "What a prick."

"Yeah. Workin' all the angles."

"Shit."

Shaw drained his snifter. He looked at Mason and said, "You still don't have to do it. Listen to Muriel."

Mason looked straight at Shaw. "Damn. Be nice if it was that easy. You really think I can tell the Chief of D, no? All this talk about what's he got on me and how much he knows and what do we have to do . . . it's all b.s. Everybody sitting here knows they gonna do what the man wants. Nobody wants to deal with the consequences of *not* doing it."

Mason pointed an extra large finger at Shaw.

"And the other side is obvious, too. Everybody wants the juice they gonna get if the Chief of D owes 'em."

"Yeah."

"Either way, the Chief of D wins."

"What do you mean?"

"You know what I mean."

"I do?"

"Yeah, you do. You know damn well how DeLuca has this figured. He's got a big problem out there. He throws you and the rest of us into it, maybe we stop it sooner than it would be otherwise. He wins. Maybe we don't. He throws us out. Maybe we get shot up and disappear from his police force. He can sure as hell live with that one, too. What the hell has he got to lose?"

"Nothing."

"Right," said Mason. "And what do we have to lose? Chances are, everything. And if we survive, we end up with nightmares for the rest of our lives. How long it take you to stop thinking and dreaming about the last thing?"

"About two years for it to finally leave me most of the time. I still think about it and get sick. If I'm not really goddamn careful, I sink into obsessive thinking about it that can go on for days. Shrink says that's a sign of depression."

"They give you drugs for it?"

"At first. Back when it happened. Didn't seem to do much, but they told me it could take a long time before they kicked in. I said fuck that. The goddamn stuff interfered with my drinking, too. I couldn't take them. What about you?"

"God and Muriel helped me out of it more than anything. That and time. I don't want to go through anything like that again, Shaw."

"You think I do."

Mason sat back and finished his drink. Shaw noticed now that the booze and the late hour were beginning to hit him.

"We're in for a war, Mase."

"I expect so."

"Well, war has its spoils. We come out of this alive, I'm going to make sure we get all our veteran's benefits, you know what I mean?"

"Hmm. Then we got to do more than beat those boys in Brooklyn. We got to beat The Shark, too."

While Loyd Shaw was finishing his meeting in Tribeca, Archie Reynolds was winding up his own gathering in yet another motel on Ditmars Street.

Archie knew his next move against the Muslims
would have to wait until he met the ceaseless demands
of his drug business. He had Reggie Whack shuttled
his surviving gang members in twos and threes, giving
each group the same message: stay off the streets.
Don't worry about the Muslims. Keep the crackheads
from gathering in The Pit. Move the sales down to the
ground floors. Steer customers to windows around the
complex. Sell out the windows. Keep everything moving.

When the last group filed out, Reggie asked his boss,
"Now wha, what?"

"Now the motherfuckers gonna really learn what hell
is like."

By the time Loyd Shaw finally shook Orestes Mason's
hand and walked out of the restaurant, he was grateful
that his apartment was only three blocks away, but almost instantly uneasy at the realization that Jane would
be home and certainly be annoyed at him for coming
home so late, once again smelling of whiskey and cigarettes.

Ah, yes, thought Shaw, Jane. Can't upset the big
breadwinner. The big-time lawyer who had made it to
the big law firm despite all the odds. Made it the hard
way. Yeah, she made it all right. Not like you, asshole.

Thinking about Jane, thinking about going home, an

image popped into Shaw's mind, a picture of him standing at his front door, sticking his key into the lock and finding that it no longer turned. He supposed that some day it might come to that. He believed that Jane had it in her to change the locks on him.

It was not the kind of thing he wanted to be imagining while he walked through the streets tired, angry, tense, and half-drunk on earthy Irish whiskey.

He suddenly had a nearly overwhelming urge to keep on drinking. He pictured it, sitting at some dive bar, drinking by himself, brooding about the mess he was in.

He turned into a deli on Hudson and bought a pack of cigarettes, lit one up and took a deep drag. It tasted just as good as he wanted it to.

Shaw knew every bar in the neighborhood. He thought about an old Irish bar within walking distance and even thought about which bar stool he should occupy, seeing himself having two, maybe three more drinks, then saying screw you to all of them, getting in his car, and driving all night, zooming along empty early morning highways all the way up to his studio. Drive until he sobered up; then sleep with the phone turned off for as long as he wanted; then get up and paint red paintings for as long as it took to lose himself in the color, the texture, the smell of the red acrylic paint.

He pictured it all, walking along the night-filled streets of the city. But instead of a bar, Shaw found himself standing outside his front door, turning familiar keys in familiar locks that still opened for him.

He stepped into the loft apartment and quietly closed the door behind him. Shaw knew that sound. He knew how loudly the hinges squeaked and how much the wooden floors creaked, no matter how quietly he tried to move. And he knew there was no way he could keep the sounds from waking Jane. She slept too lightly.

When Shaw climbed into bed, she kept her back turned to him as she asked, "Are you in trouble?"

Shaw decided although Jane's question revealed her usual perceptiveness, it didn't carry her usual accusatory tone.

"Yeah. Probably."

"Probably?"

"Well, definitely, but I've got a way I can work it out."

"Really."

Skepticism had leaked in, revealing now Jane's true feelings. One word, *really* and the slight glimmer of warmth and concern she had conveyed disappeared.

Shaw answered, "Yeah. Really. One way or another."

Jane sensed something in his tone. Quietly she simply said, "Okay."

And at that particular moment some part of the old Jane, the Jane whom Shaw once loved, emerged. Shaw knew it would not last, and he knew that would be more his fault than hers. He would be gone long periods without explanation. She would be hurt. He would be angry, short, tense, unable to deal with her at all. Shaw knew it would soon get bad. But for that one single moment her "okay" felt like a sort of blanket absolution. Like the kind priests give to assembled troops before they run off to get shot. No recitation of specific sins required. No queries as to the exact level of guilt. No definite acts of contrition required.

She just said, "Okay." And that was it.

Shaw slept fitfully, waiting for the first city light to leak under his window shade. He wanted to be up, to begin facing what lay before him, but he waited until Jane left the apartment. She was always up and out very early.

He went through his morning routine. Trying to shake off the loneliness that suddenly surrounded him, and the slight achy hangover from too much liquor the night before. He stared in the mirror, razor in hand, looking past his face into the crevices around his mouth, examining the crow's feet around his bloodshot eyes. Shaw knew that what he would do this day, and the next day, and the next until it was done, would change him. Up until now, even though he had come to loathe the Job and all it had brought into and taken out of his life, Shaw had tried to follow the rules. But now, what he was about to do in Brownsville would change all that. The irony stung him. To stay on the Job until he could leave with what he had earned over twenty years, he and his crew of outcasts would work like outlaws. The regular detectives assigned to the case would proceed in their customary, plodding fashion, according to the rules. Following procedure. Shaw and his men wouldn't even think about the rules. They would go after everybody at once, anyway they could, as fast and hard as they could.

Time to start. Shaw knew where. He would start with the commissioner's daughter, Justine Burton.

Shaw had an appointment to meet her at nine o'clock at her community center. Since the department's cars were going to be sent to the seven-three, and Shaw had no intention of driving his own car to Brownsville, he took the subway. He figured it would also give him an opportunity to walk the neighborhood a little.

According to the street and subway maps he'd checked, the New Lots subway station was closest to Justine's community center. About four blocks away. So Shaw rode the A train uptown to Fourteenth Street, a multilevel hub where several train lines interconnected and the Brooklyn L train terminated. He walked down the grimy concrete stairs to the lower platform and stepped into the waiting L train.

After a few minutes wait, the train lurched once and pulled out, sliding across Manhattan, rumbling under the East River, and then finally up into the early morning light of Brooklyn.

The train traveled against the morning commute of passengers into Manhattan, so Shaw's subway car wasn't very crowded, but with each successive stop in Brooklyn the passengers became less white, less Manhattan. More black, more Brooklyn.

Until that morning, April in New York had felt more like March, as if the city were unable to leave behind a winter that had buried it in snow and ice. On that morning, the first trace of real warmth permeated the air.

As the L train creaked along the elevated tracks, Shaw suddenly spotted a huge bank of fog off to the north. Fog? For a moment, he assumed he must be near water. Couldn't be, he told himself. He pictured the subway map. He was traveling right through the center of the borough. What the hell is this fog doing here? he asked himself. His already unsettled state became more unsettled, slightly disoriented.

As the train rounded a bend, he peered deeper into the fog and finally saw what was causing the strange phenomenon. They were passing a large tract of open land covered in the remnants of snow and ice left over from a succession of winter storms. The warm air passing over the cold ground had created the unsettling bank of fog.

But what was this open tract of land in the middle of Brooklyn? Shaw knew he wasn't near Prospect Park. As the cloud bank thinned out a little, he saw a scene out of a Dracula movie. The open land belonged to a cemetery. Actually, not just one cemetery, but a jumble

of interconnected cemeteries: Cemetery of the Ever-
greens, Trinity Cemetery, Mount Judah Cemetery, Sa-
lem Field Cemetery, and on and on. There seemed to
be a million old graves, headstones, and mausoleums
in there. Crypts from way back. Shaw began to picture
heaps of dead bones rotting in the ground under a cold
blanket of acid fog. Death was the last thing he wanted
to be reminded of that morning. He knew black men
were killing each other in New Lots. Shooting, beating,
burning each other. But he hadn't let the images fill his
mind. Up to that point, it had all been told to him or
he had read about it in DeLuca's reports. Somehow the
huge tract of graves acted as a catalyst, triggering a
dread in Shaw. Shaw asked himself if it was a fear of
dying or killing. Or both.

If the cemeteries were the final resting place of the
dead, Brownsville seemed like the final stop for the
living. As Shaw's train creaked along heading into
Brownsville, his view from the elevated track revealed
a neighborhood in which nothing seemed new or alive
or vibrant. No new cars, no new buildings, no new
streets. Even the paint on signs and stoplights seemed
old. And what wasn't old, was dead. Buildings abandoned, left to fall into ruin. Others simply burned out
and left to crumble. There were small pockets of life
amidst the ruins. A food store, a car repair shop, a used
furniture store, all poor neighborhood businesses. And
everything in between was old, ruined, dead space.

The subway pulled into the New Lots station. Shaw
stepped out, alone, onto the elevated platform. Welcome to Brownsville. Even the air seemed dead.

And it didn't take long for his discomfort to in-
crease. From the elevated tracks, he could see the
burnt-out body shop. It looked like an open black sore
back in the alley that ran parallel to the elevated tracks.
The westbound train on the other side of the tracks

screeched into the station sounding like another scream, but this time it seemed to Shaw as if he heard the screams of burning men. Despite the warm air, Shaw felt a shiver run from the back of his neck down his back. He rolled his shoulders and shook his head, trying to banish the feelings that had suddenly gripped him.

"Shit," he muttered to himself.

He moved forward, heading for the exit. Trying to just get on with it. He didn't get very far. The moment he reached the top of the stairwell leading down to street level, at the bottom step an angry black face turned toward him. One of the neighborhood home-boys, staking out the station for marks.

He glared at Shaw from the top step right down to the point where Shaw had to walk past him. Shaw knew that the young man was deciding whether or not to make a move on him. A fast mugging, and he might have what he needed for the day.

After his episode with the gangsta rap boys on Tilden Avenue, Shaw was in no mood to mix it up again with a young black man. He ignored him. But when Shaw stepped into the station there were three more just like him. They stood inside the station house, which was so old, beat up, dirty, and neglected that the only thing new was the bullet-proof booth that housed the token clerk. And even that was covered in graffiti.

Now the entire situation became clear. The first one back in the stairwell was the lookout. He would pick the mark, follow him into the station, and give a sign to the others. They'd either take him in the station or follow him out onto the street.

Shaw felt a sickening mix of anger and fear seep into him. Here we go again, he thought. Fuck it. Look right at them. Right the fuck at them.

There were three of them clustered in the station,

enveloped in puffed-up down jackets, baggy clothes, hoods, heavy boots, elaborate basketball shoes. They seemed to Shaw more like a three-headed beast than three young black men.

Shaw didn't try to look tough or angry. But he did concentrate on looking right at them, carefully picking out their faces, their eyes. He kept his expression neutral, not challenging them so they would have to go for him as a matter of pride. No, just look at them, Shaw told himself. Even though he could feel his heart pounding, just look at them so they know you're not to be played with. Don't even think about walking by quietly with your head down, Shaw told himself. Think about the Glock on your hip and the backup under your left armpit. Think about drawing it quickly, pulling back the slide, and pointing it. Don't think about them.

They glared at Shaw, not wanting to lose the opportunity to terrify him, even if they decided not to mug him. They let Shaw pass. Better to pick somebody easier.

Shaw pushed open the swinging door, noting that the glass had been bashed out, and stepped onto the sidewalk.

Outside wasn't much better than inside the subway station. Shaw felt as if he'd stepped out into an abandoned no-man's-land in the middle of a war zone. He stood in the dim morning light under the elevated train viaduct looking to his right and left, trying to get some sense of where he stood. There was nothing much to see. No people, no busy commuters rushing to work, no street signs. There was nothing but a few one- and two-story buildings that might or might not have been unoccupied, along with the boarded-up buildings, burned-out buildings, and rubble-strewn empty lots.

Within his range of vision only two places seemed to be occupied: a block or so off to his right stood a street-corner bodega. To Shaw's left he could see a newsstand-candy store. So where the hell was New Lots Apartments: four stories, five buildings, hundreds of people?

Shaw's memory of the map he'd studied told him New Lots Apartments was to his left, so he set off in that direction, hoping he was heading toward the complex. That meant walking past the newsstand-candy store where another group of neighborhood toughs had gathered.

Shaw thought about the constitutional right to assembly. They had that right, didn't they? But they weren't assembling for morning prayers, or peaceful protest, or to discuss the events of the world. They were just waiting. Hanging out. And now they had something to do: check out the white man and give him a hard time.

Shaw wondered what difference it would make if he were black, a person who lived in this neighborhood. He thought, yeah, it'd make a difference. At least he wouldn't be looking around for street signs that weren't there. If he lived in this neighborbood at least he'd know where the hell he was.

The usual litany of silent curses filled Shaw's head as he realized standing under the subway tracks looking lost wasn't going to make it any easier. He stomped off toward the newsstand, heading for the bad boys hanging out.

As he walked toward the intersection, Shaw finally spotted a first sign of normal life in the neighborhood. A gypsy cab turned toward him and headed for the station entrance. The cab stopped, and Shaw turned to watch an older man, his wife, and their adult daughter step out of the car. They were black, neatly dressed, obviously on their way to work. And obviously experienced enough to know that walking to the subway was not a good idea.

So what the hell am I walking around for? Shaw asked himself. Because you've come to save guys like the ones ready to jump you from killing themselves.

Shaw didn't make it even halfway to the intersection before five pairs of eyes were on him. By the time he came parallel to newsstand-candy store on the opposite side of the street, one of the homeboys had already peeled away from the group and started trailing him.

Shaw unzipped his leather jacket so that it would be easier to reach the Glock. Christ, he thought, this is ridiculous. I've been here five minutes and I'm ready to pull my gun for the second time.

He heard the footsteps trailing him. He told himself, come on, this guy knows you're a cop. He has to know. Why the hell is he doing this? And then Shaw imagined the other four falling in behind him. And Shaw pictured them swarming him. And one of them getting his gun. And not being able to get to his backup before one of them punched his face or kicked his head. And if he did get his gun, then what? A close-range shoot-out on the street?

No way. Shaw suddenly turned around and the guy behind him stopped short. He was way too close to Shaw. Less than six feet behind.

Shaw figured him for no more than sixteen. A teenager, old enough to intimidate, too young to know better. Shaw's sudden move surprised the kid, but he lifted his chin and looked at Shaw with his version of a bad-ass stare. He was dressed homeboy style: baggy blue jeans, unlaced sneakers, a black leather coat. Everything so big on him he seemed engulfed in his clothes, his head stuck back inside the high collar of his jacket, half hidden, feral.

Shaw took a step toward him and pointed a finger at him. "Get the fuck away from me. I'm a cop. You don't want anything to do with me."

The bad-ass glare flickered a moment, then came back not quite so bad.

Shaw didn't wait for an answer. He didn't want one. He turned and walked away, listening for any sudden movement behind him, listening for the footsteps to start up after him. But he heard nothing. He had won.

The gypsy cab who had let the family off at the subway station came back in Shaw's direction and passed him. The driver looked at Shaw, waiting for Shaw to wave him down because he knew it was crazy for a white man to be walking alone in this Brownsville neighborhood. But Shaw waved him off. Fuck that, nobody's driving me off. Not their way, not your way, buddy.

He reached the corner and finally saw a street sign. He'd been walking on Van Sinderen Avenue. The cross street, Hegeman, off to the right. Further up Van Sinderen a beat-up ghetto supermarket slumped in the middle of the block. Shaw caught sight of a woman with three young children exiting the supermarket. The mother carried two brown bags of groceries. The oldest child, a boy about six, carried a third bag. His two little sisters, three and four tagged behind the mother.

Shaw estimated the mother couldn't have been more than twenty years old.

Shaw watch the young woman head in his direction. Probably toward New Lots, since there wasn't much else around him.

Shaw crossed the street diagonally and there it was, sitting in the middle of Brownsville like a squat red brick fortress. No wonder the Blue-Tops had taken it over. The five buildings comprising New Lots were the only structures of any substance within sight, obviously the major enclave in the neighborhood. If you wanted to sell anything to anybody, this' was the place to sell it. If a crack gang had established itself in that complex, nobody was going to get them out of there without a fight.

As Shaw approached the buildings, he saw two blue NYPD sawhorses set up in front of the gated entrance to the complex and one squad car parked in front on New Lots Avenue. Inside the blue and white sat two cops. One drank coffee. The other had his head down, studying the word jumble puzzle in the *New York Post*.

The woman and three kids with their groceries walked toward the new iron gate. The older girl ran ahead into the courtyard defined by the five buildings that surrounded it. Shaw's eyes followed her as she hooked up with a group of girls about her age. He noticed dozens of kids ranging from toddlers to teenagers inside the open space between buildings. He could make out only one cluster of three mothers sitting on a bench. For a moment, New Lots seemed almost like a school. The courtyard almost like a playground.

Shaw turned right and headed for the community center. He spotted no more cops on the street. No police presence away from the front entrance. But as he came parallel with the eastern building of the complex, Shaw saw a pair of black men coming his way. They both wore black pants and combat boots. One man wore a military field jacket, the other a long black leather jacket. Both had full beards. Both wore Kufi skullcaps. One of them carried a radio unit. Muslim security guards. Shaw immediately felt safer. The Muslims were on the street, not stuck in a squad car.

By the time he walked to the north side of the complex and turned onto Rockaway, Shaw didn't feel so foolish about his decision to walk alone on the streets of Brownsville. In ten minutes he had learned a great deal.

As the Caring Community Center and Shelter came into sight, Shaw quickly learned even more about the police department's priorities with regard to New Lots. Four hundred tenants got two cops sitting in a squad car. Justine Burton got five uniformed cops standing guard outside her center, on their feet on the street; plus two squad cars parked at the far end of the block with more cops inside; and an unmarked car parked in front of the center occupied by three detectives from Intelligence, the commissioner's personal security people. Blue sawhorses extended along the entire length of the four, one-story prefab buildings that comprised the center.

Shaw flashed his shield at the cop standing outside the front door to the center. The cop checked the shield more carefully than Shaw expected he would, then stepped aside. Yet another officer standing inside opened a second door after Shaw displayed his shield.

Shaw started to reformulate the goal of his meeting. He had come to convince the commissioner's daughter to get out of the neighborhood until the troubles were resolved. Man, he said to himself, this is probably the safest spot in the city right now.

Inside the center, quiet reigned. Shaw checked his watch. Three minutes to nine. Nobody was around to give directions so he walked down the same corridor Rachman Abdul X had chased Archie Reynolds through, checking out offices as he passed them. In two of them, he saw sleeping bodies laid across plastic chairs, all women and children. He wondered why they didn't just sleep on the floor, and the answer came to him quickly. They didn't want to share the floor with whatever might be sharing it with them.

Shaw reached the waiting area. A mother and three young children were just waking up out there. The young woman was dressed in baggy jeans and a powder blue sweatshirt, but the bulky clothing still couldn't hide how thin and frail she had become. Her hair

needed combing. Her skin looked sallow and ashen.
The kids seemed normal enough. Shaw estimated they
were about three, four, and six. All boys, all dressed in
jeans and T-shirts, still sleepy and slightly cranky.
Their ordinary aspect seemed to heighten their mother's plight. Shaw felt she might as well have had a sign
on her that said, LOST IT ALL TO CRACK. She seemed
embarrassed that Shaw was there to witness her situation. He tried to act as if it were completely normal
that a young woman with three kids began her day
waking up on plastic chairs in a homeless shelter.

An intake worker sat at a battered desk in the waiting
area. Despite the early hour, the young woman looked
bright and alert, her hair pulled back into a tight bun,
her neat clothes complementing her trim body. Shaw
had the impression this was her first job. He also had
the feeling this was the same young black woman who
had ducked under the chair Archie Reynolds had
thrown through the window above her head. Good for
you, thought Shaw. Don't let the murderous fuck run
you out.

A sheet of plywood had replaced the glass, making
things more gloomy in the waiting area, but more con-
ducive to sleeping.

Shaw quietly asked, "Is Ms. Burton in? I'm Detective Shaw. I have an appointment at nine."

The young woman at the desk nodded and pointed
to a connecting doorway on the right. A couple of steps
past the doorway and Shaw reached an open door on
his left.

Justine Burton sat at her desk silhouetted by the
morning light, speaking into her phone. Shaw had been
looking forward to seeing her. He had heard that the
commissioner's daughter was a beautiful woman. But
Shaw decided beautiful was a lazy way to describe her.
Justine Burton was beyond beautiful. Shaw stopped

outside her office so he could have more time to look at her.

At first, even though she was sitting, her height and bearing reminded Shaw of an imperious, black supermodel. But he quickly discarded that first impression. There was more to Justine Burton. She was older than a model, which gave her stature beyond the physical. And her voice imparted additional status. It sounded soft, refined, and engaging, but suffused with directness and confidence.

After a few moments, she noticed Shaw in her peripheral vision, turned and motioned him in, pointing to a chair next to her desk. Then she turned away from him to finish her phone conversation. Shaw didn't mind waiting. It gave him more time to look at her.

He doled it out to himself, starting with her left hand holding the phone receiver to her ear. In the morning sunlight, Shaw decided her hand looked like an elegant, burnished piece of renaissance sculpture. Something labored over by an artist who wanted to render one simple perfect piece that would embody beauty, grace, and femininity. The skin was smooth. The fingers long. The wrist delicate, but imbued with strength. The color of her skin, a creamy light brown, seemed to absorb the glow of the early sun.

After the hand, Shaw wanted more, but satisfied himself with the silhouetted profile. He could just make out the strong lines of her forehead and cheek.

Then, without any warning, no preamble to her good-bye, she ended her conversation, hung up, and turned much too quickly for Shaw to prepare himself.

"I take it you're Detective Shaw?"

Shaw simply nodded, still trying to formulate the right word for her. Stunning? No. Beautiful. He kept coming back to that simple yet inadequate word. Finally, he settled on, striking.

Shaw hoped her looks hadn't made her insufferable. Not to mention her position as the daughter of a powerful man. But even if she did turn out to be spoiled, he decided he could still enjoy himself. Just gazing at her skin was quite a pleasure. He thought that her skin might be the most amazing part of her. There was a sheen to it. And although obviously darker than his, its texture and tone were so extraordinary that Shaw decided her skin seemed to transcend color.

He found that he had to clear his throat before he spoke.

"Yes, Loyd Shaw, Ms. Burton. One *l*. Uh, I hope I'm not coming at a bad time."

That elicited no response.

Of course this is a bad time. Why the hell else would I be here?

A moment of awkward silence emerged. No matter how good Justine Burton looked, she obviously didn't feel very well. Now that she had turned toward Shaw, he could see a surgical dressing on the right side of her face starting just beneath the corner of her mouth and extending down under her chin and jaw. Her shoulder and arm seemed to be causing her discomfort. She rested her right arm in her lap. She appeared tired. Also uneasy and perhaps a bit impatient.

"I'm sorry. I guess if it were a good time I wouldn't be here."

"Right."

"Well, I have a few questions, if you don't mind."

She shifted uncomfortably in her chair. "You said it was important that I speak with you, so go ahead."

"Are you in much pain?"

"That's your first question?"

"Well, you don't look too comfortable."

She frowned at him for a moment, but the frown quickly turned into a rueful smile.

"I'm not. My damn chin hurts. They're suppose to take the stitches out tomorrow. They pull on my skin. Especially if I smile. Which I'm not doing much lately. And if I move my arm, my back and shoulder hurt like hell."

"You should put your arm in a sling."

"I don't like the way that looks."

Shaw thought, if you don't like the way a sling looks, you're going to be real happy with stitches in your face.

"The way it looks?"

"I'd rather not be reminded of it."

"I can understand that."

More silence. Justine Burton didn't feel compelled to fill in the empty spaces.

"So, uh, I was going to ask you a few questions that you've already been asked just to kind of warm up a little, but why don't we skip that and go right to what I want to know?"

"Yes, let's. I haven't been sleeping well lately with my injuries, and I'm not in the mood to have another cop ask me if I can identify the man who came through here when you already know who he is."

"Archie Reynolds."

"Yes."

"Do you know him?"

"Not personally."

"How did you find out we know it was him?"

At that Justine simply gave Shaw a look that said, don't you know who I am, or are you just stupid?

"Well, I'm not sure that your father keeps you informed of—"

"He probably doesn't tell me half of what he knows, but he sure as hell told me about Archie Reynolds."

"What did he tell you?"

"That's not important. I know who he is. I know

what his crack business does to the women in this neighborhood."

"And that is?"

"It degrades them to a level that is hardly imaginable, Detective Shaw."

"And their children, too, of course."

For a moment, Justine softened.

"Yes. You don't see it as much, but they suffer more than anybody."

"At least the adults start with a choice. Maybe not much of a choice, but—" Shaw stopped himself. "I'm sure you know more about all that than I do."

"I've seen more than I want to, firsthand."

"And that's why you're here?"

"That's why I'm here, Detective Shaw. These women need help. Their children need help. And I'm here to give it to them. Right now this isn't much more than an emergency shelter, for battered women in emergency situations. But I'm interested in providing much more than that."

"Uh-huh."

"The only way these people can survive is with a full range of services: health care, jobs, living skills, drug counseling, rehab, shelter. It just won't work any other way."

"That seems ambitious."

"It is. But if I can make it work here, I can make it work anywhere. Anywhere in the city."

"You don't seem to have nearly enough room for all that."

"I don't."

"So—"

"So where am I going to get it? Is that your question?"

"Yes."

"Where do you think? You seem like an intelligent person."

"For a cop?"

"Hey, I've known a few cops in my day."

"And what's your opinion of them?"

"Is that relevant?"

"No. Just curious."

"Well, most of 'em don't stare at me quite as openly as you do."

"Is that because they're more polite or more worried about your father?"

"I don't know."

"I probably don't sound like I mean it, but I am sorry for being so blatant."

"It's all right. I still find it flattering."

"I'm glad to hear that. You've got a fairly direct gaze yourself."

"I try to see into people. I'm not afraid to look."

"Am I holding up okay?"

"Haven't seen anything I don't like, which is usually the case by now."

"I'm flattered."

"So now that we're both flattered, Detective, have you gotten to the part you really wanted to ask me about?"

"Just about."

"I don't have too much more time."

"Okay. How much of New Lots Apartments are you getting for your community center?"

"Thank you for getting to the point. Who said I was getting part of New Lots for my center?"

"Well, aren't you?"

Justine paused for just a beat before she admitted it. "Yes."

"How'd you swing it?"

"Believe me it wasn't easy. It never is. It doesn't

matter where you are, it's still nimby, nimby, nimby."

"Not in my backyard."

"Right. But this yard is so bad, I finally pulled it all together: the political, financial, and community support. Arbor Realty agreed to give me twenty apartments and the ground floor in Building A. And maybe additional offices somewhere in the complex."

"Uh-huh."

"What's that supposed to mean? 'Uh-huh.' "

"Things are a little more understandable now."

"Why?"

"Well, I don't suppose it's a total secret that you're going to be moving over into New Lots Apartments."

"No. It's not."

"So we can assume Archie Reynolds knows that?"

"Why?"

"Because he came in here and stuck a gun in your face and threatened you."

"What? Like he's gonna run me out of here?"

"He wouldn't have had to run you out if he'd shot you."

"So why didn't he?"

"The report I read said his gun was empty."

"Look, my impression was that people were chasing him and he simply ran through here."

"No. He came in here intentionally. He planned it."

"How do you know?"

"His getaway car was on the street that runs along the other side of your buildings, ready and waiting. The reports said that he ran through the apartment complex across the street and came out through a gangway onto Rockaway. I just walked past that spot. His getaway car could have been waiting for him right there. Instead, it was all the way on the other side of this set of trailers. He knew where he was going. Right in here. I suspect if he'd had time to reload, you'd be dead."

Shaw watched Justine's face. Some of her bravado seemed to ebb away. He asked, "Where were your security people?"

"I have two security guards. One for the day shift, one for the night shift. The day guard was on his lunch break."

"No, where were your people from the force?"

"I'm not guarded twenty-four hours a day. At least not until now. It's my father who gets full coverage. I don't want that. Up until now they just checked with me on a regular basis. And there was no indication that there would be any trouble."

"You didn't think there might be problems out here?"

Justine paused for a moment, then said, "They told me I'd be safe."

"Who told you that?"

"The realty company said they were taking care of the security problems out here."

"How? With their Muslims?"

"Yes. They are supposed to be very good at that."

"Exactly who told you the problems out here would be taken care of?"

"A man named Bloom. Leon Bloom."

"And you took his word for it that everything was fine out here?"

"He seemed very confident. Very sure."

"But he was wrong. This time the Muslims didn't scare anybody off. This time the bad guys fought back."

"Apparently."

"But you didn't know that these Blue-Tops weren't running scared so you didn't make arrangements to have your security people look after you."

"Look, I told you, I'm not normally guarded closely. It's my father who gets the protection, not me."

"Well your father isn't trying to set up a community center in a housing complex run by a crack gang in a war with an outlaw Muslim security company, is he?"

Justine's rueful smile emerged, but she quickly stifled it.

"Damn it. I told you it hurts when I smile."

"Sorry."

"Look, I know it sounds a little naive. But I really had no idea."

"Your people should have known what you all are dealing with out here."

"Well, they do now, don't they? That's why you're here, isn't it?"

"I'm not with the Intelligence Division."

"What division do you work with?"

"I'm on special assignment here."

"What's your job, Detective Shaw?"

"Stopping this war and making sure nothing happens to you."

"I see. And how are you going to do that?"

"By asking you to—"

"To what? Go home and keep my head under the covers until NYPD cleans up this neighborhood and makes it all safe."

"Something like that."

"And what are these women and children who stream in here every day and night supposed to do while I wait for that to happen?" Justine did not wait for Shaw to answer. "You really think everything is going to be just fine after you get done out here with whatever you're supposed to be doing? You've already locked up half the men in the neighborhood, and it's still just as bad as ever, maybe worse. What are *you* going to do that's any different?"

"Well—"

"As far as I can tell, locking up the only ones who can provide a real solution is stupid."

"You mean the men in the community."

"Yes. The men. How is it possible to build strong families out here without men? Without the fathers of these children? Not every man in Brownsville is a violent drug dealer who preys on women."

"So what do we do with the ones who are, like Archie Reynolds?"

"You tell me."

"We lock him up, that's what we do. We lock him up. For the rest of his life, if possible."

"What a surprise."

"You already have me figured, don't you?"

"Well, don't I? What do you see when you look at a young black man? You tell me."

"It depends on the young black man I'm looking at. Hey, I live in America, Ms. Burton. I see a lot—"

"A lot of what?"

"A lot of black people. Seen and heard and read and lived with and worked with. Just because I'm a cop doesn't mean I don't know about Malcolm and Martin Luther King and Miles and Mingus and Mandela. Or my friend Orestes Mason."

"Oh, some of your best friends are black?"

"Just the ones whose last names begin with M. What kind of a question is that? Doesn't it get tiresome assuming every white person you meet is a racist?"

"Not as tiresome as finding out they are."

Justine sat back in her chair.

"You want to know what's really tired? Constantly seeing white cops come into black neighborhoods under the pretext of law enforcement and all it ends up meaning is more black men get killed or jailed."

"There are a lot of black men in America who have nothing to do with the police. Hey, there is no America without black men, but unfortunately, there's no peace in America with young, violent, disenfranchised black men. I don't have to tell you that, do I?

"Trust me Ms. Burton, I don't believe every one of them should be locked up. Maybe half of them should be in drug rehab or job training instead of jail. Maybe not. But this guy, Archie Reynolds, Ms. Burton, *he* belongs *under* the goddamn jail. He shot two unarmed innocent black men trying to earn a living, face-to-face right out on New Lots Avenue. He led a bunch of others into an ambush that killed one and seriously wounded two. He's a murdering psychopath who scarred your face and hurt you and would have killed you if he'd had another bullet in his gun. He belongs in jail."

"Well."

Shaw couldn't tell from her reaction if he had gone overboard with his speech.

Shaw said, "Sorry. I don't exactly know where all that came from."

"I suspect from a good place. Perhaps I put you in a category you shouldn't be in."

"No problem."

"Now you've got me worried."

"What do you mean?"

"Now you've got me believing you know what you're talking about."

Shaw shrugged. "I don't know all of it. But it's obvious this guy and the members of this gang don't hesitate to kill people. And he seems smart enough to plan an attack that killed three and wounded two, terrorized the people in this place and almost took care of you, too. Not bad for about five minutes of work. He's not your regular crack-dealing thug. He's not the kind of person I would want to be targeting me."

"And you're sure he's targeting me?"

"Yes, I'm sure. But even if I weren't, you'd better figure it that way until this gang is out of here."

"Why me? New Lots Apartments would have changed with or without me. Arbor Realty had possession of that property before I made my pitch."

"You know that. But who knows what this crack gang thinks. And let's be honest, that real estate company realized getting the place cleaned up would happen sooner and more surely with the Police Commissioner's daughter working in their property. Archie Reynolds knows it, too. Unless, of course, we've all misjudged Arbor Realty's altruism and sense of community service, and they would have turned over twenty apartments and the ground floor to anybody who asked for them."

Justine shifted in her chair, seeming to position her arm in a way it wouldn't hurt.

"I don't think you misjudge much of anything, Detective."

"But you're not backing off, are you?"

"Do you have any idea what I can do with that space? I can provide housing, day care, vocational training, drug counseling, psychiatric services. Get some of these women out from under their addiction. Give them a chance to stop selling their bodies, killing themselves, ruining their children. I might even have enough space for a small clinic."

"At least save some if you can't save them all."

"Exactly. Yesterday we got a call from a woman who said her daughter had disappeared. Twenty-four years old. But it wasn't the daughter the woman was worried about. It was the daughter's four children. She gave us the daughter's address, right across the street in New Lots. We broke into the apartment. Two of the children had been locked in a bedroom for almost three days, six and four years old. The four-year-old was so

malnourished and dehydrated they think she might
have sustained brain damage. Both kids were filthy,
obviously abused. The boy's hands and fingernails
were bloody from trying to beat and scratch open the
bedroom door. An eight-month infant was lying in a
crib, naked, covered in its own mess, wheezing. It had
double pneumonia, lying uncovered like that. I have no
idea if that baby is going to live. They still haven't
found the oldest boy. He's all of eight years old. They
think she took him with her on her binge."

"Why?"

"Use him as currency. Give him away to the drug
dealers around here so they could use him as a mes-
senger. Or maybe for some other abomination that
might suit them. You know where the mother was?"

"Somewhere smoking crack for three days."

"Somewhere? She was across the courtyard from her
own apartment in New Lots, not more than two hundred feet from her babies. Does anybody realize how
insane that is or is it just me? Do you realize how easy
it would be to eliminate untold misery around here?"
Justine motioned with her hand. "I don't have to go
outside these four square blocks. I have the resources.
I can do something about this. The people who need
me are right here. All I need is the space."

"And you intend to get it."

"Damn right I do. You think that goddamn vile crack
gang belongs in New Lots Apartments instead of me?"

"No."

"No, sir, they don't."

"And you want that space."

"I want that space."

"And you're not giving up."

"No I am not."

"Then I've only got one more question."

"What?"

"How many more people do you think are going to have to die before you get it?"

For the first time in the conversation, Justine Burton looked away. But just for a few moments. Then she turned back and said, "I suppose more than I want to know. I would hope to God, Detective Shaw, that you aren't a killer they've sent in. I hope to God you might be the kind of man who could prevent anybody from dying over this."

"You mean anybody else. There are already twelve people who have died over this. You heard what the Muslims did yesterday in response to the ambush, didn't you?"

Justine did not answer.

Shaw's voice softened. "I'm not a killer. But I don't think anybody is going to stop this without spilling blood."

"Well then, Detective Shaw, let me ask *you* one more question."

"What?"

"How many more women and children are going to die if I *don't* get New Lots?"

22

After he left Justine Burton, Loyd Shaw spoke to the three detectives assigned to her and confirmed that she would be watched around the clock. Shaw knew the detectives had no interest in listening to him, or he to them, but he wanted make sure when they saw his face they would know which side he was on.

Shaw's meeting with the commissioner's daughter had done nothing to improve his mood, but it had certainly clarified the issues for him. Justine Burton knew what she wanted. So did The Shark, DeLuca. Shaw asked himself, so what the hell do you want? Besides your job, reputation, and pension.

The answer came so naturally to him that he wondered why he had even needed to ask the question. Now that he had come into the neighborhood, talked to Justine Burton, seen the people, the mothers and children, watched that family get on the subway and head off to earn a living, Shaw wanted to stop the killing.

By the time he had reached the east side of the complex, he spotted the two-man Muslim security patrol he'd seen earlier. He headed directly for them. They made Shaw for a cop in about five seconds. Shaw made a point of politely introducing himself.

"Excuse me, gentlemen, my named is Loyd Shaw. I'm with the NYPD. I'd like to speak to your boss. Is he around?"

Instead of flashing his gold shield, Shaw held out his police identification card. It felt less threatening. Less like the usual white cop flashing his authority.

Shaw stood holding his police ID, and the Muslims stood stiffly in front of him, waiting to see if Shaw tried to push them. He didn't. Finally, one of the guards told him, "Ground floor, Building A. Our office is there."

"Thanks."

The second guard pointed toward the front of the complex around the corner to the right.

As Shaw approached the front gate, again, he couldn't help notice how many children inhabited the area in and around New Lots. It seemed as if they were everywhere. Running around. Dodging between cars. Popping in and out of the courtyard. Their presence seemed to be an indelible part of New Lots Apartments. He wondered why more of them weren't in school. He didn't know that the schools in the neighborhood were so crowded the children attended in shifts. In the afternoon, most of the kids he saw would be in school. Then their counterparts would fill the courtyard of New Lots.

The two regular MS-2 guards manning the new front gate made sure to check Shaw's ID before they hit the switch that unlocked the new ten-foot iron gate.

Shaw stood for a moment looking at the buildings that comprised the complex—five of them arranged into a giant U. Four buildings, A, B, C, and D, paired off facing each other and a fifth larger building, E, running across the back.

Shaw walked into the teeming courtyard, The Pit, wondering how none of the kids had been injured during the two drive-bys and the ambush. Shaw knew that luck wouldn't last forever. If the bullets kept flying, one would find a child.

Shaw found the ground-floor MS-2 office, a basically bare room. Nothing softened the battleship gray paint and harsh fluorescent ceiling fixtures. Furniture consisted of a desk and two folding, gray, metal chairs and a battered file cabinet. One phone sat on the desk along with several two-way radios recharging in a rack.

Again, Shaw found himself standing in the doorway of an office. But unlike Justine, Rachman Abdul X was not on the phone. He was on his knees, facing east, his prayer rug under him, arms extended, palms up, praying.

Shaw's reaction surprised him. Rachman's praying made him angry. It seemed like an act. A hypocritical mumbly, mumbly mumbly act. He looked at Rachman and thought, Mr. Muslim here is the boss of guys who burn people to death and beat people to death and prop them up in public for display. It seemed an affront that this same man would engage in prayer.

Rachman seemed to sense Shaw's presence behind him. And Shaw's hostility. He quickly finished his prayers. Shaw waited while Rachman rolled up his rug. When Rachman turned to give Shaw his bad-guy stare, Shaw made sure not to start by apologizing for interrupting.

"Are you done?"

"Yes. Who are you? More police?"

"My name is Loyd Shaw, one *l*. Yeah, NYPD. And you are?"

"Rachman Abdul X."

For a second, Shaw felt like asking Rachman his real name, but he squelched the urge. Shaw looked at Rachman and again thought about that body shop and its seven piles of human ashes and burnt bones.

"So which do you prefer, Mr. Rachman, Mr. Abdul, or Mr. X?"

Rachman stared at Shaw, waiting to see if there would be any smile or smirk, any sign of overt disrespect.

Shaw kept his face blank even though he really

didn't care if Rachman thought he was being disrespectful. In fact, part of Shaw wished Rachman would take offense and try something. Part of Shaw wanted to go at this stolid black man who stood trying to intimidate him with his bad-guy look. Shaw thought about provoking him into taking a swing or making a threat, and then punch him in the throat, put a gun to his head, cuff him, and arrest him. Just take him out of the equation right now. Take out one of the killers, right now.

Rachman was much too disciplined to rise to the bait. He held his hands in front of him, right hand holding his left wrist and spoke evenly.

"Rachman will be fine."

"Are you in charge of the security operation here?"

"Yes."

"Then I'd like to ask you a few questions. Is that all right?"

"Why are so many police coming around now?"

"You know, Mr. Rachman, normally I don't mind when I ask someone a question and they answer with a question. It gets the conversation going. But to tell you the truth, I don't want you asking me any questions. I just want to know if you're going to answer mine."

"I see."

"Yeah, you fucking see. And you see why there's more cops around here, too. There are too many people being shot and burned to death and beaten to death around here, aren't there?"

Rachman's jaw clenched, but he managed to keep his voice even.

"There were too many before you all started showing up."

"Maybe so, but when you get two, three, nine at a time—that tends to create a police presence. Do you have an objection to police showing up around here?"

"Not if they are just and lawful. But we don't want police coming down on us just because we are trying to defend ourselves or clean the criminals out of this place."

"I see. And what exactly do you mean by clean out?"

"I mean—do what nobody else will. Nobody else wanted to have anything to do with this place before we got here. No police ever came in here. Not even when they be called."

"So now we're suppose to argue about whether or not that gives you the right to take the law into your own hands."

"Why argue?"

"Right. Why argue? You mind that the police are here now?"

"No. I want them here. Every day. If you all had been here every day before, there would be no dead bodies now."

"Yeah, it's our fault. I admit it. We forced you into this situation. We should have had a policeman on every block, twenty-four hours a day. Should have thought of that a long time ago. Be that as it may, Mr. Rachman, it still doesn't give you the right to do most of what you do."

"We abide by just authority in all regards, Mr. Shaw."

"What's the qualifier mean?"

"Say what?"

"*Just* authority. That implies that you consider some authority *unjust*. Just for the hell of it, let me ask you: What authority gives you the right to beat people to death, to shoot them, to burn them alive. I mean, I'm not saying you yourself did that. But what authority might somebody need to justify those acts?"

"It's wrong to take a life for no reason. It's wrongful

to take the law into one's own hands. But the greatest wrong is to be oppressed and do nothing. To have your life threatened, to have your own people killed, and then to lay down your head to your enemies. That is the greatest sin. The world has already seen what happens when a group of people does that. The result is genocide, which is exactly what is happening to my people."

"So the solution is to kill more of your people?"

"Only those who oppress us. Of any color."

Shaw nodded at the implied threat. "Any color?"

"Any color."

"White or black?"

Rachman repeated, "White or black."

"By any means necessary," said Shaw.

Rachman decided to stop answering.

Shaw said, "I know the bullshit, Mr. Rachman. End justifies the means. The lesser of two evils."

Rachman remained silent. Perhaps more to evaluate Shaw than his question. But after a moment or two, he simply answered, "Yes."

"Good," said Shaw, "I can relate to that." He took a step toward Rachman, leaning forward to emphasize his point, entering Rachman's space, challenging Rachman.

"Now relate to this: As far as I'm concerned, you and your people are way the hell up high on the list of dangerous criminals. You're murderers. Killers. Bad people. I haven't looked into your police record yet. Or the records of the people you use, but right now I'd bet big money this real estate company didn't recruit you out of any legitimate security operation. I'd bet most of your previous work experience was in prison. So I don't give a shit how much you pray, you and your people are still killers."

Shaw paused to give Rachman a chance to respond.

Rachman stood without moving or talking.

Shaw stepped back and extended his hands, palms up, empty.

"But, hey, for right now, out here, you *do* actually happen to be the lesser of two evils. When it comes to bad guys, amazingly, you come in second. So here's what I propose. I'm going to take care of the worse evil out here. Me and my men are going to hunt down Archie Reynolds and his top people, and we are going to eliminate them from your life and the life of this community. Whatever was done before by the police, or wasn't done, whatever the detectives from the local precinct didn't do or should do or won't do, I don't care. *I* am going to personally fulfill our responsibility to this community. And I don't want you in my way. You have any problem with that?"

"Why should I?"

"You like answering questions with questions. That's all right. That's close enough. My goal is to stop people out here from killing each other. You have any problem with that?"

"No."

"Good. Now while I do that, I don't want to worry about eliminating *you* from this community. So I'm asking you to keep your guns in your pockets. Stand down. Tell your people to stand down. Otherwise, it will be much more difficult for me. And I may not succeed. And if I don't succeed, that will not help you. I'm not asking you for your help. I'm asking you to stop fighting with these Blue-Tops and let us take care of it."

"Why should I believe you will?"

"Because I'm telling you. But obviously, that's not enough for you. So I suggest you just agree to wait a few days and see what happens. I don't intend to take very long doing this."

Rachman nodded.

"So are we in agreement?"

"For the moment."

"Will you honor that agreement?"

"Honor? I have no reason to believe that you're an honorable man."

"Why's that?"

"Because you're police."

"I see. Well, just tell me straight out so I know where I stand with you, what are you going to do? You going to hold off in your vigilante war to see what I'm going to do? Or are you just going to keep on killing people?"

Rachman paused again as if he were really making a decision. Shaw went along with Rachman's act, but he already knew Rachman's answer. Shaw had already concluded that Rachman was in the wait-and-see phase. The Muslim's method seemed evident. Go in. Threaten people. If you get any opposition, come down very hard and very fast on your enemies. Then wait, daring your enemies to strike back. Rachman could have just said yes and lost nothing. Shaw wasn't trying to get Rachman's agreement. He was simply trying to assess how stubborn Rachman would be.

Rachman made a show of finally nodding and solemnly uttering, "I'll wait and see."

Shaw couldn't resist pushing him.

"Meaning?"

"I won't go after my enemies. But, if they come after me, I'll defend myself. And I'll defend this property as long as it's under my protection."

Shaw nodded, as if he too were deciding something. Finally, he said, "Good enough, Mr. Rachman."

"Just call me Rachman."

"Uh-huh. By the way, who owns this property now? Who is hiring you to protect New Lots Apartments? What is it? Arbor Realty?"

"Yes. Arbor Realty."

"Who's in charge of that? Who do you report to?"

Rachman bristled. Shaw guessed the notion of reporting to anybody galled Rachman.

"What's his name? Bloom?"

"Why do you ask me if you already know?"

Because I want you to know I'm calling on the guy who gives you your money, that's why, thought Shaw.

"Just verifying it, I guess. Where can I find him?"

"His office is in Crown Heights. I've never been there. Check the phone book."

"The phone book? Never thought of that."

Shaw lay his card on Rachman's desk and wrote down the number of the 73rd Precinct on it. He didn't bother to hand it to Rachman because he wasn't in the mood to see Rachman refuse to touch it. Shaw had what he wanted. For now.

23

Loyd Shaw left Rachman X's office and stood on New Lots Avenue until he spotted a gypsy cab. The drive to the 73rd Precinct took about five minutes. He found the office that had been set aside for his team. They should have been assigned an office twice the size, but he didn't protest because he knew the five of them would rarely be in there at the same time.

Everyone had arrived on time.

Inside their office, four desks had been pushed together facing each other, creating an island in the middle of the green cinder-block room. There were also four phones, a file cabinet, one long table against the wall, and no windows. Standard issue.

The new precinct had replaced a crumbling old fortress that had generally been referred to by the cops who worked there as a shithole. In the new seven-three the plumbing worked, the lighting was adequate, there was room for parking. It would do.

Walter Wang struggled with setting up over twenty-thousand-dollars worth of electronic equipment on the long table set against the far wall of the crowded room. The others sat and watched him.

Shaw said, "Walter, looks like you got everything you need."

"Yeah."

"Did you get that other stuff?"

"In the cars."

"You get everything on my list?"

"Yeah."

"Where are the cars?"

"Precinct lot. Keys on the wall."

Walter wrestled a seventeen-inch color monitor onto the table, shoving it into position between a scanner, fax machine, a tower model CPU, a laptop computer, and a rat's nest of cables, power cords, and surge suppressers.

Shaw left him to his work.

The others had each taken one of the desks. Shaw took the desk across from Orestes Mason. James Sperling and Tony Impelliteri faced each across their respective desks. Just like that, they were partnered up.

"Welcome to Brownsville, boys."

Nobody bothered to respond.

Shaw took a moment to look over his team in daylight.

Impelliteri sat back in his chair, feet propped on his desk. He wore his usual plainclothes cop garb: black jeans and T-shirt, a V-necked cashmere sweater, and a gold chili pepper dangling from a gold chain.

Sperling sat motionless and expressionless. He looked like an aging preppy in his neatly creased khaki pants, loafers, blue button-down oxford shirt, and blue blazer. Mason upheld the senior detective's style: dressed for work in gray herringbone sport coat, shirt, tie, slacks, and sensible wing-tip shoes.

Shaw dressed somewhere between Sperling and Impelliteri. He wore black jeans, but his shirt had a collar.

Walter Wang favored a different style. He wore an ill-fitting Brooks Brothers suit and a cheap standard white shirt, but with a tie that looked as if somebody else had bought it for him. With its interlocking pattern of rectangular shapes in shades of brown that ranged from deep chocolate to copper, Shaw thought it was actually quite a handsome tie. He thought about asking Wang where he got it, but didn't bother.

"All right, let's get to it. The object of the game is to get as many Blue-Tops out of commission as possible. Are we clear on that?"

They nodded.

Shaw yanked out a page he'd brought from De-Luca's file and taped it on the wall.

"This is a list of twelve assholes along with their NYSID numbers. DeLuca and his people in Career Criminals and Gangs have identified them as Blue-Tops boys. This is not a complete list. They estimate the active membership goes about thirty-five to forty. But like I said last night, we're restricting ourselves to the leaders."

Shaw took out a set of mug shots and arrest sheets that Conklin had provided from the Bureau of Criminal Identification, BCI, and the Photo Division, both at One Police. He began taping them on the wall next to the list of names.

"Out of this dozen, here are the top guys. I want them first. Cut off the head, the rest will die off. Obviously, we'll take what we can get, but these guys are first.

"Number one, Archie Reynolds, aka Archie Ar. He's the head guy. According to interviews with the Muslims, he's the one who shot the two guards outside the complex last Friday and set up the ambush. I don't think anybody has heard or seen of him since. He got away clean after busting up that community center.

"Number two, Reginal Wilson, aka Reggie Whack. He's second in command. A manager. Apparently, he's one of three managers. Don't know anything about him, but I do have his arrest records and pictures. He looks like the original gangster type to me. Haven't seen any young guys with their hair conked straight like this. Looks like he has his done by the same guy who does Al Sharpton's. His parole record indicates he's got a bad stuttering problem. That might help you ID him.

"Number three, Ellard Watkins, street name Weight, as in heavyweight. This guy goes three hundred plus."

Impelliteri piped up, "Looks closer to four hundred to me."

Shaw continued, "I don't have much on him. Don't even have his records, yet. I'm sure he's known on the street.

"Number four, Ronald Jenkins—"

Mason cut him off. "We got a message ten minutes ago about him. They identified his remains. He was one of the guys burned up in the body-shop fire."

"They identified him already?"

"They got 'em all sorted out except for one. They're sending us what they have. Chief of D's jobs go to the head of the line."

"I guess so. Well, that's one less we have to worry about. I take it none of the others we're looking for was in there."

"Not so far," said Mason.

"Maybe the last pile of burnt shit is Archie Reynolds."

"Don't bet on it, Tony," said Shaw. "Okay, new number four, Melvin Brown, street named Melly Mel, or smelly smell or some such nonsense. He's one of their enforcers. Probably the guy in charge of the drive-by shootings."

Shaw returned to his desk. "According to DeLuca these are the top guys in this particular crack gang. As I said, this gang isn't real big, but it is particularly vicious. They don't negotiate. They just shoot. That's why the other crews leave them alone. Also, they pretty much confine themselves to Brownsville. New Lots Apartments is by far their biggest operation."

Impelliteri interrupted and slid another mug shot and arrest sheet to Shaw.

"Before I came out, I talked to a buddy of mine who works in Gangs. This is a copy of stuff from his personal file, so we didn't get it from him. Put this asshole on the wall. Name's Sanchez. He's another one of their enforcers. Comes through their Dominican suppliers. He works freelance, but he's definitely hooked in with this group."

Shaw got up and pinned Sanchez's picture and sheet on the bulletin board.

"Good. Good work. Carmen Sanchez."

Impelliteri kept talking. "They don't know too much about his background except that he's suspected of killing about twenty guys. My source tells me, when things get shitty, the suppliers make him available and they point him at somebody they want taken care of. I'd say this is one of those times."

"Where's he live?" asked Mason.

"Bronx. They think. When he's not out of town."

"Then what," asked Mason. "He go hide out in the islands."

"Exactly. Dominican Republic."

Shaw asked. "Any warrants out on him?"

"Hell, yes. Federal and state. Both for murder."

"All right. If he's a hitter, I gotta believe they're calling him in on this. And I gotta believe they're not going to just slink off and let these Muslims get away with burning their place down with them in it. They're going to hit back. I want to take them out before they get a chance."

Shaw returned to his desk across from Mason and sat down, flipped open a legal pad, and began making notes.

"Okay, let's just take a second here to get organized. Let me ask you guys a couple of questions.

"First question, Walter, have you found warrants on any of these guys?"

Wang stopped attaching cables and opened a manila folder. He added his paper to the case, looking at each page. Shaw noticed that Wang became completely engrossed in whatever he was doing. He talked more to himself than to the others, looking at the various printouts he had collected.

"Nothing on Archie Reynolds, yet. I only got through like two databases in FATN. Just State and City, and not even all the courts. I still got district attorney warrants to check, Motor Vehicle, outside agencies, I mean you know, I only had a couple of hours and there weren't terminals available right away. Not even talking about out-of-state yet. But I had a good guy I know on it with me, so we got some shit done—"

"I know, I know, you're just starting, but what did you get? Anything?"

"Okay, I got some things on the Whack guy . . . Reginal Wilson, and the fat guy, Ellard Watkins. Nothing yet on Melvin Brown, although I just started one thing on him. Course, nothing on Sanchez, but you already got stuff on him, which is good 'cuz this fucking city has like a million Sanchezes."

"What? Like there ain't a million Browns out there?" asked Impelliteri.

"Yeah, takes a long time."

"What are the warrants for, Walter?"

"Uh, let's see. Reginal Wilson got one for possession and sale of a controlled substance—"

Impelliteri said, "Bingo, seven to fifteen."

Shaw asked, "What else?"

"Couple of bench warrants out on him for little shit."

"Anything on the other guys."

"Got one out on Ellard Watkins for rape."

Impelliteri piped up, "Rape? Fat, four-hundred-pound fuck goes out and rapes someone?"

Mason mused, "I guess if you weighed that much that's the only way you can get some."

"How's he rape someone? He probably can't even find his dick under the folds."

"Okay, Impelliteri, let's skip that image if you don't mind. Rape will do nicely, thanks Walter. That it?"

"So far."

"Okay, any preference on who wants who?" asked Shaw.

Impelliteri said, "I got the line on him so I guess me and Sperling should look for Sanchez."

"Okay, but he doesn't sound like he's going to be around the territory here. Take your pick on the other two: Reggie Whack or Watkins."

"I'll take Whack. I shoot some four-hundred-pound cocksucker I don't want to get a hernia rolling him over to check him out."

Sperling said, "Good thinking."

"Hey," said Impelliteri. "The man of few words speaks. And when he speaks, he speaks the truth."

Sperling didn't respond to the compliment.

"Okay, Mase," said Shaw, "we'll take care of the heavyweight."

"Fine with me. I don't picture him running very fast."

"All right, you guys know the drill. Find their cars, find their girlfriends, their ex-girlfriends, find their mothers, their kids, where they like to hang out, buy their gas, get their morning coffee and take a shit, fill their prescriptions, do their laundry, whatever. Just find them. And if you can't find the guys on the top of our list, find the others. And if you find one of the others, use him to find the top guys. *But*—"

"But what?" said Impelliteri.

"This is important. When you find them, bring them into *this* precinct and hold them here. Don't take them to Central Booking until I'm done with them. Don't let the desk sergeant or somebody on midnight to eight ship them off to Central Booking until I say so. I don't want these guys whipping through the turnstile and getting back on the street. I want to assign them to an ADA that will keep them locked up tight, at least until they go to trial. I don't want any of these cocksuckers bailed out. We get them, we keep them. Understood?"

"We shoot 'em, ain't gonna be no turnstile to worry about."

"I didn't hear that, Impelliteri."

"Yeah, and I didn't say it."

"Walter?"

Wang was down under the table looking for a phone jack. He stuck his head out. "Yes."

"Listen up for a second." Shaw turned to the others. "Walter secured a cell phone for each team and a portable radio for each of us. Take down the phone number for this office. Walter, you will be the central point of communications. If we can't get each other, we'll call in to you. Got it."

"Yeah."

"The rest of the stuff is in the cars?"

"Yeah."

"Are the radios tuned to our own frequency?"

"Yeah. Don't change 'em."

Impelliteri said, "Probably a million Pakistani cabdrivers on the same band."

"No. No way," said Walter.

"All right, guys, when we're on the air, just use first names."

"What the fuck is your first name, Shaw?"

"Loyd, Anthony. One *l*."

"And Mason's?"

"Orestes."

"Oh, like those names won't stick out. Tony and James, no problem, but someone hears Orestes and Loyd over the air? Forget about it."

"All right, all right, just use our fucking initials or something. I don't give a shit. Just make sure everyone in the precinct doesn't know who we are and what we're doing out there." Shaw continued. "Walter, while we're gone, get on those other three Blue-Tops. And then start on the list. And any other names we feed to you."

"Shit. I be here forever."

"Goddamn right. Don't expect to go home except for clothes. In fact, you'd better bring a change of clothing in here and a razor. And it doesn't have to be a suit, man. Relax a little. There's going to be no time off for any of us until this job is done or DeLuca says it's over. You got everything you need here to do your searches?"

"Yeah, I don't have to be at Central Warrants. I got my own modem, and I got the codes to get into Central from here. But don't tell anyone. You're not suppose to be able to do that."

"Yeah, well that's the first of many things I'm sure we'll be doing that we aren't suppose to. And don't forget to bullshit up our fives."

Impelliteri raised his hand. "Question."

"What?"

"You got any money? We're gonna need money."

Shaw knew Impelliteri was right. It was the biggest thing he had asked of Conklin and it seemed to be the easiest thing for Conklin to provide. Shaw pulled out a stack of used hundred dollar bills.

"Each team has a grand."

He tossed a pack of bills to Impelliteri.

"Now you're talking, boss. Now we can make something happen out there, right Sperl?"

"Use it wisely," said Shaw. "Every penny."

Wang chimed in right away. "Hey, where's my cut?"

Shaw peeled off one bill.

"Here's a hundred for food. Impelliteri, give him a hundred."

"Fuck that."

Wang frowned. Impelliteri laughed. "Hey, just kidding Kung Fu." He handed over the bill. "This'll keep you in chow mein for the whole deal. Enjoy."

"Fuck you, you wop dago bastard."

Wang had stuttered and spit out the epithet so quickly that his underlying Chinese accent popped through. The nerd had turned. Everybody laughed, including Impelliteri.

Shaw said, "That's right, Walter. Don't let him fuck with you. Now get your magic little Asian fingers flying on that keyboard."

Mason raised a hand. "One thing."

"What, Mase?"

"Speaking of everybody else in the precinct. How much we gonna be trippin' over the precinct detectives out there? How much do they know? What are they supposed to be doing?"

"I don't know. And I can't worry about it. I want to be off this thing before anybody starts wondering about us."

"Good luck," said Impelliteri.

Shaw turned to the others. "Forget about the precinct guys. Forget about everything in your lives except these Blue-Tops bastards. Get the top guys as soon as you can and the little guys while you're developing leads. The guy with the most Blue-Tops wins. I don't give a shit how you do it. I don't give a shit if three months from now your arrests don't stand up. I want these guys locked up and I want names. Get 'em from these assholes, get 'em from your connections, get 'em any way you can."

Sperling finally spoke. "One more question, Shaw."

"Yeah?"

"The main thing is to get the main man here."

"Archie Reynolds? Yeah."

"Well, if we go after his lieutenants and managers and enforcers, that's going to send Mr. Reynolds deep into a hole where we can't find him. Or it's going to make him run."

"I don't think this guy is the type to bury himself."

Impelliteri spoke up. "Seems like he's been pretty quiet since the Muslims fucked up his buddies."

"Maybe. Or maybe he's meeting with his suppliers and his hitters, planning his next move. Or maybe he's trying to find a way to get his business running somewhere else and then come back after the Muslims. It really doesn't matter. We go for whoever we can get now. If we flush him out and nail his ass, fine. If he runs to another state, that's fine, too. Either way, he stops killing people."

"I'd rather get the man," said Mason.

"So would I. But one thing I want you to remember, this gang is in the middle of a war. They've probably already gone for cover. Or at least they're going to be very careful about being out on the street. But when you do find them, and I know we will, you make goddamn sure you watch yourself. The first thing they're going to do is shoot."

Impelliteri said, "Fuck 'em. They get to shoot on me first, they deserve to get away. And just remember, Shaw, nobody is gonna mistake me and Sperling for black Muslims. You better make sure your partner there doesn't go around wearin' his Kunte robes and Kufi cap."

Mason had been looking at DeLuca's file through his battered reading glasses. He looked over at Impelliteri and peered over the top of his spectacles.

"Hey, Impelliteri."

"What?"

Mason said, "I'm a Baptist." But said it in a way to clearly indicate he would settle for no more of Impelliteri's misplaced wit.

But Impelliteri wouldn't be cowed. As he left the office he turned, raised a fist and said, "Right on, brother. Come on, Sperling."

Shaw and Mason watched them go, then Shaw asked Mason, "You got a copy of the warrant Wang had found on Watkins?"

Mason was already looking it over.

Shaw pointed to it, "There was an address listed, maybe we should start there."

Mason said, "You'd better come up with something better than that."

"Yeah, I know. Think about it. There's something we have to do first. Let me just check with Walter for a second."

"Walter?"

"Yes?"

"How long until you're all set up?"

Wang was already making clickety-click noises with his keyboard and sliding his mouse around. Shaw heard the weird echoey noise modems make when they are establishing a connection. Wang's nose was aimed at his screen and his expression had already turned blank with a far-off, computer-geek gaze. He spoke to Shaw without looking at him.

"I'm in."

"In where?"

"Field Assistant Terminal Network."

Mason and Shaw exchanged looks.

"Mase, did you know that's what *F, A, T, N* stood for?"

"I knew about the *T, N* part," said Mason. "But I never knew the other."

"Is that right, Walter?"

Wang answered with a smirk.

Shaw said, "I think we've lost him to cyberspace."

"Fine with me, if he gets good information out of it."

"Walter, concentrate on Archie Reynolds. But get something for us on Ellard Watkins, too. I'll call you in a couple of hours. Have something for me will you?"

"Yeah, yeah."

"Both of their NYSID numbers are in DeLuca's file."

"I know, I know."

Wang had already lost interest in any conversations. He tapped and clicked his way deeper into the police database.

"Walter, you got me a phone monitor?"

The best Walter could do was grunt, "Car trunk."

Shaw grabbed the remaining set of car keys and headed out with Mason. On the way to the precinct parking lot, Shaw told Mason what he had planned.

"I want to run down this real estate guy who's paying the Muslims."

"What for?"

"Couple of reasons. You know how to work one of those phone monitor boxes?"

"Not really."

Shaw gave Mason a quick lesson on the way.

Reggie Whack got the call to come pick Archie up at the Hotel Doral in Manhattan. Whatever arrangements Archie had made, he said nothing about it. For the next two hours, about the same time Shaw met with his crew at the seven-three, Archie directed Reggie to a series of hardware stores, gas stations, and grocery stores. They ended up behind a salvage yard about five blocks east of New Lots, unloading five five-gallon, red plastic containers, each containing four gallons of gasoline. Archie set the cans down and screwed off their tops. While Reggie unpacked bags filled with boxes of mothballs and Knox gelatin and liquid laundry detergent, Archie muttered to himself, "Motherfuckers. Fucking try to burn me out. Nigger ghetto bullshit. Niggers want to burn out the Jew motherfuckers who ripping you off, go on. Burn up the white man's prison when you riot, I give a shit. Burn out the Blue-Tops? Burn out Archie Ar? No fucking way, man.

"They want to see something burn? I'll fucking show 'em how to burn."

Archie pulled twenty boxes of mothballs out of the hardware-store bags and dropped the boxes on the ground. He methodically stomped on the boxes, motioning for Reggie to do the same.

Archie distributed the crushed mothballs into each of the gasoline cans. Then divided his supply of gelatin and detergent and poured that into the cans, too.

"So what's this?" asked Reggie.

"My special blend. Ar-Man napalm."

"Nay, nay, napalm?"

"Homemade version."

"What the fuck, man, that shit ay, ay, ain't gonna eh, eh, explode in my Jeep is it?"

"No, motherfucker. That ain't the point. This shit just makes the gas nice and thick. Like jelly. You pour it on, it stays put. And it don't go out. You light this motherfucker, it's gonna burn. Burn all night long. Fuckers want to see something burn, I'll show 'em how to burn people out."

For the first time since the body-shop massacre, Reggie smiled his gold-toothed smile.

"When we gah, gah, gonna do that?" asked Reggie.

"When I say. When the time is right. But right now we got to take care of other business."

"What business?"

"The crack business, motherfucker. First we make sure the new system be working. Make sure nobody too fucked up about what happened. *Then* we take care of these Muslim cocksuckers and that Uncle Tom bitch once and for all."

They loaded the cans into the back of the Jeep. Reggie asked, "Na, na, now where?"

"New Lots," said Archie. "Where the fuck else we gonna go?"

Loyd Shaw found Leon Bloom's office on Prospect Place in Crown Heights. The address belonged to a ground floor storefront office. If this is a real estate office, thought Shaw, there's never been one like it.

The place looked as if it hadn't been cleaned in twenty years. When he entered, Shaw saw a long, narrow room. A counter across the full width blocked access. Behind the counter lay chaos. Several large photocopy machines ran ceaselessly. Phones at four desks rang constantly. Piles of paper spilled out on every vertical surface. Shaw counted five men and two women packed into the small space. The men dressed in their white shirts, black vests and pants, all wearing yarmulkes, some wearing tzistzis, the women in long skirts, blouses, sweaters, and wigs.

For all Shaw knew, in addition to a copy shop and stationery supply business, they could have been running an import-export firm, travel agency, and real estate office in the ground-floor space.

Shaw wasn't interested in wading through the mayhem to find out. In fact, Shaw didn't even want to be there. He had rushed over from the precinct to catch the end of the lunch hour so that he could get Bloom out of his office.

A wholesomely attractive young lady told Shaw the Mr. Bloom was not in his office.

"Where is he? Lunch?" asked Shaw.

She told Shaw he could find Mr. Bloom at an address one block west.

From the look of Bloom's coworkers, Shaw expected to find the man participating in some sort of cabalistic study of the Torah with a minyan of learned rabbis.

As Shaw walked through the relatively quiet Crown Heights neighborhood, Mason followed in one of the dark blue Chevy Caprices that Conklin had supplied the team.

Shaw turned around to make sure Mason wasn't following too closely. He wanted the car out of sight when he found Bloom.

While he walked west toward the address the young woman had given him, Shaw thought about the ecumenical relationship between Orthodox Jews and black American Muslims. Shaw knew a little bit about the Old Testament, but not nearly enough about the Koran to make a comparison. The fact that they had formed an alliance intrigued him. Not to mention that Rachman had appropriated the lessons of the Holocaust to justify his murderous violence. Shaw wondered if Bloom had influenced Rachman's thinking, but quickly decided it wasn't likely that any white man could influence Rachman's thinking.

As soon as Shaw arrived at the location, he stopped worrying about interrupting a lunch-hour debate on Talmudic law. Bloom was not in a temple. He was in a bar finishing the last third of a three-martini lunch. The only evidence of food in front of him was a small pile of olive pits.

Bloom sat on a stool at the far end of the bar, sipping his gin and smoking filtered Camels. Bloom was the perfect picture of a relaxed man. His tie lay undone, draped across his chest and belly, his collar loosened, his jacket hanging over the back of his bar stool. The only trace of religious orthodoxy was Bloom's yarmulke, which he wore faithfully on the top of his large, round head.

Shaw introduced himself and noted that Bloom didn't seemed surprised at all to be sought out by a police detective. Shaw told himself, why should he be with all the dead bodies dropping around him? And why the hell should that interrupt his peace of mind? It was only *shvartzers* and workmen dropping.

"So, Mr. Bloom, let me ask you a few questions."

Bloom answered, "Go ahead." But it sounded like, "gahed."

"I understand you've taken over the management of New Lots Apartments."

"Not me personally, thank God, but the company I work for, Arbor Realty. We specialize in restoring properties in trouble."

"Trouble?"

"Yes. You know what I mean."

"I suppose. Now as part of this restoration, you employ an outside security company."

"Yes, although we do help some of them with licensing and payroll."

"You process the payroll?"

"Yes."

"Uh-huh, and where do you recruit these fellows? I find it fascinating that African Americans who are followers of Islam are working with Orthodox Jews."

Bloom shrugged and smiled. He seemed delighted that Shaw would be making an issue of it.

"Why not? We're not prejudiced against anybody. Some are Muslims, some are not. The people we work with are dedicated individuals willing to help the people of their community."

"What motivates them?"

Bloom shrugged again.

Shaw thought, this guy loves shrugging. Must help him convey how mysterious and wonderful life can be.

"Who can say?" said Bloom. "Many of them believe they are doing God's work."

"God works in mysterious ways, huh, Mr. Bloom?"

"Please, I'm not qualified to comment on God's ways."

Shaw had been leaning back casually against the bar, facing away from Bloom. Now he turned to the man, his voice hardening, and said, "Yeah, well you'd better comment on why you murderous fucks think you can get away with using a bunch of vigilante felons to kill people you would rather not have occupying your rental property."

Bloom stopped shrugging. Even with three martinis under his straining belt Shaw's sudden change seemed to unnerve him.

"What?"

Shaw resisted the urge to slap Leon Bloom.

"You heard me. How do you think you can hire people to commit murder and get away with it?"

"What are you? Crazy?"

"I'm not crazy."

"You're talking crazy. You expect me to take you seriously with that kind of question?"

"You goddamn right I expect you to take me seriously. I'm talking about people dying here. I'm serious as a fucking heart attack."

Now instead of shrugging, Bloom started spluttering.

"It's, it's not a serious question, a question like that. What do you mean commit murder? If someone shoots a gun at you and you shoot back, that's not murder, that's self-defense."

"Oh. Oh, right. Self-defense. I knew we'd get there pretty quick. You're saying the murders these Muslims committed were in self-defense."

"Who said my men—"

"Shut up. I'm not done. I want to know where self-defense comes in when you drag people out of an alley and beat them to death? How is it self-defense when you lock human beings up in a body shop and burn them to death?"

"I don't know what you're talking about."

"Vaguely reminiscent of shoving people into ovens, don't you think? How does that constitute self-defense?"

"This conversation is over."

"No it isn't. Don't cloak yourself in some bullshit Holocaust outrage. You look at what you're behind and you fucking answer me, fat boy, or you will not walk out of this bar."

Bloom dropped all pretext of innocence and offense. His eyes narrowed and he looked directly at Shaw.

"Who are you?"

"I told you my name, Detective Loyd Shaw. One *l*."

"You can't talk to me like this. You can't threaten me."

"Why the fuck can't I? You're aiding and abetting murder."

"What do you want?"

That hadn't taken too long, thought Shaw.

Shaw forced a smile and leaned back again. "Thank you for asking, Mr. Bloom. I really don't want too much. Go on, finish your drink."

Bloom pushed his martini glass away and waited.

Shaw nodded as if now they understood each other.

"I apologize for my last remarks. I got carried away. Let's start over. Regarding self-defense. According to the report I read, this all started when you sent your Muslims into New Lots to shoot up one of that drug gang's apartments. What would that be considered? A warning of some sort? I mean, not that you know exactly what I'm talking about. Hypothetically. Off the record. What would that be? A warning?"

Bloom decided to answer. Or at least tell the man what he wanted to hear until he left.

"Yes," Bloom said. "A warning."

"And after the warning is given, presumably you have even more right to defend yourself. Self-defense."

"Presumably."

Shaw edged closer to Bloom, but this time he dropped all posturing, spoke very quietly, looking right into Bloom's face.

"Okay, Mr. Bloom, here comes *my* warning. You ready? Because after I give you my warning, I'm going to have more right than ever to wage a vigorous defense, a very vigorous and direct defense, you know what I mean?"

Shaw looked directly at the fat, disheveled man, staring right into his eyes. Standing right in front of him, not sitting. He wanted to penetrate the gin and any feeling of protection and complacency Bloom might still possess.

Shaw slowly reached under his jacket and extracted his Glock. He pressed the hard muzzle into Bloom's belly. He blocked his move with his body so that the bartender wouldn't start dialing 911.

"How does it go, Bloom?" Shaw lifted the Glock up a few inches. "I read the report on how they shot up that crack den. A couple of hundred bullets and no bodies. I've seen that shit. First you shoot over their heads. Next time it's in their heads? Is that how it goes? Is that the warning?"

"I don't know."

"Okay, know this. Know my warning, Mr. Bloom. I don't want any more murderers shooting guns in Brownsville. I don't want your vigilantes shooting or beating people in Brownsville. I'm warning you. You shut that down, or I will come after *you*. Not that ex-con Rachman Abdul X. Not the usual targets. I'll come after you. Me. Loyd Shaw. Nobody will stop me. Nobody from the police department. Nobody from the Muslims. Nobody. Do you hear me? Do you understand my warning to you?"

Shaw maintained eye contact with Bloom, who had begun to sweat slightly.

"You're crazy."

"That's what they tell me. Do you understand me?"

"Yes."

"You're sure. You're absolutely sure?"

"Yes."

"Okay then."

Shaw slowly removed the gun from Bloom's ample belly and shoved the Glock back into his belt. He sat down on the empty bar stool next to Bloom.

"Okay, that's the nasty part. Now here's the nice part. Are you still with me?"

"Yes."

"You tell your little private army to stop their war out there because I am going to take care of their enemies. I am going to eliminate this vicious little crack gang and its leaders. Now I do the dirty work. I already talked to your man Rachman this morning and told him I will do this. Now I want *you* to tell him to stand down."

"Yes."

"That way, Mr. Bloom, you and your Muslims don't have to be the murderers."

"You're going to be the murderer? Is that what you're saying? Because you know as well as I do, Mr. Detective, you know those animals won't stop until they are dead."

"Don't tell me what I know or don't know. I fucking know what I need to. And you'd better know it's time to stop."

Bloom asked, "Are you done?"

"Only if you assure me that you completely understand me."

"What's not to understand? I don't think the police department really works this way. If your superiors knew—"

"Shut up, Bloom. Just tell me now. Are we together on this or not?"

"Sure, sure, why not? Anything you say."

"Then do me one service. Do just one thing to help me."

"What?"

"Tell your Muslim boys to give me whatever information they have on this crack gang. You know, instruct them that it makes sense to help me. Give them that line about the enemy of your enemy is your friend. Tell them it's the smart thing to do. Tell them whatever you have to, but tell them to give me information. I want to know everything they know about the Blue-Tops."

"I can tell them, but I can't guarantee they'll listen to me. I can't make them cooperate with the police. They don't really like the police, Mr. Detective. And from what I'm seeing, I can't say that I blame them. You act like some Cossack, coming in here with your threats and accusations."

Shaw sighed.

"I do hope you understand, Mr. Bloom. Cossacks are what it's going to take with this. If I were you, I'd get used to it. Just make sure you do what I tell you."

Shaw stood up and patted Bloom's fat back.

"Talk to Mr. Rachman. No big rush. Anytime today. I'll see him later tonight. Okay?"

And with that Shaw turned and walked out of the bar.

*   *   *

Shaw reached the Caprice parked across the street just in time. Mason had the monitor fired up, tuning in, trying to pick up the radio signal from Bloom's cellular phone as it bounced off the radio transmission cell. That's why Shaw wanted Bloom out of his office. He wanted Bloom to use his cell phone.

Luckily it wasn't one of the newer digital models. The analog transmission was easier to intercept. Bloom hadn't wasted any time making the phone call Shaw wanted him to make. Shaw just managed to place his tape recorder in front of the monitor's speaker in time to pick up the conversation.

Mason had his reading glasses perched on his broad nose, carefully writing down the model number and phone number of Bloom's cellular phone as it appeared on the monitor's LCD readout.

Shaw watched the numbers scroll and listened. The normal bit of static faded in and out, but the monitor snatched the conversation he wanted to hear right out of the air. He listened to the doleful, steady voice of Lieutenant Conklin respond to the tense exasperated voice of Leon Bloom.

Bloom was telling Conklin all about Loyd, one *l*, Shaw. Bloom wanted to know what to do. He wanted to be told that someone would make Shaw go away and leave him alone. He wanted to know why Shaw had harassed and threatened him.

Bloom had a lot of questions. Conklin had a lot of smarts. He didn't invoke his boss's name once. And everything he did say was carefully calculated. He told Bloom to consider Shaw part of the solution. He told Bloom that it was always wise to cooperate with the police, but that his concerns were duly noted. Conklin wouldn't speak too openly over the airwaves, but it was good enough for starters.

Shaw would have liked Bloom to invoke Justine

Burton's name. And/or her father's name. The man had to believe he had a major load of protection if he thought he could unleash armed felons to kill the Blue-Tops boys. Shaw would have like to hear him invoke that protection so he could capture it on tape. But Conklin cut the conversation short.

Mason switched off the monitoring equipment and gave Shaw a tired, seen-it-all look.

"You really want to step in this shit?"

"We have a choice? This guy Bloom thinks he can get away with murder. You think that comes from no-where?"

"Now you going after the commissioner, too?"

"I'll go after whoever I have to, Mase."

"Jeezus."

"I know. We're in this now." Shaw held up the tape recorder. "We go wherever it leads us."

"Yeah, and where would that be, exactly."

"Right now?"

"Yeah."

Shaw rubbed his stomach.

"Someplace where I can get something to eat."

Shaw and Mason hit a McDonald's drive-through and came away with four bags of food. Shaw didn't even bother looking at the menu or at what he pulled out of the bag to eat while he called in to their office in the seven-three.

"Walter, what's happening?"

"I got stuff on Watkins. Turn on the fax in your car and I'll modem it to you."

"A fax? I have a fax in this car?"

"Yeah. See that thing that looks like a keyboard with a screen."

Shaw looked around and saw a piece of equipment where a cellular phone might be hooked up. He had never seen a police car of any kind with a fax in it. He realized Wang must have stayed up most of the night getting the array of equipment he had secured. Wang walked Shaw through the steps and within a minute the contraption started emitting a grinding noise and oozed out a sticky length of fax paper bearing information that would put them on the trail of Weight Watkins.

The printout came through Walter's computer via a database deep in the bowels of the NYPD computer network. Shaw studied the fax carefully and decided Walter Wang knew how to work minor miracles.

26

By the time Tony Impelliteri and James Sperling left the temporary office in the seven-three, Impelliteri had already taken over most of the decisions. He was at the wheel of one of the twin Caprices Wang had procured, and before they even pulled out of the precinct parking lot, Impelliteri started telling Sperling his plan.

"Sperl, you and I have to talk."

"Uh-huh."

"Well, not really. You listen and grunt if you disagree."

"Go."

Impelliteri talked fast and drove even faster. Sperling didn't bother to ask where he was going.

"Look, my view on this is very simple. I ain't waltzing around the streets of fuckin' Brownsville looking for a bunch of crack-dealing niggers. It ain't gonna work. The second our white asses hit the street, the word goes out. They'll be gone before we turn the corner and for goddamn sure some knucklehead is gonna take a shot at us just for laughs."

"Yes."

"So I got a different plan."

"Which is?"

"I'm glad you asked. I prefer we make them come to us."

"Them being these Blue-Tops guys we're looking for?"

"Who else?"

Sperling asked, "How do you figure we can do that?"

"It's gonna take a little running around, but what the

fuck. You'll see. This is one where I call in a few markers. You hungry?"

"Yes."

"Come on, we'll take a little chip out of our expense money."

Impelliteri drove east out of Brownsville to an Italian restaurant near Aqueduct Racetrack. Impelliteri walked in, sat at a table for four. Sperling took the chair opposite Impelliteri and settled back, not even bothering to pick up the menu.

Impelliteri completely ignored the fact that Sperling looked to be the type who hardly ate. He ordered antipasto and fried calamari with fra diavolo sauce for starters. Then salad. Then roasted whole red snapper with side dishes of black linguini in garlic and oil sauce. Impelliteri polished off most of a bottle of Chianti Classico Riserva and finished the meal with melon and prosciutto.

Sperling didn't drink, barely ate and, as expected, spoke very little during the meal. Impelliteri left Sperling to his silence while he made a series of phone calls on the restaurant owner's cordless phone.

Nobody brought a bill for the meal, but Impelliteri dropped a fifty-dollar tip on the table and led the way back to the car.

"Okay, Sperl, we gotta make a few stops. Everything is set up except for running down the Kilo Queen."

"Who?"

"Never mind, you'll see. By the way, you mind me calling you Sperl?"

"I prefer James."

"How about Jimmy?"

"Suit yourself."

"Okay, Sperl . . . just kidding, James, we gotta head over to my precinct and get a bunch of mug shots a pal of mine picke up for us at Photo Division. They match the guys on that list Shaw laid on us. Then we make a few stops, and we get to work."

Impelliteri drove the Caprice almost as if the siren and lights were flashing. They made their rounds very quickly.

They picked up copies of ten mug shots at the East New York precinct, then in quick succession stopped at two bars, a pool hall, a beauty parlor, and a Caribbean-French restaurant that catered to Haitians. They finally found the Kilo Queen in the back room of a car-service company on Dumont Avenue, just over the dividing line between East New York and Brownsville.

As they headed for the car-service office, Sperling emerged from his shell to ask, "Now do I get to know who this person is?"

"Can't tell you."

"She deals in kilos?"

"Yep."

"Of what?"

"Mostly coke. But she's been known to locate heroin if needed."

"Kilos."

"Exactly. No small deals. But nothing too big. She's right in the middle."

Impelliteri paused at the doorway and warned Sperling, "Hey, in case you get a wild urge to suddenly launch into a big conversation, don't. Don't say anything unless she asks you a question."

"Okay. Are we cops?"

"Hell yeah, we're cops. She knows who I am. And one more thing."

"What?"

"She's not exactly a she. She's more of an it."

Sperling's only reaction to that bit of information was a slightly raised eyebrow.

They entered at street level through a reinforced glass door, walked up one flight of stairs, and turned into the expected beat-up, dimly lit, dirty-paint office. A poorly constructed wood and glass partition separated the main section of the office from a small waiting area. On one side of the partition, three chain-smoking car-service drivers in cheap sport coats and wrinkled pants stood waiting to start their shifts. They checked in with a dark-skinned, Middle Eastern man who stood on the other side of the partition making notes on time sheets. He could have been anything from an Israeli to a Pakistani and looked as if he hadn't slept in about three days.

Another swarthy type sat at a console shouting incessantly into a microphone broadcasting addresses and assignments. The language sounded Arabic.

None of it mattered to Impelliteri, not even the hard stares he received when he entered. He hardly broke stride as he pointed to the back and said, "Margo."

They buzzed him in past the partition. Sperling followed close behind. At the far end of the office, they walked through another door more formidable than any other they had passed through. They entered a back office about the same as the office in front, except for the occupants.

By far, the most unusual thing about the office was its occupant, the Kilo Queen. Even Sperling had to admit that the queen did have a somewhat regal presence. Queen Margo was a flamboyant transsexual draped in an androgynous red rayon blouse-shirt opened low enough to reveal a distinct cleavage.

It wasn't clear whether this somewhat impressive décolletage was the result of silicone, saline, hormones, or all three. Her ensemble included bright yellow bolero pants and leopard-skin slippers. Her accessories consisted of fake Paloma Picasso earrings, strings of brightly colored Mardi Gras necklaces, and fashionable barrettes strategically placed in her heavily pomaded, marcelled hair. The hair color alone was interesting, a unique combination of reddish black with platinum highlights. Makeup included matching dark lipstick and nail polish, generous mascara, and blue eye shadow.

Margo was a handsome Hispanic man, dressed as a homosexual version of a woman who seemed to be imitating a very effeminate man.

The only part not immediately entertaining was the 9-mm Smith & Wesson semiautomatic pistol next to the phone Margo spoke into with a heavy Hispanic, decidedly effeminate accent.

The other occupant of the office, a beefy bodyguard, sat against the far wall. Unlike Margo, there was nothing charming about him. His name was Benny. He wore a dark suit too tight for his steroid-built body, a black vest and white shirt open at the collar. He looked at Impelliteri and Sperling as if they smelled bad and he was getting ready to throw them out with the rest of the garbage.

Margo sat at a neat desk speaking in quick burst of Spanglish using a combination of code, obscure references, and obscure analogies.

Margo took due notice of Impelliteri and Sperling, frowning at Impelliteri in order to convey her displeasure. The chilly reception didn't seem to bother Impelliteri or surprise Sperling.

Queen Margo finished her conversation, arranged herself and asked, "So what the fuck is with you, Anthony? I know you ain't coming in here with good news. I already got three phones calls telling me you're looking for me. What do you want?"

"Hey, I would have called you direct, but I don't have your current number."

"Whatever. I give a shit what you don't got." Margo suddenly turned to Sperling. "Who's your friend?"

"That's James."

Margo extended her hand. Sperling took it and received a surprisingly firm handshake instead of something more demure. Margo said, "Nice to meet you. What did you do to get hooked up with him? I know the cops ain't putting no good policeman with that one."

Sperling responded with a shrug.

Margo spun quickly on her swivel chair and told her bodyguard, "Benny, be a doll and go get us some coffee." Back to Impelliteri and Sperling, "You all want coffee?"

They said yes. Benny lumbered off.

Margo said, "Talk to me before my phone starts ringing." She turned to Sperling, pointed to Impelliteri, and said, "Now listen closely to the bullshit this one here comes up with. It's amazing how guys with cute asses think they can say anything, do anything, and get away with it." She turned back to Impelliteri. "Like I'm one of your chippy girlfriends you can bullshit anytime you want. Go on. What kind of trouble are you in now?"

"Margo, don't be such a hard-ass."

"Come on, baby." She tapped her wrist. "Time is money. Don't take any more of mine than you have to."

Impelliteri pointed at Margo. "Hey, this is worth your time. You want me to leave, just tell me."

"All right, all right, don't get your balls in an uproar for chrissake. Talk to me, baby."

"I'm looking for bad guys. If I find them, I can help solve a problem. I solve the problem, I get a big chip redeemable with very powerful people."

"Really. How powerful?"

Impelliteri didn't hold back.

"Chief of D."

"Oh, really?"

"Really. This could be a shot at moving from the shit list to the A-list real quick. But I gotta produce."

"Well, well, well, so what does God want?"

"Somebody is trying to bust up a crack gang that took over a housing complex in Brownsville. A bunch called the Blue-Tops. You ever hear of em?"

"Yes."

"Ever do business with them?"

"Maybe."

"Margo, please, don't fuck around now. This is serious. I'm callin' in all the chips on this one. You want in? You want to help me with this?"

"Why is the Chief of D interested in this?"

"Why should you care? He is. That's all."

The Kilo Queen grew quiet. Impelliteri had brought her an opportunity. A line into the Chief of D could be extremely valuable. But would it be worth the price Impelliteri wanted her to pay?

"Blue-Tops are the bad guys you're after?"

"Yes."

"You want my help with that?"

"Yeah. No pressure. You want to help, great. If not, no hard feelings."

"Bullshit. I say no, maybe you don't become my enemy, but you won't forget."

Margo and Impelliteri exchanged looks, but Impelliteri didn't say anything.

"But if you strike gold here, you going to have one big *pendejo* on your side, amigo."

"Exactly."

"But you fuck up, *El Jefe* don't owe nobody, and I got more bad boys on my sweet ass than I could handle with even two or three Bennys."

"Well, tell you truth, Margo, it ain't that hard a decision. This particular group is going down. It's goin' down with or without your help and with or without me. The word has come from on high. So the only question is whether or not you and me want to reap some of the rewards or let somebody else come along and take what's ours to get."

Margo looked at Sperling. "What do you say, *El Morte*?"

Sperling answered simply without attitude or challenge. "Yes or no and we'll be on our way."

Impelliteri said, "Hey, I've already given you profitable information. You just found out there's going to be a shortage of supply in Brownsville. You want to fill it? There's money there."

"There's always a shortage in Brownsville. Just depends on how much. So now things will be fucked up for a while. I don't time the market, honey. I just keep my regular thing goin'.

"And just because you say these Blue-Tops guys may be going down, how many are they gonna take with them? The first ones in take the first hit, honey. I was never one to think about the long term. It's mañana I'm worried about."

"Right. But it's today you gotta decide. So what's it going to be, Margo?"

"What's the play? As if I didn't know."

"Well, we gotta get these cockroaches to come to us, so I was thinking, maybe we have a sale. Something good enough to draw the mutts we're looking for, but not too much to make anybody suspicious."

"Wait a minute, you want to sell my shit for less?"

"Yeah."

"I'm not losing money on this. My budget does not call for losing money for anybody. Not you, not the Chief of D, not nobody, honey."

"Who said anything about losing money? I got you covered. Gimme you're best wholesale price, and I'll cover a few hundred off that to make the offer attractive. You won't lose anything."

"Losin' profit is the same as losin' money, baby."

"Hey, Margo, nuthin's for free, huh? This is for the nonprofit organization, okay? You gotta make some investment here."

"How much of an investment?"

"You tell me. How many keys you gotta sell at a discount to attract attention? This gang is gonna come apart real soon. Some of them will be breaking off to find a new supply. If you're selling at a good price while they're looking, they'll come to you."

Margo pursed her lips and frowned while she made her calculations.

"All right. Maybe there's enough in this for me to fuck with the price a little. Make some new connections. Offering good prices in bad times isn't a bad idea, you know."

Impelliteri turned to Sperling, "See, man, that's why they call her the Kilo Queen. She knows how to do business."

"Don't fuckin' con me, Anthony. You leave my business to me. If I get jammed up, I might hit you for a few hundred, okay, honey?"

"Fine. Put the word out."

"How am I gonna know who's who on your hit parade?"

Impelliteri slid the mug shots to Margo.

"Those are the names and faces I'm lookin' for. Tell me when you think you got a line on any of these guys. I'll get the fuck over here and take care of them."

"I don't want you taking care of anybody within two blocks of wherever I'm workin'. You understand?"

"Understood."

"And this doesn't go on for more than a week."

"Hey, I'm not interested in anything that's gonna even take that long."

"All right. I'm in." Margo smiled revealing a set of gleaming white teeth that looked much too perfect to be real. "Seal it with a kiss, honey."

"Thanks, Margo, I trust you."

"Come on."

"Hey, you ain't even getting a handshake out of me."

"For such a tough guy, you got no guts."

"You fuckin' got that right."

"All right Mr. Crime Buster, you run along now with your silent partner, here. I'll put the word out—"

". . . in the direction of Brownsville—"

"Yeah, yeah. I'll put the word out. I'll get some extras. We'll see what happens. But you don't fuck with my regulars or anybody I say don't fuck with, I don't care if they're Blue-Tops, Red-Tops, Four Tops, any kind of fucking *pendejo*-tops."

"Deal."

"Okay. We'll make it work. I don't mind the Chief of D owes you and you owe me."

"Okay, Margo. Good. One last thing."

"Now what?"

"You know a guy named Reginal Wilson. Calls himself Reggie Whack?"

"Reginal Wilson, is that his real name?"

"Yeah."

"Reggie Whack, I know who he is."

"Know where I can find him?"

"He's not a nice person, Anthony."

"Yeah, neither am I. Where can I find him."

Margo sighed. This was not part of the deal. Impelliteri was asking for more. But Margo was not surprised.

"All right. I don't know where he stays. My memory

tells me he's one of these dogs fucking women all over the damn city. Who knows where his lays his head? But he's got a sister. Maybe you can work her for a lead. She works over on Sutter. A beauty shop called African Woman. No, it's Afro Lady. Something like that."

"Sutter and what?"

"Uh, 'round Amboy or Bristol. Over from the Tilden Housing."

"Okay, what's she look like."

"Skinny, no tits, but cute. Light-skinned. Kinda rust-colored hair. Wears glasses."

"How tall?"

"Jeezus, *pendejo*, how the fuck do I know? Average."

"What's her name?"

"Lilly. No, no, it's Milly. Milly. That's it, Milly."

Margo had allowed her phone to go unanswered for two calls. When it started ringing a third time she told Impelliteri, "I gotta work, Anthony."

"Okay, Margo. Appreciate it. I'll check back tomorrow. You gonna be here?"

"Yeah, but after that I'll let you know."

And that was it. Impelliteri had his honey trap set. And he was on the trail of Reggie Whack.

The phone call from Archie Reynolds had come while Whitey Williams stood hunched over his two-burner stove stirring a pot of Campbell's bean soup in a stained saucepan. He listened to Archie's instructions, turned the burner off, and left, leaving the soup to go cold and congeal in the pan.

Five minutes later, Whitey walked into the storeroom in the back of the bodega across from the complex. Archie sat in an old-fashioned, wooden office chair, the kind with a padded, green seat, high-slatted back and big rolling wheels. He wore a tight-fitting white tank top under a blue rayon shirt left unbuttoned. His slacks were light wool, also blue. Archie propped his feet up onto a stack of corrugated boxes. Whitey noticed the Gucci buckle on the black slip-ons.

Reggie Whack sat off to the side, chewing a toothpick, his outfit the customary oversized denim jeans, Tommy Hilfiger sweatshirt, and black watch cap with the Knicks logo.

A faint odor of gasoline and mothballs lingered in the air, but Whitey didn't dare ask about it.

Neither of them motioned for Whitey to find a seat in the crowded room. Whitey didn't indicate any displeasure. He had heard about the massacre in the body shop. He wasn't about to do or say anything to set Archie off.

Archie asked his questions without explanation or repetition, as if he wanted to get it over with quickly. Whitey answered quickly, but there seemed to be a few points Archie wanted to go over again to make sure.

"So tell me about these Muslims motherfuckers again? They for real?"

"Real Muslims?"

"Yeah."

"I don't know a whole lot about that Islam stuff, but the ones who are Muslims seem like they take that shit real seriously. Fact is, though, a lot of them guards ain't Muslims at all."

"No?"

"Hell no. Just the heavy hitters. Lots of 'em jus' regular guys tryin' to work."

"So just the shooters are Muslim."

"From what I can tell."

"Where's their mosque or temple or what have you?"

"Bushwick Avenue is what I hear. Over west near Greene. The brown building with the thing on the top."

"Right. How many of them are there?"

"In the temple?"

"No motherfucker, in this guard company."

"All together, I don't know. I can jus' count the ones workin' 'round here. Every day I see two guards in the lobby of A and B, two at the front gate, and four on outside patrols. But they got three shifts."

"So outside they work two and two?"

"Outside?"

"Yeah."

"Right," said Whitey. "They always patrol outside in pairs."

"Nothing inside."

Whitey shook his head. "No, they have some inside, too. At least two in the lobbies like I said, but they be regular guards. Then, ever since they started buildin' that fence, they got a few more roamin' around in A and B looking after the construction workers. Those guys got guns."

Archie interrupted the old man. He had heard enough.

"Yeah, awright. Bushwick Avenue. I know the place. Okay, old man, keep on it."

Archie had finished with Whitey, but Whitey didn't leave. He stood in front of Archie, waiting, suppressing the little bit of dignity he had left in his old bones.

Whitey's lingering set off a flash of anger in Archie. He knew what Whitey was doing. Waiting for his handout, for doing nothing more than report the words that floated freely among the women and elderly residents of New Lots Apartments. Whitey provided nothing more than what gossips talked about, or little kids heard, or what a new guard would tell a shuffling old man who had ordinary questions. It didn't seem like something Archie should really need to buy. But here was Whitey, standing in front of him, waiting, doing everything short of putting his hand out. It was worse than paying off old fool bums who squeegeed the windshield on Archie's Saab. Another drop in the bucket of acid that ate away at Archie's gut.

He stuffed a ten-dollar bill in the old man's shirt pocket.

Once the money was in his pocket, Whitey asked, "Anything else, boss?"

Archie knew the old man used the word *boss* deliberately.

"No, you got nothing else for me, Whitey. What the fuck else can you do for me?"

Whitey took a step back. Reggie spit out his toothpick and stood up, as if to signal the old man to move along.

"Nuthin', I suppose," said Whitey. "But you never know."

"Fuck I don't know. Go on, old man. Get the fuck out."

As Whitey moved on out from the storeroom, Archie called after him, "Hey, what about the pohleeceman's daughter? What the fuck is she doing? She still coming around?"

Whitey turned back and said, "Oh, yeah, she's still around. Every day. Got a whole mess of cops around her. Guess she feels safe now. She's still over there."

Whitey waited for the vitriol that information would bring out of Archie, but Archie would not give him the satisfaction. He simply nodded his head and watched Whitey walk out to the counter to buy something. He had extra money now. Enough for cheese and bologna and bread to go with his soup. Enough for a can of beer, too.

Reggie asked, "So what we gah, gah, gonna do next, Arch?"

Archie grimaced, shifting the anger around inside him so it wouldn't paralyze his thinking.

"You got Weight and Melly set up?"

"Yeah, we me, me, meeting them later."

"Good." Archie shifted in his chair, unable to let it go, the last bit of information on the commissioner's daughter. "Goddamn that bitch. Got the fuckin' nerve to be still comin' 'round here. You know this is going down this way 'cause of her ass."

"I s'pose."

"Fuck her. She can have all the cops on her she wants. We got time to show her who runs this fuckin' neighborhood. Come on. Get your car."

Reggie followed Archie's instructions and drove north several blocks on East Ninety-eighth Street. They came back south on Rockaway Avenue, avoiding the police around Justine's center, but still managing to get close enough so that they could see the center's north exit.

Archie smirked at his ability to be so close and yet stay undetected by the police.

Archie and Reggie sat in the Jeep watching. Within fifteen minutes they had seen two women exit, but Archie waited patiently for exactly what he wanted. Another five minutes passed and two more women emerged from the end door accompanied by three children between them. Archie recognized both the women and he knew what they had come out for.

As they passed Reggie's car, Archie rolled down the passenger-side window and said, "Yo."

They turned and Archie motioned for them to come to him. They didn't hesitate for much more than a second or two. They were looking at the source of crack cocaine for the whole neighborhood and crack had brought them onto the street.

One woman was black, the other white; their children were a mix of both. Both women had the tense, bleary-eyed, beaten-down appearance of people under the intense pressure of a crippling need for crack cocaine.

The white woman hung back behind the black woman, figuring Archie would be more prone to deal with her. But Archie wasn't interested in selling crack. He was interested in humiliation and terror.

"Hey, cracker. Yeah, you come over here. Tell your sister to stand over there and watch them kids."

Her black friend gathered the kids around her. She didn't want to witness whatever was about to happen so she kept her back to the car, trying to block the children's view. She should have turned around and made the children face her, away from the car, but she wasn't thinking clearly.

The white woman shuffled to the passenger-side window, her head down. Archie looked at the black roots revealed by the part in her dirty platinum hair.

"Lift yo head up, honey, and tell me your name."

She looked up, "Lorraine."

"You know my name?"

Lorraine nodded.

"What's my name?"

"Archie."

"That's right, baby, you know what I do?"

Lorraine shrugged. She wore a V-necked sweater that was too small for her, dirty blue jeans, and worn-out tennis shoes. She wrapped a thin raincoat around her body, trying to hide herself from Archie's gaze and help conceal the slight shaking that gripped her.

"I asked you a question, do you know what I do?"

"I guess."

"You guess?"

"You sell."

"Sell what?"

"Crack."

"That's right, baby. And that's what you lookin' for out here, ain't it."

"Yeah."

"You need some rock?"

Lorraine looked directly at Archie now. She tried to smile, revealing bad teeth along with the tension filling her because she was so close to what she desperately wanted, so close yet afraid of what she would have to endure in order to get it.

Archie reached over and took something out of Reggie's hand. He shifted and raised his left hand to the car window, showing Lorraine three small plastic vials capped with the familiar blue tops. Each vial held a twenty-dollar dose of rock. Seeing them made Lorraine's stomach ache.

"How much money you got?"

"Twenty."

"Between the two of you?"

"Yeah."

Lorraine's nose ran slightly. She sniffed and wiped it with the back of her hand.

"Well gimme the fuckin' twenty."

Lorraine quickly pulled out a crumpled bill from her raincoat pocket. She handed it to Archie, who snatched it away from her with his right hand as he closed his left hand holding the three vials.

Lorraine shuffled her feet and clenched her jaw. She felt like screaming, *Give me the fucking rock, you asshole*. But she didn't.

"You want the one or all three?"

"You want to give me all three, I'll take 'em."

"But you only gave me twenty."

"Then give me the one."

"But you want the other two."

"I don't have any more money."

"What you got?"

Lorraine paused ever so slightly. There was still a shred of dignity left in her, and her kids were no more than twenty feet way. But she swallowed her dignity and said, "What you want?"

"How about you suck my big black dick and my friend's. Two dicks, two vials."

Lorraine's cheek ticked with tension. Maybe if the kids hadn't been with her she would have decided more quickly. She looked around behind her, checking to see how close they stood. The boy was eight. The girl five. The boy boldly peeked around her friend's leg, but the black woman moved his head back. Lorraine was getting ready to say, "Okay," but Reggie spoke up first.

"Fuck that, man. She's stanky. Ai, ai, ain't gonna let no stank cra, cra, cracker bitch cop my joint."

Lorraine slumped forward, her shoulders hunched, almost unable to bear the wave of anger and loss that hit her.

Then Archie seemed to offer her another chance. He motioned for Lorraine to come closer.

"Come here."

When she stepped closer, Archie grabbed her throat.

"Open your fuckin' mouth, bitch."

At first, she thought Archie wanted her to show that her mouth was suitable for his penis. She started to open her mouth. But suddenly, he squeezed his thumb into her throat, and Lorraine had no choice but to open her mouth wide as she gagged and desperately tried to suck in air. Archie leaned forward, hawked, and spat a load of phlegm into her open mouth.

And still he held her throat, pulling her closer. She could not swallow, could not spit it out. The warm excrescence sat in her mouth, sickening her.

"Now you listen to me, bitch, and you tell your friend and all those other crackhead bitches like you who go into that shithole you came out of, I see any of you in that place you'll never buy another rock in this neighborhood. You go in that place, I'll cut you off. And if I feel like it, I'll cut your fucking throats, too. You understand me?"

Lorraine nodded, crying now, choking, humiliated, burning with fear and hate, hoping her children hadn't seen what was being done to her.

"And you tell 'em who gave you this warning, me, the Ar-Man, Archie Reynolds. You decide what you want more: me, your shit-ass lives, and my crack; or that Uncle Tom bitch letting you sleep on her floor and kiss her light, bright ass. Got it?"

Lorraine didn't even know if she nodded. The pain had made her close her eyes.

"Look at me."

She did, and Archie shoved one vial in her mouth and pushed her away.

Lorraine bent over, spitting out the vial and Archie's phlegm, crying now openly, spitting and choking on his slobber and her tears and humiliation while she tried to wipe the vial clean against her dirty raincoat.

The fax on Ellard Watkins totaled almost four pages. By the time the last page eked out of the Caprice's fax machine, Loyd Shaw had given up on the McDonald's food.

The pages told Shaw and Mason just about everything law enforcement agencies had on Ellard "Weight" Watkins. His arrest record went back to 1978, mostly drug related and assault charges. There was an NYPD career criminal file on him, as well as state and federal records. Shaw noted that Ellard's arrest and incarceration ratio ran about average, which meant he served time for about three percent of his arrests. The pages were impersonal. The facts they showed were interchangeable with thousands of criminals like him. But Shaw knew that if Weight Watkins had risen to become one of the Blue-Tops managers, he must have hurt a lot of people along the way. He certainly had to be capable of killing.

Shaw and Mason sat in the front seat of the parked Caprice, reading the pages, shoving the ridiculous amount of wrappings and Styrofoam and cardboard from their drive-through meal into the stained McDonald's bag.

Shaw rolled down the car window to let out some of the pungent food odors. As Shaw finished one page of the fax, he handed it to Mason.

Mason wore a beat-up pair of tortoiseshell reading glasses. They gave him a professorial air. As he read about Ellard Watkins, he made a few notes in the small stenographer's notebook he carried around stuck in the side pocket of his sport coat, a gray herringbone. Shaw kept his thoughts to himself and let Mason work on the facts in his old-school cop, thorough, plodding way.

Shaw didn't know who Ellard Watkins was. But from the facts on Walter's printouts, and the blurry arrest photo, an image of the Blue-Top manager began to form in his mind. Watkins weighed over three hundred pounds, but Shaw did not picture somebody who was fat. He pictured a big man who intimidated with his size. When Shaw imagined Watkins at trial, or in his cell at Dannemora, or walking the streets of Brownsville, it was easy to imagine him as hard and mean and brutal.

Mason finished his last note and pulled off his glasses.

Shaw said, "I want to get the first one, Mase."

"Why?"

"I don't know. I just do. I'll bet Walter got us the information on our guy first."

"You want to beat Impelliteri. Show 'em the old dogs still can do it."

"Maybe."

Mason shrugged. "I just want this over as quick as possible. These are bad people. Any ideas?"

"Every time he's been arrested he's given a Brooklyn address."

"Right. But sittin' on those addresses ain't going to make anything happen quickly."

"No, but those addresses tell me he's a Brooklyn boy. I'll bet he doesn't go into Manhattan much."

"Maybe."

"What does he drive?"

Mason checked his notes. Then he shuffled through the fax pages.

"DMV has no record of a car owned by him. Last arrest reported he was picked up driving a ninety-one

Lincoln Continental. You want to look for the car?"

"No. No, I just keep thinking about him. Big car. Big guy. Big, fat Brooklyn boy. Weight Watkins." Shaw lapsed into silence, then sat upright and said, "Come on, I got an idea."

"What?"

"I need a Brooklyn Yellow Pages. And I'm still hungry."

"After all that?"

"I can't eat that shit. Come on."

First, they found a Chinese restaurant, then they found a Yellow Pages in the owner's office. Both detectives had to flash their shields at the suspicious owner before he would give over his copy of the phone book.

Once they got the book, they sat at a table and shoveled food into their mouths from three plates of Chinese food while Shaw flipped through the phone book. They'd eaten a late lunch. Now they were eating an early dinner.

As Shaw looked through the phone book, he remembered an old advertising slogan, "If it's out there, it's in here." It was in there, Shaw just had to find out where. It wasn't under "Clothing." It wasn't under "Apparel." It was under "Men's." He figured there'd be quite a number of listings under "Men's." The book told Shaw that particular category wasn't all that important. Lawyers and escort services dwarfed the listings under "Men's." The only listing under the topic was "Men's Clothing." Just for the hell of it, Shaw flipped to "Women's." "Women's" had four listings. He told himself, they always had better bathrooms, too. Hey, who says the world is fair?

The Yellow Pages told Shaw what he wanted to know, including the number of fat-man clothing stores in Brooklyn. There they were, euphemistically referred to as big, tall, portly, right between "Mending Clothes" and "Mental Health." Rather convenient, thought Shaw, if you're a crazy fat guy who busts up his clothes.

After consulting with Mason, they eliminated the portly shop in Bay Ridge, figuring it would cater to big, tall, portly Italians, called the others and inquired as to the racial mix of their clientele. They decided two of the stores might provide them with a lead. One was open until eight, the other until nine o'clock. It was a little after five. They finished their Tsingtao beers and were just about to head out when Shaw's police radio squawked.

It was Walter Wang.

"Yeah, Walter, go ahead."

"I got Justine Burton on the line, she wants to talk to you. Sounds like she's on a cell phone."

"Get the number. Tell her I'll call her right back."

Justine answered on the first ring. Her voice mixed with the background noise her cell phone picked up, but Shaw could still hear the anger in it.

"Detective Shaw?"

"Yes."

"I need to talk to you."

"In person?"

"Yes. I'd prefer that."

"Where are you?"

"I'm in my car. I'm heading into Manhattan."

"Where are you going?"

"To see my father. But I want to talk to you first."

"All right."

Shaw didn't waste time asking her what was going on. He exchanged locations with Justine and they figured out a place where they could meet on Ocean Parkway.

Mason asked, "What's that all about?"

"Commissioner's daughter. She sounds pissed."

"At us?"

"I can't see why. But who knows? She's on her way to complain to daddy."

"Damn."

"Yeah, that's all we need now. Let's see if I can calm her down."

Shaw found Justine in a quiet Italian neighborhood bar-restaurant waiting for him. She sat at a table in the back. Her three-man security squad from the Intelligence Division sat out front near the bar. Mason waited in the car outside.

Shaw nodded at the detectives. They looked back at him as if to say, "She's all yours."

Shaw took a seat across from Justine. She sat rigidly on the other side of the checkerboard tablecloth, now wearing the jacket to her suit. With her white silk blouse and a single strand of pearls, Shaw thought she looked like she should be working in a Park Avenue law firm. It occurred to him that her very appearance could set off someone like Archie Reynolds.

There was one other couple in the back dining area. Shaw had the impression they were a boss and his secretary. The couple held hands and stared into each others eyes, sneaking kisses like high school kids playing hooky. Shaw couldn't have cared less what they were doing, but their adolescent behavior served to emphasize Justine's stern demeanor.

Even angry, she looked beautiful. For the first time, Shaw noticed her hair. It seemed to him more Hispanic than African-American. No, he thought, American Indian. Straight, thick, and black. But she must have permed it slightly since there was a soft wave to it. Or maybe she had straightened it into a soft wave. Whatever she had done, it was perfect for her oval face, straight nose, and high cheekbones. Ah, that nose and cheekbones, that's what said American Indian to him.

And then, all such fleeting thoughts disappeared when Shaw watched Justine lift her coffee cup with two hands in order to keep her anger from shaking the liquid over the rim of the cup.

Shaw asked, "What happened?"

"Before I tell you, I'm going to warn you that I don't think I have ever been quite this angry or disgusted in my life. So I apologize in advance if you think my anger is directed at you. I'm just livid. I'm sorry."

"At what?"

"At Archie Reynolds. And at you because you haven't done anything about him, even though that's absurd since it's been less than one day."

Shaw didn't comment. He simply asked, "What did he do?"

She told Shaw the story she had managed to pull out of Lorraine's friend after one of her social workers saw Lorraine dragging her kids out of the center. And she told Shaw what Archie Reynolds had promised to do to any woman who dared stay at her shelter.

Shaw listened. Justine's reticence to speak about unspeakable acts made her story even more disturbing to him than if he had witnessed it himself.

By the time she finished, Shaw noted her tightly pursed mouth and clenched jaw.

"He's a fucking animal, Justine. He's just an animal. No, he's worse. He plans this shit."

The waitress came by to refill Justine's coffee cup and Shaw told her, "Bring me a shot of Maker's Mark, please. Straight up."

Without prompting, Justine said, "Make it two."

After a few moments of silence, during which the image of Archie spitting into a poor woman's mouth continued searing itself into Shaw's brain, Justine spoke quietly.

"I hardly know this man and I hate him so much it makes my stomach ache. It's not bad enough what he does to these women with his drugs. It's not bad enough what they do to themselves because of it. Now he tells them they can't even seek a modicum of shelter, a night's sleep in a place where someone isn't going to come home drunk or angry and beat them up."

"Look," Shaw said, "he isn't doing this just to hurt them. He's doing it to send you a message. To show you that you can't come into his neighborhood and take away what's his. He's trying to show you who is in control."

Justine glared at Shaw and said, "I know, damn it. I know. But why doesn't he have the goddamn nerve to come to me and tell me? Why does he have to go through them?"

"Because you've got three detectives with you and a half dozen uniformed cops around you. And he *did* come to you and tell you. He came with his gun in his hand and told you to get out. You didn't listen."

"I can't let that animal run me out."

"I know. I know. Did that woman leave?"

"I tried to calm her down. I tried to convince her to stay."

"Did you?"

"I don't know. She was still there when I left. Could I guarantee her that nothing would happen to her? Could I tell her that the man would be arrested?"

"Yes. That's exactly what you could have told her."

"I can't guarantee her that. You know that."

"Why the hell can't you? You think I'm out here playing a game. That fucking guy is already dead. He's a walking dead man."

Suddenly, Justine grabbed Shaw's wrist. The strength in her long fingers surprised him.

"But you said it yourself this morning. How many people are going to die before he does? How many women are going to get hurt. You understand what I'm dealing with, don't you? I don't mean to put this all on you, but you understand what I'm trying to do."

"Yes. Of course."

She looked at Shaw as if she wanted to believe him, but couldn't allow herself to.

"What are you going to do?" she asked.

"I'm going to track him down, track down his gang, find every lead I can get on him, and keep after him until he's dead, gone, or locked up. I don't know how long it will take, when it will happen exactly, but it *will* happen. If I don't nail him, someone else will."

She released her grip on Shaw's wrist and sat back in her chair. She seemed to fade away, her mind going someplace else. Shaw couldn't tell whether or not she believed his speech.

Shaw tapped the side of her hand to get her attention. And maybe to see if she would allow him to touch her.

"Justine."

She allowed the touch and the use of her first name. She focused on Shaw, and he said, "Did you hear me?"

And then she surprised Shaw by grabbing his hand, looking straight into his eyes and saying, "Yes. I heard you."

"Did you believe me?"

"I believe *you* believe it."

She gave his hand a final squeeze, perhaps by way of telling Shaw he had gotten as much agreement from her as he was going to get.

"You're going to see your father now?"

"Yes."

"If you're going to keep those women in your center,

ask your father for patrols on the streets around you, not just in front of the center and at the ends of the block. But if you want to be really be smart, move them to other shelters. Don't put yourself or them in unnecessary danger. If you could move everything to another locale until this is over, I think you should do that."

"I won't let him run me out."

"I'm not telling you to run. I'm telling you to be smart. Take away his targets. Help everyone survive while we beat him. You and your clients."

Justine picked up her bourbon and took a long sip. Shaw drained his shot glass and chased it with lukewarm coffee while she thought over what Shaw said.

"I don't know why I picked you, Shaw."

"You didn't. The Chief of Detectives did."

"No. He may have given you the job, but I picked you to focus on. There's plenty of uniformed guys and detectives working on this, but I picked you. There's something different about you and about the way you're working. I don't get that normal cop procedure feel about you. You're not in the normal loop, are you?"

"No."

"What are you? Some sort of special-assignment cop?"

"I don't know. I guess so."

"It's not your responsibility any more than anyone else's, but for better or worse, you're the guy it's on as far as I'm concerned."

"That's fine with me."

"Good. I don't want you to think I'm exerting unfair pressure on you."

"I didn't say it was fair. I just said it was fine. Believe me, there's so much pressure on me, yours doesn't make a whole lot of difference."

"Well, sorry if I add a little more."

She took another sip of her bourbon while she prepared for her next statement.

"You make a lot of sense, Shaw. You also seem to have the ability to calm me down."

"Maybe it's the Maker's."

She smiled. "No. Not yet, anyhow. It's you."

"Well, I take that as a compliment."

"You should. I don't pay compliments to very many men."

"Why is that?"

"There aren't too many I think deserve it. Actually, there aren't very many men who want to deal with me."

"And vice versa?"

"Right."

"And why is that?"

"I don't know. Maybe I make them nervous."

"Gee, that's surprising. You're only a stunning six foot black woman who's probably twice as smart as most men, who's got a pair of eyes like lasers, and who happens to be the police commissioner's daughter. Why should anybody be reluctant to deal with you or get involved?"

Justine smiled again. Shaw was beginning to enjoy making her smile.

"Involved? You talking about my social life or professional life?"

"Both. I just threw in the involved part 'cuz I was fishing."

"I see. So I don't make you nervous?"

Shaw said, "I'm past nervous."

"What does that mean?"

"I'm not in your league. What do I have to be nervous about?"

"What do you mean, you're not in my league?"

"Well, I'm a cop. I don't imagine you make it a policy to get involved with cops."

"You're right."

"I'm also white. Not implying that you're prejudiced, but I assume your preference is black men."

"Not necessarily. Black men bring their own problems to the equation, believe me."

"And technically, I'm married. You're not married I take it."

"No, I'm not married. What do you mean, technically?"

Shaw looked at his empty shot glass and resisted the urge to order another.

"If my wife and I weren't so busy, we'd have filed for a divorce quite a while ago."

"Do you live together?"

"We're under the same roof, sometimes."

"I think I've heard this one before."

"I wouldn't be surprised. But what are we talking about anyhow?"

"How old are you, Shaw?"

"Older than you."

"You don't really look it. You're in pretty good shape."

"Thanks. How old are you?"

"Thirty-four."

Shaw's reaction told her he thought she was younger.

"Yeah, I'm getting up there. The clock is just about ticked out."

"You were never married?"

"Close once. That was enough."

Shaw said, "I'm forty-two. So other than being older, white, a cop, *technically* married, and this being the wrong time . . . there's no problem. When's our first date?"

Justine answered without skipping a beat.

"When this is over."

Shaw stopped for several beats before he responded. "Did I just hear what I think I did?"

"You're the one who decided to fish."

"You serious?"

"I don't joke around about dates."

"*Now* I'm nervous," said Shaw.

"Bullshit."

"Well, maybe a little. What's this? More motivation?"

"Take it whatever way you want. When this is over, we go out to dinner and drink as much damn bourbon as we want."

Shaw reached over and offered his hand. He had an urge to touch Justine Burton for real. She gripped his hand and shook it once.

"Deal," Shaw said.

"Deal. But one more thing."

"What?"

"I can't just leave the center, you know. Women come there all the time. I couldn't live with myself thinking someone will come to that door and it will be locked."

"Does it have to be you? Can't you just keep someone there to direct them to another place?"

"It has to be me at least part of the time. I can't let others do for me what I won't do."

"Then keep it to the minimum. Keep a low profile. Get people out of there to other safe places as soon as you can. And tell the women who are there who still need drugs to have someone else get it for them. Have their boyfriends or people who won't be seen coming out of your shelter get it for them."

Justine listened and nodded. She frowned a bit, thinking over what Shaw had said.

"All right?" Shaw asked.

She looked up at him and finally nodded her head

in agreement. "Okay, Shaw, I'll do what you say. But please, let me know how you're doing."

She pulled out a card and began writing phone numbers on it. "Here's my cell phone and my home phone. Call me if anything I should know about happens."

"I will. Gotta go."

"Okay. Thanks."

Shaw stood up to leave.

"Hey."

"What?"

"I forgot your first name. What's your first name, Shaw?"

"Loyd. One *l*."

"That's right. One *l*." She nodded as if she approved. "Nice. It fits you. Why'd they name you that?"

"I don't know, after my grandfather I think. Where'd they get Justine? From justice?"

"My father never would admit that to me, but probably."

"Well, it suits you."

"Thanks. Don't leave me wondering about what's happening out there. I know how cops hate to answer to anybody, but please call me."

"I will."

Mason was napping when Shaw returned to the car. The sound of the door opening woke him. He leaned forward and started the car, back on the case, just like that.

As they drove to the clothing store, Shaw told him about Justine's latest problem with Archie. Mason just shook his head and held his comments. He's right, thought Shaw. There was nothing to say. It was now a question of doing something about it.

They arrived at the fat man's clothing store in a no-nonsense mood. Fortunately, there weren't any big boys searching for clothing in the store so Shaw and Mason didn't have to ruffle too many feathers cornering the manager and his two salesmen. All three eyed Weight Watkins's mug shot. All three identified him.

Shaw asked, "You have any records on him? Credit card number? Address? Phone?"

The salesman who seemed to know Watkins best said, "He always pays in cash, but I got a phone number where I call him when his clothes are ready. After we tailor 'em."

He left to get the phone number, while Shaw thought about fat men climbing into oversized pants. The salesman returned with a phone number for Ellard Watkins.

Shaw called the phone number in to Walter Wang, and he made the connection with the Coles Directory Service. They pulled up an address in Brownsville that matched the phone number.

Shaw asked the salesman if anybody ever delivered to that address.

"No. We don't deliver."

"How often does he buy clothes?"

"Oh, maybe once a month. He shops pretty regular."

"And you always call when the clothes are ready?"

"Sometimes. Sometimes he just comes in."

Shaw turned to Mason.

"Mase call up the number and make like this salesman here. See if you can find out if he's home."

Mason asked the salesman, "You don't have anything ready now, do you?"

"Nope."

Shaw could see that the salesmen and manager were anxious to be done with them. It had probably dawned on them that there might be terrible repercussions for leading the police to Weight Watkins. Tough shit. That's the price you pay when you sell to portly criminals, thought Shaw.

Mason dialed the phone and got an answer.

"Hello, this is Classic Clothing calling for Mr. Watkins. Is he available? . . . Uh-huh . . . Uh-huh."

Shaw watched the concerned look on the salesman's face when Mason mentioned the name of the store. He turned back to watch Mason. He enjoyed seeing his old partner at work. He knew Orestes Mason was a tough man. Genuinely tough. Physically and emotionally. Shaw had seen Mason go through bad times and hard guys, not much fazed by either. But Mason intrigued Shaw because despite it all, Mason maintained a quiet, thoughtful demeanor, and a disarmingly gentle voice and manner, which he put to good use on the phone call.

Shaw could easily envision Mason teaching at a quiet black college in the South. Running it down in that slow thoughtful way. Advising slightly militant African-American coeds with their firmly politically correct agendas. Gently leading them toward a more realistic view of life.

Shaw suddenly realized that that he didn't want the horror and violence of the Blue-Tops–Muslim war to touch Mason. He wanted the department to owe them. He wanted Albert J. DeLuca to be beholden to this good, honest, forthright black man. But he didn't want Mason bloodied.

The manager came over and handed Mason copies

of the most recent sales receipt for Watkins. The second salesman drifted over and decided to eavesdrop on the call. Despite their fears, they, too, couldn't resist watching Mason in action.

"Well, uh, who am I speaking to? Mrs. Watkins? Oh, I see, Mr. Watkins's mother. Well, Mrs. Watkins, we were just going over our records here and we noticed that on the last outfit your son bought—uh-huh. Right. As I was saying, Ellard was supposed to get half price on a second pair of pants, but we charged him full price. Uh-huh. Right. So when he gets in, just let him know he has a credit here for, let me see, eighty six dollars. Right. Classic Clothing. When do you expect him in? Okay. Well, give him that message, if you would please, ma'am. Thanks."

Mason hung up the phone.

"So?"

"That was his Moms. She says Ellard comes in and out whenever. Can't say when he'll be around again, but she'll give him the message."

Not great, thought Shaw, but considering how much effort they had put in, not bad.

Shaw turned to the salesmen.

"Gentlemen, thanks for your help. I'd like to ask you to keep our inquiries to yourselves. If Mr. Watkins should happen in here within the next couple of days stall him over that refund and call me right away. We'll be here in five minutes. Five minutes, tops. It's very important."

Shaw gave the manager one of his altered business cards. He doubted he'd ever hear from them again.

By nine o'clock, Shaw and Mason were parked around the corner from Mrs. Watkins's house, right in the heart of Brownsville on Lott Avenue, within walking distance of New Lots Apartments.

It was a long shot that Weight Watkins would be at his mother's, but Shaw didn't have any other shot to take.

They had circled the block once to get a fix on the house. Like most of the residents on the block, Mrs. Watkins lived in a run-down, cheaply constructed, two-story flat. The house was just an old box of a place held up by a sagging wood frame covered in plywood and then finished with cheap asphalt shingle siding, top and sides.

There were more substantial houses in the area. And there were worse. But every occupied house, including Mrs. Watkins's, had been augmented with wrought-iron bars covering doors and windows. The iron enclosures were the most substantial structures in the whole neighborhood. And they were everywhere . . . cut and formed and bolted over every window, every door, over all possible points of entry into the little houses.

Some of the houses were entirely protected with iron-bar barricades that extended from the ground all the way up to the roofs. It made it seem as if each of the houses had been caught in a giant birdcage.

It occurred to Shaw that if Ellard Watkins were inside that house, he was already behind bars.

There were two ways to find out if Watkins was home. Sit and wait for hours or days and hope to see him arrive or leave. Or go into the damn house and find out.

Shaw sat with Mason in the Caprice thinking about getting into the house. Since the neighborhood was dangerous enough to require a facade of iron bars on the outside, it was a sure bet most of these people had a brace of weapons inside.

Mason waited for Shaw's decision.

He asked Mason, "What's today's date?"

"The fifth."

"Tuesday, right?"

"Tuesday."

Shaw thought it over.

"I want to get that door open without busting it down. How about you go on up and knock on the door and tell them you're from the landlord? Tell them you're collecting this month's rent. I'll bet Mrs. Watkins hasn't paid it yet."

Mason looked at his watch. It was a fairly reasonable hour to come collect the rent. A little past eight o'clock.

"What if she already paid it?"

"Mmmm, well, just tell her your records show different. Tell her to open the door so you can show her."

Shaw could see his idea wasn't sitting well with Mason.

Mason said, "I don't know. What if the landlord never comes in here to get his money? Let me think. It's too late to be from Con Ed. Nobody in this neighborhood is lettin' the cable company in. I got a feeling she knows who she pays the rent to. She ain't gonna open the door for someone she's never seen before."

"Well, think up something. I don't want to sit here all night."

Mason didn't argue. He wanted to get it over with, too. Waiting on it made it worse.

"Come on," said Shaw. "Let's get the vests on."

They dug two bulletproof vests out of the car trunk and wrestled into them. Shaw zipped up his leather jacket to cover his vest. Mason buttoned up his sport coat, but couldn't quite cover his. In the waning light, it almost look like some sort of sweater under the large man's jacket.

Suddenly Mason announced, "I got it. Come on."

They left the car where it was, knowing that if they pulled up in the unmarked, they would be identified as a police car before they even stepped out.

Shaw waited to take out his Glock until they reached the front door. He pointed it down, next to his right leg, blocking it from sight, standing off to the right, thinking weird thoughts about the semantics of backing up his partner while standing next to him instead of behind him.

Mason carefully took out his Sig and knocked gently on the front door with his free hand. There was no buzzer, no nameplate, no way to know who lived in the house. They listened for sounds inside. Shaw wondered how they received their mail without a mailbox or name on the door.

Mason knocked again and said, "Mrs. Watkins. It's the Public Health Office."

He turned to Shaw and waved off the questioning look.

Shaw heard creaking floors and an elderly woman's voice finally came back faintly.

"Who is it?"

"It's the Public Health Office, from Kings County, Mrs. Watkins. We'd like to speak to you for just a moment."

" 'Bout what?"

"It's about your son, Ellard."

"What about him?"

"I'd rather not be shouting through the door, Mrs. Watkins. It's kind of personal. I have to speak to your son."

" 'Bout what?"

Mason hesitated for effect then said, "It's about a sexual disease that might have been transmitted to him."

Yeah, from that woman he raped, thought Shaw.

The old lady wasn't going to open the door for anybody, but Mason's news hit one of her buttons. She turned away from the door and shouted her son's name.

That was all Mason and Shaw needed to hear. Mason laid his two hundred sixty pounds into the door. Shaw added his two-fifteen. Both of them bounced off Mrs. Watkins's stout door. Shaw slammed into the door again, harder, with Mason rearing back and kicking just above the door handle. They heard the frame crack, but it took two more hits before they finally busted all the locks out of the frame.

Ellard was not in sight. But they both heard a rumbling pounding sound heading up a set of stairs.

Mrs. Watkins stood about ten feet off to the right, angry, defiant. Shaw expected a stout woman. She was thin, with a face wrinkled and ugly as an old shar-pei.

"Get the fuck out my house," she yelled.

Shaw yelled back, "Police, move!" as he ran through her living room toward the stairs. He angled in front of Mason, but his larger partner wasn't far behind him.

They just reached the stairs when they heard the soul-numbing sound of a shell being pumped into the chamber of a shotgun. They both dropped flat on the stairs as Watkins leaned around into the stairwell and fired a deafening blast. Most of the shot stayed in a tight burst, flying over their heads.

Shaw had seen the carnage a shotgun could cause. A blast at such close range could take out entire sections of a human body. Shaw cringed, imagining the top of his head about to be blown away with the next blast.

Fighting the terror to steady his aim, from his prone position Shaw pointed his Glock toward the top of the stairs and started pulling the trigger. And kept pulling the trigger, aiming at the wall on the right side, blasting out chunks of lathe and plaster, hoping to keep Watkins from chambering another round and this time aiming when he leaned around to shoot at them.

Shaw had seventeen rounds in the Glock. The fire and blasts from his gun blinded and deafened him in the narrow stairwell, but after about seven shots, he felt the wall next to him shake. Weight Watkins was on the move. Shaw jumped up, almost fell, but Mason grabbed him and steadied him as they ran up the short flight of stairs.

All Shaw could think of was to move fast and get the son of a bitch in front of him so he could shoot Watkins before Watkins shot them.

Shaw reached the top of the stairs, hoping there was nobody else up there to get in his way, some kid popping out of a bedroom or a woman jumping out, because he was ready to shoot anything that moved.

Shaw made it to the landing just in time to see Watkins turn into one of the bedrooms and slam the door behind him. He pegged one shot at the doorway just to make sure Watkins didn't pop back out with his shotgun. Mason ran past and slammed up flat against the wall flanking the bedroom door. Shaw took up the same position on the other side. His heart pounded so forcefully in his chest that Shaw feared he might blow an artery inside his head and die even if Watkins didn't shoot.

He managed to get enough wind in him to yell, "Watkins. It's the police. Throw the gun down. You can't win this. Come out."

Watkins answered with another blast that exploded a hole in the bedroom door the size of dinner plate. Then another and another. Three fast blasts.

Shaw expected Watkins to keep pumping and blasting away blindly, but he stopped. Mason and Shaw had the same thought. He was reloading.

Mason turned and kicked the remains of the door out of his way and immediately dropped down into a shooter's crouch. He still hadn't fired a shot. Shaw leaned over above him, pointing his Glock into the room, but there was nothing in sight but a beat-up bed and gun smoke. They saw that the bedroom opened onto a second-floor back porch. Watkins was already out the door and rumbling across the deck.

They ran after him and caught sight of Weight just as he reached a wooden railing. Watkins hoisted one huge leg over the railing, then the other.

Shaw shouted, "Don't move."

But he did. Without even looking back, Watkins jumped over to the roof of a one-story building next to his house. The distance from his porch to the roof spanned no more than two or three feet so Weight Watkins didn't have to launch himself very far. But it was a good six feet below him. The enormous man landed with such force that the roof of the dilapidated structure never had a chance. Ellard Watkins landed with a crashing thud and went right through the roof.

Mason yelled, "Good Lord!"

Shaw muttered, "Jeesuz Christ."

A sickening thud sounded from the interior and a plume of dust billowed up from the dark hole. Shaw peered over the porch, but couldn't see a thing.

He didn't think it possible that Watkins would survive unscathed, but Shaw wasn't taking any chances that he might get up and stagger out the front door of whatever he had landed in.

Shaw and Mason ran back down the stairs and out of the house. Mrs. Watkins had disappeared. It occurred to Shaw that she might be shuffling out of her bedroom with her own shotgun, but they made it out of her house without her pegging a shot at them. Shaw did not want to face the repercussions of shooting an elderly black woman in her own home.

They hustled around the corner and found the building Watkins had cannonballed through. It appeared to be the remains of an old brick garage, so decrepit that mortar and bricks were falling out everywhere. Watkins had shaken a few more bricks loose with his escape attempt.

Someone had nailed dilapidated sections of plywood over the areas where the bricks had completely fallen out. Rotting wooden double-garage doors blocked the entrance. At one time they had been red, but now the remaining paint reminded Shaw of a big, falling-apart scab. The old doors were nailed and braced shut, but both Shaw and Mason clearly heard sounds of pain emanating from inside.

Shaw stepped back to see if there was an obvious way into the structure. Mason stepped forward and ripped a section of the old door off on the first try.

Shaw peered inside. He saw nothing, but heard soft grunts. The kind that come from fighting off intense pain.

They entered the dark, musty interior, stepping over rubble and trash. A good section of the roof had fallen in on Watkins. Shaw could see that the Blue-Top manager had broken at least one leg, since the closer leg jutted out from under the big man at an impossible angle. He hoped Watkins had broken both.

There was just enough light to see Ellard lying in a pile, much of which consisted of him.

Shaw wanted to make sure Ellard didn't have a gun in his pocket, so he and Mason pulled off enough debris to ask him.

Watkins began cursing the cops in a particularly vile way. Shaw tried to ignore it, but he could see that it wasn't making Mason very happy.

Shaw yelled, "You got any more guns on you, Ellard?"

"Fuck you."

"The hell with him," said Shaw.

He reached under the rubble and found Watkins's right hand, just managed to fit one cuff around the huge wrist, pulled Watkins right arm out of the rubble and cuffed him to the remains of a pipe jutting out of the wall.

"Screw it. Let him lay there."

They called the precinct and asked for assistance, then sat on the curb waiting. It took five cops and two EMS workers to free Watkins from the rubble and roll him onto a stretcher. Mason and Shaw did not help. But Shaw did stay on it until he conferred with the assistant district attorney who caught the case. Shaw wanted to make sure that Ellard Watkins was on his way back to prison, broken leg and all. It didn't take much convincing. Shaw knew felons who shoot at cops— even cops like Shaw and Mason—don't get out on bail.

30

While Shaw and Mason tracked down Ellard Watkins, Tony Impelliteri and James Sperling were parked outside Afro Lady beauty salon trying to figure out their next move.

Impelliteri asked Sperling, "So how we gonna get in there and find out what's up? You need a haircut?"

"No."

"How about a bikini wax?"

"No, I hate that waxing. I just shave."

"Hey, the Sperl cracks a joke. You comin' around, James?"

"Maybe."

Sperling settled into the front seat, seeming to fold up his painfully thin body for an extended wait.

Sperling's button-down appearance and quiet demeanor made Impelliteri think he might be a prude, which was all the incentive Impelliteri needed.

"So what do you think, James, do most black women prefer to wax or shave their private areas?"

"I haven't really given it much thought."

"Well, thinking about it now, what do you think. I would imagine kinky hair is harder to wax."

"I wouldn't know."

"Well, I tell you one thing. Waxing pussy is a job I think I could do pretty well."

"Well, Impelliteri, tell you what. Maybe this could provide a reason for you to go into Afro Lady and apply for a job."

"Nah, I got that covered." Impelliteri checked his watch. "Shouldn't be too long. I reached out a little while back for someone I know to meet me here."

"Who'd you ask? Margo?"

"Ha-ha. She's probably been eighty-sixed from there already."

"I would think Margo would be very appreciative of Afro Lady's services."

"Yeah, but how much of their clientele would appreciate her act? And I didn't think you took much notice of the beauty shop services Margo might need."

"I notice what there is to notice. How come Margo knew so much about the Chief of Detectives?"

"Who said she did?"

"Nobody. Nobody had to. And nobody had to say anything about why a cop attached to a homicide squad knows a drug dealer either. But she did and you do, so what's the deal?"

"What do you mean?"

"Why do I have the feeling Margo is a cop?"

For once, Impelliteri had nothing to say, which was answer enough for Sperling.

"Interesting," said Sperling.

"You're pretty good, James. You figured that shit out in one shot. Guys out there have been gettin' burned by Margo for years and they haven't nailed her yet." Impelliteri pointed to Sperling's head. "Damn, James, you don't say much but you got some shit going on up there, don't you? Yeah, Margo is a cop. Deep, deep fucking undercover cop. I'm not supposed to know about it. Neither are you. I just found out by luck."

"What's her story?"

"Her name used to be Martin Hernandez. He and I went through the police academy together. I just knew him pretty well because he was in my unit. No biggie. Then about four years ago, I run into this Margo character. The Kilo Queen. Had to do with a shooting. A drug hit. Margo was just a person who might have information. So I'm doing this interview and I get that feeling, you know, that I know this person. And I'm sittin' there trying to figure out how the hell do I know this fucking freak. Underneath all the hormones and makeup and shit, she's still Martin Hernandez, but for the life of me I can't figure it out."

"She never changed the plumbing I'll bet."

"No. She's a chick with a dick all right. Anyhow, I'm looking at her sideways, which ain't an unusual reaction to her and, bang, it just fuckin' hit me."

"You recognized her."

"Yeah. The voice, something she said. The minute I got it, she saw that I got it. We weren't in any immediately threatening situation, I mean it wasn't like a buy-and-bust deal or anything, but it was obvious the people around her didn't have the slightest fuckin' idea who she really was."

"And for once you kept your mouth shut."

"What do you mean for once?"

"Well, I suppose there might have been other occasions."

"Fuck you. Anyhow, I ran her down about a week later. I gave the bitch hell. I mean I really played it up and, believe me, you can't fuck around with Margo too much, she'll shoot you. But she was grateful that I didn't bust her cover, so she filled me in. Turns out, dig this, they took the guy right out of the police academy. They must have known he was on the fence way back then. They never assigned him to a precinct. Put him undercover right away. The guy has never worked a day in uniform. I bet only a handful of people on our side know Margo is a cop. She's busted a lot of guys and none of 'em ever suspected."

"Interesting."

"Yeah. Not many like that out there. She and I get

along. We help each other out. Margo's a good person to know."

A police squad car pulled up and a black woman stepped out of the passenger's side, ducked down to window level, and made sure the it was Impelliteri sitting in the car. Only then did she turn and wave off her ride. As the squad car pulled away she sashayed over to Impelliteri's car. She had a sexy Tina Turner sway in her walk and wry smile that revealed gleaming, white teeth. She wore ankle boots, black jeans, a white knit top that showed off her trim figure, and a New York Mets baseball cap. Her hair was tied up in a ponytail and the ponytail had been pulled through the adjustable band on her hat. Over her shoulder hung a handbag that held her police ID and gun.

She leaned down to Impelliteri's window level and said, "So what kinda trouble you gettin' me into now, bad boy."

"Rita! Get in the car."

By the time she slid into the backseat of their car, Sperling had no doubt that the woman knew exactly how to handle herself and men.

Impelliteri introduced them. "James Sperling, this is Detective Rita Easton. Easton from East New York. One of our best and a close personal friend of mine."

She shook Sperling's outstretched hand and told him, "Emphasis on friend, James. Forget that close and personal part. Detective Impelliteri and I are strictly friends."

"But the best of friends, right, Rita?"

"Oh, of course. Nothing less. So what can I do for you two in exchange for a complete fashion makeover?"

"Come on, Rita, you don't want to mess with your gorgeous looks. Your skin, your hair, everything is already perfect. How about a manicure? Maybe a bikini wax?"

"Gimme the damn hundred dollars you promised, Anthony. I want to see how far a hundred dollars goes in Afro Lady. And tell me what you want."

Impelliteri told her. She went in. An hour later, she came out. The hundred stayed.

This time the baseball cap hung from the strap of her handbag. Her hair had been cut and styled. Her nails gleamed with a polish that seemed to match a fresh application of lipstick.

Impelliteri didn't waste too much time on compliments.

"You look great, Rita, what'd you find out?"

"That's it? I look great. She completely redid my hair, manicure, pedicure—"

"Bikini wax?"

"Shut up."

"Yeah, yeah. Fabulous. What'd you find out?"

Sperling took the time to look and said, "Rita, it's very nice. Absolutely complements the shape of your face. And the texture is lovely. Very soft and inviting."

Rita punched Impelliteri's shoulder and said, "Listen to your partner and take a lesson."

"Hey, he's a fag, what can I tell you. Was she in there, honey? This Milly babe."

"No. She works there, but she's not working today."

"What?"

"You heard me."

"And you spent all this time in there spending my hundred dollars?"

"You only wish it was your hundred. Now be quiet and let me talk. I gotta get back. It's better she wasn't there. Girls love to talk behind other people's backs. Milly has problems. Crack problems. That's why she's in and out. But the owner won't fire her because of who her brother is."

"Right."

"But you don't need to worry about Milly, anyhow. They say the brother hardly ever comes around there."

"Shit."

"The one you want to find is Reggie's girlfriend."

"I'll take that."

"Where do we find her?" asked Sperling.

"The Bronx. She only came in here once and didn't like it. She's Hispanic. Name is Angie. Lives in Mott Haven, the Bronx. A hundred fortieth street. Somewhere around in there."

"Oh, that's good. I got a first name and a street somewhere around the Bronx."

"So? You lazy? You can't find him with that? You want me to do everything for you?"

"What else you got? Tell me you got something else."

"Yeah. Be nice."

"Anything for you, Rita."

"That's better."

" 'Cept another hundred."

"*Quelle surprise.* All right, listen up. Reggie Whack drives a Jeep Grand Cherokee. It's green. He also sees a girl named Darleece at the projects over in Fort Greene." She turned to Sperling. "Green Jeep. Fort Greene. See how I make it easy for him?"

Sperling smiled.

Rita continued. "Reggie and Darleece have a baby together."

"Ah, right," said Impelliteri. "His baby-momma."

"One of 'em, anyhow."

"The project in Fort Greene. What's that? The Walt Whitman Houses?" asked Impelliteri.

"Yeah, that's it."

"Darleece?"

"Right."

"How do you spell that, Rita?"

"Who knows? And, last but not least, our dog boy Reggie has another woman named Tyeesha in Flatbush."

"Flatbush?"

"That's all I got on Tyeesha."

"How many kids has she got?"

"I don't know. Don't start with your racist bullshit, Anthony."

"Racist? I wish once in a goddamn while these mongrel dogs would come up with something new. Every fuckin' one of 'em has five or six women, all popping out bastards, in every shithole in New York. Now I gotta drive all the fuck over Brooklyn and the Bronx to find out where this death-dealing cocksucker is parking his dick tonight?"

Rita had a warning note in her voice. "Anthony."

Impelliteri turned to Sperling, "And see, this is all racist, James. I'm a fucking racist because I think this guy is a murderous, death-dealing dog that should be eliminated from the face of the earth, along with all his fucking, fatherless children before they turn into death-dealing cocksuckers, too."

"My, my, aren't we in a good mood."

Impelliteri smiled and said, "Rita, you are one of the most beautiful women in the world and someone could spend a million dollars on you in that beauty parlor and you'd still come out lookin' like two million. And I know you'll forgive my outburst, but you know and I know that every fucking word of it is true."

She shook her head. A rueful smile passed quickly, but Rita would not comment further except to say, "You take care of yourself, Anthony. You too, James. The one thing I will say is you better watch out for this guy. By the way those girls talked in there, you better believe he didn't get his name for no reason. Reggie Whack is a killer. You know the reputation of this Blue-Tops gang, Anthony, and this guy is one of their worst. So you do what you gotta do, but just take care. Find one of those girls, you'll find him. I gotta go. Gimme a ride back to the precinct, will you."

Impelliteri fired up the Caprice.

"You got it."

"And drive like a human being, Anthony." Rita primped a bit. "I don't want to mess up my new do."

Reggie Whack's green Jeep Cherokee wasn't parked near either of his girlfriends. It sat double-parked outside a Chino-Latino restaurant on lower Broadway near Houston Street in Manhattan.

Archie Reynolds had called in the enforcer his Dominican supplier provided on a freelance basis, Carmen Sanchez.

Carmen Sanchez hadn't even bothered to double-park. He drove his 1,000-cc motorcycle right up on the sidewalk and dropped it in front of the restaurant doorway. He couldn't care less that passersby had to walk around it.

The maître d' saw Sanchez leave the bike in front of his restaurant, right on the crowded street, nearly blocking his front door. But when Sanchez entered, the maître d' took one look at Sanchez and decided to keep his mouth shut. It wasn't that Sanchez was physically imposing. He was short, with the bandy-legged body of an Amazon Indian. It was simply the way Sanchez looked at the maître d'—with crazy eyes that said, give me one reason to hurt you. Sanchez looked as if he lived to kill and maim.

Sanchez sat at a window table with Archie Reynolds and Reggie Whack. He shoved beans and fried pork into his mouth, looking at Archie Reynolds with his hooded, menacing eyes. Sanchez nodded every so often at the words coming out of Archie's mouth, but barely bothered to listen. Normal, clearly spoken English generally eluded him. Archie's ghetto-speak meant almost nothing to him.

Archie and Reggie sipped Dos Equis beers while Sanchez ate. They had finished their meals. Sanchez chewed his way through his second helping.

Sanchez shoveled and swallowed. Archie talked and sipped.

As far as Sanchez was concerned, Archie talked too much. Archie took pride in his plan. Sanchez did not need a plan. Archie enjoyed the anticipation. Sanchez hardly thought about it before or after. He used a very simple method. He drove his cycle up to his victim—on a sidewalk, next to a car window, in the middle of the street. It didn't much matter. He pulled out a weapon: gun, machine pistol, shotgun. That didn't much matter, either. He pulled the trigger until he was absolutely sure the victim had died.

Sanchez wore a full-cycle helmet so nobody ever got a good look at him. He drove his motorcycle very fast, so nobody ever caught him. And every few weeks he changed bikes.

Sanchez had killed so many victims he'd lost count. When too many people were looking for him, he would simply leave for home in the Dominican Republic until it quieted down. Then he would come back and kill again.

So while Archie described Rachman Abdul X and where he lived and how the MS-2 operation ran and what he wanted to do to the Muslims, Sanchez ate and occasionally nodded, but without listening.

After he washed down his last mouthful, Sanchez wiped the pork grease from his lips and said, "So, Poppy, jus' show me the ones, okay. I take care of it."

"Aaaright, but I want to kill the burly motherfucker myself."

"So kill him. Fuck it."

"I'll have the other things all set. You just shoot 'em

up. Set 'em off. Then take care of the assholes on the street."

"Yeah, yeah, okay. *A qué hora?*"

"My source tell me he usually gets home about one o'clock. We meet in front of his house at midnight." Archie slid an address to Sanchez. "I meet you there with everything we need."

"Midnight?"

"Yes," said Archie. "*Dos horas* from now, amigo."

Sanchez frowned. "The information is good?"

"Hey, people owe me this information. They give me wrong fucking information, they gonna be dead. Lucky they ain't dead already, all this bullshit unleashed. That's the place."

"Why we wait so long? Go where he at now."

Archie checked his watch. Almost ten o'clock.

"No, no. Got to be at his place. Got to do the other shit, too. You can wait. Hey, I ain't had any good sleep for four fucking days. Motherfuckers burnin' up my headquarters. Police doggin' everybody. I can't go home. I been duckin' and hidin', movin' around. Shit, man, I got all kinds a shit to do before I meet you. Ain't gonna do us no good to get there if he ain't home, anyhow. We do this the way I want, we do it all in one night.

"Don't worry about it. We get busy, we do it all, we don't have to be draggin' this out. Go see a movie or somethin', Sanchez. Relax. Have some more beer."

Archie dropped a fifty-dollar bill on the table. "I'll see you over there."

Sanchez bobbed his head up and down once. He watched Archie and Reggie leave the restaurant. He looked at his watch. He had no problem killing human beings, but it annoyed him that he had to kill two hours.

*   *   *

When Loyd Shaw and Orestes Mason returned to the seven-three after processing Ellard Watkins, it was nearly eleven o'clock. Tony Impelliteri and James Sperling sat at their desks peering through printouts listing hundreds of parking tickets. The two teams had been working steadily almost eleven hours. Walter Wang had started right after they had eaten dinner on Monday. He had been at it almost thirty hours.

Walter continued sending bursts of keystrokes into his CPU, staring at the screen, watching for information to flow back to him, but he looked as if he were reaching the end of his endurance.

The small office smelled of cold pepperoni pizza and stale cigarettes.

Impelliteri sipped a bottle of Budweiser and added more cigarette smoke to the enclosed room.

Shaw picked up a warm beer from a six-pack on Impelliteri's desk and bummed a cigarette.

Impelliteri handed Shaw his pack without looking up from his printout.

"We almost got it," he said.

"Got what?" Shaw asked.

"A location for Reggie Whack. We found out he drives a green Jeep Cherokee. Walter the Wizard located the goddamn plate number."

"How'd you do that?"

"Did a search for Wilsons and Jeeps."

"You can do that?"

Walter chimed in, "*I* can do that."

Impelliteri said, "You have no fucking idea how many Wilsons with Jeeps there are in New York City."

"But only one registered to Mildred Wilson," said Sperling.

"Who's that?" Mason asked.

"Reggie's mongrel sister, Milly," Impelliteri answered.

"So what's that get you?"

"Not much, but if we match the plate number with locations of his girlfriends, we got a shot."

"You looking at parking tickets?" asked Mason.

"Yep. We got two locations. One in Fort Greene, the other in Mott Haven. Walter ran down every parking ticket issued in the last month in those two areas."

"How many is that?" asked Mason

"Not that many. Couple hundred. Nobody in those fucking neighborhoods pays 'em anyhow." Impelliteri straightened up. "Bingo, we have a match. How's this: one hundred forty-third street, Bronx. That's near the spic bitch he's fucking, right?"

"You mean Hispanic woman he's having sexual intercourse with outside of marriage?" asked Sperling.

"Whatever. Look, license number XVR six seven nine. Green Jeep Cherokee. Registered to Mildred Wilson. Two parking tickets on that street. We got you Reggie, you fucking, mongrel, n-word dog."

Mason asked, "That's where he shacks up with his girlfriend?"

Impelliteri ran his finger along the small type giving the details on the parking tickets.

"Yeah, look. Two tickets in the last ten days. Both of them on the same street. Both of them issued between eight and eight-thirty in the morning. Right when they come by giving out tickets for alternate-side parking violations. Fucker is too lazy to get up and move his car."

Sperling looked up from his printout.

"I've got a ticket for the same vehicle near those Fort Greene projects."

"No shit. What time?"

"Says ten A.M. It's for parking in a restricted area."

"Probably a fire hydrant, the fuck. Reggie's a busy man. He's gonna be in one of those two places. I got a feeling about this one. He's fucking the Bronx piece of ass one night, his baby-momma Darleece the next. Dog boy is running to safe places outside the hood to lay his head down. Detective Sperling and I be making an early morning wake-up call."

"Good. Good work. Anything else going?" asked Shaw.

"Yeah, we got something set up. We'll be pulling in mutts, right after we get this Reggie fuck. You guys have any luck?"

Mason spoke up.

"We got Ellard Watkins a few hours ago."

"No shit. Did you shoot him?"

"No," answered Mason. "Detective Shaw tried like hell, but he ran out his house. He tried to jump over onto a roof and went through it."

"Went through it?"

"Like a cannonball dropped from way high up."

"Shit! Great. Did he kill his fat ass?"

"Not yet," Shaw said, "But he's busted up enough so that he won't be a problem for quite a while. Won't even be a problem in whatever prison they send him to for quite a while."

Shaw checked his watch. Eleven-twenty. It was time to get over to New Lots Apartments and see Rachman. He figured that Leon Bloom had put the word in by now and wanted to see what he could get out of Rachman about Archie.

"Walter, you find out anything more about Archie Reynolds?"

Wang rubbed his eyes and told him, "All I got is his arrest records and an address his parole report lists in Brownsville, but I doubt you'll find him there. That's it. No driver's license, no credit card records, no vehicle registration. I got calls into the Career Criminal Identification Unit on him to see if they can give us a lead, but I haven't heard back yet. I also got a call into an FBI guy I know who might have access to information we don't. Haven't heard back from him either. This gang isn't the target of any task force or DEA investigations I can find. I checked outside records in six states. So far nothing."

Impelliteri spoke up.

"I talked to a guy I know in Gangs earlier this afternoon when we were running around."

"He know anything?"

"Nothing that would help us find him. But this guy got pretty serious when I brought up this Archie dude's name."

"How so?"

"Said nobody knows a whole lot about him. Said he doesn't live in the hood. Moves in and out. Not one of the regular homeboy types. Born and raised here. Knows everybody, but seems like he's moved up and on. Comes in to tend to business, then goes back out. But every fuckin' body in this hood is afraid of the dude."

"Why's that?" asked Mason.

"Cuz the guy shoots first and asks questions later. He has no compunction about taking anybody out. On his side. On the other side. He gets suspicious. He loses a shipment. Some money is missing. Anything. Any reason. He just kills everybody involved. Or has 'em killed. I can't exactly explain everything he was saying, but it's like Archie Reynolds runs things like an outsider. I don't know. Dangerous dude. If you get a line on him, my advice is just shoot him down the second you see him. Or chances are you'll be the one going down first."

Shaw didn't comment on Impelliteri's information. He simply took it in and asked Wang, "Anything on this enforcer, Sanchez?"

"I just started him. If he's Dominican, I figure he goes in and out of the country a lot. Most of those guys go home and hide out when things get hot. So I'm working on visas and passports and customs reports."

"And what about Melvin Melly Mel or whatever the hell his name is?"

Wang stored something in a computer file, sat back in his chair, rubbed his eyes, and turned to face the others.

"I was talking to some of the precinct detectives assigned to the drive-bys and the shooting over in New Lots. One of said them they had a lead on Melvin, so I'm concentrating on the others."

"Okay. That's smart. Concentrate on the others. Your plate is full with those guys. Maybe the precinct guys can do something for us."

"Yeah," said Impelliteri, "as soon as they assemble fifty fucking guys to surround him and take him in."

"Anthony, if they can get one that's one we don't have to worry about. Walter, stay with what you're doing. By the way, did you get to our fives?"

Walter's mouth actually dropped open.

"Okay, take it easy Walter. Just reminding you. Do 'em when you can. Don't let 'em pile up. Here's some notes on what Mason and I did today. I left out pulling a gun on a civilian, firing without filing reports, illegal monitoring of cellular phone transmissions, entering a premise without probable cause, and a few other no-nos."

Impelliteri laughed. "Sounds good."

Shaw said, "And today ain't even over. Walter, just write 'em up from what you got there. You're doing great. Why don't you finish whatever you're doing and go home. Grab a few hours sleep and some clothes and get back by around eight tomorrow morning. And you don't have to wear a suit, you know. Wear something you'll be comfortable in."

"I'm comfortable."

"Suit yourself," said Impelliteri.

Shaw looked at Walter. There was no reaction.

"Suit yourself. Get it? Suit. Yourself."

"Oh. Yeah."

"Hey, what am I thinking? You hardly speak English."

"Fuck you, Impelliteri."

"Shaw, did you teach him both words all at once, you know, fuck you, or first fuck then you?"

Walter spluttered, "No asshole, your momma taught me."

Impelliteri laughed. "Whoa, Kung Fu. Way to go, you sound like a—"

"Watch it," said Mason.

"Homeboy. I was gonna say homeboy, Mason, I swear."

Mason dismissed Impelliteri with a wave and leaned back in his chair, folded his arms across his ample stomach, and closed his eyes. Sperling sat expressionless, legs crossed, simply waiting. Even Impelliteri gave it up, leaned back in his chair, and propped his feet on his desk.

Shaw sat at his desk checking over how he felt. Lousy. The cigarettes didn't help. The McDonald's meal and Chinese food had congealed in his stomach. He had that washed-out feeling that sets in after the rage and adrenaline are gone.

Shaw thought about how hard he had tried to shoot Weight Watkins. How much he had *wanted* to shoot him after Watkins shot at them with that goddamn shotgun. Hadn't even thought about not shooting him. But you'd have spent the rest of your life thinking about it, seeing the bullet wounds in his big dark body if you'd hit him, though, wouldn't you? he thought.

Shaw thought about shooting Archie Reynolds on sight. He didn't want to live with that image either.

Shaw suddenly had an urge for a shot of whiskey to go with his beer. He wanted to feel the energy the alcohol could give as well as the numbing insulation from all the mayhem and chaos gathering around him.

"Is there anything to drink around here?"

Everyone looked at Shaw as if he had asked a stupid question.

"Anybody think to buy a bottle for our office?"

Walter said, "Are you nuts? Liquor isn't allowed in the precinct."

Shaw looked at Wang as if he were from Mars. Impelliteri dropped his feet and stared at Wang. Mason shook his head at Wang's comment. Even Sperling looked perplexed.

Shaw said, "Not allowed? Not allowed? Hey, *we're* not allowed in this fucking precinct, the shit we're pulling off."

Impelliteri started laughing. Then Mason and Shaw. The laughter even infected Sperling.

In about ten seconds, none of them could stop. In one crystal clear moment it hit them. The exhilaration of it, the absurdity, the danger, the fatigue, the freedom of it. They laughed until tears rolled. Wang started laughing, not really knowing why since the joke seemed to be on him. The laughter wore them out and lifted them up at the same time. It felt good. Shaw enjoyed it, both the laughing and the sharing of it.

The wave passed, finally. Mason wiped his eyes and settled into himself with a few last chuckles.

"Shit, fuck," said Impelliteri. "Don't take it seriously Fu Manchu, we do it because we love you."

"Whatever."

Impelliteri asked, "So what's next, Shaw?"

"I'm going to go over and have a word with the head Muslim guy. He knows more about Archie Reynolds than we do. I want his help."

"Good fucking luck."

"No, I think he might be in the mood to cooperate. I put a little pressure on his boss earlier today. Maybe he'll listen."

"Who? The Muslims or the boss?" Mason asked.

"Both."

"You want some company?" asked Impelliteri.

"Sure."

Impelliteri turned to Sperling. "You want to come with us or go sleep?"

Sperling gave a slight tip of the head and said, "All right. I want to see the place causing all this trouble."

Shaw mustered up what energy he had left and stood up.

"Let's go."

Shaw pointed to the papers and files scattered over the desks and said, "Walter, before you go, just make sure nothing is laying out here that somebody walking by shouldn't see. Contacts you want kept private. Whatever."

Walter was glued to the screen again, but he nodded and said, "Okay. Don't worry."

They all left the office and headed for their cars.

Shaw led the way over to New Lots Apartments.

32

By ten-thirty, Archie Reynolds and Reggie Whack were back in Brownsville, carefully cruising the streets, avoiding the Muslims, trying to make contact with their boys.

At first, Archie thought there had to be something wrong with his cell phone.

"Reggie, where the fuck is everybody? Nobody's answering their beeps."

"Mo, most of the guys is, is in New Lots getting sh, sh, shit together. Who you beepin'?"

Archie pointed to a pay phone on the wall outside a small grocery on Bergen Street.

"Pull over to that phone and call my number. See if this fuckin' thing is working."

Reggie double-parked. He punched in the numbers, turned to the Jeep to watch if Archie's cell phone rang. He saw Archie put the phone to his head and heard Archie's frustrated voice.

"Yeah, okay. Fuck it."

Reggie hopped back into the driver's seat.

"Who, who, who'd you beep, man?"

"Weight, Melly Mel, then Big Marvin and Toussant. I just need a couple of motherfuckers. Let the rest keep working."

"Maybe they b, b, busy, man."

"Aaaright, fuck it. Come on.

"Drive over to that little park on Stone. Then the pizza place on Linden. Stay clear of those Muslim motherfuckers around New Lots. Get your piece in your lap. Be ready to shoot anybody gives us any shit. I'll just have to do a little recruiting."

"For what?"

"For some bullshit I want to create over here by the project while we be doin' our thing, man. Don't worry about it. Fuckin' kids aroun' here want to make some money, the Ar man be happy to provide the opportunity. You got those pieces we took out from my house?"

"In the b, b, back there, under the spare."

"Das all I need, brother. Be funny watchin' these big bad Muslim boys shooting some ten-, eleven-year-old."

Loyd Shaw and his men found Rachman X out near the New Lots Apartments' main gate. Rachman didn't appear particularly happy to see Shaw, much less Shaw with Mason, Impelliteri, and Sperling.

Anthony Impelliteri and James Sperling stayed just long enough to see that Shaw wasn't attempting a show of force. They drifted off to have a look around.

Orestes Mason stood near Shaw, exuding his usual calming influence.

"Mr. Rachman," Shaw said, trying to sound friendly, "How are you tonight?"

"Fine."

"Any problems today?"

"Nothing unusual."

"Long day."

"I usually leave at midnight."

"Glad I caught you. I have some good news for you."

"What's that?"

"We picked up one of the Blue-Tops managers, Ellard Watkins."

"Good."

"He won't be bothering you or anybody else for a long time."

"Good."

"We've got a line on the last Blue-Top manager and the last of the enforcers. I wouldn't be surprised if we don't get as least one of them in the next day or two."

"Uh-huh."

"Maybe a few of the street-level guys, too."

"You want to get them, put your badge on and come into these buildings with us."

"Is that where they are?"

"They're still selling in there."

"I'll be happy to join you for the cleanup. Soon as I get the main guy. He's the one I want. Archie Reynolds."

Rachman just nodded his head.

Shaw continued. "Detective Mason here and I would like to find him."

Rachman looked at Mason, back at Shaw, but didn't offer any comment.

"So I was wondering, have you thought over our conversation earlier? Have you come up with anything that might be of help?"

Rachman frowned. They both knew Shaw had put the screws to Bloom. And they both knew Shaw would do the same to Rachman if he didn't cooperate.

"Well?" asked Shaw.

Rachman appeared to be making a decision. Shaw waited.

Finally, Rachman said, "What are you doing right now?"

"Now? Talking to you. You're what I'm doing. I'm not doing anything else. Don't have anything else that's more important than you, Mr. Rachman."

"I have to go home, now. Go home and see my children and my women. Come with me. We can talk there and the person who can help you lives nearby."

"Great. Hang on a just a second. Let me find out where my other guys are."

Shaw pulled out the radio which had been sagging in his rear pants pocket and called out for Impelliteri and Sperling. Impelliteri's voice came back through the static.

"Yo."

"A, we're leaving now. You staying?"

"Yeah. Me and S want to look around. Probably catch a couple hours sleep back at the place, then go out dog hunting."

"See you."

Impelliteri turned down his radio and looked for Sperling, spotting him crouched down looking at various bullet holes scarring The Pit.

Impelliteri told Sperling, "Shaw and Mason are taking off. Jeezus, look at the size of these fuckin' holes."

Sperling said, "AK-forty-seven, even the compact rounds, are about the size of half your little finger. That's a lot of steel. Traveling at over two thousand feet per second, makes a devastating impact. Ever see a body hit by one of those bullets?"

"No."

"They can easily take the entire top of your skull off. Put a hole in you the size of a fist."

"No shit."

Sperling stood in The Pit, examining the bullet holes that seemed to be everywhere. Then he looked up, shifting his gaze from the top floor of Building A to the top floor of Building D.

"They had two shooters. One on each side."

"Yeah?"

Sperling muttered to himself, "One one thousand."

"What?"

"One one thousand," Sperling repeated. "That's a second. Those assault rifles fire a little over ten rounds per second.

"Fuck of a lot of firepower. How many in a clip?"

"Thirty-two."

"Christ. Fuckers probably had no idea the damage they could do."

Sperling shook his head. "No. No way. They were just pointing and pulling the trigger. Look at these spread out patterns. Just doing what they've seen on TV and the movies a million times. No idea of what it really means."

Impelliteri started counting to himself. "One one thousand, two one thousand, three one thousand. Thirty-two fucking rounds."

Sperling and Impelliteri exchanged looks.

"Let's get the fuck out of here, James."

33

Loyd Shaw drove the Caprice, following closely behind Rachman X's battered Ford LTD, not paying much attention to where they were headed. They drove north out of Brownsville to Bushwick Avenue and turned west. After about five minutes, they arrived in Rachman's neighborhood.

As with most New York detectives, Shaw was accustomed to entering neighborhoods where he felt as if he'd arrived in another country. Chinese, Dominican, Indian, Russian, Venezuelan—every ethnic group had their own neighborhood. But this was one neighborhood he'd never been to. He imagined that if he'd ever been to a Third World Muslim country, he would have said that's where he'd landed.

A one-story mosque dominated the enclave. It was a completely nondescript, concrete-block building except for the rounded roof and the Islamic crescent moon symbol topping it. A sign in Arabic script over the doorway named the place. Most of the buildings in the surrounding two-block area had been painted a dark brown with white trim, thus designating them as part of the same Muslim community.

Black men dressed much like the ones guarding the perimeter of New Lots Apartments patrolled the streets in teams of two. Shaw saw one woman walking into an apartment building covered from head to ankle in long, flowing garb, except for a small opening that revealed her eyes.

Rachman and his people had taken over their own

small chunk of New York. It was disorienting and yet encouraging at the same time.

Rachman's apartment was located two buildings south of the mosque. A fire hydrant had created enough open space amidst the parked cars in front of Rachman's building so that he could drive his car over the curb and park it in the narrow opening between two apartment buildings. Shaw followed his lead and parked behind him, noting how Rachman had carved out his own parking area in the crowded neighborhood.

Rachman walked back to the Caprice and asked that Mason stay outside while he and Shaw talked inside.

Mason said, "No problem," folded his arms over his stomach, lay back against his headrest, and closed his eyes.

Shaw followed Rachman into a three-story apartment building, up the stairs to the second floor. After just a few moments inside the building, he had the sense that it was filled with women and children. There was a welcoming scent of curry-flavored cooking in the air mixed with a tinge of used diapers. Despite the foreign feel to the people and place, typically American kid's stuff scattered the hallways; battered big-wheel tricycles, volleyballs, baby carriages, strollers.

Inside the building it seemed quiet and restless at the same time. It was time for sleep, but Shaw had the feeling that nobody here rested completely.

Rachman unlocked his front door. It took a bit of time to turn all the keys. When they entered, a small woman dressed in fundamentalist garb stood in the narrow hallway waiting for Rachman. When she saw a white man with Rachman, a stranger, she bowed her head, not out of respect, but to hide her face.

Rachman told her, "I'll be up for a while. How are the children?"

"Fine, dear."

"Everyone asleep?"

"Yes."

"Aleya and Darsel?"

"They're in the kitchen."

"Tell them I'll see them later."

"They have food for you."

"Later."

The woman headed off toward the back of the apartment, leaving the men to their business. Rachman hadn't bothered to introduce Shaw or explain his presence. Shaw followed him through a neat living room to a dining room area. Furnishings were sparse and simple. Everything appeared to be well tended and clean, the furniture protected by plastic covers.

Shaw asked Rachman how many kids he had.

"Fourteen," was the answer.

"Your wife must be made of iron."

"Wives. I have four wives."

Uh-huh. That made more sense, thought Shaw. Four into fourteen came out to be only 3.5 kids per woman. He felt like saying, Gee, I didn't know you could have more than one wife, but kept his mouth shut.

Shaw said, "You must be a busy man."

"Have a seat," was Rachman's response.

They sat at his dining-room table. The moment of slight familiarity had passed.

"Tell me what you want."

Shaw got right to it.

"I want Archie Reynolds. And I want as many of the punks that work for him as I can get. I have a list of names. I need locations."

Shaw pulled out his list of Blue-Tops gang-bangers.

"I need to know where I can find these guys, starting with Archie Reynolds. Where they sleep. Where they buy their groceries. Where they hang out. Any place I can find them."

Rachman picked up the list and looked it over. As he read the other names he started talking about Archie Reynolds.

"Archie Reynolds does not live among those he exploits. He lives in Saddle Brook, New Jersey. The name of the street is Oak or Maple. I forget exactly. The person I'm going to send you to will give you his exact address, but I don't believe it will help you much. Archie won't go to his home. Not now. Not until this is over. We've heard he's been on our streets recently, but nobody has actually seen him. Just before you arrived at New Lots, we got word he was around. I sent people out looking for him. Maybe we'll get lucky, but I doubt it. He doesn't stay in one place for very long."

"Who's this man you want me to see?"

"Yousseff. Outside, two doors to the right. You'll want to stop over there after you leave me. He might be home. Might not be."

Rachman started writing an address in careful script on the bottom of the list Shaw had handed to him. Shaw watched the apartment number appear after he wrote the address. He thought maybe Bloom had come through for him. Or maybe the fact that they had put Ellard Watkins off the streets did it.

Either way, Shaw didn't care. Rachman was giving him access to information. Information gathered by black men. Former criminals. Men who knew the streets and had access to people Shaw and his men could never cultivate. Information meant everything. At that moment, Shaw felt as if he could win this one. And then they heard the explosion.

They both knew what it was. Loyd Shaw decided it probably sounded very much like the gasoline that had exploded in the Blue-Tops' body shop. But this time, the fire burned in the Muslims' mosque.

Rachman X jumped to his feet first. Shaw took a second to grab his list before he ran after him, then blew past Rachman and out the door when Rachman stopped to pull a shotgun out of his front closet.

As he took the stairs two at a time, Shaw had an image of black women in Muslim garb covering children with their bodies. This was the attack they had been told would come. This was what united them and bent them to the disciplines and dictates they followed. The holy war had become a self-fulfilling prophecy.

As Shaw banged open the lobby door, he heard the ripping sound of automatic-weapons fire and then the roar of a motorcycle engine. Even as he pulled out both his Glocks, he knew he was no match for machine pistols or assault rifles. He hunched over to make himself a smaller target and ran toward the burning mosque.

There was so much black smoke billowing out of the structure that Shaw couldn't see anything near the building, but he kept hearing gunfire and a motorcycle engine.

Shaw looked for Mason and saw him on the corner across from the mosque. Flames silhouetted Orestes Mason's big frame into one blocklike shape. Suddenly, the motorcycle roared louder and came barreling out of the flames right toward Mason.

Two of Rachman's gunmen chased the motorcyclist, firing handguns. Mason was in his path. It looked like Mason was going to either shoot the driver or get hit by the oncoming bike. Suddenly, the bike braked and whipped around facing the other direction. The driver, Sanchez, pulled out a machine pistol and fired off bursts at the Muslim guards chasing him. Mason aimed his Sig and carefully pulled off two shots. Sanchez twisted around and let a burst off at Mason, who was already diving down behind a parked car for cover.

Shaw raised his guns, ran toward the cycle, and started shooting at Sanchez with both Glocks. Shaw knew he'd have to be very lucky to hit the assassin nearly thirty yards away while running, but all he really wanted to do was make sure the shooter didn't turn and fire more rounds at Mason. Shaw kept firing until he nearly reached Mason.

Sanchez shoved the machine pistol into his leather jacket, slammed the bike into gear, and revved the engine. There was no one in between him and Shaw, so Shaw continued to fire.

Sanchez popped the clutch and screeched back toward the flames. The front wheel lifted, then dropped and he roared off. Shaw stopped shooting and suddenly from behind he heard a vicious series of pistol shots and an almost simultaneous shotgun blast. He turned and saw Rachman go down, a figure standing over him, pumping bullets into Rachman.

Mason, now behind Shaw, was up on one knee, already turning toward the man shooting into Rachman, aiming his gun.

Mason started shooting just as Shaw brought his Glocks around, pointed and pulled, but it was too late.

The murderer had already bolted between Rachman's apartment building and the one next to it.

Mason was up and running toward Rachman. Mason's first burst was very fast for a man his age and size, but Shaw quickly caught up to him. Mason knew Shaw's guns were almost empty. He yelled, "See to Rachman," and veered to their right.

Shaw made it to Rachman just as Mason reached the space between the two apartments where the shooter had disappeared.

Mason stayed back against the wall of the building, composing himself, then carefully turned into the space. Bullets immediately blasted into the brickwork near him. Mason ducked back, then leaned out and pulled off two shots.

Shaw dropped down next to Rachman, shoved one Glock into his waist, then used his free hand to jam a fresh clip into the other gun.

He bent over to see if Rachman was still breathing. Amazingly, he was. Rachman was down, bleeding, but undeniably alive. He suddenly growled with rage and pain. Rachman tried to sit up, grabbing for his shotgun, grunting again at the pain as he tried to breath, telling Shaw, "Archie. It was Archie Reynolds."

Shaw pushed him back down on the ground and said, "Don't move. Don't fucking move and don't fucking die."

Mason turned into the space between the buildings again and pulled off two more shots, then spun back as return fire hit around him.

Now Mason's gun was empty. He holstered it and reached for his backup. Shaw ran up behind Mason and yelled, "Rachman is still alive. Get an ambulance and backup."

Shaw pushed Mason down into a crouch, leaned over him, and squeezed off four shots into the area between the buildings. Then he broke out around Mason and ran forward to a place between the buildings where a jutting corner offered him cover.

Shaw's pupils had contracted from the gunfire, but he was still able to see a figure pop out about fifteen yards in front of him and run. He bolted out after him. It was Archie. He had a good lead on Shaw, but was within sight. Shaw didn't care if Archie turned and shot at him. He didn't care about anything. All he wanted to do was get close enough so that he could stop and steady himself and get one good shot at Archie. Shoot him down. Shoot him in the face or in the back. He didn't care.

Shaw knew he had almost a full clip so he pulled off another three shots, aiming wildly while he ran, trying to make Archie dodge and slow down, trying to think straight and make sure he had bullets left when he got closer.

Shaw didn't think any of his shots had hit the body moving in front of him, but he saw Archie duck, then trip and slide. He was down. He closed the distance between them, and a green Jeep parked on the street behind Rachman's building came into view.

Archie scrambled to his feet. Shaw fired once more, hoping to hit him or send him back down, as he kept running for him. Archie stumbled, trying to get his footing. Shaw still wasn't very close, but he stopped, gripped his Glock in two hands, tried to steady himself and squeezed shots until the Glock was empty.

Shaw was breathing too hard; Archie was moving too fast, but it looked like one of his shots connected. Archie ducked, banged into a wall, and went down. Shaw sprinted for Archie. Archie was already starting to get up. In one last desperate burst, Shaw lunged at Archie, grabbed for him, had his shoulder, gripped Archie's arm, but Archie spun and smacked the side of Shaw's head with the empty gun in his hand.

Shaw went down. Archie tore away from his grasp, just as Reggie Whack walked from behind the Jeep and started shooting slow, steady blasts from a 9-mm automatic.

Archie's blow actually saved Shaw. Reggie's shots went over Shaw's head as he fell back. Shaw hit the ground hard, but managed to roll away from Reggie's shots. Archie ran for the Jeep. Reggie stopped shooting until Archie made it out of the line of fire.

Shaw made it to the wall, twisted against it, reaching for his last magazine. He leaned out and fired at Reggie, who had been peering into the dark, trying to see Shaw. Reggie returned Shaw's fire, but scampered back.

Archie had jumped into the Jeep. He yelled out at Reggie, "Forget that motherfucker, we got to go do the rest. Come on."

Reggie jumped into the Jeep just as Archie floored the accelerator.

Shaw spent a moment, feeling around for blood on his body, but he knew he hadn't been hit. He checked the magazine in the Glock, got to his feet, and hustled back to where he had left Mason.

The street had quickly filled with black men, mostly Muslims, mostly bearded, wearing their skullcaps. All of them seemed to be armed. The fire raged at the mosque, bathing the area in a deadly, greasy firelight. Billows of acrid, black smoke produced by Archie's homemade napalm merged with the dark night sky. Sirens screamed in the distance.

Shaw knew that within minutes the area would be jammed with fire engines and other emergency vehicles. He yelled into his radio for all units to stop a green Jeep Cherokee, but there were way too many commands being broadcast for his shouts to get through clearly.

Mason and the Muslims clustered around Rachman. Rachman's blood had flooded the ground under him.

Shaw feared that the ambulance would never get to them quickly enough. Even if they had already dispatched an ambulance, it could get jammed behind the police vehicles and fire trucks rushing toward the scene.

Shaw yelled at the men nearest him to help with Rachman.

"Put him in my car. I'm a cop. Come on. We'll get him to a hospital. Come on, come on, don't let him bleed to death here. We can't wait for an ambulance. Come on, goddamnit. Get him off the fucking ground."

They wouldn't listen to Shaw. He grabbed one man by the arm and pulled him toward Rachman. He was about to get a fist in the face when Mason's big booming voiced broke through the chaos.

"Let's go!" he yelled, while he grabbed Rachman under the armpits and lifted the big man's torso off the ground.

The others could either fight for possession of Rachman or watch him be dragged away by Mason.

One more, "Let's go!" did it. The men grabbed for their leader, lifting an arm, a leg, some managed to get their hands under Rachman's bleeding body. Rachman sagged in their arms, grunted with pain and passed out.

Shaw scrambled ahead of them and pulled open the backdoor of his car. They slid Rachman onto the back seat on a thick smear of his own blood.

Shaw climbed behind the wheel and fired the engine, turned on his siren and flashers. Mason shouldered his way into the passenger seat and Shaw bulled his way out of there, heading down Bushwick Avenue as the first fire engine came into sight.

This is fucking crazy," Shaw yelled at Mason. "Fucking insane."

Orestes Mason answered with a grunt. Shaw glanced away from the streets hurtling past and looked at Mason, saw his face twisted with pain, his stomach and lap covered in blood.

"Mase. You're hit?"

"Yeah."

"Shit. Where?"

Shaw reached over to hold Mason's shoulder.

"My left side."

Mason pressed his right hand against the wound while bracing himself against the dashboard with the left.

The Caprice banged into a sewer top and Mason hissed in pain.

"Shit! How bad is it?"

"I don't know. I'm soaked in blood down to my drawers, and it hurts like a son of a bitch."

"What's the fastest way to Kings County?"

"Turn right on Nostrand up here, then left on New York."

"Who was it hit you? That prick on the motorcycle?"

"No. Idiot spraying bullets around like that. Damn rounds flying everywhere. No, it was that bastard Archie put a round in me when I leaned into that gangway to get a shot at him."

"Shit! Think you got a bullet in him?"

Mason shook his head no.

Shaw slammed his hand into the wheel. "Fuck!"

Mason said, "Rachman just kept saying, get Archie. Get Archie. That's all he kept saying to me when you went after him. Get Archie, get Archie. You hit him?"

Shaw answered, "I might have. I unloaded everything I had at him, but I was running, and he was running. I'd had to have been real lucky. He made it back to his car."

"I figured."

"Green Jeep Cherokee parked behind Rachman's."

"Reggie Whack."

"Yeah. Impelliteri got the car right. Guy came out blasting. I was empty. I had to drop back. Archie made it to the car and that was it."

Mason just shook his head. He had nothing more to say. Shaw turned around to take a quick look at Rachman X. He was still breathing, but in rasping gasps. Shaw reached behind and grabbed Rachman's shoulder. "Don't you die on me, goddamn it. Don't you fucking die, Rachman. We'll be there in two fucking minutes."

Rachman's eyes were closed. His clothes were soaked in blood.

"You fucking die on me I'll throw you right out in the gutter, goddamn it."

Shaw pitched the car into a turn too fast, bounced against a curb, straightened out, and fishtailed down the street. Mason growled at him, "Slow down, damn it. You'll kill us before we get there."

Shaw slowed down a little, but not for long. He told himself, screw slowing down. There weren't many cars on the street. Nothing to stop him. Shaw knew the only way he could stave off more death and pain now was with speed. Race ahead of it. Outrun the darkness pulling Rachman into death. Speed away from the pain filling Mason.

Shaw wanted doctors, now. Doctors and nurses and drugs and transfusions and help.

They screeched into the emergency room driveway with so much speed the Caprice almost slid through the wide swinging doors of the receiving area.

Shaw held his shield high and yelled and ordered, but the hospital personnel ignored him. The blood everywhere spoke louder than Shaw ever could.

The hospital personnel had both men out of the car, on stretchers, and into the ER in less than two minutes.

A team of doctors and nurses descended on Rachman, while a nurse and an orderly wheeled Mason into another section.

Shaw watched the doctors and nurses surround Rachman in a tightly choreographed assault. One nurse began scissoring off Rachman's bloody clothes. A doctor shoved a breathing tube down his throat, others pushed IV lines into his arms, wrapped pressure cuffs around his legs, plunged syringes into him, attached monitors; moving, pushing, shoving, cutting, bulling their way past all resistance, all the while yelling orders and responses at each other, and like Shaw, rushing, rushing as if only speed could keep them ahead of the death about to envelop Rachman.

There was nothing remotely gentle in their treatment. It was a fight, a battle, a maelstrom of medicine launched against the dirty, deadly little bullets that had blasted out of Archie Reynolds's gun and ripped into Rachman's body.

Shaw edged his way around the commotion to find Mason. His wounded partner sat on a bed in a corner of the ER set off by curtains. A nurse and an orderly were helping him out of his bloody clothes. Mason would not let them cut his clothes off. There wasn't a dry cleaning establishment in New York that could clean that much blood out of somebody's clothes, but Mason wasn't going to let anybody cut up his clothes.

Shaw took charge of Mason's belongings, rolling up his shirt, pants, and jacket, making sure nothing fell out of the pockets. He wrapped Mason's holster rig around the pile and jammed his guns tightly into their holsters.

At that moment, nobody knew about the shooting. But Shaw knew once the word went out, an avalanche of police brass and questions would descend on them. And Shaw did not want that to happen.

Taking charge of Mason's clothes and property was about all Shaw could do for his wounded partner. As they wheeled him out Shaw said, "Take it easy, Mase, don't worry," knowing that he sounded useless and inane.

At that moment, Mase looked every one of his fifty-odd years. His face had sagged and his rich brown skin color had turned ashy and dull. Everything seemed to have hit him all at once. For a moment, a dread feeling passed through Shaw. What if they couldn't stop the bleeding? What if Mason's heart gave out under the stress and shock? What the hell would he do if Mason died?

"Fuck it, fuck it," Shaw said out loud. Stop thinking about what could happen to Mason. Start thinking again about Archie Reynolds.

Shaw made his way back to his car. He stored Mason's property in the trunk, then started making calls. First, he roused Conklin and told him he had to suppress the usual investigation that would unfold as soon as the hospital reported Rachman's and Mason's gunshot wounds. Conklin said, "I'll take care of it," and hung up.

Then Shaw called his team. He used the cell phone

and the radio, calling, paging, broadcasting to them. He wanted the others. He wanted Impelliteri and Sperling and Wang. He wanted them in the hospital, with their guns. Now.

Loyd Shaw found the waiting room on the surgical floor and sat down to wait out word on his friend, Orestes Mason.

The minute he sat down in the quiet room, images of shotgun blasts and gunfire and burning mosques filled his head, interspersed with imagined visions of Mason and Rachman Abdul X laid out on operating-room tables bathed by surreal white light. Doctors slicing into them, poking around in bloody, torn-up flesh looking for bullets.

But it didn't take long before he became haunted by the specter of Archie Reynolds. He kept seeing the dark, slim form running ahead of him, feeling Archie's shoulder under his hand. He had actually had a hand on Archie. Had seen him. Had him, if only for brief moments, in his gun sight. Finally knew what Archie looked like, who he was. And Shaw wanted him. Wanted him back in his hands. He imagined grabbing Archie's throat, punching his face until his fist broke bones, punching him until his eyes rolled to the back of his head, then wrenching his arms around and slapping handcuffs on him so fast and so tight that Archie Reynolds would wake up screaming.

Just let me get the cuffs on him, thought Shaw. Let me get him before anyone stops me. Get him before he has a chance to shoot at me and I have to shoot back at him. Get Mason out of this hospital and Archie into a jail before Albert J. DeLuca pulls me off and tells me I fucked up and sends me to another kind of hell.

*   *   *

Anthony Impelliteri and James Sperling found Shaw in the surgical ward waiting room, sucking down acrid coffee, waiting on word about Mason and Rachman. Walter Wang was still on his way.

Shaw told them what had happened. Impelliteri started pacing around the room, muttering curses and threats about shooting Blue-Tops. Sperling shoved himself onto in a beat-up, food-stained chair and stared at nothing, saying nothing except, "I hate hospitals."

About ten minutes after they arrived, Shaw's cell phone rang. It was Justine Burton.

"Shaw?"

"Yes."

"I need to talk to you. I need you over here."

"Where?"

"My center."

"You're still there?"

"I came back. You said I could call you. I need to talk to you."

"What happened?"

"Please, all hell has broken loose, can you just come over here?"

"Look, one of my men has been shot, I—"

"What happened?"

"He's all right. He's in the hospital. Kings County. We're waiting."

"You're nearby. Can you come over here? Just for a few minutes."

Shaw told the others, "This shit doesn't end. Stay here until you get word on Mason. I should be back before he gets out of surgery."

Shaw saw the flashing lights surrounding Justine's center from three blocks away. He didn't allow himself to speculate about what had brought them. He parked outside the cordon of police and emergency vehicles, leaving his flasher blinking.

Outside, he saw a knot of uniformed cops and detectives checking bullet holes in the wall at the far end of the center.

As Shaw approached Justine's office, he saw two of the three detectives assigned to her sitting in the waiting area outside her office.

He asked one of them, "What happened?"

"It's fucked up. The neighborhood's been going nuts. Another drive-by went down across the street near the entrance to the complex. Random shootings. Somebody has been pegging bullets into this place all night long. Muslims are going nuts. Seems like everyone's going crazy."

"Anybody hit?"

"One lady in the dormitory section down at the end got shot in the arm. She isn't going to die from it, but it's a messy wound. Bunch of hysterical women carrying on. They won't leave; they can't stay; we're waiting for the Queen of Sheba to make a decision."

Shaw let that remark go and asked, "How is she?"

"Not happy."

He stepped into the office and closed the door behind him. Justine sat at her desk. The tension in her face made her more austere, but somehow even more attractive to Shaw.

He said, "I heard what happened."

She focused on Shaw, but instead of her usual penetrating gaze he saw her mask drop a little bit. This wasn't the confident woman Shaw had seen before. Shaw could see the woman Justine underneath Justine Burton, Police Commissioner's daughter.

"Loyd, thank you for coming. I need someone to tell me when this is going to stop. What do you know? I can't get anything out of anybody. I have to know."

"Did they catch any of the people shooting at the place?"

"A ten-year-old boy. Dead."

"Dead? How?"

"They say the Muslims saw him up on the roof across the street, up on one of the New Lots buildings. Shooting from up there. They went after him. They said he ran and fell. I heard one of the uniformed cops say they probably threw him off the roof. They found a gun near his body."

"Christ."

Shaw moved a chair next to Justine's desk and sat beside her. The moment he came close enough, she reached over and grasped his forearm and asked, "What the hell am I supposed to do, Loyd? I can't let people keep dying over this. I can't let them run me out. What is happening? What should I do?"

Shaw put his hand on top of hers and tried to sound calm.

"Take it easy, Justine. It's just, just—"

"Just what?"

"Look, you have to—"

"They've been shooting all over this neighborhood tonight. What is this man doing? Is anybody close to finding him? Stopping him? Are you?"

"Listen, Justine, he's trying to terrorize you. It's shit. Just bullshit. What he's doing—giving guns to ten-year-olds. It's desperation. His hitters must be on the run. We got one tonight. The precinct guys have another on the run. He's reaching the end."

"So he uses children?"

"They're cheaper than adults. Less likely that the cops or Muslims would stop them on sight. I'm sorry. I know it seems insane."

"You've got to stop this, Shaw. I tried to talk to my father. He won't come here. Said he can't display favoritism. He said they're doing everything they can, but nobody can tell me anything. I don't know if my father is really doing something or if he's just as helpless against this insanity as everybody else."

"He's not helpless. And you didn't call him to find out what the police are doing. You know everybody is on this thing like crazy. You asked him because you need—"

"Something else. A father? Somebody."

"Yes. You should go home, Justine. Get out of here. Get some sleep. Wait until the morning and then start getting these women out of here until this thing is over."

"When is that going to be?"

"When I get Archie Reynolds."

"And when is that going to be?"

"Soon. Believe me, it will be soon."

Justine looked away. Saying more to herself than Shaw, "This is insane. Just insane."

"Then get your people and your clients out of here."

She turned back to Shaw, nearly shouting, "I can't place fourteen women and eleven children in a day. After I talked to you, I didn't go into Manhattan. I came back here and had a meeting with the women. I told them not to worry, but that tomorrow I'll start finding other placement for them. And then before they could even get to sleep, the shooting started.

"Now they're more terrified than ever. They're afraid to leave. They think the minute they set foot out there someone will shoot them. They're afraid to stay and get shot through the window cowering in here. There's no place for them, Shaw. What am I going to do? If I keep this place open it's going to just go on. If I close it they win. But I can't guarantee anybody's safety here."

Justine talked so rapidly and her emotions escalated

so quickly, Shaw didn't attempt to respond. He reached for her shoulder and shook her gently, once, to get her to stop.

The slight physical jarring stopped her, giving her a moment to orient herself. But not talking allowed the feelings to overcome her. She turned away from Shaw, her chin trembling slightly. Shaw saw the first tear ooze out the side of her eye.

Angrily, she stood up, steeling herself, stepping away from Shaw as she quickly wiped away the tear. She did not want to cry in front of Shaw.

"Goddamn it," she said, "what the hell have I started here?"

Shaw stood and took a step toward her.

"Justine, don't. You didn't start this."

Justine turned to him now. Feeling his concern and kindness, she came to him, and without affectation she put her hands on his shoulders, as if to thank him. She lay her forehead against his chest and let out a quivering breath.

"Oh, God," she said. Just giving in to it now. Letting the tension, fatigue, and fear bring the tears to her eyes. Letting the emotions course through her now that her face was hidden.

Shaw held her, gently, patting her on the back, feeling awkward, not quite sure what he should do, but very sure that he wanted to do whatever he could for Justine.

Shaw wanted to be the comforting presence she needed. He wanted to do the right thing and just help her, calm her down, but without warning she moved completely into his arms. He felt her tall elegant body and full breasts pressing into him, and her arms around him, and that austerely beautiful face pressed against his chest, and he couldn't stop it. The sexual attraction took over. He had to fight the urge to hold her closer, to allow a deeper intimacy between them. He stood completely still and kept patting her on the back, keeping it neutral, asexual, but knowing it had already gone too far.

He kept saying, "It's okay. It's·okay."

And she continued clinging to him, increasing her hold on him. She held him so tightly that there was nothing Shaw could do. He had an insane urge to run his hands up and down her back and caress her, and then without warning she relaxed suddenly and stood back from him and looked Shaw directly in the eyes. He looked right back at her. And then she titled her head and came forward and she kissed him. Just on the side of his mouth, but not quite on the cheek either. He felt her soft full lips on the corner of his and the brush of the bandage on her face against his chin.

He stood still, letting her do what she had to. He kissed her back, just slightly so she would˙ know he wasn't offended or put off. It must have been the right thing to do, because she relaxed more and again stepped back from him, but her left hand remained on his shoulder. Shaw held her by the elbows and looked at her. Justine waited for him to say something.

"It will be all right," he said.

"Why? Tell me."

For a˙ moment, Shaw thought ˎhe should tell her how sure he was that Archie would be stopped. How sure he was that the Muslims or the cops would soon get him. He knew he could sound very convincing about the forces lined up against Archie. But deep inside he knew it was a lie. He knew Archie Reynolds had already consigned himself to his fate. Archie Reynolds knew he had lost New Lots. And Archie Reynolds knew he would soon die. And therefore Archie had the one advantage that any terrorist has against a superior force. Death would not deter him and as he rushed toward the inevitable end without regard to his life, Shaw knew Archie Reynolds could do terrible damage to others.

Shaw did not want to lie to Justine. But he would not tell her the terrible truth. He didn't even want to admit it to himself.

"We found Archie tonight. He got away. He might be wounded, might not be. But he's on the run now, Justine. He can't go on like this much longer. He can't keep this up. Not now. One way or another, he'll die. Or he'll spend the rest of his life in jail."

"I hope it's all right. My asking you to come here. I can't talk to these other cops. Everything they do is because of who I am. Everything they say. I can't trust them. I need you. I need to trust someone."

"You can trust me."

"Don't hold it against me."

"Of course not."

"And don't hold the other against me."

"What?"

"What I did just now."

"Why would I hold that against you?"

"Because . . ."

Justine hesitated to answer. Shaw asked gently. "Why? Why would I hold it against you?"

"I don't know. Because it's not right."

"Why?"

"Because it can't—"

"Be any more than just that moment?"

"Yes."

"It's still an honor."

Her soft brown eyes widened for just a moment and for a second it looked as if she might cry again. And then, she moved forward and kissed him again. This time lightly. On his cheek.

"Thank you," she said.

"You're welcome."

And then she let out a long slow breath and flashed a quick smile and said, "You keep doing the right thing, don't you?"

"It's easier with the right woman."

"Well—"

"Yeah. Well."

She let it go and said, "All right. I'm okay."

"Good."

Justine rubbed Shaw's cheek and said, "You scratch."

"Haven't had much time for grooming."

Shaw touched her chin where his stubble had scraped her, and she let him. She seemed to be happy that he did.

"Sorry."

"Don't be."

She moved back to her desk and started to gather her suit jacket and purse.

"I'm glad I called you. You said I could call you."

"Absolutely."

"You're giving me good advice. I'm no use to anyone here tonight. I'll get some sleep and deal with this insanity tomorrow. Better in daylight than now."

"Exactly."

Shaw walked her out of her office and handed her over to her guards. The third detective had returned. All three of the men stood up when she entered the waiting area. The way they surrounded Justine and their demeanor made Shaw feel that he didn't need to remind them to be careful.

Justine had returned to being Justine Burton. She told the detectives, "Let's go." They headed out. Shaw trailed behind them, watched them escort Justine to her car then headed back to Kings County with another load of feeling and emotions swirling in his head.

* * *

Impelliteri and Sperling were as Shaw had left them in the waiting room. Walter had arrived.

A minute or so after Shaw joined his men, a nurse still dressed in her green surgical clothes shuffled in on her slippers and told the detectives they could see the doctor. All four followed her out of the waiting room and she led them to the recovery area.

The surgeon in charge seemed awfully young to Shaw. But at least he spoke English. His name was Fishman. Ira Fishman. For no other reason except crude stereotyping, Shaw felt reassured that Mason had a Jewish doctor.

Fishman told them that the bullet had entered Mason's left side at a weird angle and lodged itself in the fleshy pad of skin above his left hip. He told them he thought the bullet had been deflected off another object, probably the street, which accounted for its strange entry angle and the fact that it hadn't gone all the way through.

"Did you get it out?"

"Of course. Piece of cake. The hard part was making sure nothing important was hit."

"Was there?"

"No. No damage to his ribs, stomach, major blood vessels, and other internal organs, but we had to cut a bit of a path in him to get it out and clean everything up."

"He'll be okay, right?"

"Yeah. If you're going to get shot, that's a pretty good place. Don't you guys wear vests?"

Nobody bothered to answer.

Impelliteri pressed. "He's going to be okay, right?"

"As long as nothing gets infected."

The doctor left. Shaw and the others walked into the recovery room to look over their wounded partner.

Mason lay motionless under the hospital sheets in a dim room full of prostrate dark-skinned bodies, medical equipment, sterile smells, and pain. His color had returned, and he seemed comfortable, sunk in, deep under the anesthesia and whatever else they had pumped into him.

Shaw called Mason's wife, Muriel, and downplayed her husband's wound even more than the surgeon had and felt foolish for doing so. A husband shot and lying in the hospital is a disaster to any wife no matter what anybody says. Shaw told her Orestes was all right at least five times before he had the feeling she believed him. He told her not to come before nine or ten in the morning, since Mase would certainly be sleeping until then, but he knew she'd be dressed and standing next to her husband long before that.

Shaw told Walter to stay with Mason. He gave him instructions on how to explain to Muriel why the normal contingent of police brass and union reps and politicos who normally turn out when a cop is shot would not be there. Shaw had no idea if Muriel would care or would complain. He just hoped Mason would wake up soon and keep her calm. He didn't need an hysterical wife calling Mason's CO or anybody else.

Shaw, Impelliteri, and Sperling found Rachman's operating room where they caught a young doctor coming out. This doctor was more what Shaw expected at a public hospital. He was Pakistani. Apparently he had finished his part of the job. He told Shaw Rachman would be under the knife for at least another four hours.

"He was shot with twenty-twos so no big blunt entry wounds, but they spin around and tear through tissue. Creates a great deal of damage to blood vessels, organs, bones. He had at least six bullets in him, maybe more. We do not have them all out yet."

"Will he live?"

"I don't know. Possibly. If we don't kill him trying to repair everything."

The doctor shuffled off in his operating-room slippers without another word.

Shaw knew that even if Rachman lived, he'd be in no condition to do anything for them now. But it didn't matter. Now that the shootings at New Lots and the mosque were over, Shaw knew the ones he wanted to talk to would be coming soon. That's why he had called in his men. Shaw wanted all the guns he had with him.

Fifteen minutes after Loyd Shaw spoke to the Pakistani doctor, they arrived.

Yousseff, John X, plus four gunmen. All of them in the MS-2 style: beards, combat boots, baggy, dark clothing, heavy coats, and skullcaps. All except Yousseff, who wore a baggy, black suit and looked neither to his right or left, but directly at Shaw.

They walked into the waiting room. Shaw stood up. The Muslims looked at Shaw and stopped. Shaw nodded to Impelliteri, who had positioned himself near the door. Impelliteri kicked up the doorstop. As the door swung shut, Sperling positioned himself next to the Muslims, not a trace of emotion on his face, arms folded across his chest, hands under his armpits, gripping the butts of his guns holstered under his blue blazer.

Shaw said to himself, God love you, you gaunt, wasted bastard.

They were outnumbered, but Shaw felt secure. Impelliteri stood behind the Muslims. Shaw in front of them. Sperling next to them. As far as Shaw was concerned, they had the Muslims surrounded.

An elderly, black couple sat off in the corner of the waiting room. One of their grandchildren had been injured—for all Shaw knew, another casualty of the Blue-Tops—Muslim war. They curled up in their corner and tried to make believe they were invisible. But they never took their wary eyes off the hard men standing in the small waiting room. They knew they were witnessing a showdown.

When Impelliteri kicked the door shut, it seemed as if the scene would explode right then and there. The Muslims were just as keyed up as Shaw and his men. One of the gunmen turned and started to go for the closed door. Impelliteri stepped in front of him.

"Back off."

Impelliteri wanted the Muslim to try something. Gun, fists, feet, it didn't matter.

Just before they clashed, and everyone started shooting, a voice snapped out, "Wait."

It came from the wiry man in the baggy suit.

Shaw asked him, "Are you in charge? After Rachman?"

Yousseff squinted at Shaw for a moment, looking him over through his thick, wire-rimmed glasses. It was clear Yousseff and Shaw were the leaders.

"Yes. Who are you?"

"Detective Loyd Shaw. And you. You're Yousseff?"

"Yes."

"I was with Rachman when they came tonight. Rachman was sending me over to talk to you. Two doors right of his place. I was on my way over to you when they attacked."

"What happened to our brother?"

"Archie Reynolds shot him."

"You saw it?"

"Yes, I saw it. He ambushed Rachman. My partner and I drove him off. He got away. We brought Rachman here."

Yousseff nodded.

Shaw said, "Don't thank us," and meant it.

Yousseff snapped back, "What do you want?"

"I want Archie Reynolds."

"So do we."

"I want him first."

Youseff stiffened.

"Do you know what else happened tonight?"

"Some of it."

"Another attack. Snipers. Our men shot at. Young ones shooting at us from hiding places."

"Kids?"

"Archie Reynolds recruited them. Gave them money and a gun. Offered a reward."

"How do you know?"

"Because they told us."

"I heard you threw one of them off a roof. What happened? He wouldn't talk?"

"He didn't have to talk. We found out what we needed to know from the others."

"I guess beatings work pretty good on ten-year-olds."

Yousseff did not respond.

"Any sign of Archie Reynolds?"

"No."

"You know where I can find Archie Reynolds."

Yousseff dismissed Shaw with a wave of his hand.

"There is no *where*. You won't find him. You want to know where he lives? He lives at eight-four-six-two Sycamore Place in Saddle Brook. So what? You think he'll be there? If he stops anywhere, to eat or sleep, it won't be in Brownsville. He'll never be in the same car twice. If he comes into Brownsville, you'll never see him. If you were any good, you would have killed him at the mosque."

"How did he know where and when to find Rachman?"

"We're not sure."

"Are you going to help me find him?"

"Why should we? Are you going to help us?"

"What the hell do you think we're doing? Why refuse it? You have what, fifty men? A hundred? Two hundred? We have thousands. City, State, Feds if we want them. We have the power, not you."

Yousseff dismissed Shaw with a sneer and another wave of his hand. "Yes, now. But a week from now you'll have a few squads cruising through our neighborhood, never stopping, never setting foot on the streets. You have nothing. You have no idea what's going on and you never will."

"Then tell me. Tell me what's going on."

"Look to your own for what you want to know. Don't ask me. What did the doctors say? Will Rachman live?"

Shaw answered, "Maybe."

"Good. So will you, unless you get in our way. Tell your man to open this door."

"What?"

Shaw moved toward Yousseff.

Yousseff stepped back. The gunmen reached inside their coats. But before they had their weapons out, both Impelliteri and Sperling had their guns in their hands. Four guns, cocked and pointed, just like that. Impelliteri aimed one Glock at Yousseff's head, the other at John X. He knew which targets to pick. Sperling aimed his two guns at the four others. The Muslim gunmen froze.

Shaw yelled at Yousseff, holding himself back from grabbing his skinny throat, "What did you say? Say it again you prick. Say it again and I'll fucking kill you right now. Say it! Say you'll kill me!"

Shaw knew without any doubt that if Impelliteri and Sperling hadn't gotten their guns out so quickly, they might already be dead now. It made him even more enraged. At that moment Yousseff slowly raised his hands.

"I meant it as a friendly warning. I meant no disrespect."

"Bullshit, you little asshole. You fucking threatened me, you little vigilante fuck. Fuck you."

Yousseff glared at Shaw, but he kept his hands up.

Shaw stood where he was, struggling to control himself.

Nobody moved. Shaw felt himself coming back. His murderous rage ebbed. Suddenly, everyone realized Shaw would not risk the blood that would ensue if he went for Yousseff.

He quietly told the man, "Don't ever threaten me or my men again. You may think you're a fucking hero on a divine mission, but you're just a murderous little ex-con vigilante as far as I'm concerned. And don't you ever fucking tell one of my men to open a door for you. Do you understand?"

For a moment, Shaw thought he might have pushed Yousseff too far, but he slowly turned toward Impelliteri and said, "I apologize."

"All right then," Shaw said.

Shaw nodded at Impelliteri. The cop hesitated for just a moment, then shoved one of his guns in his belt and opened the door, never taking his eyes or his other gun off Yousseff.

The Muslims slowly moved out. Yousseff filed out last. Impelliteri kept the gun pointed at Yousseff's head the entire time, but Yousseff never blinked. As the small man reached the door Impelliteri just nodded at him as if to say, I'll shoot you in a heartbeat.

And then Yousseff was gone. And the knot in Shaw's upper back slowly began to loosen. But Yousseff's words kept pounding in his head, "Look to your own."

38

It should have been more difficult for Archie Reynolds to find out where Justine Burton lived. He got it on the very first try.

After shooting Rachman, Archie had Reggie Whack drop him off on a quiet street in Queens where he stole a blue Honda Civic. He picked the Honda because it was so unobtrusive. Then he simply drove back into Brownsville and parked within sight of the community center. With all the police and ambulances and commotion, no one noticed him. He sat low in his seat, gazing just above the steering wheel waiting, watching, passing time by guessing where she lived. Striver's Row in Harlem? One of the middle-class black neighborhoods in Queens like St. Albans?

Spotting Justine couldn't have been easier. The four men escorting her out of the center were hard to miss. And one of the men certainly attracted his attention. Three of the four wore suits. Only one wore black jeans and a dark brown leather jacket. The same one that had shot at him and Reggie. Archie had nearly changed his plans right then and there. He had actually pulled out the Beretta, started up the Honda, and tried to figure out the best way to cruise up to that guy in the jacket and put one in his head. A cop, thought Archie. The fucking cops be working with the Muslims now. Shaw had walked off to his car by himself. Archie had almost been sure he could have done Shaw and gotten away before anyone had even noticed the cop go down. He had eased the Honda into gear and rolled away from the curb. But at the last moment, he braked. Archie's need to hurt Justine outweighed his desire to shoot Shaw.

Archie had waited for Justine's Ford Taurus to head off, tailed by the unmarked police car. He'd followed them from a good distance across Eastern Parkway, onto the Prospect Expressway, then through the Brooklyn Battery Tunnel. When she'd pulled off the West Side Highway into the small streets of the West Village, Archie had sneered. Just like this fuckin' bitch to be livin' in this white Yuppie neighborhood.

There were plenty of parking spots good until eight A.M. on the Village streets. Archie had slid the Honda into one of them as Justine parked her car in an open-air lot on Washington Street. The detective riding with her had escorted her to their unmarked. Then they drove her one short block to a recently renovated building on Horatio between Washington Street and the West Side Highway. A place rather prententiously named the West Coast Apartments, as if the grimy West Side Highway constituted a coastline.

Archie hadn't even had to leave his car to see where they took her.

One detective had walked her into the building. The other two had stayed outside, parked at the curb.

Archie had to admit the location made sense for her. A black woman like her certainly wouldn't stand out in the Greenwich Village neighborhood. Travel to her center in Brownsville was simple. As long as she had the money to live there. Archie wondered about that now as he stepped out of the Honda.

He walked over to her building, then slowly walked all the way around, checking entrances, looking up at the few lit windows, wondering which one might be Justine's.

He took note of the several bars on Washington Street near Justine's building that were still open and doing good business. Nearby on Gansevoort Street, the all-night diner, Florent, attracted customers until the early-morning hours. Right on the corner of her building a twenty-four-hour deli attracted customers around the clock. And by four in the morning when the last bars closed, the meat market district, just one block north, was up and running.

The neighborhood never slept.

Archie simply had to keep moving, be part of the general flow of people, and nothing would seem out of the ordinary to the detectives parked in front of Justine's building, not even when he passed the front entrance of the building.

Archie had the audacity to cruise by the entrance twice as he made his plans. And also by the service entrance up near the corner. Justine's guards didn't take any notice of him. They didn't even see him when he stood on Washington Street guessing the window up on the eighth floor belonged to that bitch Justine, one of the only two lit up at that hour.

Only when the door closed behind Yousseff and the others did Impelliteri and Sperling holster their guns.

As usual, Impelliteri had the final word.

"Assholes."

Sperling dropped back into his chair. Shaw rolled his head, trying to release some of the tension. Impelliteri stood by the door, still not quite able to let it go.

Shaw checked his watch.

"You guys going after Reggie Whack?"

The question focused Impelliteri's attention back on the real job. He also checked his watch. Nearly three A.M.

"Yeah. It's about the right time to head out there. We got a whole hour's sleep before you called."

"At the precinct?"

"Yeah. Neither one of us felt like bothering to go home. Just end up coming right back out. What are you going to do?"

"Try and find out what the fuck that guy meant by, 'look to your own.' "

Impelliteri and Sperling tried the Bronx address first, because Reggie had collected more parking tickets there. They cruised the neighborhood looking for the Jeep, but didn't spot it on any of the surrounding streets. After an hour of searching punctuated by Impelliteri's cursing, they drove back into Brooklyn and headed for Fort Greene. After five minutes cruising around the Walt Whitman housing project, they spotted it. It wasn't very difficult.

Impelliteri pointed to it, not parked at a fire hydrant or driveway, but right in the middle of the project courtyard.

"Jeezus, can you believe that crazy fuck? Parks it right out in the open like that."

Sperling answered, "Yes."

"People around here have to know who owns that car. Thing would have been stripped down to the frame by now otherwise. Guy must have a scary rep."

Sperling squinted at the car. "I suppose."

He asked Sperling, "You think the Brownie who wrote him up had the balls to walk in there and do it?"

"Some of those meter maids can be pretty tough."

"Yeah, most of them big mammas know how to handle they-selves."

Impelliteri drove the Caprice over the sidewalk and positioned the car so it blocked one exit out of the courtyard.

"So, we wait for him?" asked Sperling.

"Fuck, no. I ain't waiting for that asshole to wake up."

Impelliteri got out and rummaged around in his trunk until he found a tire iron and headed for the Jeep.

Upstairs in a cluttered one-bedroom project apartment, Reggie Whack, Darleece, their infant baby, and Darleece's five-year-old son by another man slept peacefully. The kids slept in one bed. Reggie and Darleece in another. All in the same room. It was long before their wake-up time, only five in the morning. Even Darleece's pit bull bitch slept curled up in a pile of dirty laundry that had collected in the corner of the stuffy, dingy bedroom.

Normally, a car alarm sounding in Fort Greene wouldn't wake anybody. But with the car parked right in the project's courtyard, it couldn't be ignored.

Reggie had smoked some weed and downed two cans of malt liquor to calm his nerves and ease his stutter after the mosque ambush. So when the alarm squealed out its repertoire of beeps and wails and bleats, Reggie hardly stirred.

Impelliteri had used the tire iron on the driver's side window. The window shattered without making much noise. But it did set off the car's alarm. The alarm continued to sound through a two-minute cycle then ended midwail. Impelliteri immediately shattered a headlight and kicked the side of the car to start the alarm again.

Reggie turned over. The alarm finally awakened him, but he had no desire to open his eyes.

It didn't seem possible, but along with the alarm someone seemed to be yelling his name. And then, mixed in with the wailing and the yelling came the sound of iron smashing sheet metal.

Reggie sat up suddenly and looked out the window. Impelliteri smashed the Jeep with an overhand blow that knocked a crease across the entire width of the hood.

Sperling squatted down near the back of the Jeep, his cocked SIG-Sauer in hand, waiting.

Impelliteri hit the Jeep twice more and yelled Reggie's name again.

Impelliteri was about to ask Sperling if he thought it possible for someone to sleep through the noise, when Reggie burst into the courtyard.

He ran with his gun extended, barefoot and shirtless, firing shots at Impelliteri.

Impelliteri had his Glock ready in his free hand, but he didn't beat Sperling, who quickly stood up, mumbled a warning, dropped into a shooter's crouch and squeezed off two quick shots at his target. His moving target.

Impelliteri had expected Sperling to be one of the best shooters in the NYPD. In fact, Sperling was *the* best shooter. He put two bullets into Reggie Whack's moving head from almost twenty yards. Most of Reggie's head disappeared. His feet flew out from under him. He died before he hit the ground.

Impelliteri hadn't even raised the Glock.

"*Goddamn*, James."

Even more impressive were the shots Sperling fired when the pit bull bitch burst out of the open door.

Reggie had been a hard target. The animal was an impossible target. She streaked across the courtyard, low to the ground, intent on launching herself at Sperling or Impelliteri or both. Sperling's first shot missed, his second caught the dog at the top of its right leg. The dog yelped, skidded, gathered itself, and kept coming, limping, but still on the run. Impelliteri opened up, too, but Sperling's third shot slammed into the dog's chest and she dropped.

The dog's feet kept moving. Impelliteri had a better chance at the stationary target and finally got a couple of slugs into the dying dog.

"Well," said Impelliteri, "that's that."

Sperling looked over at Reggie.

"I assume he's the guy?"

Impelliteri walked over and moved what was left of Reggie's head so he could see the remains of his face.

"I don't know. I see a gold tooth in there. He have a gold tooth?"

"He wasn't smiling in his mug shot."

"He ain't smiling now, that's for sure."

From up high came the screams of Darleece, a big woman, leaning out the window, crying and wailing, "Reggie. Reggie. They kilt my Reggie."

Impelliteri looked up and listened to Darleece, looked back at the corpse, and muttered. "It's him."

"And I assume that's Darleece. So now what?" asked Sperling.

"You never gone through a shooting aftermath before?"

"No."

"Well, get ready to have your day ruined. If the uniformed guys don't get here soon, we're supposed to call the supervising officer at the precinct and tell him to haul his ass out here. Then we wait for the crime unit, wait for our supervisors, wait for the precinct detectives, wait for the DEA guys, the union, it's fuckin' unbelievable. When they get done with all their bullshit and interviewing us, we have go to the hospital and get checked for stress and all that shit. I've done it twice before. It fucking takes forever."

"I don't want to do that," said Sperling.

"What, you want to just walk?"

"Well, I don't know."

"It's gonna cause us untold hassles if we walk."

"I don't want to go through all that. In fact, I won't."

"So? What do you suggest?"

Sperling thought it over for a moment.

"Call Shaw. Or call Wang. Get him to call DeLuca's guy. What's his name, Conklin. Let's see if DeLuca really is God."

Just then, a blue-and-white screeched into the courtyard with two more following close behind.

Impelliteri held his shield up, as did Sperling. They identified themselves, then ignored the uniforms while they talked to Wang on their radio. Thirty minutes later, when the area had become inundated with police personnel, Conklin showed up with a team of detectives from DeLuca's office.

Conklin spoke to Impelliteri and Sperling for a couple of minutes. He looked at Reggie. Saw the gun still in his hand. Looked at the dog. Noted it was a pit bull. He walked over to the commanding officer on the scene. He spoke for a few minutes, introduced a team of detectives assigned to the Chief's office. Then he came back and told Impelliteri and Sperling they could leave. The case was now officially under the jurisdiction of the Chief of Detective's office. No more precinct cops. No more questions.

Impelliteri looked at Sperling. Sperling smiled for the first time since they had met.

39

Loyd Shaw had slept through the demise of Reggie Whack, in his unmarked car outside Justine Burton's apartment building, waiting for a reasonable time to see her. Shaw had set his wristwatch alarm for seven. Three hours of sitting-up sleep had helped cut the fatigue, but it had been hell waking up.

He feared he might simply fall back asleep, so he got out of the Caprice and breathed deeply and stretched. He checked his watch. Looked around. Wednesday morning, six o'clock, overcast, cool morning air. The streets were empty of people and traffic, quiet except for a refrigerated meat truck parked about a block away outside a meat-packing warehouse. The truck's engine had been left running to power the refrigeration unit.

Shaw called Justine's apartment on his cellular phone. He expected her to be sleeping, but she answered on the second ring.

"It's Shaw. We should talk."

"Now?"

"Yeah. I'm parked outside. Are you up?"

"Up and down all night." There was a pause before she said, "Okay. You might as well come up here. Eight F."

"Do you want coffee or anything from the deli?"

"Coffee. Light."

Shaw thought a light cup of rich coffee would just about match the color of her skin.

"Okay. Be up in five."

While the deli man poured the coffee, Shaw imagined how Justine would be dressed. He figured her for pajamas and a robe. A woman with a body like Justine's would take care to cover it up at night. He entertained himself with an image of her sleeping nude. Then switched to a lace black teddy. Then stopped.

Shaw had felt her body against his. Had looked it over. Had touched her skin. It wasn't good for him to think about Justine Burton in bed, dressed, undressed, or even dressed and under the covers.

He'd guessed wrong. He hadn't pictured a nightgown. When she opened the door, she wore a terrycloth robe and cotton nightgown that reached about midcalf. Shaw still couldn't get over that skin, what little there was showing.

After the nightgown and robe, he half expected fuzzy slippers on her feet, but she wore something that looked like suede clogs with cork soles. Lightweight and easy to slip on.

"Well," she said, "the image is absolutely shot after this."

"You look fine to me."

"Liar."

Shaw wasn't lying. At home without the formalities of her work wardrobe and surroundings her manner was more relaxed and feminine. More sensual.

He handed her a brown bag.

"There's some Danish in there, too."

"Thanks. I just need the coffee. I didn't sleep much last night."

She took the bag and led him into a standard issue one-bedroom, single-girl, simply furnished, Sheetrock-box apartment. The only outstanding features were higher than normal ceilings and an interesting view over the rooftops of the low West Village brownstones and town houses.

They sat at Justine's kitchen table for two.

"So what's important enough to bring you to me first thing in the morning? Tell me you got Archie Reynolds."

Shaw thought about that phrase for a moment, "bring you to me," but let it pass.

"No. Not yet. I need to ask you a few things."

"It couldn't wait?"

"Nothing can wait."

"What happened?"

"You mean besides that mess around your center last night? I told you one of my men was shot. He'll be all right. I didn't tell you about Rachman Abdul X, the man in charge of the Muslim security company. He got shot six times by Archie Reynolds."

"Oh, no."

"The guy's a bull; he's still alive. Might stay that way if he doesn't get shot again. They set fire to the Muslim's mosque on Bushwick, then ambushed Rachman. I don't know how many people were shot out there. How many in New Lots. Two of my men are still out there. Don't know what they've run into yet. It's been a bad night."

Justine didn't comment. She simply nodded.

"Justine, if there's anything that you know about this that I don't, I'm asking you to tell me."

"What do you mean?"

"I'm getting some weird feedback out there. Comments that I don't understand."

"Like what?"

"Let me ask you something first. What do you know about Arbor Realty?"

"Not much."

"Did they come to you or did you find them?"

"I found them. I had inquiries into every community and district planning board in the city trying to find a location. I had the money, a Federal grant with matching state and city funds, but I didn't have the space. So I put out the word everywhere I could. A woman named Cecily Adams in City Planning told me about Arbor Realty. She knew Arbor Realty from an apartment building they took over in Bed-Stuy, and she knew about their deal for New Lots Apartments. She gave me a lead. I followed it."

"To where? Who did you talk to?"

"Leon Bloom."

"How does an outfit like Arbor Realty get an apartment complex like New Lots Apartments?"

"There are a number of private companies taking over what used to be public housing. When a place goes under, it used to be the city took possession in lieu of back taxes. They stopped doing that unofficially several years ago. Officially in ninety-five. There were just too many."

"So whoever wants to assume the debt, gets it?"

"Yes, but it's not always that easy. There's a lot of negotiating that goes on, mostly with the banks who hold the mortgages. And it's usually HUD that backs the loans, so they're involved, too. It's complicated. But the fact is, the city and banks are fairly eager to get rid of these places and they make it a good enough deal so that there's competition for them."

"So who wins?"

"Basically, whoever offers the debt holders the best deal."

"Was there competition for New Lots Apartments?"

"Not much. Arbor Realty doesn't go for the good properties. It goes for the problem properties. The ones nobody else wants."

"So they get them cheaper."

"Way cheaper."

"And they invest a few bucks in an outlaw Muslim security force to clean it up."

"No. Most of their investment comes from the renovation. They almost always get reimbursed for the security contracts."

"They do?"

"Most of the time HUD kicks in to pay for security."

"Unbelievable."

"I don't think many would go through what it takes to clean these places out unless they had some backing. Look at what's going on now. If you don't succeed in cleaning out the place, you never make back your investment."

Shaw sat at the table absorbing what Justine had told him.

"Bloom knew who you were, obviously."

"Of course."

"Did your father ever talk to him?"

"Not that I know of."

"So he didn't exert any pressure on Arbor Realty?"

"If he did, I didn't hear about it. I don't think he had to. And I sure as hell didn't ask him to."

"Is your father going to profit from this in any way?"

"Hey, Shaw, you're—"

"I'm sorry. I don't know your father. Just tell me I'm wrong and I'll shut up about it. I'm trying to figure out why Arbor Realty thinks they can bring in a criminal group of vigilantes and get away with it."

"Maybe because they've done it before."

"You mean in Bed-Stuy?"

"And other properties. I don't know all their holdings, but New Lots isn't the first."

"It's still the same question. Why did they think they could do it before?"

"Maybe just because it worked easier before. And who's going to complain about someone cleaning up a bad neighborhood?"

"Okay. Let's say you're right. But this time when

the shit hit the fan, we didn't shut them down. The Chief of D, with your father, knowing what they were doing, went beyond the call to help them out."

"What do you mean?"

"The Chief of Detectives pulled together a squad of men who aren't exactly your normal, everyday cops."

"You."

"And four others. We're not working through the regular chain of command. We're not doing things by the book. And when I put pressure on this Bloom guy, the first person he called was the Chief of Detective's contact, a fixer named Conklin. And then tonight, after all hell broke loose, the Muslims told me to look to my own."

"Look to your own?"

"Yes. I'm not a member of the Elks Club. If somebody tells me to look to my own, I'm gonna look at cops. What the hell is going on, Justine? Who's in bed with who?"

"You mean DeLuca and Arbor Realty?"

"DeLuca, your father, I don't know."

"My father isn't. I can't speak for DeLuca. But if they are or aren't, what difference does it make?"

"You don't think it makes a difference?"

"In what context? For you I mean. Does it make a difference why DeLuca put you in this position?"

"Bottom line, maybe none. But if I'm going to die out there, I'd like to know what's really going on."

Justine sat back in her chair and looked at Shaw. He had the feeling she was deciding something.

"All right. What are the possibilities? Let's say for argument's sake that my father and the Chief of Detectives are helping this realty company more than they normally would. I'm not saying they are, but if they are, you want to know why. Beyond the fact that I'm involved."

"Right."

"Maybe my father plans to run for mayor and needs campaign financing from them. Maybe DeLuca wants to retire and be head of their security operation. Or, what the hell, New Lots Apartments is going to be profitable, maybe it's simply payoffs under the table. Cops have been paid off before. If not with money, then jobs, loans, there's lots of ways to pay."

"So which is it?"

Justine leaned forward and gave Shaw one of her direct looks.

"Shaw, I don't know. I honestly don't know. I don't think my father ever took a dime in his life. You know more about DeLuca than I do. What's his reputation?"

Shaw didn't answer.

"Maybe my father is just being overprotective. Pick whatever nefarious plot you want, it all gets down to the same question."

"Which is?"

"Would you still be involved?"

Shaw gave it a couple of seconds just to be sure, but it didn't take much effort to say, "Yes."

"Okay. Why?"

"Besides saving my pension and playing the hero?"

"Is there more?"

"Yes."

"What?"

"You."

The word came out of his mouth almost before he knew it, before he could stop it, as if the word had a will of its own.

"What?"

"I guess I'm doing it, at least partly, for you."

"Oh, Loyd. I didn't ask for that."

"Not in so many words you didn't. But come on, Justine, you've been watching me look at you like I'm dumbstruck. You call, I come running. You shake my hand and propose a date, I say sure; you kiss me, I kiss you back. I'm not supposed to think there's something going on between us?"

"There is."

And there it was. Right out. Directly from her. Shaw didn't comment, because he didn't want to do anything that would allow her to change or ameliorate what she had just said. But she kept looking at him, wanting a response from him to the truth she had just admitted.

"Well," he said, "so I guess I can stop pretending there isn't."

"Right. So now what?"

"I, I don't know. I mean . . . when this thing started out, it was real simple for me. The Chief of D had enough on me to end my career with a nod of his head. End my chance at a pension, plus make good on a bunch of other grim threats. So, he gives me a shot at a reprieve. Go out there and stop this thing and all is forgiven.

"I figure, with the right guys, a little luck, move fast, work smart, I've got a chance. Get in, get out.

"Then I see that place. I see all those kids running around, women, regular people trying to get to work. Trying to just live. It's a shithole, they're surrounded by shit. I know what goes on in that goddamn neighborhood. Unimaginable degradation. Overdoses. Everybody peddling dope. Girls young enough to be our kids peddling themselves. People either just trapped in that mess or people trying to live in it like it's a real neighborhood, like any other. They don't deserve what's come down on them, so naturally I want to stop it.

"And then they start shooting at me. At my partner. I want to shoot back. But I'm thinking about you and your anger about more young black men dying. And I picture putting a bullet in somebody. And living with that. And on one side it feels like the last goddamn thing I want to do. On the other, it's like, goddamn it, just get a fucking bullet in him before he gets one in you. Just shoot first and keep on shooting.

"Then this murderous fuck Archie stands over a man and shoots him six goddamn times and puts a bullet in my partner and I want to put a bullet in him so bad my fucking head aches.

"And suddenly this guy tells me to look to my own. And I'm wondering how many people do I have to worry about. Who can I trust? And now you're part of it. You're someone I don't want hurt by this. And I know as sure as I'm sitting here, this maniac Archie Reynolds wants to hurt you. Shoot you, for god's sake."

Shaw stopped talking, surprised at how much had spilled out of him.

Justine just sat, looking at him, nodding as if she understood every word.

Shaw took a deep breath and came back to the original question.

"So, what do we do now? We don't do one goddamn thing until this is over. Until you're safe. Until those people out there in New Lots and Brownsville get at least some relief from the endless violence and danger that fills their lives every fucking day. So, yeah, the answer is yes, I'm in this no matter what. As long as you're in it, I'm in it. But I'd still like to know what's really going on."

Justine took his hand.

"Shaw, I don't know anything more than I told you. I'll see what I can find out. I don't know if it will help, but I'll do what I can."

"Okay. Good. Thanks."

"If you're doing this, at least partly, for me, it's the least I can do."

Shaw nodded, accepting her statement. She held his hand in both of hers and kept talking.

"And I know this is wrong. It's the wrong time. You're probably the wrong person. I'm probably just clinging to you, because I'm scared. You know I'm not some tough ghetto kid. I don't do well with guns pointed at me and getting knocked around and shot at. I'm scared. So I need you. And I'm attracted to you. And I admire you. So even though this is all wrong, I can't stop. I won't stop."

"I don't want you to stop."

"And I can't make any promises. Maybe even after this is over, this goes nowhere."

"I'm not asking for any promises."

"When this is all over, we probably will be, too."

"What happens, happens."

She touched his face and said, "Well then, Loyd . . ."

"What?"

"You'd better go shave."

"Shave?"

Justine just looked at Shaw, giving him time to absorb what she meant. After a moment, Shaw smiled. "Sorry. I'm not exactly at my sharpest."

He shaved, and showered and shampooed and scrubbed until he was sure to get the stink of blood and gunpowder and sweat off his body, if not off his clothes. While Shaw stood in the shower, the door opened. Justine entered and set out a clean towel for him and gathered up his clothes and left.

Shaw stepped out. There was a condom sitting on top of a large, fluffy, pink bath towel. He found it charming and competent at the same time. It was comforting to know the single set had worked out a method for handling such matters.

He dried himself and wrapped Justine's towel around

his waist and stepped out of the steamy bathroom. He heard Justine's voice off to his left.

"I'm in here."

Shaw walked down a short hall and turned into her bedroom. She had drawn the blinds and turned the louvers so that just a touch of early morning daylight entered the room. Justine sat up against the headboard, the covers drawn to her waist. There was no terry-cloth robe. No nightgown. Just Justine. All of her.

Shaw actually found that he had trouble breathing. Her shoulders, long lean arms, perfect, full breasts, taut stomach, that silky smooth café au lait skin . . . it all mesmerized him. He just stood for a few moments, taking her in, realizing that Justine didn't mind at all how much he stood and looked at her.

She asked, "Do we have time?"

"Hey, as long as it's been for me, this won't take very long."

And then Justine Burton laughed. A big, bright, beautiful smile lit up her face and she laughed. It was marvelous.

And it was incredible.

Shaw had made her promise to wake him in an hour. He'd never had a better hour's sleep in his life. Justine had drained him, not only of his lust, but for the brief hour, she had relieved the swirl of dark emotions plaguing him and taken away his inhibitions and doubts. She had wrung him out and restored him at the same time. And when it was time to wake him, she did it with a hot towel, first wiping Shaw's face and lips, then his chest and then, very gently, his genitals. She dried him and kissed him and said, "Time to climb back in those dirty clothes and do what you got to do, baby."

Baby. It sounded good. Especially the way she said it.

Shaw croaked, "Thanks."

When he left, he didn't say good-bye. Didn't offer any more advice or warnings. And didn't tell her about recording their conversation.

He'd switched on the recorder when she turned around to take the coffee and Danish out of the brown paper bag. Shaw assuaged his guilt by telling himself that he left the recorder on because he couldn't risk Justine seeing him turn it off. The guilt he felt for not erasing it went unassuaged.

James Sperling and Tony Impelliteri did the sleep-in-the-car routine, too, logging in three hours before Queen Margo found them parked across the street from her car-service office.

She rapped on the window and yelled, "What the fuck you doing parked outside my place?"

Sperling almost shot her. He had his gun out and pointing at her after the second rap.

Margo jumped back. Benny went for his piece. Impelliteri woke up fast and gently pushed Sperling's gun toward the floor.

"Easy, partner."

Margo told Benny, "Keep your shit in your pocket, damn it."

Impelliteri stepped out of the car.

"Christ, Margo, don't be rapping on my window like that. You fuckin' give me a heart attack with that shit."

"Don't you be parked outside my place. You think I'm gonna do any fuckin' business with an unmarked and two ragged-out detectives sitting here. You look like shit. You need a bath."

"Come on, we had a hard night. We were just waiting to catch you, Margo. You never answered any of my messages."

"I didn't have anything to tell you."

"Well, you could call and fucking tell me that, couldn't you?"

"I don't waste my time like that."

"All right, all right. You still got nothing?"

"No. I don't still got nothing. I got something. I got plenty of Something, baby."

"What?"

"Shit, you wouldn't believe it, *pendejo*. Like rats from a sinking ship these Blue-Tops *maricóns*. I got three fucking calls for dope. That operation is going down the shitter, baby, and everybody knows it."

"Yeah?"

"Hell, yeah. All the two-bit, low-rung guys in that little gang are striking out on their own. Trying to get a kilo or two to fill the need. Nobody's watching the store in New Lots. No supply coming in. Everything going out."

"That's what you hear?"

"That's what I know, sugar. You stay around today, you get some guys."

"Good."

"But not on my fucking doorstep. Park someplace else."

"I'll go around the corner."

"Good. I'll call you when any of the guys you're looking for show up. Gimme your cell phone number."

"Right. I'll follow them home or something. I won't bust anybody so's they know it was you."

"Thanks. But to tell you the truth, I wouldn't worry too much about it. Give them a little room, but believe me, none of these guys will be surprised if they get busted. The precinct detectives are all over these guys. Plus a bunch from Narcotics and Homicide and Major Cases and who the fuck knows who else."

"No shit."

"No shit. You're not the only bad boys in on this."

Impelliteri spoke quietly, even though no one was close enough to hear him. "So, Margo, anybody else contacting you for help on this?"

"None of your fucking business. I'm helping you,

ain't I? I told you I would and I am. Let the others go fuck themselves. Comes down to it, you the one I know will do the right thing when payback time comes, right, honey?"

"Right. Good. Call me on my cellular and we'll do it neat and clean."

"*Ciao.*"

Margo strode off with Benny rumbling along behind her. Just before she entered the car-service office, she turned back to make sure Impelliteri had cleared out.

As they drove around the corner, Impelliteri turned to Sperling.

"Listen, James, we'll spend some time around here, okay."

"Yeah."

"Let these knuckleheads come to us, okay?"

"Sure."

"But do me a favor."

"What?"

"Don't shoot anybody unless you really, really have to, James. I don't know how many times we can pull that trick with the Chief of D's guy, okay?"

"Right."

After Shaw left Justine's, he stopped at his loft for a change of clothes.

The coffee he'd sipped with Justine had turned sour in his empty stomach. He hadn't eaten anything since the bad Chinese meal. He still didn't feel like eating anything. He grabbed a bottle of Pepto from his kitchen cabinet and swigged down a mouthful while he dialed in a page to Walter.

Walter called back and Shaw sipped more of the pink stuff as he talked to him.

"Walter."

"Yes."

"It's Shaw. What's happening at the hospital?"

"Huh."

Shaw swallowed.

"It's Shaw, goddamn it. What's happening at the hospital?"

"They just finished with Rachman. He's in the intensive care."

"He's still breathing, huh?"

"Yeah. Barely. Got some of his brothers watching over him."

"That's nice. How's Mason?"

"Looks okay to me. He woke up about a half hour ago, talked to his wife, and went back to sleep."

"She's not hysterical or anything?"

"No."

"All right. Any people from the Job show up?"

"Yeah, but DeLuca's guy Conklin was here."

"Mr. Fix-it."

"Everything got quiet real quick. But he has a message for you."

"What?"

"Call him. DeLuca wants to talk to you. Pissed you aren't answering your beeper."

Yeah, like I'm going to keep my beeper on while I'm in bed with Justine Burton, thought Shaw.

"I'll take care of it. You go back to the seven-three. See what's going on there."

"Okay."

"If Impelliteri and Sperling show up with any bad guys, make sure they get processed right."

"Okay."

"You got a pencil?"

"What?"

"Take the shit out of your ears, Walter."

"I can't get you. Are you eating something?"

"Yeah, wait a minute."

Shaw gagged down one more swallow, wanting enough bismuth in his aching stomach to kill whatever evil brewed down there, then rinsed his mouth out with a handful of tap water.

"Okay, listen up. I'm going to catch some sleep. In the meantime, do these things. Get an alert out on Sanchez. Ten to one, he was the prick on the motorcycle shooting up the mosque last night. Make it all points, man. Especially the Port Authority Police. I want them watching for him at every fucking airport and bus terminal and railroad station, including Newark, especially for any flights to the Dominican Republic or anywhere in the Caribbean. There's a guy I know named Josh Dove at the Port Authority Police. He's got rank. Tell him it's for me. I want everything shut down on this guy Sanchez. Make sure he has pictures or whatever else he needs. I don't want Sanchez leaving the country."

"Okay."

"And put it out over FATN. I want every cop and every detective in every precinct to know about Sanchez. Alert the Feds, too. This guy does not leave New York."

"Yeah, yeah, okay. I got it."

"Keep searching for anything that will lead us to Archie Reynolds."

"Yeah."

"And when you get a spare moment, I want you to do background checks on Arbor Realty."

"What do you want to know?"

"Who owns it, who runs it, what properties they manage. Can you do that?"

"Take me a long time, but I know a guy who can do it pretty fast."

"Who's that?"

"My cousin, Jimmy Wang. He's a fixer at the Building Department. You know what that is?"

"No. And I don't much care. If he can do it, get him on it."

"We got money for Jimmy?"

"I thought you said he was your cousin."

"Got to take care of cousins, man."

"I'll throw him a couple of hundred, but I want to go to the head of the fucking line."

For some reason, the comment made Walter laugh. Which was good. Shaw figured the little guy must be ready to drop. But if he could laugh, he could work.

"I'll be there in a few hours. Beep me if you need me. But only if you need me. I want to clean up and grab another hour of sleep."

"When am I suppose to sleep?"

"You slept last night. I saw you leave. You went home and slept didn't you?"

"Yeah. Three whole hours."

"You're young. That's plenty. You'd probably feel better if you'd have stayed awake."

"Not me."

"Drink coffee. Take drugs. Do whatever the fuck you have to do, Walter, but stay on it."

"Okay."

"Okay. And don't forget about our fives."

Shaw hung up before Walter could protest.

He sat back in a reclining chair looking out a window that faced an open parking lot. Not much of a view, but by Manhattan standards, any view better than an airshaft was a major plus.

Shaw's apartment took up half the floor of a converted loft building. Of course, he had to build the place from scratch, get it before real estate prices exploded, and live in a neighborhood with no neighbors for about ten years, but he ended up one of the "lucky" ones. He had space and light. Shaw also had a woman whom he dreaded seeing in the apartment. And now, suddenly, Shaw also had a nearly unquenchable desire for Justine Burton, making it even more painful to contemplate dealing with Jane.

Shaw knew that whatever was going on between him and Justine could burn out quickly. But he also knew he didn't want it to. He knew that as long as Justine Burton would have him, he would want her. And he knew he would continuing wanting her, even after she no longer wanted him.

Why? he asked himself. Why risk it? Her looks and her body were almost enough in themselves. But there was more to it. Shaw wanted the woman behind the looks. The woman who generated that smart, penetrating gaze. The woman who could go right ahead and treat him like a man, without pretense or guile or qualification. Shaw didn't know if that ability came from her black culture or just from her, but it made him want Justine Burton, fiercely.

Which meant Shaw had to deal with Jane now instead of just letting it linger on. Whether Justine Burton lasted or not, Shaw knew the time had finally come to end his dead end with Jane. He was ruined now. Now he knew what else there could be for him. If it were going to be any woman, it would have to be a Justine Burton woman.

That was the hard part. Knowing that he couldn't settle any more. Allowing it to go on with Jane just so he wouldn't have to bother fighting over a desirable Tribeca loft wasn't worth the price anymore. Not that it was going to be much of a fight. Jane had the money and the law. Shaw had sweat equity and a Glock. If he wanted to remain civilized, he was going to lose.

It didn't help his sour mood.

Shaw sat there, looking out at his view, still smelling

and tasting and feeling Justine, thinking about the turn his life had taken, knowing that nothing could come of it until he took care of Archie Reynolds and DeLuca's demands.

DeLuca. He was a dark presence hanging over Shaw. He couldn't put off calling DeLuca any longer. And besides, Shaw did wonder what the hell DeLuca was going to let himself say over the phone about New Lots Apartments and Archie Reynolds and killer Muslims.

Shaw popped a fresh minicassette into his recorder and attached a little suction cup accessory that made it easy to record off the phone receiver.

The first sound over the phone was the Fred Gwynne rumble that came out of Conklin's mouth.

"Conklin."

"Shaw."

"Hold on."

"Okay."

They understood each other.

DeLuca's voice came over the phone. "Shaw."

"Yeah."

"What the fuck is going on?"

"Just what you said—"

DeLuca interrupted. "Don't tell me what I said, tell me what you're doing."

"Going after the Blue-Tops. We got one of the managers last night, my guys are closing in on the second."

"They found him. He's dead."

"Oh. Good. Then we got two managers. I hear the precinct guys are nailing up the third one. The fourth one went down in that body shop fire. Today we move down to the next echelon of guys. Between us and the Muslim brothers and regular cops, in two days there won't be anything left of the Blue-Tops."

"Yeah, and what about number one?"

"Who, Archie Reynolds?"

"Answer my question."

"I'm on him. He's next. He's history."

"Don't fuck with me on this Shaw. I want this over. I got reports of all hell breaking loose last night."

"It's a fucking war, Chief, what do you think is going to happen? Nobody is sleeping; nobody is backing off. It's only been a day and a half for chrissake."

"Get it done. I don't want one goddamn more report of shots being fired at that location. Get that guy. Get it over."

"Yeah."

"And stay the fuck away from the woman. You got no business there."

"What are you talking about?"

"You know what I'm talking about."

"If I think she has information, I'm going to ask her."

"She doesn't. And she's out of bounds. Don't even think about it."

Click.

Fucking DeLuca.

He turned off his tape recorder and added the latest cassette to his collection. DeLuca hadn't really said anything incriminating. He hadn't even spoken his name. But Shaw had him talking directly about an issue he almost certainly did not want to be connected with. It was something.

Shaw turned off his police radio, phone, everything but his beeper, which he sincerely hoped would not wake him. Sitting in his dirty clothes made him want to shower again, but Shaw decided he'd save that to help him wake up.

He closed his eyes and a jarring jumble of images swept through his mind: Ellard Watkins's shotgun exploding over his head, Mason bleeding, Archie pumping bullets into Rachman, streets racing by, flames, a naked Justine sitting up in her bed looking at him, Walter staring at his computer screen, the desolate, burned-out streets of Brownsville filled with drugs and pain and misery, that endless cemetery . . . the whole dangerous, unruly mess of it. And then he was out.

Loyd Shaw slept. Walter Wang worked. Tony Impelliteri and James Sperling watched and waited. After Queen Margo rousted them, they parked a block west of the car service, facing the entrance. The East New York street looked dismal, even though the sun had finally broken through the overcast sky. Ripped-up plastic garbage bags, broken glass, and scraps of newspapers lay in the gutter, on the sidewalk, everywhere. Even though it was only April, weeds had already sprouted through the cracked sidewalks, untrammelled, on the nearly abandoned streets. To their left, a long brick wall, barely interrupted by doors or windows filled most of the block. On their right, a jumble of run-down, three-story flats filled half the block. An empty lot filled with tall grass, weeds, and garbage took up the remainder.

They waited and watched.

A crack whore, so gaunt even a baggy sweatshirt failed to conceal her bony frame, led a customer into the empty lot. They disappeared in the weeds and garbage. Neither Impelliteri or Sperling wanted to imagine what she was doing in there to earn her endless doses of rock.

Impelliteri checked his watch. Nearly eleven. They had been waiting almost two hours. He thought, maybe it's too early for the dealers to be out and about.

Just then, a baby blue BMW stopped for a traffic light, about half a car length behind Impelliteri's dark blue Caprice.

Impelliteri had been flipping through his pile of

crime photos and mug shots for most of the past hour. He knew the faces of the Blue-Tops boys he was after. The car service was on a one-way street, so the traffic heading there had to pass Impelliteri's Caprice to get to the front door.

Impelliteri was quite aware that BMWs did not fit into that neighborhood, so naturally when he saw the gleaming car, he looked over the passengers very carefully. They looked familiar.

Impelliteri quietly told Sperling, "Slide down until these fucks pass us."

The BMW rolled by and Impelliteri punched in Margo's number.

"Margo."

"Speak up."

"Listen, there's two guys that just drove past us about a block away from your place. I think they're headed for you. They looked like two of my mutts."

"So?"

"So stay on the phone with me until they walk in. If you recognized them, tell me. I'll take 'em out when they leave."

"Why not before they come in here, dammnit."

"Hey, we get 'em after they leave, you get an instant return on the merch and we take care of your price discount."

"Oh. Okay, honey. See, I always knew you were a smart one. Wait a minute."

Margo came back on the line.

"Are they in a blue BMW?"

"Yeah."

"Yeah, it's parked right outside. They must be coming up now."

"Both of 'em?"

"Uh-huh," Margo's voice suddenly became more businesslike. "Okay, then, that will be fine."

"They just walk in?"

"That's right."

"Good. You know them."

"Uh-huh."

"Blue-Tops."

"That's right."

"Okay, Margo. Cool."

Impelliteri turned to Sperling. "You want to drive, or you want to shoot?"

Sperling smiled.

Impelliteri drove to the Beamer parked outside the car service. Sperling got out and slipped into the backseat. Impelliteri continued driving about a half block ahead and sat waiting, watching through his rearview mirror.

Two men came out. One carrying a white garbage bag. By the size and heft of the bag, Impelliteri figured it held at least two kilos.

The BMW pulled away from the curb. Impelliteri let it pass and followed them for two blocks. Far enough. He floored the accelerator and turned the Caprice in front of the BMW so quickly they didn't have time to brake before their bumper banged into the side of the Caprice.

The marks took it for a rip-off or at least a car jacking, but before they could pull their guns, Sperling sat up in the backseat of the BMW and pressed a SIG into each of their heads.

Impelliteri swaggered over with a big smile, flashed his badge, and announced, "You're fucking under arrest, meatheads."

The driver turned around and yelled at Sperling, "What the fuck is this? You can't be hiding in my motherfucking car."

"Why not?" asked Impelliteri. "There some rule against that?"

"It's bogus man."

"Shut the fuck up, asshole."

In three minutes, the two would-be drug dealers were handcuffed and sitting in the backseat of the Caprice, waiting with Impelliteri and Sperling at the same spot where they had started near the car-service office.

After five minutes, the driver complained.

"Hey, man, when you takin' us in? I can't sit here in these handcuffs like this. Come on, man."

Impelliteri pulled out his Glock and held it two inches from the man's face.

"Listen, asshole. I already told you to shut the fuck up. You say another word, I'll shoot you. I've got your gun. I've got you. I'll shoot you in your stupid head and shove you out in the gutter. Then I'll take the cuffs off and say you tried to shoot me. You got that? Just nod."

The Blue-Top nodded.

He turned to Sperling. "Hell, James, I think this is going to work."

Sperling merely nodded.

"Like dropping your line in the water when the blues are running."

"Uh-huh."

"Get it. Blues. Bluefish. Blue-Tops. Get it?"

"I got it."

"What's the matter? You pissed because you couldn't shoot them?"

Sperling thought about that for a moment before he turned to Impelliteri and gave him a thoughtful answer.

"Well, you may be right. No arrest, no booking, no idiotic trial where the defendant has every advantage, where all our evidence gets thrown out, where every witness lies. Bam! Over, done with, finished."

"More like bam, bam." said Impelliteri, "Pity they can't all be that simple, huh?"

"Yes. A pity."

Just as Impelliteri started another riff, another car pulled up. Another group going for the bait. Over the next four hours they nabbed five more would-be dealers responding to Margo's sale. Impelliteri and Sperling didn't have nearly enough handcuffs.

Shaw arrived at the seven-three precinct a little before three o'clock, just as Impelliteri and Sperling paraded their catch into the precinct.

They'd called the precinct cops to come and help them chain the prisoners together. In they trudged, seven captured criminals, Impelliteri trailing behind carrying seven pairs of shoes strung together like scalps.

Shaw watched the procession and smiled.

Back in the squad room, Tony Impelliteri regaled Walter Wang and Loyd Shaw with his tale of conquest. Sperling said nothing to take center stage from Impelliteri, yet by his silence seemed to verify every pronouncement his partner made.

Shaw allowed it to go on for about ten minutes. He was happy to tell them they had achieved something damn impressive. Seven collars. All with drugs. Six of them turning out to be on their list of Blue-Tops.

Shaw told them they had done a great job. And then he told them, "Okay, before we celebrate there's one little thing left to do, otherwise the rest of it doesn't mean shit."

"What's that?"

"Nail Archie Reynolds."

That ended the celebration quickly.

"I talked to DeLuca this morning. I keep getting the same message: get Archie Reynolds."

"Okay, okay," said Impelliteri, "let's get the fucking guy and be done with this."

Shaw asked Walter, "You come up with anything helpful?"

"Nothing. I went through just about everything: Federal, NY State, every state east of the Mississippi and California. Only new thing I got is a traffic ticket in South Carolina."

"How old?"

Walter shuffled through a pile of computer printouts until he came up with a piece of paper.

"Two months ago."

Impelliteri said, "Probably down there buying guns."

"I don't suppose he was driving his own car, was he?"

"Nope," said Wang. "Rental. But he didn't rent it. Reginal Wilson rented it."

"Well he's fucking dead and so is that lead," said Impelliteri.

Shaw asked Walter, "Anything happen with that guy Melvin Brown?"

"Yeah. Precinct detectives found him in Virginia. Hiding out at his aunt's."

"Great. When is he coming back?"

"Don't know. He's fighting extradition. They got him for parole violations. He's going back for the last bit on a fifteen to twenty-five."

"Fuck, he won't be up here for at least a week."

"Screw it," said Shaw. "We've got no time for it. Fuck him, fuck that computer, fuck Reggie Whack, fuck all of them. We do this the old-fashioned way. We got six guys, right? Six from the gang?"

"Six," said Impelliteri.

"All right. One of those pricks is going to turn. One of them or all of them are going to tell us something, some goddamn thing about how or where we can find Archie fucking Reynolds. So let's get some interrogation rooms and let's start talking to these mutts. Did you keep those guys together when you arrested them?"

"Shit, we had to. There was no place to put 'em."

"For how long?"

"Well, five of 'em sat together for a couple of hours."

"Shit. That probably eliminates using them against each other."

"Hey, you know they're gonna lawyer up anyhow."

"Not until I say they can. All right, let's get a feel

for who might play ball, then take it from there. We'll divide them into two groups. You three each take one guy, and I'll rotate between them. Then we'll do the other three."

The Blue-Tops didn't surprise Shaw. They were all convicted felons. And they all felt they had an obligation to be tough and uncooperative.

Of the first group, Shaw rejected two immediately, wavered on the third, ended up rejecting him and picking the other three.

After making his picks, Shaw, Sperling, and Impelliteri met back in the temporary squad room.

"Okay, fellas, here's the next move. We get these bums down to Central Booking. There's a good supervising ADA working today I can get on this. He'll cooperate with us. His office is at Central Booking. He asked if we could do our thing there, which is okay with me. Keep them separate, take them down, go through the booking deal, then we concentrate on three guys: Marvin, Jacobs, and Mitchell."

Impelliteri asked, "Hey man, I gotta clean up, take a shit, get myself together. Any chance we can catch some sleep?"

"Clean up while we're waiting for transportation to pick these guys up for us. You got clean clothes with you?"

"No. Neither one of us have been home since we started."

"Fuck it. Buy a couple of shirts on the way to Central Booking. Clean up in the locker room there. You'll probably have time to catch some sleep in the waiting room while I talk to my ADA."

"That place is a shithole."

"Tell me about it."

"See ya. Come on, James."

Impelliteri and Sperling shuffled out. Shaw turned to

Walter, whose Asian complexion seemed to be turning slightly green. His eyes were hidden behind two narrow slits. Shaw figured he had maybe two or three hours before he crashed.

"How ya doin', Walter?"

"Fine."

"Good."

"How are we doing on Arbor Realty?"

"It's coming. I should have all the reports on properties they manage. I'm doing a Lexis/Nexis search on outstanding liens and lawsuits. My cousin is on it down at Buildings."

"What about their corporate structure?"

"It's a real estate partnership."

"I want names of everyone who's a partner or shareholder."

"No shareholders. It's a partnership."

"Then partners. Anyone with an interest in it. Anyone who takes money out of the place."

Wang shrugged his shoulders. "I don't know. There's a million ways to get money out of a place. A million more if it's a partnership."

"Find out who's inside, who gets the money. As much as you can."

"That could take forever. You looking for anybody in particular?"

"Yeah. Commissioner Burton, any members of his family including his daughter, Justine Burton, his wife, brothers, other kids, anybody connected to him. And DeLuca. Albert J. DeLuca and anybody connected to him."

"Shit, you crazy, man. Those guys."

"Yeah. Those guys. Push off that rock and see what crawls out."

Walter turned back to his keyboard. The possibility of uncovering something about the commissioner and

Chief of Detectives seemed to energize him. He knew as well as Shaw did the advantages they would gain if they discovered that information.

As Shaw left the squad room, he actually saw Walter dialing the phone with his left hand as he slid and clicked his mouse with his right hand. Walter was a virtuoso.

Just before Shaw made it out the door, Walter called out, "Hey don't forget."

"What?"

"That guy Marvin. Ellis Marvin."

"What about him?"

"I think he's the brother of the one they found with a bullet in his head early on."

"What?"

"Marvin and Marvin. Same name." Walter rummaged through a pile of paper on his desk. "I checked. They're brothers."

"Shit!"

Shaw had missed it. Walter, in his dead-tired fog, hadn't. But he'd almost forgotten to point it out. They came that close to blowing it.

Shaw rummaged through Walter's piles of papers until he came up with the original complaint report documenting the discovery of Little Marvin's body. It was in DeLuca's original file. The bullet. Something about the bullet had been unusual.

Shaw shuffled through the papers until he found the coroner's report. Bingo! They'd pulled a .22-caliber round out of James Marvin's brain. Twenty-two had seemed too small for a gang related shooter. Nine millimeters, 45s, bigger guns were more in vogue. Now who put that bullet there?

Another raft of papers took Shaw through the first shooting at New Lots Apartments. One of the MS-2 guards had been shot in the head. And yes, there it was. A .22.

Nobody had ordered a comparison of the bullets as far as Shaw knew, but he didn't need forensics to tell him anything further. He knew who had shot James "Little" Marvin. And now he knew how he was going to find Archie Reynolds.

"Hey, Walter."

"What?"

"Good work."

"Thanks."

Shaw didn't think that Walter even knew what he was thanking him for. He'd explain it to him later.

43

Archie Ar's final conversation with Whitey Williams took place over the phone. By the time Archie called him from his room at the Vista Hotel, he knew it would be suicide to come into New Lots to talk to Whitey in person.

"Old man."

"Yeah."

"What take you so long to answer the damn phone?"

"Can't hardly hear it, boss. Cops and yelling and all kinds of nonsense going on aroun' here."

"Yeah, what's happening? Can't get any callbacks from in there."

"Looks like they be tryin' to clean out New Lots today, Archie."

"Who?"

Whitey shuffled over to his window. The cord on the old wall phone in his kitchen just about reached his window overlooking The Pit. He watched the activities in the courtyard as he described it to Archie.

"Got a whole mess of them Muslim security dudes all around the complex and in the courtyard. Got a shitload of cops going in and out of everywhere, too. A bunch of 'em in damn riot gear. Vests and big plastic shields and all. Emergency vehicles parked right down in The Pit. Look like a war down there, except no one's fighting it."

"What the cops doin'?"

"They going in and out, rousting everybody."

"Sounds like a shakedown in a prison."

"I guess so."

"Ain't gonna do 'em no good. No way they got search warrants for all those places. Totally illegal. Can't arrest nobody that way."

"Well, I see some guys coming out in handcuffs."

"Any of my people?"

"If any of your boys in there, I'd say they coming out of there. One way or another."

"Probably not many of 'em left anyhow. They find any of my stash."

"I can't tell. Sounds like they tearin' up a few places."

"Sounds like the end of that deal to me."

"Looks like."

"Fuck 'em."

"Any a yo' people still about?"

"You my people, Whitey. You still there ain't you?"

"Yeah, Archie, I'm still here."

"So long, old man."

Archie hung up.

Whitey slowly replaced the silent phone. He knew he'd never see Archie Reynolds again. Probably never see any of those Blue-Tops boys. Word had come down about Weight Watkins and Reggie Whack and Melvin Brown. The rest of the gang was on the run.

Kids all over the complex were yelling, "Five-Oh, five-oh." Between the cops and the Muslims, the Blue-Tops were done with New Lots Apartments. And Archie was done with Whitey.

The old man sighed, wiped a hand over his tired face, and continued doing what he had always done. He watched the world outside, from inside. And he thought about getting along without Archie's money.

Eventually, it all came down to money. Drug money or lunch money or rent money. Who would pay Whitey to watch now? Who would make it possible for Whitey to eat three meals a day instead of one? Or pay for the phone next month? Or for decent shoes on his feet when winter came around again? What if they raised the rent once they got the place fixed up? What if? How much? When? Who?

Change. Whitey knew it never ever changed for the better in New Lots. Not really.

After his short conversation with Whitey, Archie checked out of the Vista Hotel in downtown Manhattan and walked across the West Side Highway, continuing a few blocks uptown along the river until he arrived at an open-air parking lot. He paid his parking fee and climbed into the black Saab.

Archie assumed a description of the Saab had been posted in most of the city precincts, but he counted on the cops in Manhattan to be less inclined to look for him than Brooklyn cops. He also knew he only needed to drive up the West Side Highway to the Henry Hudson, to a chop shop in Washington Heights. Pretty much a straight line. It was worth the risk. The time had come to cash in his chips, make a few last minute arrangements, and sell the Saab.

Shaw headed to Central Booking on Gold Street in downtown Brooklyn, the last stop in the arrest process and Shaw's last chance to get a lead on Archie Reynolds.

If he could have picked any place to make his play, Shaw would have chosen Central Booking because it was so grim and utterly demoralizing.

Most cops figure that criminals who have been through the system aren't affected by the booking process. Shaw didn't buy that. Shaw believed that even hardened criminals going through Central Booking felt the fear and dread.

They felt it because they knew that by the time they

arrived at Central Booking, they were facing jail time. The average, straight citizen who's never done jail time can't imagine it. But a criminal who knows he's going back into the system, knows what jail time means. It means weeks or months or years of being surrounded by dangerous violent criminals, strict regimentation, and soul-numbing degradation.

Shaw turned the Caprice into the narrow alley that led to Central Booking's entrance. He sat for a moment staring at the bleak, heartless doorway, not a front entrance, not a doorway leading into an institutional lobby, just a dark, prison, back-alley doorway in the corner of a cramped, asphalt parking lot.

Back there, as if it were too shameful to have the entrance in front of the building, was a single door set in a ragged brick wall. The door was metal clad, always open, revealing another door made of iron bars and reinforced blocks of glass. A single lightbulb burned over the entrance, day and night, reminding everyone that inside a world existed where day and night were totally interchangeable.

That entrance in the corner of that dirty, cramped, back-alley parking lot, told it all. Walk through there, your life changed.

Shaw stepped out of the car and through the door. He knew he would walk back out and it still made him cringe. Some men walked in that doorway, from there went to a detention cell, to Rikers, to a prison upstate, never, ever setting foot on the streets again.

Shaw wanted his three Blue-Tops bad boys to walk through that door and think about that. He'd seen more than one felon who was supposed to be a tough guy hesitate at that doorway. He'd seen more than one break down right there.

Shaw heard the van transporting his criminals pull into the lot. He stood in the hallway and waited, then watched Ellis Marvin, Toussant Jacobs, and Willie Mitchell cross the threshold, heads down, hands cuffed. If they felt anything, none of them showed it.

The cops who had transported them deposited Shaw's prisoners with the clerk who locked them up in separate cells. Shaw went upstairs to find his ADA, a fellow named Charles Edgerton.

Mr. Edgerton was a black man who had such strength of character and bearing that he had managed to maintain his equanimity and dignified manner while performing one of the most chaotic, soul-wrenching jobs on earth.

Shaw knew he could never have done Edgerton's job without eventually punching out someone, probably starting with lying defense attorneys, incompetent ADAs, lazy judges, and remorseless criminals.

Shaw believed that most of the workings of the criminal justice system were mindless contrivances. The mindless routine took its toll. But however mindless and mundane, the system had the power to imprison people, to change their lives forever and that took the greatest toll on the people who worked the system. Somehow, Charles Edgerton had withstood the burdens of his Sisyphean job and still managed to remain civilized. Shaw considered him a true gentleman.

So when Shaw dealt with Charles Edgerton he extended him the greatest respect. He spoke and acted carefully. Even when the clerk told Shaw he would have to wait for Edgerton, Shaw remained respectful. He accepted sentence to the cops' waiting area without complaint or comment.

Shaw waited in the cops' room, a combination locker room, waiting room, bedroom, eating room, smoking room, belching, talking, farting, and complaining room. There were benches and lockers and a few long tables and beat-up chairs. Cops would do just about anything in that room while they waited for the ADAs to interview them. Some got drunk. Some talked. Some ate. Others smoked. Some did all of it in the hours they had to kill.

Shaw picked a chair back near a window, away from the general commotion and quickly nodded off. Forty minutes later a voice yelling into the waiting area roused him. He followed a civilian to Edgerton's cubicle, trying to muster up his energy and wake himself.

The piles of folders and papers on Edgerton's desk and floor told Shaw his workload had not decreased. Edgerton sat amid the paper in a white shirt, tie undone, looking about the same as he had for so many years.

Shaw had always figured Charles for an ex-athlete. A football player. A college standout, but too smart to sacrifice his body for the pros. Now in his late forties, his close-cropped hair just beginning to gray, Charles had become an imposing figure with the extra weight that middle age usually brings. His chair creaked as he stood to shake Shaw's hand.

Shaw gripped the meaty hand and returned the firm, but cordial handshake.

"Charles, good to see you."

"Thank you, Detective Shaw."

"How's the family?"

"Fine, just fine. Thank you for asking. What can I do for you?"

That was Charles, polite, but to the point.

"I know you're busy Charles, so I'll try to be as brief as possible, but there is quite a bit of background here."

Charles Edgerton sat patiently through Shaw's explanation. He listened. He didn't simply sit waiting for Shaw to finish talking. He didn't allow any phone calls to interrupt. Charles Edgerton sat in his beat-up chair, a chair that seemed to suffer under his large frame, and listened.

When Shaw finished, Edgerton asked, "So what do you want from them?"

"I have to get a lead on Archie Reynolds. I've got to nail this guy. Fast."

"What are you going to offer them in return?"

"I'm not totally sure. We'll have enough on each of them to put them away for a long time."

"You *will* have? We have to have it right now, Detective Shaw. Not sometime. Have to have all the ducks lined up or their lawyers aren't going to go for it. Won't go for it unless you have what it takes to nail them right now."

"Charles, let me make the offer."

"What's that going to be?"

"Not much. Nothing you can't live with. Just let me do it. Back me up with their lawyers. I won't offer anything you won't want to give. I'll be straight up. I haven't got time for any back and forth. Either it works first time or I move on."

"Okay. Go on and make your play. I'll go along unless it looks like it might hurt me."

"Fine. That's all I need. Just one other thing."

"What?"

"Make sure you flag these guys so none of them slips out. I have no idea if any of them can come up with significant bail money, but there're drugs behind all this so that means there's money. Please, don't let a judge ruin this for me, Charles. They have to stay in for a good long time before anybody starts to get cute. No turnstiles."

"I'll keep an eye on them."

"Charles, don't let someone screw up the paperwork or make a stupid mistake that springs one of them."

"I understand. We'll be careful with them."

Shaw nodded once as if to confirm it.

"Thanks."

They shook hands. Shaw rode the elevator back down to the bowels of the building, formulating his pitch as he stared blankly at the interior walls of the elevator. Somebody had scraped off most of the paint and left it that way, like a wound on the elevator wall that wouldn't heal. Shaw assumed it had been done to get rid of graffiti. The cure seemed hardly better than the illness. The analogy was not lost on Shaw. Shaw knew what he was about to do—something almost as ugly as the crimes he was trying to stop. Like using Muslim ex-cons to eradicate crack dealers. Or Justine dealing in back rooms so she could do good on the street. Or Shaw taking DeLuca's deal so he could go on living and working.

The lesser of two evils. Do what you gotta do. Can't make an omelette without breaking eggs. The moral evasions, the platitudes closed in on Shaw, but he continued to push them out of his way.

The bruised elevator landed with a thud.

Shaw walked through the cold, narrow corridors, finding Sperling and Impelliteri waiting near the check-in area.

They had stopped on the way to Central Booking to buy clean shirts. Impelliteri had simply bought a clean, black T-shirt to wear under his cashmere sweater. Sperling had opted for a long-sleeved polo shirt. He wore it buttoned to the top, under his blue blazer. It made him appear much more casual, less button-down, more a match in style and sensibility to Impelliteri.

Shaw told them everything was set and the three proceeded into the first interrogation room.

Shaw asked Impelliteri and Sperling to stay with him. He had to work himself into a rage sufficient to threaten a man with death and really mean it. What he was about to do meant wanting, really desiring to kill somebody. Shaw allowed himself to be enveloped by the seductive power of the desire. He allowed himself to enjoy the feeling, especially since it involved men as dangerous and disposable as Ellis Marvin, Toussant Jacobs, and Willie Mitchell.

Shaw wanted to kill them. And yet, he didn't want to. He knew the psychological toll that would be extracted from him when he genuinely, truly, absolutely threatened to take away the life of a man sitting in front of him. And Shaw knew that he would work with the rage that always simmered somewhere in him. And he knew that if they opposed him, he might explode and his hands would be on them.

So Shaw wanted Impelliteri and Sperling there. To hold him back, as well as infect him with their callous attitude about killing men like the ones he was about to confront.

The three men walked into a small, barricaded room where Toussant Jacobs sat dozing. In his disheveled repose, with his long dreadlocks and Bob Marley face, he looked harmless. Shaw tried to picture him holding a gun or a crack pipe, or hitting his woman, something, anything so that he would deserve condemnation.

Shaw kicked Toussant's chair to wake him. He jerked and woke with a start and looked at Shaw in a way that told Shaw he was being rude.

"Cool, mon, jus' dozing, ya know."

Shaw stared at the man and knew he couldn't do it. Toussant Jacobs seemed too damned harmless. Or maybe he simply seemed too useless. Too lacking in force to affect what was happening. He was going away for a long time. That was his life. So be it, thought Shaw. If he lives or dies it won't be on my head.

"Toussant."

"Yes, boss."

"You're going away for a long time. A long time."

"Yes, boss."

"Do you want to help yourself a little?"

"Sure, boss. I be happy to do any lickle t'ing I can do for ya."

"Tell me now, so I don't waste my time—do you know how I can find Archie Reynolds?"

Toussant Jacobs sat up and scratched his head, ran his hand over his face, tried to appear as if he were genuinely giving it some thought.

"Come on, Toussant."

"Well, boss, you know he be living in New Jersey. I know dat."

"Yeah, where?"

"Well, I was nevah dat close to da Ar-Man, ya know."

"Okay, Jacobs, go back to sleep."

Toussant frowned as they left him. Perhaps he began to realize how little he mattered even to Shaw.

There was no interrogation room available for Willie Mitchell so they met with him in his cell. He greeted Shaw with a smirk. The smirk helped. The rage blossomed in Shaw like a devil ascending and he kicked Mitchell right in his chest.

"Hey!"

Shaw got right up to him and stuck his finger in Mitchell's face.

"No, you piece of shit, you hey. You fucking hey this. No smirks out of you. No bullshit. No noise. Nothing. You fucking sit there and you listen to me. And you fucking decide if you believe me. You listen and shut up. Then when I come back in here, you tell me what I want to know or you tell me fuck off and take what I swear on the eyes of every person I ever loved, I will do to you."

Shaw watched the hate blossom in Mitchell's eyes. Fine, he thought. Hate me. Just make sure you hear me.

"Are you listening? Just fucking nod. Don't talk. Tell me now if you want to hear me out."

Mitchell nodded. Good.

"There are two facts I want you to burn in your tired, ignorant, unused, stupid brain. Two hard facts. Number one, you are going to prison for a long time. I've got drug possession with intent to sell; I've got weapons charges; I've got attempted murder; I've got murder; I've got conspiracy; I've got racketeering; I've got more than I need to put you away for a long time. And if you think anywhere in the dim recesses of your mind that I don't have that, just know this—I have every fucking kind of witness I need to say whatever the fuck I want them to. I can put you wherever the fuck I need you to be. I can eyewitness you at the New Lots drive-bys, the ambush in The Pit, the body-shop burning, the mosque attack, any goddamn thing I want, I got.

"Number two, I will make sure you go someplace where they will kill you. I'll find the prison with the gangs you Blue-Tops fucked with. I'll find the prison filled with Muslims who will take it as a sacred duty to avenge their brethren. If you fucked somebody in the sixth grade I'll find him, too, and put him in that cell with you. I swear to you, I will make sure that the time you serve will be the worst time, the worst hell you've ever faced. If it doesn't kill you, it will maim you first then kill you. You'll be tortured, bitched out, and killed off within a year."

Shaw looked closely at Mitchell, searching for the fear, trying to see if the hate in his eyes had allowed room for the fear. He couldn't tell if it was there or not.

"Now, here's my deal. I can't, I won't do anything

about the time they'll give you. But I will do something about *where* you serve your time, if you give me what I want. What I'm asking is simple. Not much at all. But I won't waste my time with you. I'm leaving here now and making the same offer to your pals. First guy who says yes and convinces me he can help me, gets the deal. You decide. I'll be back. When I step in here again I want to hear either yes or no and then we'll talk. Just one word, yes or no. Ten minutes."

As Shaw walked out, he had that shaky, letdown feeling that sets in after the rage wears off. He didn't have much left for Ellis Marvin, except the truth.

As it turned out, he didn't need much.

Ellis had something the others didn't. He had a brain. That makes it much worse when you are facing a life in prison. Shaw could see the calculations, the emotion, the realizations flitting through Ellis's mind. It was in his eyes. Shaw didn't need the rage. He gave Ellis what he had—a tired truth.

"Ellis," he asked, "are you interested in a deal? Just tell me yes or no because I'm too damn tired and disgusted to go back and forth. Yes or no?"

"Yeah. Sure."

"Archie Reynolds shot your brother, didn't he?"

Ellis just stared at Shaw.

"No, no, I'm not asking you, I'm telling you. I don't need you as a witness to that. That's not what this is. There's no lawyer here. I'm not looking for a statement out of you. This is just us. Off the record. Archie killed your brother."

Ellis nodded.

"Okay. Now, listen to me. I want Archie Reynolds. I'm figuring if he shot your brother, you want him, too. You can't get to him, now, but I can. I hate that fuck. I almost had him and I lost him. That can't happen, Ellis. Archie Reynolds is bad. He's bad for you, bad for me, bad for everybody. But right now, while we sit here, he's getting ready to kill again, to hurt people, to strike back. I can feel it. He's going to strike and then he's going to disappear. I can feel him slipping away, leaving more pain, and leaving you and all the others to pay for it. You're going back. For a long time. He killed your kin. And he just might get away with it. Don't let him do that, Ellis. Give me Archie Reynolds. I want that murderous bastard in my hands. That's all I want, Ellis. I want Archie Reynolds."

"Uh-huh. And what the fuck do I get?"

"Besides knowing you helped get the guy who killed your brother?"

"Yeah."

"You get to live."

And so Shaw made his pitch. No histrionics. Just a true promise that he would either arrange for Ellis to die in prison or live in prison.

Shaw didn't think it was a tough decision at all. Shaw figured the tough part was going to come when Ellis had to convince him the information he gave was worth hearing.

"Now look, Ellis, just be straight up with me. If this is a guess, or if you're going to sit there trying to think up some bullshit that you believe I'll believe, don't. I have no time for that. No time for some story about a pissed-off girlfriend holding his money or some mother he has stashed away or some old auntie that raised him who he has to say good-bye to before he goes. Whatever you tell me, I have to believe it, Ellis."

"Archie ain't got no girlfrens. Certainly ain't got no bitches he let hold his money."

"Whatever, man, just tell me the truth, because I gotta believe it."

"Well, you ain't goin' to believe it at first, which is why I know you gonna believe it."

Shaw did a slight double take on that and Ellis just sat there staring at him while what he had said penetrated.

Ellis Marvin was absolutely right. What he told Shaw was so believable because it seemed so unbelievable. And yet, it made perfect sense.

"If Archie be cashing in and getting ready to go on out of here, he's got to go to one person."

"Who?"

"Before I tell you, what we gonna do, put this deal in writing or something?"

"Don't worry about that. You got a lawyer coming?"

Impelliteri said, "His stooge was out there making noise to see his clients before you came down."

"All right, Ellis, I walk out of here satisfied, I hook the lawyer up with the assistant district attorney in charge and they write up something that says you go to the prison you want, any way your lawyer wants to make it happen. Choice of three places, veto, whatever. Now, what the fuck do you have for me? I need it now. Right now."

"Before Archie Reynolds be checking out, you can be damn sure he's gonna check in with the man he work for, his partner in all of this shit, the man who takes care of his money, too. He's gonna make arrangements with him."

"And who would that be?"

"That would be the Jew boy, Leon Bloom. You find that fat motherfucker, you find Archie."

44

After three seconds of stunned silence, Loyd Shaw jumped up so quickly that he knocked over his chair.

On his way out, he yelled back at Ellis Marvin, "You got yourself a deal."

Shaw barely spoke to Charles Edgerton as he left except to tell him what he had promised Ellis. Charles just gave Shaw a quiet, "all right," as Shaw hustled out of Central Booking, followed by Tony Impelliteri and James Sperling.

As they ran out to the back parking lot, Impelliteri yelled, "Where to?"

Shaw yelled back, "Crown Heights."

Shaw did not need to tell Impelliteri to drive fast, but despite Impelliteri's cursing, jamming the accelerator, slamming on the brakes, jamming the accelerator, the congested downtown Brooklyn traffic didn't allow them to make much progress.

This was not a time to be slowed down by traffic. Shaw had to find Bloom, now.

He punched his fist into the dashboard. He started to curse, but instead, realizing Walter Wang was closer to Crown Heights than they were, he got on the radio. It took three tries before Wang answered the calls.

"Yeah."

Shaw yelled so loudly into his police radio that Wang probably held his unit at arm's length.

"Are you fucking sleeping? You sound like you were sleeping."

"Maybe. I don't know. I guess I closed my eyes."

"Well, fucking wake up, Walter. This is it. We got

a lead on Archie Reynolds. Get in your car. Get over to Prospect Place in Crown Heights, Arbor Realty. It's Bloom's place. I don't remember the exact address. It's the thirteen hundred block. Somewhere in there. Just get over there and stake it out. Don't do anything. Archie could be hooking up with Bloom, or if not, Bloom should know where we can find him. If either of them show up there, just stay with them and radio us their position. Don't do anything. Just stay on them. Go. Now."

Shaw didn't wait for a response.

Impelliteri asked, "So what the fuck is up with the real estate company?"

"Leon Bloom or whoever he works for is playing both ends of this. Christ, I tried figuring this every way but this one."

"What exactly is going on, Shaw?"

"It makes perfect sense. All these bankrupt properties, places like New Lots Apartments, the city stopped taking possession of them years ago. Private investors are going after them. A place like New Lots Apartments would attract a lot of attention and competition, *except* if it's infested with crack dealing scum like the Blue-Tops."

Impelliteri said, "So these fucks at this real estate company reduce the competition by . . ."

"By using Archie Reynolds to fill the place with bad guys and dope dealers."

"It guarantees they get the property for cheap," added Sperling.

"So why the fuck don't they just tell Archie and those assholes to get out when they take over? Save everybody a lot of trouble."

"Maybe they did. Or maybe they just let the Muslims do it so they can make money on the security company, too. They got every base covered. They ruin the property or at least accelerate the process. Then they buy it up for nothing because there's no competition for it. Then they clean it out, get paid for that by HUD. Then fix it up and collect rent forever. Fuck!"

"Fuck is right. But it don't sound like they got this Archie boy completely under wraps. He's going nuts out there."

"I think Archie boy got fucked and didn't like it."

"How?" asked Impelliteri.

"I got a feeling he received his vacate notice a little earlier than he expected. My guess is when the commissioner's daughter got involved, they told him to get the hell out a lot sooner than he expected. Cuts down on his drug profits, but so what. They're not going to say no to the Police Commissioner. So Archie gets fucked."

"So he flips out and goes on the fucking warpath."

"Yeah, plus, I got a feeling the Muslims played a little too rough for Archie to swallow. Maybe a little rough for Leon Bloom, too. Somebody told Archie where to find Rachman and my money says it was this goddamn Bloom character."

Shaw pounded the dashboard again.

"Shit! Look to your own. That's what Yousseff said. I thought he meant the cops. He meant the real estate company."

"Or both," said Sperling.

"Yeah," said Shaw. "Maybe so, James. Maybe so."

Impelliteri asked, "You think the brass knows what's going on?"

"I don't know. I don't think they know about the Blue-Tops–Arbor Realty connection. I hope not."

Sperling added, "What does it matter? Ends up the same. This real estate company gets in over their heads, what do they do? They pull strings and management sends in the troops."

"And us," said Impelliteri.

"The kamikaze squad," said Sperling.

"Fuck that," said Impelliteri. "Anybody dies I got a few ahead of me on the list."

"Bloom is moving up to number one," said Shaw.

"With a bullet," said Sperling.

Impelliteri smiled. "Very good, James." Then turned to ask Shaw, "Why the fuck isn't Bloom dead already if he fucked over Archie?"

"Ellis Marvin said Archie uses him to handle his money. Archie probably can't afford to kill him. And if Bloom told him how to take out Rachman, he probably owes him for that, too. A little something to make up for his early eviction notice."

"Shit. The Muslim brothers find out about that, that's one dead Yid."

"Hey, enough of the anti-Semitic slurs, huh. Yid? Jew boy? Every time there's a scheme done with half a brain it has to be the Jews?"

Impelliteri drove the Caprice up on a curb to maneuver around stalled traffic. The three of them bounced around in the car as Shaw turned to Sperling.

"You Jewish?"

"Yes, I'm Jewish."

Shaw turned to the backseat. "Well, you must admit, James, in this particular case it does seem to be a Jewish group masterminding it."

Impelliteri added, "Hey come on, Sperl, only a Jew could figure this whole thing out. It's too fucking devious. Playing everybody off against everybody else and makin' money on every play."

"Impelliteri."

"What?"

"Fuck you."

"Hey, where's your fucking sense of humor?"

"I left it back at the Holocaust."

"All right. Take it easy. But I got news for you, Jew or no Jew, this guy Bloom is going down just like any other cocksucker who's responsible for me getting my ass put on the line to stop the bullshit he created."

"Fine with me."

Shaw said, "Fuck Bloom. Archie Reynolds is the number one bad guy. Bloom isn't out there shooting anybody. We got a long way to go before we have enough against him. We're looking for Archie Reynolds."

Impelliteri turned around to Sperling with a mischievous smile.

"Hey, James."

"What?"

Impelliteri spoke quietly and slowly. "Just remember. Bam, bam."

Sperling simply nodded.

Shaw peered at a street sign as they passed it. Estimated the distance to Crown Heights. Looked at his watch and muttered, "Come on, Archie, come on, you bastard, be there."

But Archie wasn't at Arbor Realty. He was up in the Bronx selling his Saab for cash to the owner of a chop shop who would stamp the identification number from a wreck onto the engine, get new tags and plates, and resell the Saab for twice the seven thousand he gave Archie.

Archie had his pocket money without needing to risk returning to the safe in his Saddle Brook condo. Now he began taking methodical steps to put the rest of his plan into action.

He met with his primary cocaine supplier, a Dominican named Ricardo Arcel. Arcel owned a diner in Washington Heights within walking distance of the chop shop. The cocaine shipments fit right in with the bags of produce and other supplies that were delivered daily to the diner.

Arcel knew of Archie's problems. He had arranged for Sanchez's services. Now he would help Archie with more arrangements.

They sat over coffee in a corner booth and negotiated a monthly fee for Arcel to contact his supplier, a Colombian group that controlled a small, hillside town near Bogotá. The fee would guarantee Archie their protection. And Colombia's lack of an extradition treaty with the US would guarantee he'd be out of Shaw's reach.

Next, Archie took a cab to a storage facility in downtown Manhattan where he entered a small room and collected five plastic cards and five keys. The cards admitted the bearer to five storage facilities in Manhattan and Brooklyn, the five keys opened a storage room in each of the facilities. In addition to the cards and door keys, the box contained a valid passport issued to a man named Adam Everett, but bearing Archie's picture. Archie had purchased the passport two years earlier for just such an emergency.

All that Archie had left to do was pick up Carmen Sanchez to help him at his final meeting with Leon Bloom.

Archie knew he couldn't risk hauling his cash to Colombia. Suitcases full of bills don't always get through security X-ray machines unnoticed. Archie needed Bloom to handle his payments to Arcel while he was away. And he needed Sanchez to ensure Bloom's performance.

Sanchez pulled up outside the bank at the arranged time. He drove a beat-up white 1985 Honda Accord that Archie had agreed to purchase for three thousand dollars. He planned to drive to another city and fly out of an airport where his name and picture would not be posted at every terminal.

Sanchez drove. He wore jeans and a leather motocross jacket designed in red, white, and blue to suggest an American flag. Sitting next to him was a man he introduced as his cousin Hector. He wore jeans and a sweater, as if he couldn't quite afford an outfit like Sanchez's.

Archie climbed into the backseat, thinking that the guy might really be his cousin. He had the same Amazon Indian features as Sanchez.

"Hey, man," said Archie, "we don't really need two guys for this."

"Don' worry," said Sanchez. "No charge. I break him in. After this, I go back for a while. We need someone from family here to take care of business."

"He strapped?"

"Yeah, yeah." Sanchez pulled out a Smith & Wesson 9-mm automatic with a fifteen-shot magazine. He said to Hector, "Show him."

Hector pulled out the same gun.

Archie nodded, shifting in his seat, feeling his Beretta nestled under the belt of his light wool, Jhared Barnes slacks, hidden under his fifties, retro, rayon shirt—his last set of clean clothes. Archie flexed his shoulders and settled into the passenger seat, thinking, cops try to stop us, they be in for a shitload of bullets. Not going down easy now. Not now.

Archie told Sanchez to drive over the Brooklyn Bridge.

Sanchez asked, "Brownsville?"

"No," said Archie. "Not this time, chief. I'll show you where. Just get over the bridge."

Loyd Shaw and his team were about ten blocks away from Leon Bloom's Crown Heights office when Walter Wang's voice came squawking over the radio.

"Shaw, come in."

"Yeah."

"What's Bloom look like?"

"Where are you?"

"Outside the real estate place. Guy just came out, going to his car."

"Is he a fat, sloppy guy with a scraggly red beard and a yarmulke hanging off his head?"

"That's him."

"Follow the bastard. Don't get spotted. Can you do that?"

"Of course."

"Do it. Let us know where he's going."

Shaw released the transmit button on his radio.

Tony Impelliteri cursed as the traffic brought them to a halt.

"Fuck!"

"Don't worry about it," said Shaw. "Turn off the fucking siren. We don't know where we're going yet. Just hold it."

"No fucking choice with this traffic."

The police radio squawked and Walter's voice came over.

"He's heading west on Eastern Parkway. Maybe going for the bridge. Can't tell yet."

"Stay on him. Don't get too close."

"Cool," said Impelliteri. "He's headed toward us.

We get over to Flatbush Avenue, maybe we can intercept him."

"All right. Go on."

Impelliteri revved up the car's siren and just managed to squeeze through most of the traffic. It still took them almost five minutes before they approached Flatbush Avenue.

Shaw picked up the radio microphone and called out to Wang.

"Where are you now, Walter?"

"We just passed Atlantic Avenue a couple of blocks back."

"Shit," said Impelliteri. "Now the fuck is ahead of us."

"Don't worry," said Shaw. "Just head west. We're not far behind." He pressed the transmitter and said, "Let us know if he gets on the bridge or if he stops anywhere."

"I don't think he's going for the bridge. He turned on Willoughby."

"He's in Brooklyn Heights," said James Sperling.

Five minutes later, Walter's last transmission came over.

"He's parked. He went into a bar called Slades on Montague Street."

"All right, Walter. Just stay outside. Don't go in. We'll be there in three minutes. Just wait."

"Slades," said Impelliteri. "Kind of a fern bar. Front part has a long bar, tables on the wall opposite, a few more tables in the back. Food is shit, but it'll be crowded this time of day.

"Fucking Montague Street. Busy area. Bad place for this kind of thing."

Shaw checked his watch. Nearly eight o'clock. The bar would certainly not be empty.

Impelliteri turned a sharp corner, cursing, "Every

goddamn street in this neighborhood is one-way the wrong way."

"Ask someone," said Sperling from the backseat.

"I know where it is. I just got to go around here. Every fucking time you ask someone they give you the wrong directions. You ever know a New Yorker just say, I don't fucking know? No. They tell you—"

Shaw interrupted him. "It's right there. Turn."

Impelliteri turned onto a tree-lined street, barely wide enough for a single lane of traffic and one double-parked car. Local stores and restaurants lined both sides of the street, plus chain stores—everything from a Waldenbooks to a Starbucks.

They spotted Wang double-parked about a block away in front of a Radio Shack store, across the street from Slades.

Impelliteri pulled up and Shaw leaned out his window to speak to Wang.

"How long has he been in there?"

"About ten minutes."

A driver, blocked by the two Caprices, honked his horn. Impelliteri was about to turn and tell the driver to fuck off, but Shaw grabbed his forearm and said, "Hold it. Let's not start a commotion. Sperling, get out and keep watch on the bar." He shouted over to Wang, "Walter, follow us and pull around the corner. Let's get these cars off the street."

Sperling faded back near the entrance to a supermarket across from the bar as the cars pulled away.

Within two minutes, Impelliteri, Shaw, and Wang appeared on foot heading back toward Sperling. Just before they reached him, a white Honda pulled up outside of Slades. All four detectives watched Sanchez double-park and get out, followed by Hector and Archie.

Shaw stopped and turned to face the other way as if

he were talking to Impelliteri. Wang kept walking, realized the other two had stopped, then turned around. Sperling stood where he was, transfixed, concentrating on the three men walking into the bar.

Once Archie and the others were inside, Shaw motioned for Sperling to come down the block to where they stood in front of an apartment building.

The first words out of Sperling's mouth were, "That's them. The black guy—"

Shaw finished his sentence. "Archie Reynolds."

"And one of the other two is his shooter, Sanchez," said Sperling.

"Probably."

"No. Not probably. That's him."

"We got 'em," said Impelliteri.

"Not yet we don't," said Shaw.

Shaw turned to look at the restaurant. Half the sidewalk area in front of the restaurant was filled with tables, most of which were occupied by patrons eating dinner outside. Flanking the bar's open door were two large plate-glass windows. Despite the large windows, from his angle Shaw couldn't see very far into the place. He assumed there were more people inside.

"Why the hell did they pick this place to meet?" asked Impelliteri.

"Midway between Crown Heights and Manhattan. Close to the bridge," said Sperling.

"It doesn't matter," said Shaw. "He's here now. But there's no way in hell we can take him down in there. Not even until they come past those people eating outside."

"What's the plan?" asked Wang.

"All right, listen up. I'll call for backup. But we can't wait to move until they get here. This guy is not getting away this time. We have to position ourselves now."

Shaw looked around one more time, trying to figure the best way.

"Okay, we can't take them down in that bar. We don't want to move on them while they're walking past those tables out front, so when they come out, we wait until they reach the street and head for their car. When they get near their car, they'll be clear of the people in the bar and anybody who happens to be walking by on the sidewalk.

"Both Bloom and Archie have seen me, so Anthony, James, you two go inside. Get a table where you can keep an eye on him. Walter, you wait a couple of minutes then go in after them. Get a spot by the door. I'll stay out here."

"Then what?" asked Impelliteri.

"When they leave, you two get behind them, not too close, just follow them out. I'll be by their car. When they get out in the street, you take out Sanchez and the other guy, I'll take down Archie."

"Why don't we all just wait outside?" asked Impelliteri.

"It's better to take them down from two sides, you behind them and me in front. Plus, I don't know if there's a back exit in that place or not. I doubt it, but I want this guy Archie in our sight."

Impelliteri shrugged. "Okay. Cool."

"What do I do?" asked Wang.

"You wait in there until they get out of the joint, then just get up and stand in the doorway. Have your gun in your hand. Hold it down next to your leg so no one sees it. I don't want any civilians flipping out, but have the fucking thing in your hand. If any of them breaks and tries to get back inside, you shoot them. Just fucking point and shoot. I don't want any of them getting back in there and taking a bunch of hostages."

Wang grimaced, but nodded his head. It was obvious

to everybody that Shaw's plan gave Wang the least dangerous task, but it still seemed to disturb Walter.

Shaw pressed him.

"You got it? Can you do that? Just make sure they don't get back inside?"

Wang steeled himself and blurted out, "Yeah. Yeah. I got it."

"Good. Good, Walter. You can do it. All right, everybody know what to do?"

The other three nodded.

"All right. Don't spook this guy. He's probably way revved up about now. He's been on the run. His whole operation has gone to shit. Just hang in, relax, get behind him, take out your guys, and we're done. It'll be over. We lock these pricks up and DeLuca can kiss our asses. Let's go."

Impelliteri and Sperling adjusted their guns so they could reach them quickly. Without another word, they headed for the bar.

Shaw thumbed his police radio and started to call for a supervisor. But then he switched off the radio and pulled out his cell phone. He decided he'd rather not get into an argument with the midlevel brass about how it should be done. He dialed DeLuca's number.

Impelliteri and Sperling walked into the restaurant. They passed Sanchez and Hector sitting near the front door at the corner of the long bar. They looked past them, trying to spot Archie and Bloom and saw them sitting against the far wall in back, Archie facing away from them, Bloom facing toward the front. They quickly took a table in the middle of the front room against the wall opposite the bar. Impelliteri faced Archie's table. Sperling faced the two Dominicans.

"Christ," Impelliteri said, "this place ain't very big."

"It doesn't matter," said Sperling. "This is good.

Most of the people are eating outside. I can see his shooter and the other guy. You can see our boy."

Impelliteri took a quick look around. A bartender and one waitress stood at the end of the bar near the service area. Another waitress entered from outside carrying an empty tray. Impelliteri pictured her getting in the way just as they were about to leave. He noted that all the tables in the front room opposite the bar were empty except for his and one table behind him occupied by a couple and their toddler. The baby sat proudly in its stroller, playing with a fistful of plastic keys while the mother patiently pushed bits of grilled chicken into the child's mouth.

The back area held six more tables. The space extended around the left, making the room into an L-shaped space. In addition to Archie and Bloom, two of the tables in back were filled with diners. One occupied by a man and woman, the other by a three girls and one guy. Impelliteri had the impression they were co-workers sharing a dinner out together.

Impelliteri looked down, shifted in his chair, picked up a menu.

"The sooner these guys get the fuck out of here, the better."

Sperling, as usual, displayed no emotion. He sat back in his chair and stared blankly ahead, keeping Sanchez and Hector in sight.

Impelliteri stole a look at Archie. He couldn't see his face or hear what he was saying to Bloom, but from the movement of his head, Archie seemed to be speaking intently. Impelliteri could see most of Bloom's face. The man didn't seem to be too intimidated by Archie, answering him with short sentences and shrugs. Impelliteri had the sense that Bloom was trying to placate Archie, but it didn't seem to be working.

*   *   *

"And how many times do I have to tell you it wasn't my fault?" said Bloom.

"Fuck that, goddamn it. Get my ass going in there. Set up my operation. Deal with all that bullshit and riffraff. Then less than six months later you shut the whole fucking thing down."

"You think that was my decision? You think I decided when they wanted you out? How did I know the commissioner of police's daughter would make some deal for a place in there? Once that happened, everything changed."

"Yeah, everything changed. Everything changed, but not for you motherfuckers. For me. I'm the one who got fucked."

"What's the matter with you?" said Bloom. "It's business. Things change. Sometimes for the better, sometimes worse. Today we have a change. Tomorrow it will change again. There will be more buildings. More opportunity." Bloom held up his hands, "Excuse me. I have to piss."

"Man, where the fuck you going?"

"I have to go. It's the drinks."

"You fucking drink too much."

"Yes, and I eat too much, too. Maybe I'll take a shit while I'm at it."

Archie leaned forward. "Keep it up fat boy and you'll be shitting yourself where you sit."

"All right. All right. Take it easy. Just give me a minute."

Bloom slid his chair back and maneuvered his heft out from behind the table. The bathrooms were located down a small corridor behind them, opposite the kitchen.

Sanchez leaned out from the bar to watch Bloom.

*   *   *

Sperling watched Sanchez.

Impelliteri caught the slight change of focus as Sperling watched Sanchez watching Bloom.

Sperling asked Impelliteri, "What's he looking at?

"Bloom just slid his fat ass out from the table to hit the shitter, I guess. Take it easy. Don't attract his attention."

Sperling settled back as the waitress approached them.

"What can I get you? You here for dinner?"

"Yeah," said Impelliteri.

Sperling frowned at the notion of ordering food. Impelliteri nodded toward him reassuringly.

"We're in a little rush. Let's order everything at once. Couple of Bass Ales and two burgers. You make burgers."

"Sure. How do you want them?"

With fucking Uzis, thought Impelliteri.

Archie turned to check on what was happening behind him. The movement caught Impelliteri's attention, and he inadvertently looked at Archie. Their eyes met for just a moment before Impelliteri quickly looked up at the waitress.

Archie became more restless. He stood up and walked out to the front room.

Impelliteri moved his hand under the table and gripped the butt of his gun. Archie passed their table, and Impelliteri relaxed slightly.

The waitress finished jotting down her order and left.

Impelliteri asked Sperling, "What the fuck is he doing now?"

"Talking to his buddies."

*   *   *

Archie asked Sanchez, "You get a good look at him?"

Sanchez nodded.

"That's him. Just make sure you know who he is."

Archie began to turn back to his table, just as Walter entered, just as the waitress serving the outside tables approached the door with a tray full of drinks.

For a moment, Walter, Archie, and the waitress had to move side to side to get out of each other's way.

Sperling watched Walter trying to get out of Archie's way and couldn't help but grimace. When Walter saw that he had almost bumped into Archie, his head actually snapped back. Archie looked at him for a second, turned away, and headed back to his table.

Sperling made a point to look at Impelliteri as Archie passed.

"So how about those Knicks?" said Sperling.

"Huh?"

Archie passed by.

Walter quickly took a seat near the doorway and picked up a menu.

Bloom came out of the bathroom. Bloom seemed surprised that Archie was standing and asked, "What are you doing?"

"Just shut the fuck up and sit down."

Archie and Bloom took their seats.

"So what are you going to do?" Bloom asked. "Why are we here?"

Archie took out an envelope.

"Thanks to you and all this shit with them Muslims it's too fuckin' hot for me around here. Couple a more little details, then I'm gone until this shit settles down."

Archie slid the envelope to Bloom.

"In there is five pass cards, five keys. Inside the en-

velope is a piece of paper with five addresses. Keep
that separate. The cards and keys are for five different
locked storage rooms. Cards let you in the place. Keys
open the doors."

"Yes."

"My money is divided up in those five locked rooms.
Anybody got those cards and keys can get it. You got
to handle my money for me while I'm gone. I'll call
you and tell you who to pay or where to send money.
Once I'm set up, you do it."

Bloom rolled his eyes. "This I need. You never heard
of a bank?"

"What the fuck bank is gonna deal with me? Listen—"

Bloom held up a hand to mollify Archie. "Don't worry.
I'll do it."

"You goddamn right you'll do it." Archie pointed
over his shoulder to Sanchez sitting at the bend of the
bar. "You see that guy over there?"

Bloom looked over Archie's shoulder and saw Sanchez, his dangerous animal eyes staring right at him.

"Yes. Ever since you walked in with him. Why is
he here?"

"To get a good look at you, Bloom. He knows your
face now. He been staring at it long enough. Any more
shit out of you, any more fuckups, him and his partner
there know who to shoot. And believe me, they don't
hear from me regularly, they will fucking find you and
shoot your ass."

"What is this? Now you threaten me? You think I
should do this because you threaten me? Is this how
you do business?"

Archie snarled, "You fat Jew motherfucker, where
you get off coming on to me with an attitude? You
fuck me out of this deal at New Lots. You get these
motherfuckers to burn my people out—"

Bloom raised his voice, interrupting. "That wasn't my idea. I had nothing to do with that. I told you where to find him. I didn't want any more of it."

Archie talked right over him. "And you sit there giving me shit! Me!?"

Archie's voice had become loud enough so that everyone in the restaurant could hear him.

Impelliteri muttered, "Shit, this fucker is losing it."

Sperling gripped the butt of his gun.

Sanchez stood up to get a better view of Archie.

Archie pulled out his Beretta, shouting now, yelling at Bloom, "Give me back that fucking envelope."

Bloom clutched it and shoved it into his jacket pocket, stuffing it in, knowing now that he had gone too far with Archie.

Archie reached out. "Give me the fucking envelope."

Bloom clutched it, shoving the envelope deeper into his breast pocket.

"No. I said I'd do it, I'll do it."

"Give it to me," yelled Archie.

The bartender started to come from behind the bar. Impelliteri couldn't let that happen. He stood and pointed at the bartender. "You, go back there. Get back."

Archie and Sanchez heard Impelliteri yell at the bartender and both turned toward him.

Bloom tried to scramble out from behind the table.

Sanchez went for his weapon. Sperling pulled his gun and stood up. Hector, seeing Sanchez's move, reached for his. Impelliteri pulled his Glock, yelled at Archie, "Put it down. Police, put it down."

Archie turned to Bloom who was now almost clear of the table. "You fucking set me up?"

Without another word he raised the Beretta and shot a bullet into Bloom's eye. Impelliteri aimed at Archie and squeezed off a shot just as Archie turned and fired at Impelliteri, hitting him in the left arm and spinning him back against the wall.

Sanchez turned and aimed at Impelliteri. Sperling opened fire. Turning saved Sanchez from catching the bullet dead center. It hit his far shoulder, and he slammed into the bar, as Hector open fire at Sperling.

Suddenly, it seemed as if the bar had exploded. The people inside dove to the floor, screamed, clutched their heads. The people outside panicked, knocking over tables, plowing into each other as they tried to flee the area.

Walter pulled his revolver and stood by the front door, not knowing whom to shoot, but knowing he was not going to let anyone out of the bar.

Impelliteri righted himself to fire again at Archie, but one of Hector's wild shots hit his left leg, and he collapsed onto a table behind him.

Sperling put three bullets into Hector, blowing him up onto the bar, but Sanchez recovered enough to shoot Sperling. Sperling went down hard, but turned on Sanchez and opened fire. Both men kept firing at each other from the floor.

Outside, Shaw had positioned himself near the Honda. When he heard the first shot fired, he pulled his gun and started running. He yelled into his police radio, "Ten-thirteen, ten-thirteen, officers under fire. Slades, Montague Street. Slades, Montague Street."

Shaw ran toward the bar, but banged right into a large man fleeing the outside dining area. He shoved him aside, yelling "Police, police, move." He knocked over a woman, then ducked as one of the front windows shattered, sending an explosive spray of glass out onto the sidewalk.

Even from outside, the gunfire exploding in the restaurant deafened Shaw. The bar was so filled with smoke he couldn't see inside.

Archie had scrambled behind the service area that divided the end of the bar from the back dining area. Impelliteri's shots had driven him away from Bloom's dead body, but he still wanted that envelope. Impelliteri was down on the floor, unable to move, braced behind a table with his gun pointed in Archie's direction, struggling to stay conscious, keeping his gun held in two hands, ready to shoot.

Shaw finally burst into the bar, ducking, squinting under the smoke, gun held in front of him. He ran into Walter who stood in front of the door, knocking him to the ground.

All firing had ended except for another shot from Impelliteri, aimed where he thought Archie crouched.

Shaw cursed, feeling for Walter, pushing him firmly to the ground.

"Stay down, Walter. Stay down."

"Shaw," yelled Impelliteri. "He's in the back."

Archie leaned out from his cover. Even amid the gun smoke and screams and shattered glass and blood, he recognized Shaw. He pegged two quick shots at Shaw. Impelliteri turned and fired at Archie, but Archie was already moving, launching himself into the corridor that led to the bathrooms.

Impelliteri fired two more shots.

Shaw yelled to Impelliteri, "Hold your fire."

Shaw reached Impelliteri, saw blood all over him, reached down instinctively for him. Archie disappeared past the kitchen, out the back entrance.

"Go," yelled Impelliteri. "Go. He went out the back. Get him, goddamn it."

Shaw sprang up and ran, stumbling over a woman down on the floor. He made it past the kitchen and

bathrooms, running outside to a cluttered courtyard behind the restaurant.

Archie was nowhere in sight, but Shaw thought he
heard a noise from the other side of a wooden fence, set
high up on a brick wall, dividing the restaurant's back
courtyard from the garden of the town house fronting
the next street.

Shaw looked to his right and left. More walls topped
by cyclone fencing surrounded the back area. There
were ladders, an airshaft, buckets, assorted clutter and
junk, an old sink and stove. Both fences to his right
and left were topped with razor wire. He heard the
sound of gunshots and glass shattering on the other side
of the fence. He shoved his Glock into his belt and ran
for the back wall. He had to climb the cyclone wire
fence to his right, step over to the brick wall and grab
for the top of the wooden fence.

The wood slats, pointed on top, cut into his hand,
his stomach, the side of his leg as he pulled himself up
and over. The drop down was almost fifteen feet. He
hung off the wood fence, kicked away from the wall
and let go, falling, not clearly seeing the ground, landing awkwardly. His right ankle felt as if it had been
lashed with a whip. His foot turned under and he went
down hard, smashing his right knee, slamming his right
hand into the slate stones lining the backyard patio.

He managed to get up, ignoring the pain, limping
toward a sliding glass door that had been shot open.
He ducked through the opening, sliding awkwardly on
a hundred pounds of exploded Thermopane glass covering a terra-cotta floor. He fell, feeling the sting of
glass chips cut into this hands, knees. He slid and half
crawled off the glass until he could stand, breathing
heavy, hurting, bleeding, but moving, moving forward
after Archie.

He sensed he was in a kitchen. The room was dark.

He pulled out his Glock, half expecting to be confronted by a shotgun-toting home owner. He heard sounds ahead of him, moved forward, and banged his hip on the side of a countertop. He spun to his left, just as Archie leaned around a corner and fired at Shaw's head. The flash of light blinded Shaw, he jerked back violently, falling, shooting blindly in front of him at the same time. His shoulder banged against the stone floor. He thought he heard footsteps, a door slamming.

He rolled onto his hands and knees, blinking, still blinded from the gun flash, trying to see, trying to stand. He managed to rise, staggered with vertigo, reached out blindly for a wall in the dark room, felt his way forward, moving toward where he imagined the exit to the apartment lay.

He saw a dim light ahead of him. He reached a door, half opened, pushed it wide, stepped out into a common hallway that led to the front door of the town house, bent low, looking for Archie, hoping he wasn't running into another ambush. The hallway was clear. He ran for the front door, shoved it open, and ran up a short flight of stairs to street level.

He looked to his left, saw nothing. Then to his right. Archie, running full speed, had almost a full block's lead on him.

Elegant brownstones and town houses lined the narrow, quiet street, lit only by streetlights at the corners. The sudden calmness disoriented Shaw as he ran, limped, pushed on, watching Archie nearing the intersection.

Shaw could hear sirens. It seemed as if Montague Street was filling with police vehicles, but all of it one block to his right. Up ahead, a cab had stopped at a red light. A blue and white screamed through the intersection in front of the cab, heading for Montague. The light turned green. Archie ran for the cab. The traffic light had turned green, but the cab did not move. Shaw wanted to yell for the driver to go, pull away, but the driver was too afraid to venture out into the intersection with all the sirens sounding around him.

Archie veered into the street, heading for the driver's side of the cab. Shaw raised his Glock, aimed, shot at Archie, who never even turned in Shaw's direction.

Archie reached the door of the cab, his Beretta still in his hand. He raised the gun and shot the cabbie as he turned to look at the figure who had suddenly appeared outside his window. No arguing, no fighting, no pulling open the door. One shot. The driver's foot came off the brake. The taxi lurched forward and swerved into a car parked at the curb, the engine died.

Shaw ran with everything he had. Archie pulled the dead body out of the cab, jumped in, ground the engine. The cab would not start.

Shaw ran into the street. "Stop."

The engine fired. Shaw raised the Glock. Archie shoved the cab into gear. Shaw stopped, aimed at the cab. Behind him he heard brakes screech and tires slide on the asphalt. Shaw turned. A blue and white skidded toward him. He put his free hand out, moving back, but not fast enough. The squad hit the side of his left leg, sending him up onto the hood, banging into the windshield. Shaw, the wind knocked out of him, rolled off the hood and dropped on the street. He fought for consciousness, gasping, trying to speak. He heard the cab roaring away.

He heard the cops open their doors.

He gasped, "I'm a cop. I'm on the Job. I'm on the Job," trying to get to his feet and pull out his badge as the two uniformed cops surrounded him, guns drawn.

Shaw desperately held up his badge, hoping they wouldn't shoot him, remembering the night that seemed like an eternity ago when other cops had nearly shot him on a Brooklyn street.

He heard one of the cops yell, "Don't shoot. He's a cop."

Shaw felt hands lift him.

He grunted, pointed. "He's in that cab. Get that cab."

"Are you all right?" the cop asked him.

"Get in the squad." He pointed. "Get that fucking cab."

It seemed to take forever to get back in the squad car. Archie's cab had already sped three or four blocks up the street before the cop took off after him.

Archie heard sirens. He kept his foot on the accelerator, not distinguishing between the sirens around him and the siren behind him. His only thought was to get out of the area, put distance between him and that bar and the sirens. And then he caught a glimpse of the flashing blue-and-red light behind him.

"Shit!"

He pounded the steering wheel. And then he saw the girl. About a half block ahead. Backpack. Gliding along on her in-line skates, maneuvering along the side of the street, avoiding the narrow sidewalks and curbs.

Archie smiled and pressed the already floored accelerator even harder.

Shaw and the cops heard the thud and the scream at the same time. And then they saw the body, already limp and bent, fly up in the air, hit with such frightening full force that the body arched over the roof of the cab, bouncing, crashing landing with a sickening thud in their path.

If Shaw had been driving, he might have driven right over the body. But not the cop. He braked the blue and white to a halt. The sudden stop threw Shaw into the back of the front seat. He righted himself just in time to see the last glimpse of the yellow cab as it turned right.

Both cops jumped out to see to the girl.

Shaw reached forward, fumbled for the squad car radio, thumbing the receiver, croaking a plea to stop all cabs in the area. Trying to get through the cacophony of static and babble of police transmissions. He tried. Giving the message again and again, knowing it was useless, but doing it again and again before he finally gave up and slumped back in his seat.

Tony Impelliteri sat on the floor propped up against the wall. He held a bloody napkin to his face. Two medical personnel tended to him, wrapping the bullet wounds in his arm and leg.

It had taken Loyd Shaw ten minutes to limp back to the nearly destroyed restaurant. In that time, the space had filled with cops, paramedics, and detectives, tending to the injured and the dead.

Shaw made his way over to Impelliteri.

"How bad is it?"

"Fucking bad enough. Tell me you got him, Shaw. You got him, right? Somebody got him. Tell me somebody got that cocksucker."

"No."

"Jeezus fucking Christ!"

Shaw turned away from Impelliteri and looked for Walter Wang. He sat on the floor, too, leaning against the base of the bar, legs splayed out in front him, still in a daze. Shaw saw no blood on him except for a few specks of red on the collar and front of his white shirt.

The room stank of gun smoke and excrement. At least one of the dead bodies had evacuated. As if it weren't sickening enough, Shaw heard someone behind him vomiting.

Shaw still hadn't found James Sperling. He peered into another clump of cops and medics and saw Sperling's slight body, crumpled between two tables. A tall man in a suit seemed to be examining him. Shaw pushed his way closer. Sperling looked more dead than any corpse Shaw had ever seen. Sperling hadn't been very expressive when he was alive. Now that he was dead, all the muscles in his face had gone slack and his mouth had dropped open as if he had emitted one last "oh."

Shaw stared at the dead man. He didn't say anything or attempt to move closer. He didn't feel as if he had the right to alter anything about the death James Sperling had chosen.

Shaw pulled a chair over and sat near the body. He looked around, trying to discern if anybody else had been killed. He saw the bodies of Sanchez and Hector. Saw one more cluster of people near the back and assumed they were tending to one of the patrons, not yet knowing that Leon Bloom lay dead back there.

Someone helped Walter to his feet and he came to where Shaw sat. He dropped into a chair looking as if he had forgotten his own name. He blinked and swallowed, but he continued to stare off into nowhere, saying nothing.

The paramedics had stabilized Impelliteri and lifted him onto a gurney. As they wheeled Impelliteri past, he saw Sperling, arched up against the straps holding him down and began yelling, "James! James!"

It occurred to Shaw that Impelliteri hadn't realized until that moment that Sperling had been gunned down. As the gurney rolled closer, Impelliteri reached out for Sperling. The paramedics tried to restrain him. He leaned off the gurney, grimacing in pain, yelling, "James, James."

Impelliteri had blood all over him. Sperling was covered in blood. Shaw sprang out of his seat and grabbed Impelliteri's arm saying, "No. No, Tony, don't. He's gone."

Impelliteri fought against Shaw with his remaining strength.

"Let me go. Let me go, goddamn it."

"No. No, Tony."

Impelliteri yelled at the paramedics. "Wait, god-dammn it, wait."

Shaw held on to him, blocking the way to Sperling. Impelliteri looked at Shaw, realizing that Shaw purposely stood between him and his dead partner, but not understanding why. He clutched at Shaw's arm. Shaw pushed his arm down and gripped the side of the gurney, helping the paramedics wheel him away.

"What the fuck are you doing, man?"

"It's over, Tony. Let it go."

Impelliteri looked back at Sperling one last time, then closed his one good hand around Shaw's arm and pulled Shaw down close to his face, staring at him, digging his fingers into Shaw's biceps, staring into Shaw's eyes with his one good eye burning with anger and hate.

"You get that fuck, Shaw. You get him and you fucking kill him. Do you hear me? You fucking shoot him like the murdering dog he is. Just fucking kill him."

Shaw gripped Impelliteri's wrist. Impelliteri finally let go, fell back onto his stretcher.

Shaw stood near the doorway to the restaurant, watched them wheel Impelliteri away, grimacing, wanting to tell Impelliteri why he couldn't let him touch Sperling, but knowing now was not the time.

Sperling's name had appeared on DeLuca's list of detectives because James Sperling had AIDS. James had known full well he didn't have much time before his fellow detectives found out about his infection. And he had known once that happened it would be the end. There had always been gay cops on the force. And Sperling had known he wasn't the only cop with AIDS. But he had known full well what would happen once the word got out. He had already endured the transfer to the shooting range. It would have only gotten worse. Nothing would've been said. Nothing overt would have happened. But the isolation and rejection would have continued. Slowly, inexorably, almost like the disease itself, Sperling knew he would have eventually found himself alone, working somewhere, in some administrative job that had nothing to do with being a real detective.

So Sperling had taken DeLuca's dare. Only Shaw knew why—because it gave Sperling a chance to die a cop's death. Die in the line of duty. With his fellow cops fighting next to him.

Shaw took one last look at the mess behind him, then stepped outside. He lifted a fallen chair and sat. Impelliteri's words echoed in his brain, but something had gone out of him, replaced by coldness, indifference mixed with utter deflation. He imagined pulling the trigger on Archie Reynolds and felt not even a ripple of remorse, not even a speck of reluctance.

Impelliteri was gone. Mason was gone. Sperling was gone, forever. And Walter looked to be so used up as to be gone, too.

They were so close, and now it had turned into a total, utter disaster.

As if it could be any worse, a black unmarked Ford Crown Victoria pulled up and Albert J. DeLuca stepped out.

Shaw simply sat and watched him approach.

The chief strode forward, wearing a dark suit, white shirt, blue patterned tie accented with yellow, letting his barely scuffed leather soles touch the pavement.

Albert J. DeLuca, king of all he surveys, thought Shaw. Even this bloody, stinking mess.

DeLuca spotted Shaw as he passed by, looked at him briefly and said, "Don't move."

Shaw noticed how white his shirt looked and how stylish his tie seemed, perfectly pinched under the knot so that it would lie straight and handsomely against his bright, white shirt, a shirt much too perfect and clean for this place, a place where something nasty could easily stain it.

Shaw sat there thinking, DeLuca is going to scuff the leather soles of his shiny shoes. Maybe even cut the bottoms on all the broken glass. Certainly stain them with what he's stepping in. Now won't that be a pity.

Shaw waited outside while DeLuca did his Chief of Detectives act. The walking cadaver Conklin hung back by the doorway monitoring who could come into the bar while the exalted DeLuca graced the wounded and dead with his presence.

Shaw figured it was too late to simply get up and leave. Just as well. Conklin would have tried to stop him and he would have punched his face and shoved him out of his way.

Something about the sad-faced, officious old cop deeply annoyed Shaw. The invisible fixer. The facilitator. The enabler of the evil that flowed around DeLuca, the man who made things happen that resulted in the carnage inside Slades restaurant.

Shaw thought about the bloody mess inside. Thought about the double-dealing of Leon Bloom and Arbor Realty. About DeLuca's demands. The pressures, the ebb and flow of interests. Thought about how all of it eventually meant that cops like Sperling and Impelliteri and Mason paid for it—caught the bullets and bled when it all went to hell.

At that moment, Shaw could probably have shot Conklin if provoked. He was ready to shoot just about anybody now.

He forced himself to look away from Conklin and watch the crime-scene-unit personnel and Medical Examiner's people and uniform cops milling about.

And now Shaw watched DeLuca head his way. Now the devil was going to come over and tell Shaw that he was used up and done. Fuck that, Shaw said to himself. Fuck that and fuck him.

DeLuca must have seen it on Shaw's face when he sat down at the table. He saw a man who had arrived at the edge of not caring what he said or to whom he said it. Or whom he would shoot after saying it.

But DeLuca didn't make Chief of Detectives by being inept or easily intimidated. DeLuca had the instincts and perceptions that ruthless men acquire. He knew enough to speak quietly to Shaw.

"You all right, Shaw? Did the paramedics see you?"

"Just banged up. Nothing they can do for me."

"You should go home now, Detective."

"What's that mean? I'm getting tossed in the shit pile? I'm history now?"

"Take it easy."

"Why should I take it easy? Is that your next move, DeLuca? You're done with us now?"

"I said take it easy. I can see what you've been through. I'm not here to add to it. I've covered you and your guys behind a trail of dead and wounded all over Brooklyn. Don't get stupid on me now, Shaw."

Shaw thought about his gun. Then about a punch. He pictured burying his fist in the middle of DeLuca's face. But suddenly, a moment of grace shone somewhere in his head. It was the obvious time for Shaw to revert to being Shaw. But for once in his life, for one piercing moment of lucidity, Shaw succumbed to a better instinct. He kept his hands down and his mouth shut. Shaw realized that DeLuca's considerate manner had been extended for one purpose: to get him to talk. DeLuca did not know everything Shaw knew.

Shaw breathed slowly, realizing how close he had come to blurting everything out—all the accusations, all the suspicions, all the anger. He swallowed hard, determined not to give DeLuca what he had come to get.

Instead, Shaw repeated his question.

"I'm just asking—am I history?"

DeLuca sat back in his chair and looked Shaw over. He came at him on a new tack.

"How's Impelliteri?"

"Don't know. Shot up."

DeLuca feigned concern.

"Sorry. I hear Mason is okay. He'll be discharged tomorrow."

Like a fucking politician, Shaw thought. Conklin must have prepped him with important facts just before he sat down to talk to me.

"That's good," Shaw said. "I haven't had a chance to catch up with him."

"I know."

Shaw asked, "What about Archie Reynolds? Anybody find him?"

"I don't think so. I doubt he got out of the area. We'll find him. What happened here, Shaw? Why was Leon Bloom here?"

"Ask him."

"He's dead. How'd you know he was meeting Archie Reynolds here?"

"Got a lucky break."

"What?"

"Some guys. Why are you taking me off?"

DeLuca leaned back. He knew Shaw would give him nothing.

"Why am I taking you off? Look at you. I'm taking you off because you're done, Shaw. Used up. You're fucked up. Go home. Go sit in the woods until I tell you to come back."

"Come back to what?"

"I'll let you know."

DeLuca didn't have the decency to just tell him. He didn't want to risk pushing Shaw over the edge now. Not while he sat in front of him. Too messy.

Shaw didn't care. He was just as much done with DeLuca as DeLuca was done with him.

Shaw persisted. "He got away in a cab."

"Who?"

"Archie Reynolds. Did they find the cab?"

"I don't think so."

"He could be anywhere."

"So what? Where the fuck is he gonna go?" DeLuca dumped a bloodstained envelope on the table.

"You know what those are?"

Shaw eyed the envelope.

DeLuca said, "That was in Bloom's pocket."

Shaw said nothing, but figured the cards and keys had something to do with Archie's money.

"You know what that stuff is?"

"I'd only be guessing," said Shaw.

DeLuca stood up and took one last look at Shaw.

"Good-bye, Detective. Go home."

Home, thought Shaw. Now where exactly would that be?

Before he left, Loyd Shaw walked back into the restaurant and grabbed a fifth of Jack Daniel's from the back of the bar, one that didn't have a bullet hole in it.

Nobody tried to stop him. And nobody stopped him from sipping on it as he drove back to Manhattan.

But when Shaw walked into his loft, there was something sitting on his recliner chair that stopped him mid-sip.

She knew just where to put it so he would see it.

It was one of those legal documents, the white pages stapled onto a blue cover so it all folds up into a tidy package. Shaw hated those blue covers. They only meant trouble.

Shaw didn't bother to read the legal pages. He didn't even want to touch them. But Jane had left a note on top of them. He read the note.

Dear Loyd,

It's been on my list for so long. You know I'm a list maker. That's how I do it. First it was on a mental list. Then, months and months ago it made it to my paper list. When I make up a new list, I transfer whatever I didn't do to the new list. Getting the divorce papers filed made it to a lot of new lists, Loyd. It was the all-time champ. But I finally did it. Stopped carrying that burden around. Maybe it was this last week or so that finally pushed me to get it done.

You've either been gone or acting like you weren't here even when we're in the same room. I can't con-

tinue to worry about you anymore, Loyd. It doesn't
work for me. It's not a productive part of my life. It's
a part that has to end. For both of us. I suppose I would
have preferred giving you the papers myself. But, as I
said, you haven't been around much lately. And apparently you're not working at One Police anymore so I
couldn't reach you there.

We'll have to discuss the loft. Legally, (I know you
hate that term) it's pretty much all mine since most of
the money was mine. But I know all the work you put
into it and that counts for something. Sweat equity and
all, so we should talk about it. My understanding is that
you probably can't make the mortgage payments on
your own, so as of now I'm assuming I'll have to buy
out your interest. Once this one point is agreed, we can
move forward. Let's talk.

Jane.

Shaw held the note in his hand, but refused to look
at it any longer than it took to read.

Not a productive part of her life, huh? My work was
worth *something*. Something? What?

A note. She didn't even have the guts DeLuca had.
At least he told me face to face that I'm used up and
useless.

Shaw shook his head at the arrogance of it. She was
so convinced she had the power to dictate and direct
him. Or perhaps in person she would have spoken those
things she had written and it wouldn't have sounded
nearly as heartless. And Shaw would have nodded and
allowed it to happen. And gone up to Massachusetts
and settled into the calm and quiet and painted red
paintings with his glass of warm Jack Daniel's.

Everybody wanted Shaw to go away.

He placed Jane's note on top of the heartless blue

bundle. He thought, poor Jane. Such a burden I've become. Hanging around on that list for so long. Hanging around her life. She'll pay me to leave. How good of you, Jane. That will make it all right. More fair. The lesser of two evils. That same goddamn rationalization linking all the evil shit from my broken life to my broken marriage to the broken lives of New Lots.

Shaw turned away from the blue and white pages, not wanting to think about what he would need to do in order to sign that evil little pact.

He headed for the bathroom, stripping off his clothes, leaving them where he dropped them on the floor.

Under the clean spray of the shower he told himself, fuck this loft. Whatever it was, it isn't us anymore. Let her have it.

Shaw stood wrapped in a towel, looking through his wallet until he found Justine's card. He called her apartment. No answer. Not even a machine. He checked his watch. Nearly ten. He called the community center. The person answering told him Justine was on another call. Shaw told the person it was important. Very important.

After a few minutes waiting and grinding his teeth, Justine came on the line.

"Hello?"

"It's me, Shaw."

"Oh. I wondered who it was. I just got off the phone with my father."

"You heard."

"Yes. I'm so sorry. One of your men—"

Shaw interrupted, changing the subject. For some reason, he didn't want Justine to talk about it.

"Yes, yes. You're still there?"

"I'm almost done. I've been at it all day, trying to

get these people placed. It's done now. The last ones will be out tomorrow."

"Look, Justine, you should leave now. Archie Reynolds is still out there. I doubt if he'll go near the place, but he might be over the edge now. They're going to find him. It won't be long, but I want you out of there. Get out of New Lots until this is over."

"I am. I'm just going over this with a few of my people before I send them home. We're closing down now. I'm leaving in a few minutes. I'll be fine."

"All right. Just be careful. Stick with your security detail."

"Don't worry. I will. When can I see you? What's happening with you?"

"I don't know. I'm . . . it doesn't matter. When are you getting home?"

"An hour or two."

"Okay. Call me when you get home."

"Okay, baby. I'll call."

Shaw hung up, walked to his window ignoring the pain in his ankle and leg. He stared out at the nearly empty parking lot.

"Where the fuck are you?" he said out loud.

He grabbed his phone and dialed in a page. He still had Walter Wang. He still had himself. He wasn't giving up.

He waited, carefully going over everything in his mind. It all came down to money. Archie needed money now. He was dead without it. No time for more cocaine deals. The keys to his money were now in DeLuca's hands. No way to get to his stash. He still needed money.

It took longer than Shaw expected, but eventually the phone rang back.

"Walter?"

"Yeah."

"It's Shaw. Are you all right?"

"Yeah. Yeah. I guess so."

"Where are you?"

"In some hospital out here. Waiting to talk to a doctor, I think. I don't know."

He still sounded dazed.

"Walter, did they give you any drugs. A sedative? Anything?"

"No. No. I'm just—"

"I know, you're beat. But I need you."

"What? What for?"

"You can get to a phone, right?"

"Yeah. Yeah, there's one in the room here."

"Then get a hold of your cousin in the Building's Department and ask if he got that information on Arbor Realty."

Shaw listened to a long moment of silence. He thought Wang might have fallen asleep. Or might be building up to also tell him to fuck off because it was over.

Finally, Walter answered. "What the hell, Shaw? What for?"

"Bloom's gone. Maybe Archie's moving up the line. He still needs money. And I figure he still thinks Arbor Realty, or whoever is behind it, owes him. It's all I've got, Walter."

"We got nothing."

"Walter, this is it. Just do this for me and it's over."

"I don't even know if I can find him."

"Reach out. Try his home. Get in the car and look for him. I don't care how you do it, get a hold of him."

Walter asked, "What did DeLuca say?"

"Fuck DeLuca. Don't quit on me, Walter. Do this last thing. Finish up with Arbor Realty."

Walter shot back, "I'm not a quitter."

"Then do it."

"Okay. Okay."

"Call me with whatever you get."

"Okay."

Shaw hung up.

What the hell am I doing? he wondered. Can't you just let this go?

The answer was no. Everybody might be done with Loyd Shaw, but Loyd Shaw wasn't done with Archie Reynolds.

He fell back into his bed, aching for the sleep he needed to continue. He closed his eyes. In a minute, he was gone, sunk in a deep, exhausted sleep.

When a ringing phone startled Shaw back to consciousness, it could have been ten minutes later or ten hours. Shaw had no idea the time or even the place for a few moments. He fumbled for the phone, expecting to hear Walter's voice, Justine's voice . . . any voice but the one he heard.

Archie Reynolds had raced the cab, zigzagging his way through the one-way streets, always moving away from the sound of the sirens until he found himself on a side street leading to a main thoroughfare. He slowed down, not knowing at all where he was, but knowing he had to ditch the cab, now.

He pulled over to the curb and slid from behind the wheel. He stood no more than ten yards from the corner subway station entrance at Borough Hall. He left the cab parked inconspicuously, walked to the corner and disappeared into the subway station.

Except for a barely noticeable smear of the cab-driver's blood on his dark pants and a scratch on the right side of his head, Archie appeared normal. He walked slowly down the stairs, intent on blending in with the few passengers in the station.

Now that he had escaped the scene, he began thinking about how they had found him. Who was that fucking cop? Twice now he had shown up unexpectedly. Show up again, motherfucker, and you dead. I fucking guarantee that, he thought.

Archie bought a token and took the nearest flight of steps down to the subway platform. He had no idea what train passed through the station or where it went. He leaned out over the tracks peering into the darkness, willing the train to appear.

From far off he saw the lights of the subway approaching.

"Come on, motherfucker. Come on."

The train came closer, closer.

Suddenly, Archie heard the crackle of police radios overhead. On the far side of the station, he heard footsteps descending and more radios.

He put his head down and walked toward the approaching train. He made sure not to turn his face toward the other side of the station, but out of the corner of his eye, he could see the first cops coming down the stairs. The train had almost reached the platform on his side. Another moment and it would block him from the police.

"Come on, goddamn it."

And then, just before the train entered the station, it veered off to the left, as if playing a vicious joke on Archie, heading toward another platform.

Archie cursed and ran to the end of his platform, watching the train screech into a left turn, heading off to another section in the underground terminus. He reached the end of his platform and jumped down onto the tracks, abandoning caution, running across the rails until he reached the far end of another platform for the Manhattan-bound N train. If they spotted him now, running along the tracks, it would be over.

The N train pulled into the station. Archie grabbed the grimy edge of the platform and pulled himself up onto it. The doors opened. The familiar chime sounded. Archie ran. The doors began to close. He lunged out, just managing to grab the last door on the end car before it shut tight.

The conductor saw the red warning light. Popped the doors open briefly. Archie twisted into the car, the doors slammed, and the train pulled out, headed for Manhattan. Archie slumped into a seat.

Archie had seen the dry cleaner's truck on his first visit to her apartment building. He tried to remember what time he had seen it. He checked his watch. Five after ten. There might be a chance.

As soon as Archie turned onto Horatio Street, he looked to see if the dry cleaner truck or Justine Burton's security squad were parked outside her building. He saw neither.

He continued walking past the front entrance of Justine's building toward West Street. Almost as if on cue, the dry cleaner truck came into sight, moving uptown, heading Archie's way. Archie smiled.

As the truck slowed to make the turn onto Horatio, Archie simply stepped in front of it, put his hand up, and smiled again.

Maybe if Archie had been uglier, bigger, more intimidating, the Korean kid would have driven around him. Or backed up and gotten the hell out of there. But Archie appeared to be well dressed and friendly. The blood on his dark pants did not show. So Eddie Lee stopped.

Eddie prided himself on being polite as well as hard working. He made it a point not to be abrupt or tough like many of the other Koreans who worked at the dry cleaner. None of the doormen ever had any problem with Eddie. Neither did Archie.

One quick shot, aiming up into the truck from where he stood on the street; a two block drive into the meat-packing district where he stuffed Eddie's body into a large metal drum marked REFUSE; and Archie was ready to get Justine. The bullet had stayed in Eddie's skull so there wasn't even that much blood to wipe up inside the van.

He drove the truck to the service door of Justine's apartment building, parked it, then pulled out a large laundry cart that had an overhead rack fitted to it. He carefully picked out the clean laundry for the West

Coast Apartments as well as a few extra pieces. Then he wheeled his cart to the front entrance.

When the doorman asked what happened to Eddie, Archie told him, "Eddie be sick, man. They called me from the other store to fill in."

"They have another store?"

"Yeah. Two others. One up on Washington Heights. And one in Midtown."

The doorman frowned, but hearing about a Washington Heights store seemed to explain why a black man could be filling in for Eddie.

He checked the laundry, and sure enough, the tenants names and addresses were correct. The clothes belonged at the West Coast. Apparently so did Archie.

The doorman allowed Archie to pick the pieces that belonged to West Coast and hang them on a rack behind the front desk. He even helped Archie load the return bags of dirty laundry into the cart. Then Archie dutifully headed off to the service door exit, which took him right past the set of elevators that led to Justine's apartment.

If the doorman had been really paying attention, he might have looked at the closed-circuit television screen that showed Archie riding the elevator up to the eighth floor instead of exiting out the service entrance. He never even glanced at the screen.

Archie knew the odds were good that Justine lived on the eighth floor. He remembered which lights had been shining that night. But he had to know for sure.

He arrived at the eighth floor, grabbed a hanger of clothes, and knocked on apartment doors until a voice answered from the other side. Archie knew the occupant of the apartment was looking at him from the peephole on the other side.

"Dry cleaners. Clothes for Burton."

He said it in a friendly way.

A woman's voice on the other side of the door said, "This isn't Burton. Isn't it late for a delivery?"

"This is when we deliver the night load. I'm just bringing these up for the doorman."

Still, she would not open the door. But she did answer.

"Not here. Burton is across the hall. Eight-D."

"Oh, thanks. Thanks. Sorry."

Archie smiled, turned around and rang 8-D, knowing that Justine was not home, but wanting the neighbor across the way to see and hear him trying to make the delivery.

Archie waited a moment, then wheeled his cart back toward the elevator.

Twenty minutes later, the eighth floor elevator doors opened. Justine stepped out, escorted by one detective from her three-man security squad.

Like most working women returning home, Justine had her hands full. She carried a briefcase, a purse, a small bag of groceries with her mail stuffed in it, and her apartment keys.

To make it even worse, she had her head down, trying to pick out her front-door key. She didn't see Archie. The detective stepping off about one pace behind saw Archie standing in the hallway with his dry cleaner's cart. The cop eyed him suspiciously. Not for long. Archie raised his right hand and shot the highly trained detective just above the bridge of his nose.

That's when Justine turned, hands full, confused, startled. Archie drove his fist into her solar plexus with enough force to knock out a two-hundred-pound man. On Justine's female frame, the blow had enough power to stop her heartbeat for two seconds, paralyze her diaphragm, and knock her out.

She collapsed. Archie kicked the back of her head for good measure, then grabbed her around the waist and pulled her up off the floor. Her weight made Archie curse. He shoved his knee under her hip and left thigh and levered her legs up off the floor until he had her high enough to dump her into the laundry cart.

"Fucking bitch."

He gathered his fist and smashed her face and spit on her.

"Cunt."

His rage satisfied for a moment, he gathered up her briefcase and fallen keys, groceries and mail, and threw all but the keys into the cart, aiming so that most of it hit Justine's face.

He found the key that opened her apartment door, dragged the dead cop inside, and dumped him. Just then the detective's radio crackled.

"All set, Phil?"

Archie pulled the radio out of the dead detective's jacket pocket, held the send button, and said in his best imitation of a white voice, "Yeah. All set."

The answer came back, "Okay."

"Okay, motherfucker," Archie said to himself. He turned down the volume on the radio and shoved it in his back pocket.

He slammed the apartment door and grabbed his cart. Justine had landed in the cart on her side and back, her legs thrust up, her skirt hiked up around her waist, revealing her long legs sheathed in sheer panty hose. Archie pulled her left leg over and stared at her crotch. It was worse than if Justine had been naked. She was helpless and grotesquely exposed.

"Gonna get me some a that shit, too, bitch."

He shoved and folded Justine's long legs into the cart, covered her with bags of dirty laundry and wheeled the cart onto the descending elevator.

The elevator took him to the ground floor without stopping. Archie and his dry cleaner's cart were around a bend, down a corridor, and out the service entrance in less than one minute.

The remaining two cops parked outside Justine's entrance barely noticed Archie coming out the service entrance up the street. Archie Reynolds drove off with the Police Commissioner's daughter, her security detail watching him absentmindedly.

49

When Loyd Shaw finally picked up the ringing phone, expecting to hear Justine Burton's voice or Walter Wang's, the doleful tones of Lieutenant Conklin rumbled in his ears.

"Hold for the chief."

The unexpected voice so disoriented Shaw he thought he heard someone say "hail to the chief." Even after waiting for The Shark to come on the line, he hadn't awakened enough or focused sufficiently to deal with him suddenly.

"Shaw, DeLuca."

"Yeah."

"You awake?"

"Barely."

"Report to the commissioner's office, now."

"What?"

"You heard me. Get down to One Police. Come up to the commissioner's office."

Shaw suddenly became fully awake. "Why? What's going on?"

"Just do it. You'll find out when you get here."

Shaw stood up, focusing now, taking in what he had heard.

"Wait a minute, wait a minute, what the hell is going on?"

"You'll find out when you get here. Hurry."

"Tell me why I'm coming up there or fucking forget it."

"Shaw . . ."

"You told me I was used up. Sent me home. What the fuck is going on."

"Shaw just get up here, now."

"Do I need a lawyer?"

"No you don't need a lawyer." There was a pause. Then DeLuca said, "Archie Reynolds kidnapped the commissioner's daughter. You're on the list of demands. There's a blue-and-white waiting outside your building. Get in here. Now."

The phone went dead and so did something inside Shaw.

His chest constricted all the way up to his throat. An icy shock hit his stomach, spreading down to his scrotum. Shaw suddenly had difficulty breathing.

He rubbed his hands over his face to break the hold that had suddenly gripped him. Shaw sat down, then forced himself to stand, and his heart pounded at the effort.

He muttered, "No." then it turned into a shout. "No!" and he felt a rush of fear and anxiety and anger rise in him. He concentrated on moving, finding his clothes, getting dressed, grabbing keys and money and his guns, arming himself, grabbing his cell phone and police radio, beeper, equipping himself, trying to move fast and remember to take everything he might need. Extra ammunition, he thought. No. No. They'll have anything I need. But he found himself rummaging in the bottom drawer of his dresser trying to find a spare magazine for the Glock.

He gave up trying to find the clip. There was no time for anything but to just move and keep moving so that he didn't begin screaming.

The blue-and-white, lights flashing, waited for him. He slid into the front seat, still unable to speak, but finally able to think. How did he do it? What happened? How long ago? What the fuck happened to her security detail? Questions clogged Shaw's mind, each one pushing up his anger and fear one more notch.

Ten minutes later, Shaw walked through the turnstiles in the lobby of One Police. An administrative assistant, his identification hanging from his neck, met him and escorted him into the elevator that led directly to the commissioner's office.

He finally felt he had control of himself. He began concentrating on *not* thinking about Justine. He concentrated on forcing her image out of his mind, on squelching his feelings about her. It was either that or become paralyzed by emotion.

Shaw checked his watch. Nearly midnight. He had slept barely two hours. Immediately, the thought entered his mind that he might have been with Justine by now. The image of her standing at her apartment door smiling at him, waiting for him, ripped through his mind. Shaw immediately changed the image. Stopped himself from picturing it.

By the time he entered the large outer office, Shaw felt focused and in control. Not much else seemed to be. Chaos reigned. The area teemed with police personnel, civilians, and outside law enforcement people. Bosses shouted questions or commands, sending people hurrying about. Others stood around doing nothing. Nobody seemed to be in charge.

Shaw spotted Captain Parnell and several of his former partners from Major Cases off in a corner. They were supposed to handle kidnappings, but it was obvious nobody had sought their services yet.

At least two crews from the Technical Assistance Response Unit moved about the outer office hooking up their traps and traces and recording equipment and installing extra phone lines.

The supervisor in charge of security for the commissioner stood scowling near a group of his men.

White-shirted uniform brass and civilian assistants moved throughout the large office. A couple of SWAT commanders from Emergency Services hung out, waiting for the inevitable call to swoop in and shoot somebody.

Shaw even spotted a few Federal guys, the assumption being that Archie might have crossed a state line, making the kidnapping a federal crime.

He looked around for DeLuca and the commissioner, but they were not present.

Shaw stood on the edge of the mess thinking, this is wrong. This isn't going to work. Too many people here, too little command control.

It seemed to Shaw that no one had dared to usurp the commissioner's authority, so no one took over.

There was not a scintilla of doubt in his mind that Archie intended to kill Justine Burton and there wasn't much doubt that the out-of-control operation in front of him wasn't going to do much to stop him.

The assistant who brought him up reappeared.

"Wait here. They'll be calling you in soon."

Shaw nodded his head, not paying much attention.

The assistant walked off and Shaw felt his beeper vibrate on his hip. He squinted at the small LCD screen, recognized Walter Wang's cell phone number and immediately pulled out his own phone to call him.

He stepped out into the hallway and stuck his finger in his free ear trying to block out the commotion going on behind him.

He barely made out Walter's voice.

"Hello."

"Walter, Shaw. Where are you? What's up?"

"I'm heading back over to the seven-three. My cousin called me. He got a bunch of shit on Arbor Realty."

"What did he get?"

"I don't know. He didn't even print it. He just down-loaded some files and modemed it to our computer in the seven-three."

"When?"

"He's doing it now."

"When will you have the information?"

"It should be there when I get there. I don't know what he found. I don't know long it will take to print it out. I'll be there in about fifteen minutes."

"Okay, call me when you get there. I'll leave the phone on."

Shaw felt a tap on his shoulder. He turned to find Conklin staring down at him.

"This way."

Conklin motioned him away from the outer office. At the far end of the hall, they entered a side door and stepped into a smaller, corner office.

There were fewer people in the smaller office, less noise, less commotion.

DeLuca appeared at Shaw's side and led him toward the commissioner.

William Burton, the Commissioner of Police, sat be-hind a large, wooden desk on which a single phone, a recorder, and a yellow legal pad had been placed. Shaw had seen and heard the man on many occasions. Wil-liam Burton, handsome, dignified, dressed in a gray suit, blue shirt, striped tie, looked like a police commissioner. But Shaw had no idea if William Burton had the where-withal to act like a police commissioner now.

At the moment, William Burton seemed to be busy looking through a file. Shaw assumed it was his per-sonnel file.

Two more men in suits stood off to the side of the large, wooden desk, both of them leaning against a ra-diator cover, arms crossed, mouths shut tight. Shaw recognized one of them as an FBI agent attached to the

New York office. He assumed both were federal agents.

Another tech crew consisting of three cops sat at a folding table along the far wall. Two speakers on the table crackled with static. One of the crew immediately turned down the volume. A civilian with headphones sat at the far end of the table, fielding transmissions from somewhere outside.

No one else was anywhere near the phone on the commissioner's desk, the designated phone, the one hooked up to all the traces and traps and recording devices. The phone that would bring Archie Reynolds's calls directly to the commissioner.

In every kidnapping, Shaw knew that a negotiator was a crucial element. The family member would speak, but with the negotiator's words. No family member could be in the right emotional state to deal with kidnappers. It appeared that William Burton had already broken the first rule.

Without explanation or introduction DeLuca presented Shaw.

"Commissioner, this is Detective Shaw."

Shaw stepped forward.

The commissioner looked up. He didn't stand or offer a handshake. Neither did Shaw.

Commissioner Burton got right to it.

"You've been dealing with this man, Reynolds."

"Yes."

"He has my daughter. Do you know what he wants?"

"Not all of it, no. He might have money demands or some demand for passage out. But if he has your daughter I know that he'll put a bullet in her head the instant he decides he doesn't need her. Assuming he hasn't done that already."

By the look on the commissioner's face, Shaw could tell no one else had dared to give him such a blunt prognosis.

Shaw didn't care.

"You sound very sure about that."

The challenge made Shaw jerk his head back. He looked right at the commissioner. Right in his eyes.

"I am absolutely sure about that. Archie Reynolds is a murderer. A monster. He will pull a trigger without any hesitation. Not even a second's hesitation. I consider him barely human."

The commissioner grimaced. Shaw wasn't sure if the expression was directed at him or his answer.

Shaw asked, "You're sure she's still alive."

"That's our assumption."

"Your assumption? Have you spoken to him? Has he given you his demands?" Shaw turned to DeLuca. "Don't tell me you negotiated without proof she's alive?"

No one answered Shaw's question.

Shaw turned back to the commissioner.

"Commissioner, we all know the procedure. Did you—?"

The commissioner raised a hand.

"Don't raise your voice in here, Detective. And don't ask me any questions. I'll ask the questions."

Shaw ignored the commissioner and kept talking, moving forward, hands on the desk.

"The minute he can't produce her, put her on the phone, assume she's dead. I hope you're not negotiating with him. It's not possible for a parent to do that. Even a professional."

The commissioner's voice remained calm, but Shaw could hear the anger in it.

"Are you done?"

Shaw stepped back.

Burton continued. "It appears you are part of his demands. He wants you to deliver money. You are to

wait in the outer office. Stay here and be ready to follow my instructions."

"When is he supposed to call back?"

"Soon. Go outside and wait."

The commissioner turned to DeLuca, assuming Shaw
would follow his order. Shaw did not move. Burton
began to speak to DeLuca. Shaw interrupted.

"No," said Shaw.

The commissioner turned back to him as if he hadn't
heard him.

"What?"

"You heard me. I said, no."

Now it was Burton's turn to raise his force. "You're
refusing my order?"

"You're going to kill her. I won't participate in that."

Shaw turned to leave. DeLuca grabbed his arm.

"Shaw."

He turned to face the chief, arm tense, left hand
balled into a fist at his side. The look in Shaw's eyes
made DeLuca involuntarily loosen his grip.

The commissioner's voice broke the tension.

"Chief!"

"Yes, sir."

"Get him out of here. You're right. He's a loose
cannon. I don't want him involved. He's fired. Get his
gun and badge on the way out."

DeLuca released his grip and motioned with his head
for Shaw to leave.

Shaw took one final look at the commissioner. He
knew in his heart that the man had decided to preserve
his power and image at the expense of doing the right
thing. For a moment, Shaw thought he should try again,
but DeLuca quietly told him, "Come on."

Shaw shook his head, half in disgust, half in sympathy, then walked out, DeLuca trailing close behind.

When they reached the hall, Shaw turned and continued walking, heading for the elevator, not looking back, not caring about DeLuca or the commissioner or any of it anymore. He reached the elevator and mashed the down button, feeling as if he wanted to bang his head into the wall.

He heard DeLuca say his name.

"Shaw."

He turned and faced the chief.

"You want to take my gun and badge? Come on. Try it. You gonna throw me out? Come on. You wanted me to tell you, fuck you. All right. Fuck you. Fuck all of you. You're going to kill her. Him, you, all of you."

The elevator arrived, the doors slid open. DeLuca shoved Shaw into the elevator, stepped in after him, and yelled, "Shut up." The doors closed. DeLuca turned to him, "Shaw, you're right, okay. You're right."

Shaw's anger evaporated.

DeLuca asked, "Do you have anything, Shaw? Any leads? *Anything*?"

Shaw stammered, "I, I don't know. Maybe. Not much. Maybe."

DeLuca reached into his pocket and pulled out a card and set of keys. He handed them to Shaw.

"My car, downstairs, take it. That card will let you out of the parking area. Sublevel two. The space is marked."

The elevator doors opened. Shaw stepped out. DeLuca yelled, "Go. Do what you can."

Shaw ran for DeLuca's unmarked.

Come on, bitch. Wake the fuck up."

Archie Reynolds slapped Justine Burton's face.

The pain brought her back to consciousness. The pain she felt breathing wrenched her into complete attention. It felt as if something in the middle of her rib cage had been broken.

"Get the fuck up."

Archie grabbed her wrist and dragged her across the floor of the dry cleaner's truck, pulling her out onto the street. She landed hard on the pavement, bruising her hip and skinning her knee.

Archie stepped closer and kicked her viciously.

"I said get the fuck up."

A yellow cab stood parked next to the dry cleaner's truck, engine running, back door open. Justine struggled to stand, fell on her knees.

"Get the fuck up and get in the cab."

She felt Archie's foot push her rump, sending her toward the open door of the cab. She put her hands in front of her to break the fall, but could not stop her face from hitting the steel edge. For a moment, everything went black, then more pain brought her back.

"Goddamn it."

She felt Archie lift her and push her onto the backseat. He grabbed her right arm and pulled it behind her. She felt cloth wrapping around her wrist, then her left arm roughly wrapped tight until both arms were immobilized behind her back.

"Get down on the floor."

Before she could comply, he pushed her down,

wedging her between the seats. He slammed the back door and told her, "Stay down. Don't fucking move, don't say anything."

Archie sped off as Justine lay helpless, bent over the cab's transmission hump, her full weight on her arms. She tried to sit up. The cab hit a bump, she slammed down on her bound arms. She let out a short cry of agony.

She twisted slightly on her side, gasping for breath, grunting at the next bump.

She heard Archie dialing a cell phone from the front seat. She stopped struggling, lay still and tried to hear the conversation.

"Let me talk to him. Now."

Less than five seconds passed before Archie continued.

"You got my money? Good. You got that cop? Good. Chain the fucking money to his hand and get him ready. I'll tell you where to bring it."

She heard a slight beep as Archie turned off the phone.

Justine twisted again and again, trying to get into a position that would allow her to endure the ride.

Suddenly the cab pulled over and stopped. The back door opened.

The first kick struck the top of her head. Then more kicks slammed into her shoulders, face, chest. With her arms bound behind her, she was helpless to block any of them.

"You need to learn a fucking lesson right now, bitch. You keep your ass still and your uppity mouth shut until I tell you to talk."

He punctuated nearly each word with a kick.

"You understand me, bitch?"

"Yes, yes," she sobbed.

"You sass me and I'll kill you right now. You got that?"

"Yes."

"I'll fuckin' kill you. You fucked up my thing. You're the reason all this shit started. So you shut the fuck up and stop moving."

"I'm sorry."

"Not as sorry as you gonna be."

Archie was out of breath by the time he stopped kicking her.

"Now get the fuck up on the backseat and keep your head down or I'll beat you to death."

Justine didn't dare stay on the floor. But she hurt so much, she didn't think she could move.

He yelled, "Get up! That's what you wanted, so do it."

She managed somehow to maneuver herself onto the backseat where she curled up and descended into her private agony, not daring to cry.

He had broken her nose. Her right eye had begun to swell shut. The backs of two ribs were cracked and her jaw felt as if it had been dislocated.

If she could have willed herself to die, she would have. But it would not have ended her ability to ignite Archie's terrible murderous rage. Justine had become the target of everything that made Archie hate. She was the black person he could never become. She was privileged, educated, protected, and powerful enough to take from him what he had fought and killed to get. And she was a woman.

Archie Reynolds would hate Justine Burton even after she died. He would hate Justine all the way to his own grave and beyond.

The speakers in the commissioner's inner office went silent, but Archie Reynolds's voice seem to echo in the room.

The commissioner slowly put the phone down and looked up at the men assembled in the room.

Calmly, as if it were part of his everyday routine he asked questions of each of them.

"All right. How are we organizing the teams here?"

The head of the Police Intelligence Division, Walter Peterson, responded. It was not lost on DeLuca that the man in charge of the detectives who had allowed the kidnapping in the first place had been put in charge of the field operation.

Peterson tried to sound competent.

"We have approximately twenty teams with trackers assembling in two locations. One in Manhattan, the other in Brooklyn, the two boroughs where we assume Archie has contacts. We also have approximately thirty teams with scanners taking positions on all major highways within the five boroughs trying to pick up any transmission from the kidnapper's cell phone. All teams will coordinate with our squads here and ESU personnel. We've got more people ready to go in when and where we tell them."

Go in where? DeLuca asked himself.

Burton asked, "What about aerial surveillance?"

"Too risky. Helicopters are too easy to spot. We're better in unmarked cars on the ground."

Burton pointed a finger at DeLuca and said, "I want an experienced man from Major Cases who looks like Shaw. Make him available to me. Have him dressed in similar clothes to what Shaw was wearing when he came in. Dark pants, leather jacket."

"We have to assume he knows what Shaw looks like, Commissioner."

"He'll never get close enough to know the difference."

The commissioner turned to Ricardo Mendez, head of his technical division.

"You have the transmitters ready."

"Yes, sir."

"Make sure DeLuca's man is wired."

"Yes, sir."

DeLuca stopped listening and left the room, trying to imagine who the hell he would pick to send on a payoff to a homicidal maniac.

Shaw parked DeLuca's Mercury Grand Marquis in the seven-three lot. He took the stairs to the small office on the second floor two at a time.

Wang sat in front of his computer screen shaking his head, silently muttering to himself in Chinese.

"What do you have?" asked Shaw.

"Fuck. Thirty, forty pages of shit."

"Shit? What do you mean?"

"I don't know, the text format came over fucked up. It's running all together like one big block, all mixed with symbols and shit."

Wang turned to him. "I don't know, Shaw. I've tried reformatting this three ways. It's still a mess. It could take days to fix this."

"Tell him to print it and fax it."

Wang shook his head. "Okay. I don't know. He's pissed. He's going to have to go back to his office."

Shaw dropped into a chair. He bit down on the rage. He would not yell at Wang. Could not. He had tried his best. Was trying his best.

"Don't you have anything? There's nothing?"

Wang pointed to the screen. "You want to try and pick out the text on the screen? You can see some of it."

Shaw looked at the computer screen. There were sections on it that bore lines of words, sections that flashed, sections that were nothing but a mix of symbols and letters. Sections that were simply bars of color.

Shaw stepped back and dropped into his chair. The absurdity that he had defied the commissioner, bet Justine's life on this last, desperate hope shattered him.

51

Archie Reynold's drove the taxi into a McDonald's parking lot in East Flatbush. He had been sitting, parked, for about ten minutes, thinking.

Absentmindedly, he picked up a steering-wheel lock called The Club from the floor on the passenger side.

He had to pull the lock out from under the dead driver. Archie hadn't dumped the body, not wanting to take a chance that the cops would find it and be looking for a cab.

He began tapping the long bar of steel with its sliding u-shaped lock against the steering wheel.

Justine Burton lay in the backseat, concentrating on nothing but fighting the pain. Her broken nose had swollen so badly she had to breathe through her mouth. Her tightly bound hands were beginning to swell, adding another unbearable measure of pain.

Archie dialed his cell phone. The commissioner came on the line.

"Get your cop and the money. Send him over to that plaza by the river down near Battery Park, across from the Vista Hotel. Have him stand out there, alone, by where the boats are. Nobody else. No wires, no surveillance, no bullshit. I see anybody but him, she's dead."

The commissioner answered, finally demanding to know if Justine were alive.

"I need proof my daughter is alive."

"You do, huh?"

"Yes. I do."

"Hey, fuck it. No problem."

Archie held the phone up and jabbed the end of the steering lock into Justine's pubic bone.

She let out a short shriek of pain.

"Say your name, bitch."

Justine complied instantly.

Archie spoke into the phone.

"Do it," he said. "Don't fuck up, or you'll find her on the bottom of the river."

Justine's cry of pain had clearly unnerved her father. He struggled to maintain his composure. He looked over to the tech crew, asking, "Did you pick up anything? Anything?" A note of pleading had crept into William Burton's voice.

The tech supervisor shook his head.

Somebody began laying out maps of downtown Manhattan on the long table.

The commissioner turned to DeLuca.

"Get your man ready, but don't let him leave until we tell him."

He turned to the others, "Gentlemen, how is he going to make the exchange?"

Somebody said, "Boat? Something like that. He's right near the water."

"Notify Harbor."

"He's right near the Brooklyn Battery Tunnel."

"Near the West Side Highway, too. He could go uptown or downtown, head for Jersey."

"There's a park down there, all that World Trade Center stuff, a maze of buildings, bunch of subway lines converge there."

Everybody responded, but nobody knew the answer.

Again, Archie shoved the steel bar into Justine, this time hitting her abdomen. Again he poked, this time viciously aiming between her legs.

"They gonna try to kill me, ain't they?"

Again he bruised her.

"Ain't they?"

Harder.

"Ain't they?"

"Yes. Yes!"

"Right." Archie pointed the steel bar at Justine. "They gonna try. But you remember one thing, bitch. Ain't nothing more dangerous than a nigger don't give a shit if he dies."

Archie started the car and drove out of the parking lot, and nobody else breathing on the earth had any idea where he was going or what he intended to do.

52

While helicopters, boats, mobile units, detectives, highway cops, and patrol cops organized themselves to close off downtown Manhattan, Archie Reynolds drove for about five minutes before reaching his destination. He parked the cab in between two ramshackle buildings, hid it there underneath a overhanging roof. Then he walked between the two-story houses pulling Justine Burton over the rubble and garbage that seemed to collect in every open space in Brownsville, waited until there was no one on the street, then crossed quickly and entered the one place where nobody would think to look for Justine Burton: New Lots Apartment Complex.

Archie had made it to right where he wanted to be, ready to cause the last heaping measure of pain and loss that his mean soul required before he left New Lots for good.

Desperation drove Loyd Shaw. He sat at Walter Wang's computer, scrolling through the maddening text, picking out words, lists, names, addresses, trying to make sense out of jumbled lines of numbers. The more he tried, the worse he felt. Nothing made sense.

Wang made call after call trying to get his cousin on the line.

Finally, Walter reached his limit. Shaw watched him lay the phone down, close his eyes, and drop his head in his hands.

Shaw pushed his chair back from the computer screen. He stood up, eyes closed, teeth clenched. He hit his forehead with a closed fist as if that could jar an idea or a thought or a piece of information from somewhere deep in his brain.

The mix of rage, fatigue, and frustration finally sent him down into a chair. He curled up, feet on his desk, elbows on his knees, and his head down in his fisted hands.

Shaw felt as if his head would split open. His marriage, over. His home, gone. His job, gone. Everything he and Mason, Impelliteri and Sperling and Wang had done, everything they risked to meet DeLuca's demand had all been for nothing.

But none of it meant anything compared to the possibility of losing Justine.

Shaw didn't know if it was love or lust or longing. Didn't know if was battle fatigue or merely the result of a desperate need to have something in his life above and beyond the dark, debilitating mess he had been living for what seemed like years. Shaw didn't know why, didn't know how, all he knew was that if Justine Burton died, he would have finally and utterly lost everything. It would be time to eat the Glock. Go up to Massachusetts and paint his last red painting with his own blood blown out of the back of his head.

Archie guided Justine carefully about ten yards along the perimeter fencing until they reached a specific first-floor window in Building B. Hidden behind a scraggly bush, the remains of a wooden shipping flat lay propped up against the wall. Archie stepped up, opened the window, stepped back down. He placed his gun at the back of Justine's head and said, "Get in there."

They climbed silently into the empty apartment. From there, they walked out into the hallway and exited out a side door into The Pit.

Newly installed high-intensity lights illuminated the

area, but they were well away from the guardhouse at the main entrance. Archie moved quickly across The Pit, pulling Justine along with him, and entered Building E.

The Blue-Tops had been cleaned out of Building E, but none of the renovation efforts had started. The hallways were still dark, many of the apartments still wretched, open, and empty. As Archie pushed Justine ahead of him up the dark stairwell, Justine could feel empty crack vials crunch under her feet, smell the rank odors, and hear the rodents scurry out of their way.

They quietly entered an empty apartment on the fourth floor, Archie pushing Justine ahead of him with the muzzle of his gun still pressed against the back of her head. Sufficient light from outside bled through the windows in the small room so that Archie could locate a beer bottle with a candle stuck in it. He lit the flame and the flickering light illuminated the room enough to see, but not enough to attract attention from outside.

Once the candle burned, Archie shoved Justine to the floor. He reached under her skirt and grabbed at her crotch, but Justine squeezed her legs together, preventing him from getting high enough in between her legs to grip her. This seemed to amuse Archie.

"Gonna get me hot, doin' that. You know that don't you? Gonna get yourself wet playin' like that, too, you know. Right, honey?"

Justine didn't answer.

Archie shoved his hand at her vagina twice more, laughing, then suddenly turned mean and grabbed the waist band of her panty hose, pulling them down, tearing them off her waist and over her bottom.

Justine continued to keep her legs together, trying to cover her pubic area. Archie held his Beretta in his free hand, but continued to pull and tear off the panty hose, making an awkward job of it.

Justine's hands were bound but her legs remained free. She steeled herself, ready to kick at him, fight him, determined not to let him rape her without a fight. But Archie was not initiating a rape. Not yet. He shoved his gun under his belt and stuffed the waist end of the sheer panty hose into Justine's mouth, then wrapped the legs of the panty hose around her head and tied them into a tight gag.

He pulled Justine's belt off her skirt and wrapped it around her ankles.

He stood back from her. "There. Don't need you trying anything stupid while I'm busy."

Archie moved away from her, disappearing into the shadow beyond the candlelight. Justine didn't hear a door open or close, but sensed he had left the room.

Justine immediately worked herself into a sitting position and slid back toward the wall. The movement help push her skirt down over her and allowed her to rest against the wall. She tucked her legs back and sat on her hip, trying to avoid putting any pressure on the bruised and painful areas where Archie had beaten and kicked her.

Her efforts didn't help much. Her arms were bound behind her in an awkward position, and she hurt just about everywhere. Her right eye had swollen shut, her jaw ached, and worst of all the swelling and the blood in her nostrils made it almost impossible to breathe with the pantyhose gag in her mouth.

She looked around the room. It seemed empty of any furniture except for a wooden table on the wall next to her.

She struggled against her bindings, but rapidly found herself out of breath. A cycle of panic started in her. Needing more air, she breathed harder, which made it clearer to her that her airways were terribly impaired, which caused her to become more fearful and panicky and need more air. She started to cough, then choke. She began suffocating. She desperately struggled to suck air into her nostrils, felt her heart pounding, felt the fear, and began to lose consciousness.

And she could not stand to let that happen. She would not allow herself to die that way.

She focused her will, concentrated, forced herself to calm down and breathe slowly, to pull in air through her blocked nose, to live on that thin stream of life, to calm down and to live.

She bit down on the nylon material in her mouth and flared her nostrils in defiance and told herself, God-damn it, girl, you do not let that animal beat you. Slow down. Concentrate. Don't you dare make it any easier for him to beat you.

And slowly, slowly Justine used her anger and her will to steel herself against the pain and the fear. She determinedly gathered air into her lungs bit by bit, enough so that she could blow once violently through her nostrils, expelling blood clots and mucus. It helped and she did it again, feeling the mess land on her lips and chin. She didn't bother to wipe it off on her shoulder. Good, she told herself, good. Let him see that. Make a nice sight when he tries to rape me.

Then she remembered the rape advice she had once heard. She had plenty of fear available to help her evacuate her bladder and bowels if he came to assault her. See how he likes that next time he touches me.

The vertigo and panic subsided, but she still had to struggle for air, so she began to bite and compress the synthetic material filling her mouth. Every movement of her jaw sent searing pain all the way up the side of her head, but she kept at it, compressing the material and shoving it to one side of her mouth with her tongue. She managed to open a slight space at the corner of her mouth and greedily sucked in air.

Her head began to clear more. Her strength and resolve built moment by moment. She made up her mind to fight him. When he came at her next time, she would use her long powerful legs. Or her head or shoulders or hands or teeth if she could get them free. She was going to kick and hit and lash out at him until she either beat him off or he killed her. Justine had endured enough. Maybe she knew she didn't have a chance against him. Maybe she didn't know. Maybe what she really wanted was to provoke him into killing her sooner rather than later.

And then Justine heard a noise out in the hallway, a splashing, sloshing sound, and even through her broken, clogged nose, she could smell it—gasoline mixed with naphthalene and gelatin.

53

During that last hour or so Loyd Shaw spent agonizing in the precinct squad room, he might have actually prayed in between muttering curses. Whether it was a curse or a prayer that summoned the answer, it came in such an ordinary way as to seem even more miraculous. A miracle born of simple, ordinary, grinding police work.

If anybody deserved credit, Walter Wang did.

Because he had spent so much time around the seventhree, everyone knew that Walter was working on the New Lots Apartments–Blue-Tops thing. At about five after two A.M., a detective named John O'Dwyer ambled into the squad room with a scrap of paper in his hand.

Shaw's first thought on seeing O'Dwyer was that they had sent him to get the squad room back. Shaw steeled himself for the final insult, the order to leave.

But O'Dwyer simply asked, "Any of you guys interested in talking to somebody from that New Lots place?"

Shaw looked up.

"About what?"

"I dunno. Some old guy is on the phone. He had one of Jimmy Silver's cards. Jimmy was over there after that drive-by shooting. The guy says someone should talk to him."

"The drive-bys?"

"Yeah."

Shaw almost told O'Dwyer to tell whoever it was that Silver would call him back if he needed anything.

But it seemed simpler to just pick up the phone and do it himself.

"All right, put him through."

"He's on the third line."

Shaw punched the blinking light.

"This is Detective Shaw, how can I help you?"

"My name is Williams. I live over here at New Lots Apartments."

Silence.

"Yes. Is there a problem?"

"Well, you know I used to do some work for one of the guys who kind of ran things over here."

"Ran what things?"

"You know. With the selling and all."

"Selling?"

"Uh-huh."

"What kind of work are we talking about Mr. Williams?"

"Well nothing illegal, you know. Not with moving or selling—"

"Selling crack."

"Right. I don't mess wit' any of that business."

"So what exactly did you do for him?"

"Well, you know I was paid for it."

"Right. You worked for him. He paid you."

"And now that type of work is pretty much gone."

"Yes."

"I thought maybe you all could use my services."

Shaw sat forward. "Well, maybe we can. But I'm not quite sure what you're selling."

"Is it Detective Shaw you say?"

"Yes. Loyd Shaw."

"Are you in charge?"

"Yes, Mr. Williams—"

"Whitey. They call me Whitey. I guess because of my white hair."

Shaw wanted to yell, so what? What the fuck do you want? But something in Whitey's voice, some wisdom or cunning came through. And the fact that he was sober and cautious spurred Shaw's interest.

"So you've been around a while, Mr. Williams."

"Yes I have."

"I suppose you've seen a lot over there."

"Seen just about all there is to see, Detective Shaw."

"Is that what you provided to your employer? Information?"

"Yes, sir. I did."

"And who was that you worked for?"

"Well, you know, I'd rather not say over the phone? The top guy, though, you know?"

"Was it Archie? Archie Reynolds?"

"Well, I won't say yes, but I won't say no. You understand?"

Suddenly Shaw found himself talking faster.

"And he's not around to purchase your services?"

"Not exactly."

"Whitey, if you've got information to sell, I'm buying."

"Should we talk about price?"

"I'm buying. Don't worry about price. You'll be happy with my price, I guarantee it. But I don't have time to discuss it. What do you know about Archie Reynolds?"

"I know where he is."

"Now? You know where he is right now?"

Shaw was already on his feet.

"Where, Whitey?"

"Well, now, you know—"

"Mr. Williams, I give you my solemn word as a man, I will take care of you. Trust me and tell me and do it right now."

Walter was on his feet. Shaw was already reaching into his pocket for DeLuca's car keys.

The solemn voice of the elderly savior came through the earpiece.

"He's in New Lots. Archie Reynolds walked into Building E about fifteen, twenty minutes ago. That's the last building, you know. The only one left about the same as they used to be."

"Twenty minutes?"

"Well, I been tryin' to get through to someone—"

"Was he alone?"

"No. It was kind of dark. Couldn't make out exactly who was with him, but if I was going to guess I'd say it was that woman who runs the center across the street. She's the Police Commissioner's daughter, you know. I don't know if you know that."

"Yes. Yes I do. I'm going to put you on the phone with one of my detectives now. He'll get your exact location and phone and so on. I will be seeing you soon, Mr. Williams. You're in your apartment now?"

"Yes, sir."

"You stay there. You stay on this phone and keep watch and don't move. Do not move."

Shaw handed the phone to Walter.

"Get everything you can on this guy."

"What are you going to do?"

Decision time. Life and death. No going back. And he had to decide in seconds.

Shaw looked at his watch. If he alerted the brass he knew they would come full force. Archie would hear them. He couldn't risk that. But could he possibly take this on by himself?

He told Walter, "You wait twenty minutes. Twenty minutes. Then you call into One Police. Give them the information. Archie Reynolds spotted in Building E,

New Lots, with Justine Burton. Twenty minutes from now."

Shaw shouted the last words as he ran down the stairs.

Archie backed into the apartment pouring out gobs of gelatinous gasoline. He splashed the reeking solution on the floor and walls of the room.

All of Justine's resolve disappeared. Pure, implacable fear took over. She pulled her feet back and cowered away from the splashing liquid, but a cold, sticky blob of it splattered across her legs and thigh. She could already feel the searing pain, could imagine her skin bubbling and burning when Archie ignited it.

He set down his five-gallon can and turned to her.

"Had this shit stashed up here for a while now. Got a nice can full of it emptying down the stairwell. Outside halls are wet down real nice. Gonna be real hell to pay soon. You people gonna wish you'd never messed with the Ar-Man."

Justine could do nothing but stare back at him, her mind too blank and numb to allow her to even nod.

"I take that shit out your mouth, you gonna scream?"

Justine managed to shake her head no. Anything to be able to breathe again. Anything to delay the match.

"Okay, now, don't fuck with me, bitch. Don't move while I cut this shit off you."

The wing knife opened in Archie's hand with a snap.

He came within striking range, but Justine remained motionless, and he sliced through the leg of the panty hose. Justine shook her head and spit out the gag. She didn't scream. She didn't say anything. She just sat there against the wall breathing through her mouth, practically tasting the noxious, flammable liquid.

Archie cut the belt off her legs then deftly stepped back as if expecting a kick.

"You gonna die over this thing, you know. Was it worth dying over? That stupid-ass community center of yours?"

Justine cleared her throat, responding, "What about you? Is it worth you dying over it, too?"

"Shit. Who says I'm gonna die. I got some cash in my pocket. Boost another car, drive on out of here when this place goes up. They catch me, fuck it, I won't die alone like you."

Justine didn't comment.

"So? Was it worth it?" he asked.

"Yes," she answered.

"Why? To help a bunch a crackhead bitches and their crazy, fuckin' kids they don't even give a shit about anyhow. Most of them bitches let their kids starve in rags if it means another hit on the pipe. What the fuck you think you were gonna do for 'em?"

"Help them stop."

"Stop what? Crackin' up?"

"Yes."

Archie laughed. "Sheet. What the fuck you smokin' girl. Bullshit. You know what?"

"What?"

"Those bitches go in your place? They walk right back over here and buy shit from me. They crack it up, then go back and get what they can from you. You ain't stopping shit."

"We stopped you, didn't we?"

"Yeah, who's we? You and that fat-ass Bloom and his Muslim house niggers? That motherfucker be dead now, honey. The Muslim guy, too. I shot his ass full of holes. Cops couldn't stop me. That fuckin' cop you had around you? I'll kill his ass too before this is over. I'm might just fuckin' do it before I go. I. got him where I want him, too. Got him standing out by the Hudson River, right now. I can run his ass all over this town, sidle up next to him and cap a round in his head anytime. Be gone before they know it. Shit.

"And nobody gonna stop me from burning your ass and this place to the ground. So what did you accomplish except getting everybody killed, you included? Nothing going to change. Crack ain't even leavin' this neighborhood. Ain't me it's just gonna be some other nigger selling dope. These people ain't got nothing else. Crackheads don't *want* nothing else."

Justine had enough sense not to answer him. As long as he talked, she didn't burn.

"Ain't a fuckin' thing you can give them they'll want more than crack, baby. Not one fuckin' thing. What the hell gave you the notion they do?"

Justine forced herself to speak to Archie as if he deserved her response, knowing the longer he talked, the longer she would stay alive. Maybe someone would hear them. Maybe someone would see the flickering light. Maybe she believed somewhere inside her that Shaw would find her.

"They're human aren't they? Do you really think they want to live like that? That the only thing left for them is crack?"

"What the fuck else is there for them? Jobs? Families? Place to live where someone ain't gonna take whatever they got, first chance they get? You gonna change that?"

"Maybe. Maybe for a few. For at least a few."

"Hah. You gonna need more than cops and Muslims and a place in this shithole to do that. You got fuckin' balls, girl, comin' in here like this. Causin' all this mess. But you ain't done nothing but get a lot of people killed and make the mess move to someplace else."

"I don't agree. I still think people should try."

"Yeah, right. What the fuck you know about it

anyhow? Ever try crackin' it up a little? Might do you some good."

"I don't have to try it to know how it ruins the lives of these women and children."

"Yeah, womens do love the rock, don't they?" Archie reached into his back pocket and pulled out a plastic bag filled with blue-topped vials and dropped it on the floor near Justine.

"That's the last of it. Used to have pounds of that shit stored up here. All the homeys used it up for themselves. Grabbin' what they can. You ought to try it before I burn your ass up. Be good going out high."

"Don't do this. What about the other people in this building? Why? Why do this? Just to kill me? Why hurt everybody else?"

"Shit, they'll get out when they smell this burning. And if they don't, fuck 'em. They'll remember not to mess with the Ar-Man next time."

"You do this and you'll die. They'll hunt you down wherever you go. Just leave. They don't know where you are. You can get away."

"You think they ain't gonna hunt me down anyhow? You think I'm going quietly? Put my nappy head down and shuffle off, hope the white man don't git me and make me pay? Fuck that. Come on, get your ass up, time to give your daddy a message. You want to talk to him?"

"Yes."

"Then get your ass up, girl, and don't be causing me any trouble or I just shoot you and get on wit' it."

Despite her injuries and hands bound behind her back, Justine managed to rise to her feet without Archie's help.

"Go over and stand facing that table."

*   *   *

Albert J. DeLuca's unmarked had a hugely powerful engine, a full set of flashers in the window well and grill, plus flashing strobes. Shaw touched the brake only twice during the five minutes it took him to reach New Lots.

He drove the unmarked right up to the front gate. He had his gun and badge out striding toward the guard house before the two guards on duty even stood up.

"Police, open the gate."

They buzzed him in and Shaw walked quickly to them.

"Call Yousseff. Tell him Archie Reynolds is in there and that I'm going after him. Keep that gate closed until he arrives. No one gets in, no one gets out. No one. Tell Yousseff." Shaw did not wait for a response. "Which one is Building E?"

The guard pointed to the far building located at the back of The Pit. Shaw broke into a run, looking at the building, trying to see a light, any motion, any sign, but seeing nothing but a mean, dark, menacing building. The last stop in New Lots.

Justine turned toward the table. Archie shoved her forward, pushing her off her feet. She banged into the table's edge and doubled over onto it. She wanted to kick back at Archie, but he nimbly stepped to one side and pushed her head down firmly against the tabletop, into a wet paste of napalm. She felt the noxious liquid soak through her blouse.

Still pressing her head to the table, he maneuvered around, picked up his cell phone with his free hand and dialed One Police. An operator answered and Archie announced, "This is the Ar-Man, baby, get me the pohleece commissioner."

The call went through immediately. Commissioner Burton picked up the receiver. Speakers in the inner and outer office broadcast the conversation to every man assembled.

"Commissioner Burton here."

"Yeah, Archie Reynolds here. Where's my fucking money?"

"Where are you? We can't deliver it unless we know where you are."

Archie walked back around the table, still holding Justine's head down.

"Yeah, how come I see cops crawling all over the area?"

"The man is alone. Where you said. You have my word—"

"Fuck your word."

Shaw burst into the lobby of Building E. He pushed the elevator button. Nothing. No light, no sound. He ran for the stairwell, pulled open the door and gagged at the acrid, oily smell of the doctored gasoline.

He ran up the stairs, pushed open the door to the first landing, saw nothing but darkness, ran back out to the stairwell, aching to call out Justine's name, to warn anybody still in the building, but not daring to make any noise to alert Archie. As he ran, the smell grew stronger. Instinctively, he ran up up toward the source. Up toward the source of the evil.

Archie yelled, "Fuck you and your money. How many cops you got running around down there, you chump. How many scanners you got tryin' to pick up this cell phone? Huh? Betcha got boats an' shit, cops sneaking around. You got that asshole standing out there with my money? I hope someone mugs his ass."

In his corner office at One Police, William Burton suddenly realized the true purpose of the man who held his daughter. The men around him squirmed as they watched fear finally take hold of the commissioner.

Something in him broke. He yelled, "Where's my daughter?"

As Archie moved behind Justine, even with her head pinned into the sticky gasoline, she aimed a blind kick at his crotch. It was an awkward attempt. Archie twisted away from the kick, but it still struck the side of his leg. It seemed to amuse him.

"Uh-oh! Ain't this a bitch? Your girl just tried to kick me. She's right here, motherfucker, trying to assault me. Ought to have you arrest her ass."

The commissioner stood up at his desk, yelling at the tech crew, "Find him. Find him."

Archie savagely kicked the inside of Justine's thigh, opening her legs so he could stand between them, behind her. He shoved his growing erection into her backside. Justine twisted and tried to shove him away with her leg, screaming, "Get away from me. Get away."

Archie could not hold her down with one hand. He tossed the phone onto the floor so he could use both hands to restrain her. The sounds of Justine's screams filled her father's office.

From two flights down, Shaw heard a faint noise from above. He tried to run harder, faster. His foot stepped into the slick gasoline and he went down, smashing his knee into the edge of a step.

His twisted ankle screamed again in pain.

He grabbed a handrail, feeling, stumbling, moving again, his lungs aching for air, his heart pounding, the stench of the gas burning in his throat, trying to suppress his gasps for air so he could hear better. It sounded like a woman's voice.

Justine twisted and writhed with such fury that Archie finally slammed a fist into her kidney, paralyzing her.

As he pulled her skirt up, he yelled toward the phone, "Shit man, she's a fighter. But I'm still gonna fuck her up the ass and cap a round into her head."

He pushed her skirt up over her hips and began to pull down his pants zipper.

"Man, she likes this. Bitch is wet, man! Wet an' wild, baby."

In the small office at One Police, Commissioner William Burton began raving, screaming threats and curses over the phone, but they emerged from the cell phone lying on the floor as tiny, muffled noises buried by Justine's anguished snarls and shrieks.

Walter Wang's call finally got through to the command center at One Police adding more confusion to the chaos. He yelled his message to the operator who tried to transfer the call to the command center, but no one picked up the ringing phone. No one heard anything except William Burton snarling death threats at Archie Reynolds.

Archie heard nothing, except Justine Burton.

He had his erection out. He punched at the inside of her thighs with his knees, forcing her legs open wider, pushing her down against the table. In desperation, Justine grabbed blindly with her bound hands, hoping to grasp his genitals. Archie avoided her clutching hands, then gripped the cloth binding her arms and pulled up sharply, nearly dislocating her shoulder sockets, pinning her to the table with unbearable leverage. Her face pressed harder into the doctored gasoline. The liquid burned her open wounds and her eyes. She began to gag and choke.

Shaw rounded the next flight of stairs, clearly hearing Justine's choking sobs. He burst into the hallway, saw the dim, flickering light, ran, stumbled, finally unable to stop himself, he screamed her name.

"Justine."

*   *   *

Archie stopped, turned, fumbled himself back into his pants, and went for his gun. He pulled it from his waistband, one hand still on Justine's back. He pressed the Beretta to the side of her twisting head.

With one last desperate attempt, Justine flailed, arched her back, pushing Archie backward. The gun lifted from her head. Shaw burst into the room. Archie turned, brought the gun around. Shaw launched himself and slammed blindly, smashing into Archie, knocking him off Justine.

Justine heard the impact, felt Archie's weight pushed off her, heard both men hit the floor. She rolled off the table, blinking furiously to get the stinging gasoline out of her eyes.

Archie landed on his side with Shaw on top of him, his gun hand pinned underneath him.

Justine yelled, "Shaw."

Shaw ignored her, groped for Archie, felt for his head, keeping his weight on him, leveraging himself up with his left forearm buried in Archie's neck, bringing the Glock around, aiming at Archie's face.

Justine, nearly covered now in the napalm, screamed, "Don't shoot. Don't shoot. The gasoline, don't shoot."

Shaw hesitated, Archie twisted violently, shoving Shaw off him, bringing the Beretta around. Shaw dropped the Glock and lunged for Archie's gun, grabbing for it. He felt the hammer sliding back under his hand. He just managed to wedge his finger between the hammer and the breech. He felt a fist smash into the side of his head. He tried to twist the gun out of Archie's hand and took another stinging blow to his head and ear.

Shaw yelled, "Get out, Justine, go. Go!"

Justine hesitated, looked at the burning candle, looked back at Shaw.

"Go!" he yelled.

She bolted for the doorway.

Shaw took another hit, this time a stinging blow to the temple. He felt himself losing consciousness. He couldn't take another blow. He let go of the Beretta to block the next punch. Archie pulled the trigger. Shaw slammed his forehead into Archie's face.

Archie's nose splintered, but the intense pain only enraged him. He pulled the trigger again and again but nothing happened. The gun was empty.

Shaw reared up to punch Archie, but Archie banged the empty Beretta into the side of Shaw's head, knocking him away.

Both men got to their feet, backing off, gathering their strength.

Shaw looked around, blinking blood out of his eyes, making sure Justine had gotten out. He circled to his right, making sure to block the doorway. He heard Justine out in the hallway kicking doors, screaming, "Get out. Get out."

Archie hunched over, panting, smiled at Shaw.

"Fuckin' bitch still doin' her save the po' people act. Well guess what, honkey, she ain't gonna save your ass."

Archie threw the empty Beretta at Shaw. When Shaw ducked, Archie went for his knife. Shaw heard the metallic flick and just managed to see the wing-knife blade flash open in Archie's right hand, down close to his right thigh.

Archie bent low, spitting a mix of blood and saliva at Shaw, holding the knife back near his right hip.

Shaw felt the fear constricting his throat. He could tell from Archie's position that the man knew how to use the knife. He would come in low, knife hand back, out of reach, almost invisible until he came within range, ready to punch the knife into Shaw's ribs, his liver, his kidney.

Shaw backed away. He knew sucessfully blocking the knife was nearly impossible. Archie moved forward slowly, patiently, waiting for Shaw to back into the wall where there would be no escape.

"Oh, this is going to hurt, motherfucker. You gonna wish you never messed with the Ar-Man, honkey. You gonna bleed now, asshole. Big fucking hero you are."

Shaw hit the wall. Archie smiled, ready for the kill.

And then, seeing Archie's malevolent, almost gleeful sneer, something inside Shaw snapped. Something inside Shaw made him simply refuse to die. He stopped trying to see the knife. He stood erect, arms outstretched, and told Archie Reynolds, "Come on." Then he screamed, "Come on!"

Archie feinted once with his left hand, and followed with his stabbing right hand, coming in fast. Shaw should have flinched at the feint, moving into the knife aimed at his side. But he never flinched because he had gone for Archie first.

Archie's right hand came at him, but Shaw was suddenly too close for a fatal stab. Shaw felt a searing pain at his hip, but it meant nothing to him. And then he felt both his hands on Archie's throat.

Archie reared back for another stab, but Shaw growled and lifted him off his feet, twisted, and slammed Archie into the wall. And again and again, slamming Archie's head with such force he cracked the Sheetrock. And again.

The knife dropped. Archie went limp. Shaw fell to the ground with Archie, still holding Archie's throat. Shaw straddled Archie's chest, tightened his grip on Archie's throat and squeezed. He heard Archie's choking, felt Archie weakly tearing at his arms and wrists.

He continued to squeeze, lifting Archie's head up once again and banging it down. Still Archie struggled. Shaw grunted at the effort, felt himself squeezing the life out of Archie. Shaw thought about DeLuca and Mason and Impelliteri and Sperling. He remembered the faces of children he had seen in New Lots and their tired defeated young mothers. He thought of Justine. He heard Archie choking. Focusing on his face. He felt Archie dying in his hands. He thought of Justine. And himself. And then Shaw felt his grip relaxing. Felt himself lift his hands from Archie's throat.

Shaw stood up, out of breath, dizzy now, steadying himself with one hand against the wall. He looked down at Archie. He watched his head loll to the side, saw Archie's right hand move toward his bruised throat. In a fresh rush of hate, Shaw kicked Archie behind the ear, turned him over, pulled handcuffs from his jacket, and snapped them on Archie's wrists.

He found his Glock, doused the candle, grabbed Archie by the collar and dragged him out of the darkened room.

The hallway and stairwell were filling with confused, frightened people fleeing the gasoline-soaked building, but Shaw bulled his way through, pulling Archie down the stairs, dragging him through his own napalm, wiping the floors and stairs with him.

At first, the people of New Lots let him pass, the men, women and children, the old and the young, the people Archie had brutalized, preyed on, terrorized. But by the time Shaw reached the bottom flight of stairs, they knew who Shaw dragged behind him.

Someone yelled, "Kill that bastard."

Shaw held the Glock in front of him, keeping them away from him. When he reached the lobby, he heard the first kick land on Archie. He turned and pointed the gun. The mob behind him backed off. He knew he could never drag the body through an attack. He was already losing his grip.

As Shaw dragged him into the light of the Pit, Archie regained consciousness. He struggled to get his feet under him, but Shaw kept pulling him, not letting him stand.

He backed out into the middle of The Pit and let go of Archie's collar. Archie rolled over and made it up to one knee, gasping in air through his bruised windpipe, coughing, choking on the blood still streaming from his nose. Hands cuffed behind him, he struggled to his feet. The crowd pressed closer. Someone threw a rock at him. It smacked into his shoulder. He turned and snarled, "Get back."

Someone spit at him, a woman ran out of the crowd and scratched at his face. He kicked at her, almost falling, and she scrambled away. He turned to Shaw and yelled, "Shoot me, motherfucker. You, cop, come on. Pull the fucking trigger."

Shaw took one last look at Archie Reynolds, turned, and walked away. Something like a collective snarl erupted from behind him. He heard the sounds of fists and feet on flesh. Some in the crowd had knives. He heard the wet slashing sounds. He heard Archie scream. Shaw kept walking, feeling now as if he might not make it. Suddenly, everything began hurting. And then he felt Justine at his side, holding him. Saying his name. He reached for her, clinging to her and she to him, each helping the other walk toward the main gate.

Police sirens filled the night air.

The first patrol cars were arriving. A helicopter appeared in the sky above The Pit, casting its burning searchlight into the area, trying to expose the flailing mass surrounding Archie.

As Shaw and Justine reached the main gate, someone

set fire to Archie's gasoline soaked clothes. By the time Shaw stepped out of New Lots, New Lots had turned Archie Reynolds into a bloody, broken ball of flesh and flames.

Epilogue

Over the next three days, Loyd Shaw put up with the doctors telling him how lucky he was and with the police brass putting him through five debriefings. Then he told them that's all they were getting from him and left for the studio in Massachusetts.

Before Shaw left, he attended James Sperling's funeral with Orestes Mason, Anthony Impelliteri, and Walter Wang. Mason looked good, having lost about ten pounds during his recovery. Impelliteri looked very dashing with his eye patch and cane. Walter appeared to be back to normal, perhaps a bit more distracted than usual.

The Chief of D, Albert J. DeLuca, had given Shaw word that he intended to keep his end of the bargain, but none of the men spoke about it. After the funeral they shook hands, setting a date for another dinner in a month, figuring that would be plenty soon enough to talk about what had happened.

Shaw retreated to his painting and Jack Daniel's. The whiskey felt good, but the color red didn't. He started thinking in grays and browns and black.

Five days after Shaw arrived at his studio, the phone rang. Shaw let the answering machine take the call, but when he heard Justine's voice, he grabbed the receiver.

She told him she was at the bus station in Hartford and could he come get her. She had no idea how to get any closer to Shaw's studio.

Shaw found her sitting in the bus station, a scarf

covering her head and much of her face, and dark glasses covering her eyes. Shaw made sure to be very gentle with the first embrace and kiss. And with every one after that.

They hardly spoke during the drive back. And when they arrived at the studio, they talked about everything but New Lots. They concentrated on being kind to each other.

Justine retreated to the outdoors, taking long walks with Mrs. McGovern's black Lab, Ellie. The old lady hovered around them at times, very protective of them and their privacy.

When night settled, Shaw would drink quite a bit, and Justine a little until they were able to fall into long, careful sessions of stroking and caressing. Because of her injuries, Shaw had to be very gentle with Justine, which made the sex they shared somehow more intense, more deeply satisfying.

They had survived. And they carefully embraced the opportunity to extract every bit of pleasure they could from each other.

The ugly bruises on Justine's beautiful skin broke Shaw's heart, even as his emotions for her soared beyond anything he had ever known.

Shaw had a great deal of difficulty handling what had happened to Justine. Especially at those times when he touched spots on her that still hurt. Bruises that he could not see. And she would wince on the outside and something inside Shaw would twist with searing, psychological pain.

Knowing all that had happened to her, knowing that she would live with nightmares about Archie Reynolds, filled him with the familiar feelings of anger and regret. He couldn't seem to completely escape their grip on him, no matter how many times Justine reminded him that she was alive, that she was okay, that he had saved her.

Over the days that followed, Justine and Shaw met each other, in many ways, for the first time. Shaw had never imagined how warm she could be. Even in their disarmed moments back in New York, when they went for each other, the limited time and their differences naturally separated them. Now, for the first time in Shaw's life, a woman made him feel that he was her man. And she was his woman. Shaw had come through for Justine and her stance toward him was absolute and solid.

Shaw knew that for the rest of her life, Justine would care for him, and felt enormously gratified by it. He took her devotion to him and held it like a secret prize, not speaking about it for fear it would become less real.

Time passed slowly. The first week seemed to provide them with the hours they needed for both themselves and each other.

By the middle of the second week, Shaw had begun to ease off the whiskey and accompany Justine on her afternoon walks. One bright, sunny day, they whistled for Ellie and set out for a late-afternoon walk. The April of their horrible time and had evolved into a calm, balmy May.

The first part of the walk took them about two miles along an overgrown pathway running through the scrub forest. Their turnaround spot, a small pond set in marshland clearing, nestled comfortably and quietly at the end of the trail.

They sat on a log facing the water. Justine turned her face to the waning sun and the blue sky. Shaw watched the ineluctable snatches of light play on the surface of the water. He thought about trying to paint something so thin and ephemeral as that light upon the water. The pond might have been a mile deep, but for

Shaw all the action lived right there in the play of light glittering on the surface. The weightless sunlight made everything visible and alive, yet never penetrated past even a molecule's depth.

Shaw seemed content with such thoughts, but Justine had had enough of avoidance.

"I've been talking to my father."

"Oh?"

"On your phone upstairs."

Shaw simply nodded, not saying anything. He knew he didn't have to pursue it. He knew Justine would not force him. But he also knew it was time to talk.

"So what does he say?"

"Well, quite a bit. He likes to go on. But it usually ends up with making sure I'm all right."

"And what do you tell him?"

"I tell him I am. Or I will be."

"Uh-huh."

"And I tell him about you."

"Oh."

"You're why I'm going to be all right."

Justine smiled at him.

Shaw realized he could look at Justine's smile for a lifetime and be dazzled every time he saw it.

"How does dad take that bit of information?"

"Well, he doesn't love you for it like I do, but he's grateful to you."

"You love me for *it*?"

"For it and for everything and for what's to come."

"Justine, I'm not sure the word love even begins to cover what I feel about you."

"Oh?"

"Yes."

Shaw could see that pleased her. Justine looked away, making believe she was trying to see where Mrs. McGovern's dog had wandered off.

Still looking away from Shaw, she asked, "So what's next, Loyd?"

"With us?"

"No. I'm not worried about us. With you."

"I haven't sorted it out yet."

"Why not?"

"Because most of it centers around me continuing as a cop for the next year or so, and I don't want to think about doing that."

"Why not?"

He shrugged. "I don't know. Lately, I've gotten good at not thinking about things."

"You know, they're going to let you do just about whatever you want."

"Who's they?"

"My father. DeLuca."

"Is your father sure about that?"

"I don't think there's anything about you he's sure about. He doesn't know you well enough. But he knows how much he owes you. He might not admit it to you, but he knows it."

Shaw watched the light sparkle on the lake for a few moments. Then he told Justine, "Before I left, DeLuca made sure to get me in a room alone. He had his stooge Conklin watch the door and then he gave me his speech."

"His speech."

"Yeah, it started out with telling me I had done the right thing, but in the wrong way. It went on like that. I figured he was leading up to telling me how magnanimous the department was going to be about not prosecuting me.

"I didn't really want to hear it. I told him I didn't give a damn. I told him he was full of shit. I told him I had tapes of Leon Bloom talking to his henchman, Conklin. And I told him their boy Bloom had used

Archie Reynolds and his gang to ruin that housing project. And I told him I had information that could tell me who was getting what out of Arbor Realty if I decided to pursue it. But I told him I didn't give a damn about that either. Just gave a damn that he was still trying to keep me in my place.

"I guess I ranted on about collusion and honesty and giving in to pressure from your father. I went on about sending men to die for their bullshit. I wanted him to finally know I knew the score."

"What was his reaction?"

"He sat there and listened to me, then he told me I didn't know the half of it."

"You're kidding."

"Nope. Then it was my turn to sit and listen. He told me about the Koreans."

"The Koreans?"

"That's where all Arbor Realty's money comes from. The whole area's being bought up by them. Told me they not only squeezed the department, they squeezed the mayor, threatening to drop financial support. And they weren't the only ones. He said there were also bankers, construction people, City Council members and other pols who raised hell because their campaign coffers were also threatened.

"The Koreans, the Hasidim, the press, the politicians, all of them put on pressure. There were way too many bodies dropping out there in Brownsville for a lot of people. He told me just because your father was stupid enough to let you get involved out there or just because Bloom was stupid enough to get involved with drug dealers then come running to the department, didn't make him or your father dirty."

"Did you argue with him?"

"No. Because after he told me all that, he stuck a finger at me and told me none of it meant anything."

"None of it meant anything?"

"He said whether I was right or he was right or who was or wasn't dirty—it all added up to the same thing as far as he was concerned."

"Which is?"

"Which is when you get right down to it, after everybody makes their deals or their alliances or threats, after everybody does what they want or think they can get away with, it's the cops who come in and clean it up and make it work. Guys like Impelliteri and Wang and Mason and Sperling who stand next to each other with their guns and take care of it. It was the second time he gave me his thin-blue-line speech. Without us, civilization ends. He really believes that."

"Do you?"

"I guess it's hard not to believe it, but that's not really the issue, Justine."

"What is?"

"I know there have to be people like DeLuca. And like your father. The question is, do I want to be one of them? Do I want them to put me in a situation where I have to shove everything aside, push and push and push until I have to push everything out of me that's human and pull the trigger? Do I really want to be one of the civilized killers?"

Justine looked at Shaw, thinking about what he had said.

Shaw felt he had to be perfectly clear about it so he added, "Somebody had to kill Archie Reynolds. Or at least make sure somebody else did."

And then Justine nodded. She understood.

"Well," she said, "I'm sure you'll make the right decision."

They lapsed into silence. The sun edged down, touching the treetops.

After a few minutes, Justine stood up and brushed herself off, turned to Shaw, and asked, "Shall we?"

She reached her hand out to him. He took her hand in his and said, "Yes."